Hickory Flat Public Library
2740 East Cherokee Drive
Canton, Georgia 30115

UNSUB

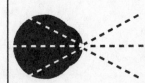

This Large Print Book carries the
Seal of Approval of N.A.V.H.

UNSUB

MEG GARDINER

THORNDIKE PRESS

A part of Gale, Cengage Learning

GALE
CENGAGE Learning®

Farmington Hills, Mich • San Francisco • New York • Waterville, Maine
Meriden, Conn • Mason, Ohio • Chicago

GALE
CENGAGE Learning®

LIBRARY OF CONGRESS CATALOGING-IN-PUBLICATION DATA

Names: Gardiner, Meg, author.
Title: Unsub / by Meg Gardiner.
Description: Large print edition. | Waterville, Maine : Thorndike Press, 2017. |
    Series: Thorndike Press large print thriller
Identifiers: LCCN 2017023990 | ISBN 9781410499608 (hardcover) | ISBN
    141049960X (hardcover)
Subjects: LCSH: Women detectives—Fiction. | Serial murder investigation—Fiction.
    | Suspense fiction. | Mystery fiction. | Large type books.
Classification: LCC PR6107.A725 U57 2017b | DDC 823/.92—dc23
LC record available at https://lccn.loc.gov/2017023990

Published in 2017 by arrangement with Dutton, an imprint of Penguin Publishing Group, a division of Penguin Random House LLC

Printed in the United States of America
1 2 3 4 5 6 7 21 20 19 18 17

For Shane Salerno

Whoever fights monsters should see to it that in the process he does not become a monster. And if you gaze long enough into an abyss, the abyss will gaze back into you.

— *Friedrich Nietzsche*

The yelling woke her, the rough voice of her father, shouting into the phone.

"Listen to me. We don't have days. We have *hours.*"

The black sky poured through the bedroom window. Shadows crawled along the ceiling.

"Don't you understand? It's in his message — Mercury rises with the sun."

Caitlin curled into a ball, hugging her bear. She knew what *Mercury* meant. It meant flashing lights and BREAKING NEWS and everybody so scared. A body bag sliding into the coroner's black van. KILLER CLAIMS EIGHTH VICTIM. It meant you could never close your eyes or turn your back. Because *he* could get you anytime, anywhere.

"He's telling us, flat out. When the sun comes up he's going to kill again."

9

And her dad had to stop it.

That's why each word Mack Hendrix spoke sounded angrier than the last. Why his shirt was dirty and he hadn't shaved in three days and when he came home for an hour he ignored dinner and the Warriors' game and her. Why he paced and stared at the walls and yelled into the phone.

The back door creaked. "Because I've goddamn worked this case for five years. I *know.*"

Caitlin slid from under the covers and crept to the window. Her dad stepped outside, lit a cigarette, and stalked across the backyard. Lights reflected on his gun and detective's shield. His shoulders were bent. That frightened her. The wind blurred his words.

She tiptoed from her room. Her parents' door was shut, Mom asleep. She slipped into the kitchen to the open window, to hear what he was saying.

". . . we work the evidence. We keep working. Or somebody dies."

She stopped. The door into the garage was open a crack.

The rule was: Never go in the garage unless Dad says it's okay. He spread files on the workbench in there. All his information. But sometimes he let her in, to help stack his papers. Her stomach knotted. She looked out the kitchen window again, into the backyard. The cigarette glowed red.

Answers were in the garage. Truth. She edged to the door and stole through.

She stopped, bare feet cold on the concrete. The walls were covered with photos.

Faces. Flesh. Open eyes. Jagged slices. Blood. Her head began to pound.

A plastic bag on a screaming face. Bite marks. Dogs. At the edges of her vision, starlight shivered. A cut. A cut, he cut with a knife in the person's chest, a dead person, she's dead.

A sound rose from her throat. He cut a picture into the woman. Stick figure. *It.*

She turned in a slow circle. She saw dangling feet. Frankenstein stitches. An arm with words scrawled on it — *despair.* Her legs started to shake. *The cuts the cuts the cuts.* The sign.

Dizzy, she turned. The photos seemed to lunge and wail. *Devilman him him.* She pressed her hands over her mouth, but the sound grew louder.

Footsteps pounded through the kitchen. The door banged open. "Jesus, no."

Her dad charged in, mouth wide, eyes burning. The sound poured from her throat, uncontrollable screams.

11

He swept her in his arms. "Don't look, Caitlin. Close your eyes."

She buried her face in his chest, but the photos howled and clawed. She sobbed, clutching him, feeling him shake. The work of the killer was everywhere. Mercury, the messenger. The Prophet.

They were surrounded.

1

Equinox
Present Day

Weapon at her side, eyes on the night, Caitlin approached the house. Fog clung to the ground, rolling thick off San Francisco Bay. It hid the stars, their faces, the view beyond.

Silently they climbed the steps to the broad porch. The March chill weeviled down Caitlin's arms. By the doorbell a faded sticker announced that JESUS SAVES, but Caitlin saw no evidence of it. *Not tonight,* she thought. Tonight, he didn't get the call.

They stacked up beside the door. Behind drawn blinds, a television burbled. Intel suggested that six people were inside. But *suggested* didn't mean *confirmed.*

Caitlin's heart beat hard against her ballistic vest. Beneath it she wore a T-shirt, jeans, and work boots. Her auburn hair was tucked beneath a ball cap. Her nerves were tuned to an ultrahigh frequency, adrenaline crackling through her like static, waiting for the sign.

The raid leader held up a fist. The team stilled.

Rios was an Oakland Police Department sergeant, built like a furnace in black tactical gear. He glanced at them over his shoulder: Oakland Police, San Francisco PD, Alameda County. Caitlin's vest read SHERIFF. Her ball cap read NARCOTICS TASK FORCE. They gave him a thumbs-up.

The moments before, the suspense, always fried her. Anticipation was hell. The hateful uncertainty. The house was two-story, decrepit, secretly humming with danger. Caitlin hugged the stucco wall, SIG Sauer warm in her hand. At her back, a young Alameda sheriff's deputy named Marston thrummed with apprehension. *Come on,* she thought. *Jesus might not get the call tonight, but we're here. Let's move.*

Rios raised his semiautomatic rifle and pounded on the door. *"Police."*

A dog barked. The TV droned. Rios drew back his arm to pound on the door again.

A gunshot from inside blew splinters across the porch.

The static in Caitlin's nerves resolved to a clear tone. *Here we go.*

Inside the house, feet pounded. Men

14

yelled. Rios tested the doorknob. Locked. He signaled the fourth man in the stack, an Oakland cop who held the Little Pig.

Caitlin braced for more gunfire. The Oakland cop, Hillyer, rounded them and aimed the Little Pig at the dead bolt. The scaled-down shotgun was loaded with a breaching round. He fired from an inch away. The dead bolt assembly blew into the house and Hillyer stepped aside. The door yawned open. The Master Key — it worked on any lock.

Rios said, "Go, go." Rifle to his shoulder, he led the formation in.

The lights were dim, the floor warped. Tight and fluid, they swept into the hall. Rios aimed ahead, then to the right.

"Right clear," he said.

Caitlin stepped to the left, pistol level. Checked her sector. "Left clear."

The hall reeked of sulfur and ammonia. At the back of the house, a battering ram smashed open the rear door.

Marston stepped past her, checked his sector. "Clear."

They closed up behind Rios, left hands on the shoulder of the person in front of them, and advanced to the wide doorway to the living room. Rios pointed. *Go.* He swung in.

"Drop it," he yelled.

A gun clattered to the floor.

Caitlin came in behind him. Again she checked her sector. Rios yelled, "Get down," and peripherally she saw a man drop to his knees. She said, "Left clear." Rios kicked a handgun away from the suspect and held his rifle on him while Marston and Hillyer swept the room.

"All clear."

Down the hall, men shouted. Footsteps raced back and forth.

Rios pointed at Caitlin and Marston and put two fingers to his eyes. "Kitchen. Go."

Caitlin returned to the hall. At the far end, men grabbed stacks of cash and fled with officers in pursuit. She advanced toward the kitchen door, weapon level, finger on the trigger. Her pulse pounded in her ears. The kid, Marston, closed up behind her.

His breath warmed her neck. She was taller than he was, five-ten, and, for the moment, a shield. In another room, someone shouted and slammed into a wall.

"Clear," an officer shouted.

The stench of ammonia burned her throat. At the threshold she stopped, concealed. Heard nothing from the kitchen. Marston's hand grabbed her shoulder. She nodded: *Ready to clear the room.* He squeezed: *I'll be right behind you.* They moved together.

She swung through the door with Marston on her heels, peripherally checking the gap between the door and the frame. Vision pulsing, SIG sweeping the room. She immediately stepped out of the doorway. The fatal funnel, path of most bullets.

"Right clear," she said.

Marston went around her. "Left clear."

Crusted dishes covered the counter. On the table sat a money scale, colorful currency straps, and a pile of cash. A trail of twenty-dollar bills wafted across the linoleum in the clammy breeze blowing through the window. The screen had been punched out. It looked like a quick getaway.

A shiver climbed Caitlin's arms. She hated having a doorway behind her. Even though the team had cleared the hall, a door always felt like a hungry mouth at her back.

And the window opened to darkness. To anyone outside, she and Marston were brightly lit targets.

Marston's knuckles were white on his gun. He was waiting for the all clear.

Beneath the chemical stench hung the reek of sweat. She eyed the darkness outside, a pantry in the corner of the room, and the twenties on the floor. The money didn't actually lead in a trail to the window.

Marston stepped toward the table. Outside, the dog barked again.

Caitlin raised her left hand, fisted. "Stop . . ."

The pantry door flew open. A man lunged out.

Shirtless, strung out, he charged toward the table. A butcher knife gleamed in his right hand. Caitlin turned to put him in her sights.

Marston was directly beyond him in her line of fire.

Screeching, the man drove the knife forward.

She launched at him, a flying dive, and tackled him around the chest. He was ripe with sour sweat. Twenties were falling from his pockets. They hit the kitchen table and slid across it. Twitching eyes. Blackened teeth. Clawing hands. She worked the momentum and rolled, flinging him with her to the floor. He shrieked like a smoke alarm.

She flipped him facedown and subdued him with a wristlock, forcing his head into the linoleum, knee shoved against his elbow. Marston stood above her, eyes on his own chest. The knife jutted from his ballistic vest.

Rios came through the door, weapon raised. He stopped at the sight of Marston

18

and of the man thrashing under Caitlin's grip amid broken dishes and crumpled cash.

Marston pulled the knife from his vest. "All clear."

Rios lowered his rifle. "The guy pop out of the toaster?"

Caitlin handcuffed the man and pulled him to his feet. "It's the meth fairy. Tweakerbell."

Rios's eyes didn't match his light tone.

"Under control," she said.

Marston touched his vest, wincing like his ribs were bruised. Rios told him to bag the knife for evidence and take the suspect into custody. As Marston led him away, Hillyer appeared in the doorway.

"House is clear," he said.

Caitlin followed Rios into the hall. The yelling and running had stopped. In the living room three men sat cuffed on the floor, backs against the wall. The SFPD officers were counting bags of crystal meth. She holstered her gun and exhaled.

Overhead came a noise. They all tilted their heads to the ceiling.

Rios pointed at Caitlin and Hillyer. "Upstairs. Two bedrooms. Go."

The tone in her head revved like a firehouse Klaxon. She didn't ask what the team had missed. She drew her gun again and

19

led Hillyer down the dingy hallway. Her vest felt heavy. So did the SIG Sauer, in a two-handed combat grip. At the foot of the stairs, Hillyer put his hand on her shoulder. *Steady.* Together they climbed.

Upstairs they cleared the hall and first bedroom. The second bedroom door was half closed. From within came muffled sounds. Caitlin leveled the SIG. *Not gonna get surprised again. Gonna be ready.*

The sounds intensified. Almost a cry. She and Hillyer stopped outside the door. They had concealment but not cover, not if whoever was inside decided to shoot them through the plywood. She tried to slow her breathing. She nodded, Hillyer squeezed her shoulder, and she flowed through the door, gun aimed at the source of the sound.

"Sheriff. Don't move."

The crying intensified. Hillyer slid around her, his weapon swinging.

"Stop. *Stop.*" She raised a fist. Grabbed Hillyer's vest. "Don't move. Don't breathe. Take your finger off the trigger." She lowered her gun. "Oh, my God."

2

Caitlin closed the front door behind her and
flipped the dead bolt. Her footsteps echoed
on the hardwood floor. A table lamp gave
the living room an amber glow. She reached
to unhook her duty belt. She couldn't get
her fingers to work the buckle. She closed
her eyes and clenched her fists. After a few
seconds the shaking eased. She unbuckled
the belt and dropped it, clattering, on the
coffee table.

Her jeans were torn, her knee swollen
where she'd hit the crank-house kitchen
floor. Her red hair was disheveled. Beneath
her white T-shirt, the scarred bullet hole in
her shoulder ached. The world seemed
bright and supersonic.

From the back of the house, Shadow came
running. Big ears alert, tongue lolling. Caitlin knelt and buried her face in Shadow's
soft exuberance and let the dog lick her
face. The tremor in her hands subsided.

She leaned back and looked at Shadow's bright eyes. "Who's a good girl?"

The mutt yipped and sat, tail wagging. She was skinny, black with white paws. Caitlin roughed her fur, then groaned to her feet.

She followed Shadow to the kitchen and filled her water bowl. The small house was warm against the foggy night. It was a rental in Rockridge, a Craftsman cottage behind a *Father Knows Best* picket fence. The Berkeley Hills rose behind it. The neighborhood was crowded, eclectic, heavy with fir trees and spilling ivy — which meant she was safely beyond the fire line. At least until the fire line burned its way downhill to her street.

In her bedroom she cleared her SIG and set it on the dresser. She shucked off her clothes and showered away the eau de meth head and the knots in her shoulders. She was pulling on clean jeans and a T-shirt when she heard a knock on the front door and a key turning in the lock.

She leaned around the doorway and saw Sean Rawlins walking down the hall toward her. She exhaled.

Sean had just come off surveillance, but he didn't take his eyes off of her. His stride was long and slow, boots clocking on the floor. His dark hair was windblown. His brown eyes were intense. His great-great-grandfather had ridden with the Chiricahua Apache into the Sierra Madre, and Caitlin thought of that look as Sean's raider stare. The take-no-shit look he gave to suspects and car salesmen. She thought he was the best-looking thing she'd ever seen.

The stare turned to a smile. He held up a bottle of tequila.

She laughed, took the bottle, and tossed back a swallow. Her chest heated. She blew out a breath.

"Perfect."

She didn't drink during the week — holidays, Warriors' championships, and *shots fired* excepted.

"There's more," he said.

"Better be."

He pulled her along the hall to the kitchen. On the counter sat a brown paper bag from a neighborhood taqueria.

"Praise Jesus," Caitlin said.

They didn't bother with plates but stood at the kitchen island bent over their tacos, spilling pico de gallo.

"There's something else," he said.

"Did I win the lotto?"

"You made the news."

His voice, usually cool, took on an edge.

He pulled up a video on his phone.

"Last thing I expected to see you carrying out of a crank house was a baby," he said.

"You never know what's behind door number three."

The screen went bright, the late news, and yeah, there she was.

Maybe the Narcotics Task Force had alerted the media about the raid. Maybe reports of gunfire had brought them out. She forgot the food and watched herself at a weird remove.

Coming out the front door of the crank house, cradling a squalling infant. Onscreen, she blinked as though caught by surprise. She had been.

When she'd rounded the doorway into the upstairs bedroom at the raid house, she had been *that* close to firing. She could still feel the pressure of her finger on the trigger as she shouted at the room — and stopped dead.

Seeing the baby, only a few months old, trying to kick her way out from under the ratty blanket heaped on the floor. Window wide, cold air heaving in. Little fists clenched by her red face, chubby legs bicycling. Caitlin had holstered her gun and scooped her up. Stunned.

Just like she looked on the video. *Under*

control, she'd told Rios. Like hell.

"For a little thing, she had a ton of fight in her. I hope that's a good sign," she said.

"Always," Sean said. "Whether you're twenty inches or five foot ten."

She gave him an appreciative look, shut off the phone, and caught a view of herself in the window. Eyes too hot. She grabbed the tequila bottle and poured another shot. It burned less than the first.

She wound an arm around Sean's waist and nodded at the ATF badge that hung on a chain around his neck.

"Off the clock," she said.

He pulled it over his head and set it on the counter. Then he picked her up and set her on the counter too. She pulled him close. He smelled like soap and the outdoors.

"You got more to bring me tonight?" she said.

He smiled, and it looked like a wicked promise. She laughed. The remnants of her stress evaporated. She kissed him. Then wrapped her arms around his shoulders and kissed him some more. He ran his fingers into her hair, tilted her head back, and kissed her neck.

Headlights swept past the window. She slid off the counter, hanging on to him, and reached to close the shutters. A car door slammed.

They paused. Turned to the window. Outside, an Alameda County sheriff's car had pulled to the curb.

They looked at each other. A cop car was never a good sign, not even at a cop's house. A heavy knock sounded.

She opened the door to the cold night.

The plainclothes officer who stood there looked like so many older cops who hung on to the job until somebody told them it was time to retire. Jowls and a slouch. His grim expression said that something was seriously wrong.

"Detective Hendrix. I need you to come with me."

The drive took a long, portentous hour, out of the city and into the dark countryside. Neither of them spoke. The headlights swept across empty fields until they rounded a bend into a frenzied bubble of red and blue. The stretch of highway where the car finally stopped was desolate. The flashing lights illuminated cornfields. A police helicopter hovered overhead. A dozen cops were in motion on the ground.

Caitlin stepped out into a cold wind. Here, the night sky was clear. Two steps from the car she could feel the tension hanging thick in the air.

She recognized the man waiting for her at the edge of the road. Backlit by swinging flashlights, coat flapping in the downwash from the helicopter, Senior Homicide Sergeant Joe Guthrie watched her approach. Hands at his sides. Breath steaming the air. Lean and sharp, with deep-set dark eyes, he had the wiry alertness of a fox. He was known as a methodical investigator who patiently probed for weaknesses and, when he found them, ripped your throat out.

He watched her carefully as she walked toward him. Measuring her. She took a deep breath and returned his steady gaze.

"There's something you need to see," he said.

Caitlin understood what that something almost certainly was. She signed the crime scene log-in sheet and steeled herself. She had seen bodies before, in the autopsy suite and in the wreckage of head-on collisions and on grimy kitchen floors, a husband bleeding out from a knife wound while his wife fought against the handcuffs, screaming, *He deserved it, the cocksucker.* Death came in numberless forms, and she could deal with all of them.

They pushed through rustling cornstalks

until they came to a small clearing. The searchlight from the helicopter swept overhead. Guthrie stepped aside to show her what lay at the center of the clearing.

It was a young woman. Her skin was paper white, her hair matted red with dried blood. She had been strangled.

The bullwhip that had choked the life out of her was twisted tightly around her neck. Red lash marks welted her arms and face, furious stripes. Her blouse, shredded by the whip, lay open, exposing the symbol pounded into her chest with shining nails.

Caitlin turned away and doubled over. She caught herself and stayed there for a long time, her hands on her knees, her eyes closed. She had to will herself to breathe.

"Detective," Guthrie said.

His voice came to her as if she were down a hundred-foot well. The night smelled of dirt and iron.

It's impossible, she told herself. But she felt every nightmare she'd ever had, roaring to life at once. *He disappeared years ago. Decades.*

She opened her eyes and turned to see it. To prove to herself that it was real. That same symbol, pounded into another victim's flesh. *His* symbol. *His* madness.

The Prophet.

The victim's face was dusty and streaked from dried tears. The thin trails of blood that ran from the nails meant she was still alive when they were pounded into her. She couldn't have been more than twenty-five.

Caitlin peered into the woman's dead eyes. Flat blue. She could feel Guthrie standing right behind her. He was watching her closely. Watching her reaction. She shut her eyes so she wouldn't see the victim's face, but an aftereffect imprinted it on her retinas. Her throat closed and light-headed sorrow swooped through her. She fought it down. All of it, until she could finally speak.

"Where's the other body?"

"Look, we don't know it's him," Guthrie said. "It could be a copycat."

"Did he phone the family?"

"That's how we knew where to find her."

Lock it down, she thought. *Don't think about her family right now. Deal with the scene.*

But she couldn't. It was all coming back to her, everything she knew about the

29

Prophet. The way he'd take two victims at a time and pose them in grotesque scenes, like mannequins in display windows from hell. The way he'd etch his signature into their flesh: the ancient sign for Mercury, messenger of the gods, guide to the underworld. He sliced it into one victim with a box cutter and poured liquid mercury into the wound.

"Where's the note?" she said.

Guthrie hesitated.

"There was always a note," she said.

Guthrie called to a nearby officer, who brought an evidence bag. The officer held it up for Caitlin. Behind the thick red sealing strip, inside the clear plastic, was a single sheet of white paper. Caitlin read the handwritten message.

All these years you thought I was gone. But
hell and heaven turn and turn again.
Angels fall, the messenger descends,
your insolence is harrowed, defiance ends.
  You
wail in fury, but the
Equinox delivers pain. It batters like a
hurricane. Tremble now — you cannot hide.

She read it slowly, twice, forcing the words to stop jumping in her vision. The wind

30

chilled her. *But the Equinox delivers pain.*

It was him.

"This week is the start of spring. The vernal equinox," she said.

Anyone who lived in the Bay Area between 1993 and 1998 knew what that meant, because it was a story played out on the front page of every newspaper, at the top of every news hour.

Eleven murders, all unsolved.

An UNSUB: the unknown subject who would come to be called the Prophet. He made women stay home instead of going out alone. He made parents bring their children in before it got dark, and keep them inside.

For five years, one of the biggest metropolitan areas in the country lived in fear, dreading the next news bulletin. Waiting for the Prophet's next victim.

Until he disappeared.

You cannot hide. Caitlin read the note again, feeling the glare of every officer in the cornfield. They were all watching her.

"The second victim," she said.

"That's why we have the chopper here. But we haven't found anyone."

From the road, another detective beckoned Guthrie. A car had pulled up, a reporter. A man with lank gray hair was try-

31

ing to get around the deputies and reach the scene. Guthrie tramped away, head down, without saying anything else.

Caitlin stared at the cornfield. Her breath frosted the night air, catching the beam of swinging flashlights. The stalks rustled as the helicopter made another sweep.

She ran the lines of the note through her head. *Turn and turn again.* She peered at the long furrow of black earth between the rows of corn. *Insolence is harrowed.* The plowed groove ran to a vanishing point and beyond into darkness.

She took her Maglite from her belt. Rubber bands from her jeans pocket. She slipped them around the toes of her boots to identify her footsteps. Feet silent on the soft earth, she followed the furrow. Slowly. Step by step, directing the beam of the flashlight ahead of her, checking each inch of the ground for footprints and signs of disturbance. Finally calming her breathing, she listened to the night. All voices were behind her. Ahead were wind and cornstalks scraping.

At the end of the row, she paused. Which way?

She could head toward the highway or into the field. If this was a game, how had the Prophet designed it?

He loved to test and taunt. He was both a blunt, bloody ax and a needle-sharp stick. She could imagine him dropping a victim's body on the centerline of a rural highway. It would be brazen and grotesque — one of his favorite styles. But if he'd done that, even at two A.M., the swarm of sheriff's vehicles and the crisscrossing helicopter would have discovered it.

And a harrow had prepared this ground. She rounded the corner to the next furrow, heading deeper into the field.

Where the furrow ended she turned again, deeper still into the corn. The voices of the detectives and uniforms, the scritching of police radios, the whine of the chopper's engine, receded. The rustling dark rose around her.

Then, at the far end of that row, her flashlight caught a glint on the dirt. She went completely still. Tried to be sure she was actually seeing it.

A trail of silvery liquid drew an arrow around the corner to the next furrow.

It gleamed under her Maglite. Definite. The liquid lay on the earth without soaking in, without even seeming to touch it. Under the beam of her flashlight it was a shifting, squirming mirror. Quicksilver. Mercury.

"Guthrie." Drawing her weapon, she turned

33

the corner and pushed through the corn-stalks.

The second victim lay ahead. Dried blood caked the silver nails pounded into his chest.

Heavily, shoving cornstalks aside, Guthrie came running. He lunged into view beside her and stopped short.

He let out a *huh,* hard and involuntary. He stared for a long moment, then shouted for the forensic techs.

"You read through the code in his message," he said to her.

She nodded. She couldn't drag her gaze from the young man sprawled on the ground.

"Is this really him? Is it even possible?" Guthrie said.

Anything's possible with the Prophet. She stared at the victim's face. Head thrown back. Arms cast wide, a posture of crucifix-ion. A fearsome angel was tattooed on his forearm.

"I wish it wasn't," she said.

Guthrie stared at the victim for a long time. When he spoke, his words seemed reluctant. "I need to talk to your father."

"No." It sounded more abrupt than she wanted.

"It's important."

"It's a bad idea. Leave him out of this."

"It would be helpful if you came along."

She shook her head. "Talking to him won't help. Taking me along won't help. Forget it."

"We're going to talk to him with or without you. With you would be better."

The wind lifted her hair. The dark seemed to hiss at her.

Guthrie turned to face her. "Your father was the lead investigator. His partner is dead. There's nobody else."

3

Guthrie's car rolled through Oakland on an empty freeway, headlights spearing the darkness, tires droning a litany in Caitlin's ears: *No, no, no.* Gray smudged the eastern horizon. A bulging folder lay on the backseat. Caitlin knew what was inside. She'd seen it before.

"This case." Guthrie drove with one hand and rubbed his jaw with the other. "Twenty years dormant. Talk about cold."

Caitlin hunched against the doorframe, absorbing the blast of the heater. Guthrie, she thought, was trying hard to guilt her into helping him with this expedition.

He glanced at her. "Most of the witnesses are dead. Half the evidence is gone."

"Lost? Stolen?"

"People took souvenirs. Sick, but not surprising."

Her shock lasted only a few seconds. Of course people took souvenirs. A serial killer

36

of the Prophet's . . . what should she call it? Stature? Enormity? People wanted a piece of him. They wanted to touch a live wire and feel the power coursing through it. Without getting burned.

She felt queasy, down to her bones.

The cornfield crime scene was in an unincorporated area of the county. That's why the call had fallen to the Alameda Sheriff's Office.

That was his method. Always had been. The Prophet was cunning and knowledgeable. Like that other infamous local killer, the Zodiac, he murdered at locations spread across the Bay Area. That meant multiple law enforcement agencies became involved. Each with its own turf to guard, its own reputation at stake. Communication had been haphazard. Evidence and lines of inquiry were hoarded or forgotten and never shared. There was not a master file on the Prophet, because half a dozen police and sheriff's departments had each run their own investigations. The huge workload, the pressure, and rivalries all led to mistakes.

Not a copycat.

Guthrie glanced at her. "What was that?"

"I think it's him."

His gaze lingered, before the bay swept into view, the Bay Bridge graceful and curving, its soaring towers lit white against the predawn sky. Beyond it, San Francisco's skyscrapers climbed the hills and reflected in gold on the black water.

They don't know, Caitlin thought. *This city's nightmare has come back, and they don't know.*

The sun broke over the horizon as they crossed the bridge. They headed south to Potrero Hill, through sharply slanting streets crowded with apartment buildings and clapboard Victorian houses. With every block they drove, the dwellings looked more rickety, less tended. A few people were already walking toward the bus stop, hands jammed deep in their coat pockets.

Guthrie rounded a corner and Caitlin pointed. "Up there on the right."

They pulled to the curb in front of a boardinghouse painted a sickly seafoam green. It was a gingerbread Victorian that would have been worth a fortune in this gentrifying part of San Francisco, if not for the peeling paint and overflowing trash cans. The street slanted sharply toward the waters of the bay, which were whitecapped and burnished in the rising sun.

The view was spectacular. But it was a universe away from the tidy ranch home in Walnut Creek where she'd grown up. Guthrie, thankfully, said not a word.

Inside the house, at a bay window that burned with the morning sun, a figure watched them, obscured by the glare. By the time they climbed the steps, the heavy front door opened.

Mack Hendrix stood in the shadowed entry hall. Caitlin raised a hand in greeting.

Mack kept his hand on the knob, like he might slam the door on them. He was weathered, slim, his hair shorn close, a prickly white. His blue flannel shirt stretched tight across his shoulders. Caitlin wondered if he was getting construction day labor again. His eyes looked clear. The mug he was holding smelled like coffee, not whiskey.

"Detective Hendrix," Guthrie said.

"I'm not a detective anymore." Mack looked at the file folder in Guthrie's hand, then at his daughter. "Why are you here?"

It wasn't a question, Caitlin knew. It was a challenge.

Guthrie stepped up to the threshold. "We've got two dead. A man and a woman."

Mack didn't even acknowledge him. He stared at Caitlin.

She said, "It's him. It's the Prophet."

Mack stood there for a minute, as blank as a concrete block. Then he turned and walked into the gloom of the hall, leaving the door open wide.

Caitlin's jaw tightened. She and Guthrie followed Mack down the hall and into the living room. The house smelled of fried food and air freshener, like a McDonald's bathroom.

Guthrie held out the fat case folder. "This is your file on the Prophet. Your murder book. Everything you know."

Mack walked slantwise to the bay window and stared out. Backlit by the garish sun, he seemed to vibrate.

" 'Everything' is never in the file," he said. "*He's* not in the file. He's . . ."

He waved as though smoke was coiling through the air, and pressed a fist to his forehead.

"That's exactly why we need you." Guthrie approached, but Mack acted like he didn't see him.

Caitlin sensed static electricity building in the room. There were rhythms, tempos, that had to be observed if Mack was to keep on track. The problem was, those tempos, those rules, changed capriciously. And you never knew what would trigger him. They'd been there less than ninety seconds and she already felt thunderheads gathering.

Guthrie said, "Give me the stuff you

40

didn't put in the file. Impressions. Hunches."

Mack shook his head. Caitlin knew that a movie had started running behind his eyes.

"What's his victimology?" Guthrie said. "What does the Mercury symbol mean to him? We gotta get up to speed fast."

"I can't help you."

"Then your private notes. Scratch paper. Jottings. Post-its."

"I burned them. Destroyed it all." Mack cut a glance at Caitlin, looked at the floor, and finally turned to her. "This case will destroy your life. Stay the hell away from it."

The circuit blew. Not Mack's — hers.

"That's real easy for you to say now," she said.

Mack leaned toward her and made air quotes. " 'Dreams of domination and control contrast with UNSUB's inner inadequacies.' " His voice became insistent. "Domination and control. Domination and control. I told you, serial killers don't quit."

"That's it? Recite his profile? Come on."

Guthrie opened the file. "You warned that he was going to escalate. You got that from reading this letter." He ran his finger along the note. " *'Mercury speaks through the sky. He controls the vertical. He controls the*

41

horizontal. He —'."

"You think I unspooled his plan just from reading that letter?" A vein throbbed in Mack's temple.

" *'He rises with the sun. And — coming up after the break! — he will rule. Tune in for your message, at seven on the dial.'* You got his schedule from that. How?"

"From my Prophet decoder ring. You heard of it. The wire in my head that picks up Radio Satan."

Caitlin clenched and unclenched her fists.

Mack spread his hands. The coffee mug was shaking. "Rise, Mercury, seven. A sky chart showed Mercury rising on the horizon seven degrees southeast of the sun the morning of April eighteenth." He gave Guthrie a scorching look. "He was going to kill that day. Everybody should have seen it, not just Captain Crazy."

"Dad. Stop," Caitlin said.

His smile was cutting. "Help. Stop. Make up your mind."

She dug her fingernails into her palms. "He's going to kill again. Maybe on April eighteenth. Less than four weeks."

"Or not. He's patient. Twenty years — he could outwait *death.*"

On a coffee table Guthrie spread photos taken at the cornfield crime scene. "He's not waiting anymore."

For a second, Mack's mouth worked silently. A wild light flared in his eyes.

Guthrie turned to him. "You hate this guy? Help us catch him."

Mack let out a roar and flung his mug across the room. It shattered against the wall, spraying coffee. "Don't show me this shit."

His shaking hands drew into fists and he squared up to Guthrie. Caitlin jumped between them, pressed her palms against her father's chest, and pushed him back.

"For God's sake. This isn't about you. Can you focus for one actual minute and think about that?" she said.

A woman in a bathrobe and moccasins appeared in the doorway. The landlady, from the scowl on her face.

"Mack," she said.

He didn't respond. He backed away from Caitlin, breathing hard, scratching at his forearms.

Caitlin said, "It's all right. I'll clean it up and pay for the mug."

The woman muttered and shuffled back down the hallway.

Mack stared at the crime scene photos. Pain darkened his face. Caitlin knew the horror show was now playing in his mind.

43

That final day. The cemetery. He continued scratching his arms. He pushed up his sleeves and clawed at his skin.

Caitlin circled to face him. "The latest victims. The woman and man" — *the kids,* she thought — "in the cornfield. They were alive when the nails were hammered in."

Mack's chest rose and fell. "I know what you're doing. You want to stop what I couldn't. Make things right. If you think that, he's already claimed his next victim."

She reddened. "It doesn't matter why I'm doing it. I need an edge. Help me."

He looked at her unsparingly. "You want me to be a cop. Caitlin Rose, you're not nine years old anymore. Don't be pathetic."

The words hit her like cold water. He leaned in, enunciating each word. "Stay away from this case. Run from it. You won't catch him."

She stared. Where his sleeves were shoved up, tattoos stood out on his forearms.

"Get out. *Go.*" He backed away.

Caitlin did too. "Sergeant Guthrie, we're done here."

She stalked into the hall without looking back. Her pulse was pounding.

When did he get those tattoos? What was he thinking?

Mack almost always wore long sleeves. So

44

did she, on duty, because her arms were marked too. But that ink — on his right arm, *Caitlin*. That shocked her. Confused her. But not as much as the tat on his left arm.

What the hell was wrong with him?

It was the Mercury symbol.

4

Caitlin jogged down the steps of the boardinghouse to the street, putting on her
sunglasses to hide her eyes. In the doorway
behind her, the landlady pocketed the cash
she'd handed over to pay for the mug and
for cleaning the rug. The morning fizzed
with sunlight. It didn't cut the chill, just put
a buzz at the back of her eyes. A headache
was ready to leap. She'd been up all night
and couldn't fight the exhaustion any longer. She knew her face was crimson.

Guthrie was on the phone, leaning against
the car, facing away from her. It took her a
second to realize that he was speaking to
her Narcotics lieutenant.

". . . waste of time," Guthrie said. "Hendrix is a basket case."

She hesitated, a stutter step. That scab just
kept getting ripped off.

It always would. She walked up to the car.
Guthrie glanced at her, seemingly embar-

rassed, and wrapped up the call. The air now felt blazing hot.

"Sergeant, I want to work this investigation," she said.

He put away his phone. "You want to be detailed to Homicide?"

"Immediately."

He took her measure again, openly, head to toe. "You know how green you are?"

"You can look up my record."

She knew what he'd find: age twenty-nine. Seven years on patrol. Took a gunshot to the shoulder during a bank robbery. Only six months as a detective, but on her first assignment in Narcotics, she apprehended the Glass House Arsonist, a crank dealer who set fire to rivals' drug labs.

Guthrie continued to eye her. Forget pride in her work. Forget her oath as an officer. Right now, it seemed, her record boiled down to Daddy's Girl. So be it.

"I'm pea green. But I have something nobody else can give you." She nodded at the boardinghouse. "His insights."

Guthrie nodded, slowly. "Can you keep your eyes open and your head down while you learn how homicide investigation works?"

"I can do whatever needs doing."

He pursed his lips. He looked wary, but

— maybe — willing to take a chance. "Your lieutenant said the same thing on the phone just now. Your transfer is already going through."

Her heart raced. "Where do I start?"

"With the cold case files."

The wind shifted, swinging around to the north. It seemed to swirl in a great arc across the bay.

The Prophet was out there. Savoring, raging, planning. Caitlin thought, *Mack's wrong. We damned well* are *going to stop you this time. We're coming, bastard.*

"You got it, boss," she said.

Sean was waiting for her when she came through the door. He was ready to head to work, badge around his neck, Glock 22 holstered on his hip. The sun blazed through the kitchen windows. He poured her a cup of coffee but she set it on the counter and buried her face in his chest.

His arms went around her. They stood for a tight minute. He held on. He knew.

"This time," she said, forcing her uncertainty to become a vow. "This time we'll stop him."

"Anything you need, Cat."

She held him tighter. "This is it. We have to shut him down. Our only chance."

He leaned back, looked her in the eye, and nodded. Cop to cop.

Special Agent Sean Rawlins had been with her for two years. He understood why the Prophet was a name she never mentioned. He knew it was the poison that had cored a hole in her life, marked her as an outsider as a kid, and driven her to become a police officer. He knew how this was hitting.

"What happened to my dad is not going to happen to me," she said. "The case is the case. My life is my life. They will not bleed together."

"I'm going to hold you to that."

"Don't worry."

The concern on his face only deepened.

He was aware that when she applied to the academy, she had written vows on a legal pad. *Dedication. Persistence. Job stays at the station.* That last one was easier said than done.

"I swear," she said.

He wasn't about to express fear. But he took her face in his hands. "Be careful."

"Compared to Narcotics, Homicide is a Zen garden. Detectives hardly even get to break the speed limit."

"Not this case."

Like a lot of cops, Sean viewed the world as a dangerous place where he could do

49

only so much to make it safe for the people in his life — Caitlin, his three-year-old daughter, and his ex-wife. He touched Caitlin's shoulder, where she'd taken the bullet years before. Then he rested his hand on her heart.

"Careful. Got it?" he said.

She nodded. She got it. *And I got you, thank God.* "Yeah. And now I've got to get to the station."

At four P.M., the halls of Sequoia High School were quiet. The buses had pulled out. A few athletic teams were practicing, and the a cappella choir. But the clean suburban campus, on the outskirts of Pleasanton, was gearing down. For the most part, teachers and custodial staff were the only ones around.

In his classroom in the math quad, Stuart Ackerman packed up for the day. He erased the board, pausing when he reached an algebraic equation some ninth graders had scribbled when he wasn't looking. *32A × 36C = 68DD.* A pair of bulging boobs drove home the joke.

Cheeky monkeys. At least the kids were engaged.

He erased the drawing almost wistfully. He knew too many guys his own age, thirty-

50

three, whose sense of humor hadn't grown beyond this kind of stuff. He himself was trying to be a complete adult. Button-down shirt and khakis, a tie except on Fridays. Hair cut stylishly short — his mom assured him — and a hipsterish stubble that the school administration never openly complained about, thanks to his students' test scores. He slotted a stack of homework into his briefcase. His forearms, he decided, were buff. Three days at the gym was doing it. Huzzah.

He was in a spring mood. Easter weekend was coming up soon.

He closed the briefcase and grabbed his keys. He thumbed his phone — the battery had run down. He looked at the desktop computer. His fingers tingled. Personal use was prohibited. *Delete Browser History* was disabled. The school could track every site he visited.

But he was feeling good. Feeling lucky. Feeling . . . *please, oh, please . . .*

Just once, he decided. Well, just once more. Just for a minute. He leaned over the keyboard and oh-so-quickly checked a website.

Hoo boy. He had a private message from Starshine69.

He sat down. What a photo.

The screen briefly flickered. He lifted his hands from the keyboard, wondering if there was a loose connection or whether Mrs. Lovado in the vice principal's office was secretly monitoring him, hunched in her dim cubicle like a KGB gnome. The screen cleared.

Starshine's message said: Silver Creek Park tomorrow 9PM.

He replied, smiling. Ready to rumble.

Outside, he swung his briefcase and jauntily aimed his key fob at the car, like James Bond pulling a quick draw. He felt almost giddy climbing into his Nissan Sentra.

As he closed the driver's door, he caught another flicker. Across the street, a black pickup idled, facing him. The driver's sunglasses, or . . . binoculars?

The pickup drove away.

Ackerman pulled into traffic behind it. He shook off the weird feeling. If the pickup was ahead, it couldn't be following him. Right?

He turned on the radio, and his anxieties about the pickup vanished. "Fight Song." He cranked the volume and sang along. What perfect timing. What a sign.

5

The Briarwood Sheriff's Station sat between sleek business parks on a broad suburban street. Caitlin swung into the parking lot at seven thirty A.M. She locked her Highlander and strode toward the building. The wind was up, rattling the spring-green leaves on the maples. Her hair was damp from the shower. She wore a snug long-sleeve white T-shirt, jeans, Dr. Martens, her badge, and her SIG Sauer P226 holstered on her hip.

A patrol car rolled past, a slick Dodge Charger, heading for the street. She nodded a greeting. When she came through the door, the civilian clerk behind the counter smiled from behind a cinnamon roll.

"Morning, Paige," Caitlin said.

"Beautiful." Paige licked icing from her thumb.

The girl was Miss Sugar High. When citizens arrived to report crimes, she greeted them cheerfully, with the predatory cuteness of a kitten. She *liked* hearing which penal code violation had brought them here. Caitlin thought the department should ship her to work at the DMV for a few weeks, to take the edge off.

Caitlin entered a code and buzzed through the door. The station's open brickwork and blond wood were deliberately calming. That worked for her, because the learning curve for new detectives was ballistic. She'd wanted to be a detective since kindergarten, when she watched her dad holster his .38, burn his mouth on his coffee, and sweep out the door to catch the bad guys. But some days she felt like the cowboy riding the H-bomb in *Dr. Strangelove.* Interrogation Methods. Protecting the Integrity of Evidence. Breaching Techniques. *Yeehaw.*

Across the floor, Guthrie whistled to her. From the intensity in his eyes, he was surfing the crest of a caffeine wave. "More files were delivered last night. Bring them up from Evidence. Team meeting in twenty."

Thirty hours after the first victim was found in the cornfield, the department had ramped up a major investigation team for the killings. Guthrie had gathered a squad of detectives and turned a back section of the station into a war room.

One wall was covered with maps, profiles,

old Identi-Kit sketches of suspects. And crime scene photos. Caitlin absorbed the new shots that had been tacked up. The cornfield, the bodies, three footprints — men's size ten — and the trail of mercury. One after another, like Stations of the Cross. She approached the wall.

It was the temple of the Prophet.

September 23, 1993. Giselle Fraser. Found dead, hanging by her wrists from a crossbeam. Wasps swarming so thick in the shack, first responders could hardly see.

March 20, 1994. David Wehner. Suffocated with a plastic bag and left at a traveling carnival. A crime scene photo showed the fun house, cotton candy stand, rides and games — Wild Mouse, Limbo, Skee-Ball — and Wehner's body, propped in the seat of a Ferris wheel. A note was pinned to his shirt. *This is a sign of what was, and is, and is to come.*

That was how the killer got his nickname. *Talking like a prophet. That's who he thinks he is.* The public latched on, and the media, and finally law enforcement.

Everybody except the killer himself. He

55

never referred to himself by any name. He only signed his messages with the Mercury symbol.

March 21, 1995. Barbara Gertz. Stabbed, dumped in a car wash.

April 12, 1996. Helen and Barry Kim, the first couple murdered. Bludgeoned, dumped in a landfill. Postmortem, their bodies were mauled by dogs.

April 26, 1997. Justine and Colin Spencer. Their bodies tumbled from the back of a dump truck delivering rocks to a construction site. The symbol was sewn into their skin with fishing wire.

That gruesome detail had been withheld from the public. It would have kept Caitlin awake for weeks, lying cold in her bed as the wind knocked the trees against the roof. She'd slept poorly for most of her childhood. She still did.

March 20, 1998. Lisa Chu. The teenager was dropped into a water treatment pond chained to a concrete parking bumper. A message was scrawled on her forearm in indelible ink.

As Caitlin stood before the photo, a faded memory grew vivid: of sitting cross-legged in front of the television, playing Barbies, when a news report broke in. A Serious News Lady talking, before a drawing of a stick man with devil horns. "The Prophet has struck again, and left a chilling new message, written on the victim's own skin: 'Infinite wrath and infinite despair.' "

Then her dad's voice, booming. "Jesus Christ, Sandy — you left the news on?"

He rushed in and turned it off. "*Goddammit.*" He chucked the remote at the wall and stomped to the kitchen and Caitlin didn't move, because his yelling made her stomach cramp. She heard him pick up the phone and when she dared peek over her shoulder, he was stalking around the kitchen. "You see it? Saunders, somebody fucking leaked it to those jackals."

Now she shook off the visceral memory of anger that had suffused the house.

April 18, 1998. Tammy and Tim Moulitsas. Calvary Cemetery.

She stared at the young couple's photos. Guthrie swept past. "Hendrix. Saddle up."

Caitlin brought up the new evidence boxes

57

on a dolly and joined the team as they assembled in the war room. The lights were harsh, the energy jagged.

Tomas Martinez wore a bowling shirt and a trilby cocked back on his shaved head. He had the easygoing bearing of a beach bartender, but his eyes, stony with dread, betrayed the decade he'd spent working Homicide. Caitlin thought the snapshots he kept on his desk, of his wife and four daughters, had something to do with that.

When she walked up he raised his chin in greeting. "Kid."

She held back *Gramps.* He was forty-three. And his voice was warm. "Detective."

Mary Shanklin set a stack of files on a table, neatened them, and gave Caitlin an assessing glance. Shanklin had come in from sheriff's office headquarters in Oakland. In her late thirties, she was known as a disciplined investigator. Her brown hair was cinched into a tight ponytail. Her lipstick was the red of a stop sign. She carried herself like a regimented Brownie leader Caitlin recalled from childhood. And like a dominatrix she'd once arrested.

"Morning, Detective," Caitlin said.

Shanklin nodded briskly. "Hendrix."

Guthrie strode in and pinned two new photos on the wall. Blowups of the cornfield victims' driver's license photos. Seeing them alive tightened Caitlin's chest.

Guthrie tapped the woman's photo. "Melody James. Age twenty-six. Disappeared from Union City Tuesday night. Finished her shift waiting tables at Olive Garden at eleven P.M. Never made it home."

He took out his phone. "Her husband got a call Thursday night at eleven fifteen. Voice mail picked up and recorded the conversation."

He thumbed his phone and pressed PLAY.

Over the outgoing message, a man's breathless voice stumbled onto the line. He sounded wide-awake and panicked. Caitlin could virtually see him clutching the phone.

"Melody?" he said.

A man replied. "No, Mr. James. But I know where she is."

Everyone on the team straightened.

"Where? Who is this?" James said.

"I saw your missing person flyer."

That voice. It rasped, coarse and grating. Shanklin gave Martinez a stony glance. He gave it back, then shook his bald head, muttering under his breath. Caitlin's skin shrank.

Was it him? Twenty years back, the Prophet had sent recordings to the police and television stations. This sounded lower,

59

rougher than she recalled. It was horrid.

The voice said, "She's out at this place on Highway 88. Fields, east of Guadalupe Road."

James spoke in a rush. "And she's okay? Did you speak to her?"

"I'm looking right at her. I think a reward —"

"She's alive. Oh, my God. Can you put her on?" James's voice sagged with relief.

Even now, even when it was too late, Caitlin wanted to grab him and knock his hand away from the phone. *Don't express relief. Don't express hope. Don't be happy. That's what sets you up for the blow he's about to deliver.*

"People said she couldn't be, but I knew it." Tears welled in James's voice. "Tell her — please, come home. I don't care why she left, or with who . . ."

"You mean the guy she ran off with?"

James paused again — shocked, or getting hold of himself. "No questions asked. Keep her there — I'm on my way."

"No rush. She's not leaving."

An audio recording clicked on. *"No. Don't hurt me . . ."*

It was a woman, sobbing.

"Stay back. Oh, God, put that down . . ."

She screamed. And screamed.

The voice returned. "She's going nowhere. I punished her." He paused. "You're welcome."

James gasped and began yelling. His wife's screams filled the room. The call went dead.

Guthrie ended the playback.

"Son of a bleeding bitch," Martinez said. "That was cold."

Shanklin stared at Melody James's photo. Against the red lipstick, Shanklin's face was white with apparent rage. "Sadistic."

Guthrie said, "The call came in from a 650 number. A prepaid cell, a burner. And our audio specialists suspect that the number was a cut-through, a call forwarded from another cell. They're on it, but we doubt we'll trace it."

Caitlin stared dazedly at Melody James's photo. An apple seemed to lodge in her throat. The driver's license photo blurred into Melody's face, tear-streaked and dirty and dead on the ground.

The killer's voice. Almost lighthearted, the stinger lurking at its edges. Male, tenor, maybe deliberately coarsened in an attempt to disguise it. The words. The taunting. Giving hope, dangling the lure.

If it wasn't him, it was somebody with the Prophet's perverse desire to inflict drawn-out pain.

She said, "Voiceprint comparison?"

Guthrie eyed her, and the boxes stacked on her desk. "The old tapes are in there somewhere. Dig them out." His gaze was pointed. "Dig everything out. Look for patterns in the evidence. Echoes between the old and new cases."

She nodded.

He moved on, to the male victim's photo. "Richard Sanchez. Age twenty-seven. Checker at a supermarket in Alameda. No wants, no warrants. Possibly connected to Melody James."

A man at the back of the room said, "Voice on the recording mentioned 'The guy she ran off with.'"

It was the boss. Lieutenant Ray Kogara, who commanded the station's Investigations Unit.

Kogara was intense and imposing. Fifty-ish, Japanese American, when he entered a room, people stepped back an inch and straightened their shoulders. His charcoal suit hung perfectly on his battering-ram frame. He strolled toward the wall, pointing at the photos of the victims.

"Did she?" he said. "Run off with him?"

Guthrie said, "No, but she may have been cheating with him. Her coworkers at Olive Garden say Sanchez was a regular customer, that Melody flirted openly with him — and that he once picked her up after her shift. I've interviewed Melody's husband. He knew of the rumors. He insists all he cares about is catching the guy who killed his wife."

"Tough on him," Kogara said.

"The night Melody disappeared, Richard Sanchez picked up takeout from the Olive Garden. We suspect that the killer was nearby, watching. Then he followed Sanchez home. Sanchez never made it inside his house. His car was parked in his garage, with the door down. Remote missing. We think the killer accessed the garage and attacked him there."

Guthrie opened a folder. "We have preliminary autopsy reports. Both victims died of strangulation. The ligature marks on their necks match the bullwhip."

He handed Kogara autopsy photos. "Abrasions on their wrists, ankles, and faces indicate they were bound and gagged with tape. Blood spatter from each victim was found on the other victim's clothing. They were whipped in close proximity."

Kogara took in the photos. Though he said nothing, his expression tightened.

Martinez shook his head. "Nasty."

Caitlin's stomach felt hollow.

Guthrie said, "Tool marks on the victims' skin indicate the nails were fired into their chests with a nail gun. We're working to identify the make and model."

"The nails?" Kogara said.

"They're four-inch common steel framing nails. Large shank, flat head, diamond point. Used for construction and framing, plus amateur carpentry. They're ubiquitous. No way to trace origin or point of sale."

"What about the whip?"

"It's old. Maybe a hundred years. We're checking online vendors, but it could have been in the killer's attic for the last century."

Kogara scanned the wall of photos. "The trail of mercury?"

Shanklin stood at parade rest, hands clasped behind her back. "I sent samples to the lab for chemical analysis. In its pure form, mercury's a silverish metal that's liquid at room temperature. What's in thermometers, electrical switches, fluorescent lamps. But in nature, it's found in compounds and inorganic salts. Purifying it isn't a home DIY project. And its sale is regulated. It's not available at Target."

"Where could he get it?"

"He could buy it online. Claim it's for a chemistry class. As long as he fakes a commercial address, he's good," she said. "Or he could have stolen it."

Kogara crossed his arms. "Can they trace a batch or lot number? Is mercury tagged?"

Caitlin straightened. "No. Only explosives are required to contain chemical taggants. Not a base metal like mercury." She eyed Shanklin. "The lab's looking for contaminants and trace?"

Shanklin's expression pinched. "No, trans fats and artificial sweeteners. Of course they are." She walked past Caitlin to the conference table at the front of the room. "Two other things about mercury. One, it's toxic. And two, if it's not sealed off, it slowly vaporizes."

Kogara turned toward Shanklin. "You mean our evidence could evaporate. Literally."

"Yes."

Caitlin felt singed. Guthrie eyed her dourly.

He turned to the others. "One more thing. Melody James and Richard Sanchez were killed someplace where the killer had room to maneuver."

He nodded at the photos on the wall. "That bullwhip is seven feet long. From the spatter and the damage it inflicted, it struck the victims at high velocity. The killer needed space to wield it. Someplace where

65

neighbors wouldn't hear. And to use a nail gun, he almost certainly needed an electrical outlet. This guy has a house. Or he has access to a shop floor where he can go after hours. He didn't commit these murders in an apartment with thin walls."

Kogara perused the autopsy photos with what looked like a subdued ache.

"If he repeats his last cycle, we only have four weeks before he kills again. He's out there, getting ready. Every minute counts." Guthrie looked at the team one by one. "Let's get to work."

As Caitlin headed for her desk, Guthrie called her aside. He looked like he had a burr in his shoe.

"Detective. Mary Shanklin has ten years in Homicide. You have one day."

"I was out of line. I know — keep my head down. And my mouth shut."

"Starting now. We don't have a second to waste." He nodded again at the boxes. "Dig, and deep. Go."

6

The water stain ran along the side of the cardboard storage box like a muddy tide. When Caitlin lifted the lid, a spider nest billowed out. She rubbed the back of her sleeve across her face. On her clipboard, she started a fresh page for her inventory. *BOX 13.*

The evidence she had organized from the original files covered a conference table. She'd been at it for five hours. She was summoning ghosts.

Some of this material she had seen before — on the worktable in the garage at her childhood home. Where Mack said, "Quiet. Close the door." Then let her stay.

The responding officers' reports. The detectives' reports. Statements by witnesses who found the victims. By the teenage girl who managed to slip from the killer's grasp and escape.

Photos of tire tracks. Of a footprint, size

nine. A map of the first crime scene, drawn freehand by the killer.

That one gave her a chill.

Crumpled and water stained, it was drawn with an engineer's precision. A compass rose indicated north. Streets were sketched with smooth curves and sharp intersections. There were hills and trees — maybe to indicate places for concealment? — and the park where the victim died. A creek. A storm drain, with its length indicated as *125 ft.* Picnic area marked with tiny tables. Playground with swings and a slide.

Written on the map was the word *PUN-ISHMENT.*

The handwriting was harsh, pressed deep into the paper. Ballpoint pen, the corners of each letter acute, sloping downward. The map came from a twilight time when the thing had started its slow roll toward horror, before anyone knew a serial killer was at work.

These boxes were an attempt to categorize unremitting hell. But hell couldn't be contained. And Guthrie was right. It was the ultimate cold case.

She needed only to skim the original inventory sheets to see how much evidence had disappeared over the last twenty-five years. Sent to storage . . . somewhere.

Destroyed when the evidence room flooded. Pilfered by cops, forensic techs, and even FBI agents. Everyone wanted a piece of the legend.

But when she excavated Box 13, she hit pay dirt: two cassette tapes labeled *Prophet phone call.*

Except she couldn't listen to them. Because the station no longer had a cassette player.

She packed up the cassettes and took them to the criminalistics lab. It was a thirty-minute drive, to a complex surrounded by eucalyptus trees in the hills off 580 in Oakland. When Caitlin signed over the cassettes, the forensic examiner, Eugene Chao, took them with efficient disinterest. Then he saw the label on the evidence bag.

"No shit?"

"None at all."

He whistled.

"I need it —"

"Last week. You'll get it. For real, for once."

"Thanks, Eugene."

Driving back to the station, she felt antsy. Investigation required diligence. Dogged, patient, grinding diligence. But a sound like a metronome beat in her head. Seconds, ticking off.

She called up voice search on her phone. "What is the date and time that Mercury next rises in the morning sky?"

"Interesting question, Caitlin."

The phone didn't know. She frowned and slowed for a traffic light. The car ahead was a red Camry.

She stared at it. "Damn."

The phone said, *"There's no need for that."*

Caitlin swung into the next lane and pulled alongside the Camry as it stopped at the light. The driver was hunched forward, tightly gripping the wheel. Caitlin honked. When the driver looked over, Caitlin pulled off her sunglasses. She pointed at a parking lot in the next block.

She whipped into the lot behind the Camry and jumped out. The driver climbed from the vehicle, gave Caitlin a punishing stare, and strode toward her. Red hair flame-hazed by the afternoon sunlight. Paisley blouse an onrushing psychedelic scream. Heels of her boots tattooing the asphalt. Typhoon Sandy.

"Are you stalking me?" Caitlin said.

"I can drive by the station anytime I want. Especially since you've lost your mind."

"Great to see you too, Mom."

"Don't do this. It destroyed your father."

Caitlin spread her hands. "That's always

your reason for stopping me. 'Don't run with scissors; it destroyed your father.' 'Don't feed the squirrels; it destroyed your father.' " She patted her mother's shoulder. "I'm not Dad."

Sandy Hendrix gave Caitlin a barbed look, and softly took her wrist. Sandy's touch sent a wave of heat coursing through Caitlin's veins. Sensory memory. Pain, warmth, shame. She inhaled and forced it to pass.

Sandy lowered her voice. "This case hurt you. And you were only on its fringes. If you take it on as an investigator, you're throwing yourself into the volcano."

Once Sandy sank her teeth into something, she didn't let go. This relentlessness had gotten her through college with a husband on patrol and a toddler at home. It almost got her to save her marriage. It gave her the strength to pull Caitlin to shore that long dark summer when she was fifteen.

Sandy held on a second longer, then let her hand drop. Her eyes never left Caitlin's.

Caitlin said, "I can't walk away. People are dying." She heard the catch in her voice and hated it. "We have to end this."

Sandy clutched her in a hug. "Baby, don't. You're the only daughter I have."

"I love you," Caitlin said. "But I have to do my job."

Sandy smiled, an injured, frightened smile, and backed away. When she neared her car, she swiped away tears, flinging them from her fingertips like they were poisonous.

Radio pumping, anticipation turning his mouth dry, Stuart Ackerman pulled into Silver Creek Park right around nine P.M. Night had fallen. The darkness felt both dangerous and protective.

The road into the park was narrow and winding. He put his phone away. He was wearing the things Starshine69 had specified. He hoped he was. The message had come through just a couple of hours ago. For a panicked second, he thought she was canceling on him. Instead, she wrote, *Be sharp. Things are going to get rough.*

A leather vest. That worked, didn't it? And gloves. Leather in general. Biker boots that he'd bought in college, still polished from the box. But he wouldn't have them on for long. He hoped. His nerves were sparking. The live oaks leaned overhead as his headlights swept a bend and he drove toward a darkened glen.

A sharp *thwack* rattled the car.

"What . . ."

He slowed. Had he hit something? The steering wheel yawed left. The yellow tire

72

pressure light pinged on. He stopped. Puzzled, he got out.

He stepped away from the door to examine the car. He saw it and stopped, baffled. That couldn't be right. His front tire had been shot, with . . .

"Are you kidding . . . ?"

From the trees, a man appeared.

One moment he wasn't there. Then he was. His face, his entire head, seemed absent. It took Ackerman a disorienting second to understand that he was seeing a man wearing a black ski mask. Calmly, the man raised . . .

Dear God.

Stuart Ackerman bolted. He spun and sprinted for the tree line. Stiff biker boots kicking up gravel, head back, panting. *Unreal, unreal, unreal, God, no . . .*

A whistle cut the air. The shot slammed Ackerman to the ground.

Oh, Jesus.

For a weird second it just felt like a hard blow. Then the pain hit, sharp and deep and wrong. He tried to rise and couldn't. He realized his mistake. He shouldn't have run for the woods. It was too far and would leave him unarmed and vulnerable, with only his feet as a means of escape. He should have gone the other way. For cover.

For an engine.

He didn't hear the man, but he sensed him. Sensed him nearer than he had been.

Move. This is serious. The pain spread, crazy bad. Something warm ran along his ribs inside his leather vest, pooled and dripped to the ground.

The car. Wounded, he turned and crawled for it. *"Help."*

The man glided toward him. "Help isn't coming."

He loomed, a wraith. His footsteps seemed silent. Ackerman crawled.

The man came to within five yards and stopped, feet braced in some kind of stance. He aimed. "Bloodthirst brings a reckoning. You made the date. You pay."

He fired another shot. Ackerman screamed. From the trees, crows burst into the night sky.

7

Just after seven A.M., Steve Ramseur eased off the two-lane highway and headed through the gate at Six Pines Ranch. The morning was blustery, clouds shredding in a red sunrise. The hills were a rich green. He hadn't seen anybody on the road. Hadn't expected to.

The cargo bed of his Ford F-250 was loaded with bales of alfalfa hay. The truck rattled over the cattle guard and up a hill through the oaks and past the pines that gave the place its name. He drove with one hand on the wheel, the other holding the travel coffee mug that rested on his belly. He wore a Stetson and a Burberry padded jacket and had the radio tuned to a Bay Area drive-time show, Chaz and T-Bone.

". . . Seven-oh-seven on a sunny day and we're gonna help you *make it,*" one of them said, as brightly as if he'd stuck his face into a bowl of speed and started gobbling. The other deejay snickered. "Doesn't matter if you want to get over or get off. You can do it with us." Their minions in the broadcasting booth laughed like donkeys.

Ramseur could never remember which guy was Chaz and which was T-Bone. It didn't matter. He listened because it reminded him of the twenty years he'd spent stuck in morning traffic on the Bay Bridge, listening to shock jocks while commuting to his office in the San Francisco Financial District. It reminded him that when he'd quit to take over the family ranch, he'd chosen wisely. Here he was, a mere thirty-five miles from the city, driving through a landscape that was virtually unchanged from the 1700s. This ranch had been in his family for centuries, since a land grant from the Spanish Crown. This was his inheritance, and his responsibility, and he loved it. He listened to Chaz and T-Bone to hear the sound of his freedom.

"So today we're talking about these murders the other night," said Chaz, or T-Bone. "The police are playing coy, but everybody thinks they were committed by the Prophet. The one and only."

"Un-freakin'-believable, man."

"Do you think it's him? After all this time?"

"Him or his ghost, or his reincarnation. Spawn of Satan."

"We'll open up the phones after the break. What do you think? Is the Prophet back?"

Cali-forn-i-crazy.

Two miles in, he slowed the truck for the crossing over the creek. The water splashed his rims, a welcome sound. He crested the next hill and smiled at the broad green sweep of the valley.

He slowed. "What in hell?"

The horses were out.

The Arabians were in the turnout pasture, running in a tight circle inside the white fence. They should have still been stabled in the show barn. Especially this time of year, in this cold. But — dammit. They were out, all ten of them, it looked like. Stamping, turning, skittish.

He accelerated down the hill to the barn. Who had let this happen? Had his daughter been out yesterday evening and forgotten to close the barn door securely? He slid out his cell phone and brought up her number.

But that made no sense. He and his wife were the last ones out here last night. The horses were secure in their stalls when they left. He had checked and double-checked. The Arabians were prized and glorious creatures, and there were wild animals in the hills. He would never . . . dammit.

He pulled up in the gravel outside the barn. He got out, left the motor running and Chaz and T-Bone blathering. "The guy was a monster but a mastermind. He made tough cops wet themselves, the stuff he did." The barn door was shut. He went through the pasture gate and tramped toward the horses. First things first: Make sure they were all right. Something was spooking them.

The chill wind grabbed the brim of his Stetson and tried to blow it away. He pulled it down as he marched across the dewy grass. The horses were turning, pacing, tails up, eyes flared. And they were drenched in sweat. Steam smoked from their backs and blew from their nostrils.

Dammit, how long had they been out here? All night?

At the far end of the pasture was a water trough. The horses were turning their backs on it. One spun and burst toward the barn, snorting and shaking its head. What the hell?

Gingerly he approached one of the fillies. "Easy, girl." He didn't want to get kicked. Or stampeded and trampled, not with them in this state. "Easy."

Gently he lay a hand against her neck. She flinched. He held it there, and stroked. She was hot. No signs of injury. No signs on any of them, as far as he could see.

The wind shifted, coming down the hill from the water trough. The horses whinnied. The sound was shrill, an alarm. They turned downwind like magnets pulled to a compass heading, and bolted past him, hooves thundering.

"Hell is . . ."

Ramseur stood alone in the field. The wind felt immensely colder than it had a minute earlier. Slowly he turned and looked at the water trough.

He stood for a long minute. Then he returned to the Ford and took the shotgun from the gun rack.

He gazed again at the water trough. Saw no movement. But he hesitated. He didn't want to cross the field and see what was there, not even with a Remington in his hand. He racked two shells into the magazine and walked slowly across the field.

The trough was eight feet long, a three-hundred-gallon galvanized-steel stock tank. The water lapped at its rim, rippling in the wind. Something black and bloated bobbed on the surface. Ramseur raised the shotgun, feeling wobbly. Jesus God. What the *hell* was sticking out of it?

Step by step he approached, pausing to

wipe his eyes clear. Twenty yards from the trough he stopped.

A body floated facedown. The water was deep red with blood. Good hell — when the wind shifted, the horses had smelled it.

He held the Remington on the trough and looked at the shaking pines, the thick chaparral, at the high ridges and the tree line. He backed up, turned, and ran toward the truck, toward wind-twisted peals of laughter coming from the drive-time radio jocks.

The man in the trough, wearing a leather vest and biker boots, floated in his own blood. His body was riddled with arrows.

A deputy responded to his 911 call, a sturdy young man driving a Chevy SUV with SAN JOAQUIN COUNTY SHERIFF in gold along the side. Within an hour, two more SUVs and the detectives' beige sedan lined the road along the pasture fence. Ramseur corralled the horses in an adjacent pasture and leaned against the front bumper of his pickup. At the water trough, forensic people in white coveralls took photos and laid out a yellow tarp on the ground. They pointed and gestured, debating how to remove the body.

Just get him out, Ramseur thought. *Get*

him gone, so I can haul the trough to the dump. Then he would burn the pasture and get a priest out here to exorcise it. Hell, the pope. And he was Presbyterian.

The white suits hefted the body clear of the tank and onto the tarp. One of the detectives danced back as water sloshed on his shoes. A deputy covered his mouth with the back of his hand. Then everyone stood as still as the pines. All of them, staring. Except Steve Ramseur, who found himself walking toward the others.

The dead man lay on his side on the yellow tarp. He was young. When the bloody water ran off his face, his skin was blue gray. The first deputy saw Ramseur coming, put up a hand, and strode in his direction, gesturing for him to stop. Ramseur kept walking. Some force compelled him. This was his land. He had to bear witness.

"Sir. Mr. Ramseur. Please," the deputy said.

Ramseur stopped. But he saw. The symbol, that astrological sign. Devil's horns were carved in the dead man's forehead.

And on his chest, where his vest was torn open, a single word. *ANSWER.*

8

Later, when the fear and alarm subsided, the authorities confirmed that the video file had arrived on the server at KDPX News at 1741 PDT. Five forty-one P.M. On the bridges, traffic was a slow-motion accordion. Over the bay, flights descended the glide path toward the runway. Along the San Francisco waterfront, the lights were coming on.

At the Cold Creek Café in the Berkeley marina, the crowd was watching the Golden State Warriors game. Caitlin walked through the door just after six, from a breezy evening tinged blue and gold, to a dazzling duel of big-screen TVs. The place was busy, but not as packed as usual. She spotted Sean on the patio. She shouldered her way past the bar and out the patio doors.

He was sitting at a picnic table with his daughter, Sadie. He shared custody, and this was a regular outing. The little girl was bundled up against the chill in a jacket with a panda bear hood. Sean had on a blue Cal hoodie. He was earnestly watching Sadie play with two My Little Ponies.

Scratch that. He was playing My Little Pony.

"Which one's that?" Caitlin said. "Glitter?"

He smiled. Sadie lit up like a Fourth of July sparkler.

"Cat!" She stood on the bench and raised one pony high over her head. "This is Pinkie Pie. Come play."

That smile, those rosy cheeks, Sadie's guileless affection — Caitlin's cares lifted. She sat down and said, "Pinkie Pie is very pretty. Does she fly?"

Sadie nodded vigorously. Her panda hood fell off and her dark hair lifted in the breeze like corn silk.

Sean handed Caitlin an electric-blue pony with a rainbow mane and enormous violet eyes. If she saw eyes like that on the street, she would have probable cause to search for LSD.

Sadie said, "They're thirsty. They have to drink water from the lake."

They tipped their ponies' faces down to the tabletop to drink. For a bad second, an image lit up Caitlin's head — the Arabian horses at the backcountry ranch, shying from the water trough where Stuart Ackerman floated, dead.

Then the wind blew Sadie's hair across her face. Caitlin reached out with her index finger, cleared it away, and pulled Sadie's panda hood back up.

"There," she said.

Sadie hopped off the bench and galloped the ponies across the patio.

"You want to get a table inside?" Caitlin said to Sean.

"The fresh air's good."

"Sadie wanted to fix your hair, didn't she?"

"There are some things a federal agent shouldn't do in a sit-down restaurant." He leaned over to kiss her. "You're chilly."

"Cold case is cold."

"Hot case?"

"Is chilling."

He signaled the waiter. "Diet Coke?"

She laid her hands flat on the picnic table. "Please."

"You hesitated. Things that heavy?"

She'd grown up in a house where drinking during the week meant the case was going badly. She reminded herself: *Job stays at the station.* She might have added, *I will be worshipped as a goddess,* since she was working on stretch goals.

"He kicked it into another gear. It's unprecedented. Three victims. Nails, arrows, carvings — that word, *Answer,*" she said. "I thought I knew what was coming. I was wrong."

She kept her voice low, though it would have been nearly impossible for anyone to hear her while the Warriors scrapped with the Thunder on the TV. An OKC forward drove the lane for a layup as the halftime buzzer sounded.

Sean eyed her coolly.

Live the legal pad dream, Caitlin. Put the job away. "How was your day?"

On the television, BREAKING NEWS interrupted the halftime show. A female anchor appeared, glaring.

"Bombshell news tonight. In the last hour, the Prophet has delivered to KDPX News a message claiming credit for the murder of Pleasanton teacher Stuart Ackerman."

Despite the cacophony in the restaurant, a few people turned toward the television, including Caitlin and Sean.

"Ackerman's body was found this morning at a ranch in rural San Joaquin County. While authorities have not released the cause of death, they confirm a key claim in the killer's message — that Ackerman was shot multiple times with a bow and arrow."

More heads turned. A man muttered, "You shitting me?" A woman said, "God, this sicko." Someone asked the waiter to turn it up.

"What you are about to see is the entire video message received by KDPX."

A hush spread across the restaurant. An image, bright and crisp, filled the TV screens.

Sean was on his feet and already halfway across the patio to pick Sadie up and get her away from the television.

The video showed a poster taped to a blank wall. Someone unseen held the camera. Harsh overhead lighting. No shadows. No audio. A message was printed on the poster.

*Arrows pierced him when he ran. For violence
   sought
violence. So he was
hunted into a river of blood.
Alameda sheriffs knew this was coming. I told
   them.
Yet they stumble and fall, fools old and young,
   into
the pit
without a prayer.
Expect no help. Punishment will rain on you*

here, now, neverending.

People gasped. "Unbelievable." "God, the cops."

Caitlin tossed cash on the table and hurried after Sean and Sadie to the door.

In the morning, Stuart Ackerman's photo filled the front page of the *San Francisco Chronicle.* Ackerman looked winsome and geeky. A teacher the kids in trigonometry class could approach with questions. In her kitchen, Caitlin flipped through local TV stations. It was wall-to-wall coverage of the murder. Outside Sequoia High School, kids were crying. Parents choked up about Ackerman's devotion to teaching. The principal brought in grief counselors.

The headlines screamed, THE PROPHET IS BACK and COPS "STUMBLE." SATANIC KILLER *WARNED* THEM.

Fear and anger were fermenting. Caitlin could smell it. An old, rancid, nauseating smell. *They stumble and fall, fools old and young, into the pit.*

That line was no accident. Did the Prophet know she was on the investigative team? The thought set a nerve crawling beneath her skin.

When she walked into the war room, the other detectives were staring into screens or

87

talking on the phone. The atmosphere seemed freighted. A morning newspaper lay on the conference table. The *East Bay Herald.* At the bottom of page one, following the lead story, a headline read:

Detective's Failures Haunt Case — and His Daughter

By Bart Fletcher

As the Prophet wreaks fresh havoc in the Bay Area, Detective Caitlin Hendrix is working to solve the case that drove her father to attempt suicide.

Her stomach dropped. She skimmed the story. The murders. The increasing horror. The public taunting, the missteps and frustrations suffered by the authorities.

Bart Fletcher. She knew the name. A sidebar described him as a pit bull crime reporter who had covered the original case. His photo was now grayed and severe. She recognized him. He was the reporter who had turned up at the cornfield, the one trying to get past the deputies and barge into the scene.

She read on, and acid rose in her throat. The main story detailed Mack's dedication to the case — and the day everything went disastrously wrong.

The Prophet's reign of terror reached its climax the evening of April 18, 1998. A 911 call from Calvary Cemetery reported a suspicious vehicle. A camper had parked outside a mausoleum. Its driver was spotted carrying some kind of handheld container inside.

Hendrix and his partner, Detective Ellis Saunders, responded. They instructed cemetery employees not to approach the driver or vehicle.

When the detectives reached the cemetery, they didn't approach either.

Instead, they parked at a distance to surveil the suspect through binoculars. They saw him walk to the door of the mausoleum, stop, and speak to somebody inside, seemingly in a conversational tone. They held back, hoping to catch him in overtly incriminating behavior.

What neither the detectives nor cemetery employees knew was that inside the mausoleum was a young couple the Prophet had kidnapped. Newlyweds Tammy and Tim Moulitsas were bound, gagged, and drenched in gasoline.

By the time the suspect lit a match and threw it inside, it was too late.

Caitlin leaned heavily against the conference table.

Hendrix and Saunders pursued the suspect, first via car and then on foot. The killer — young, white, and fast — scaled a fence and dashed onto the freeway. He managed to dart between cars, as did Detective Saunders. Mack Hendrix was sideswiped by a pickup truck. Badly battered, he climbed to his feet and limped across lanes of traffic to follow his partner into an abandoned warehouse.

There he found Ellis Saunders shot multiple times, choking to death on his own blood.

Hours later, Mack Hendrix drove his car off a bridge. He was pulled from the water, raving that he heard ghosts.

The Prophet vanished.

So, for all purposes, did Mack Hendrix's life.

He spent the next six months in a psychiatric ward. Doctors spoke of bipolar tendencies and a schizoid break. The department forced him to take medical retirement. His wife left him.

Today he lingers on the fringes, prone, sources say, to tremors, delusions, and violent outbursts. It falls on his daughter, still wet behind the ears, to succeed where he failed.

A buzz filled Caitlin's head. Then a dark suit loomed in front of her. Guthrie grabbed the paper from her hands.

"Ignore this."

"Right."

She may have said it with too much snark and not enough can-do attitude.

Guthrie rolled the paper into a tight cylinder. "Don't get sucked into this. I need you focused on the case."

"Got it."

The cemetery was a public, historic tragedy. And at least the article didn't mention her father's hallucinations, or the bugs he was convinced crawled under his skin. But how the hell had Bart Fletcher learned about Mack's psychiatric diagnosis? Had Fletcher bought off a file clerk at the hospital? Had a neighbor or relative talked to him?

"Hendrix?"

"Yes, sir."

Calm down. Stories got out. This was inevitable.

91

"Fletcher's a washed-up drunk. Forget about him." Guthrie turned to go. "If you need to punch a wall, do it outside."

"Yes, sir. On the side of the building away from where the news vans are parked."

His shoulders moved. Maybe a laugh.

"Keep working." He slapped the paper against the edge of the table and walked away.

Caitlin sat down at her desk and opened a new file: COMMUNICATIONS FROM THE PROPHET.

She started with the most recent. The letter mailed to the television station read: KDPX NEWS DESK. OAKLAND, CA. RUSH TO NEWS EDITOR. It was a white business-size envelope.

Inside was a single sheet of eight-and-a-half-by-eleven-inch paper folded in thirds. It was medium-weight printer paper without a watermark. On the page was a single line of type, in twelve-point Courier font, printed on what the lab thought was a Hewlett-Packard Officejet 4620 e-All-in-One printer. Which were cheap and ubiquitous, sold at Best Buy and Fry's and maybe the Mc-Donald's drive-through. Homeless Gladys, who slept under the freeway overpass, probably had one in her shopping cart.

The single line on the piece of paper was a URL. A link to a webpage.

KDPX would not relinquish the envelope or note without a subpoena. But its news director and the station's attorney had brought the note to the criminalistics lab and permitted detectives to examine it and the techs to run tests. The lab ran a biohazard scan. It took high-resolution photos, front and back, under normal and UV light. It checked the flap of the envelope for DNA. There was none. No surprise — the Prophet wasn't sloppy enough to lick an envelope.

The lab found several latent fingerprints on the envelope. It was working to exclude postal service personnel and the intern at KDPX who carried the letter to the news editor. The note was clean.

What caught Caitlin's eye first was the postmark. The letter had been franked at 12:07 A.M. the previous morning. It had been dropped in a drive-up mailbox outside a major USPS sorting center in Fremont. That allowed it to get whisked through the system and delivered the same day.

The mailbox was emptied every two hours. The earliest the killer could have dropped it there was ten the previous night. He had come straight from the crime

93

scene to deliver his message. He'd had the note prepared well in advance. He was moving like a machine. Hungry, relentless, eager for attention.

What she didn't understand was why he had mailed the note at all. He could have simply contacted the station online. Why take the risk that a stray fiber or hair would drop into the envelope and give forensics the chance to nail him? Why take the chance that a business near the post office would catch him on CCTV?

Then she lined up all the Prophet's messages from the nineties, in chronological order, and she saw. The first letter the Prophet ever sent, to the *East Bay Herald,* was mailed at the Fremont Processing Center.

A tiny needle seemed to jab her between the eyes. He was telling them, *It's really me.*

This wasn't an echo. It was a shout.

She typed the URL into her desktop computer. As she expected, a Jolly Roger popped up, jaw hinging up and down, laughing, and a red NO ENTRY sign flashed on-screen.

The Prophet's message had been uploaded via anonymizing software to a page designed to be accessed once, then to self-destruct. She hit EXIT and blew away the smirking skull. Then turned to the screen grab of the message itself.

Twenty years back, the Prophet sent the cops VHS tapes. Now he'd sent an electronic video message stripped of identifying data.

He was tech savvy and highly literate. He used standard grammar and had perfect spelling. He had money, and access to a compound crossbow and a reliable vehicle. She doubted he had spent the last twenty years in prison.

She leaned back. Where had he been? In the military, deployed overseas? In a monastery? Hibernating? Why did he stop killing?

Why did he start again?

Look for patterns.

Caitlin spread the Prophet's messages across her desktop in a wide fan.

Stunningly, there were twenty-seven communications from the killer, going back to the first murder. Two to the Santa Clara County sheriff. Five to the San Francisco Police Department. Three to the *San Francisco Chronicle,* two to the *East Bay Herald.* Two specifically addressed to the *Herald*'s pit bull reporter, Bart Fletcher. Interesting.

Three messages had been written in graffiti at crime scenes. Two were written in ink on victims' bodies. And eight had been sent to the Alameda County sheriff. One to Detective Ellis Saunders. Seven to Detective Mack Hendrix.

Or, as the killer styled it on the envelopes, DET. MACK HENDRIX. PERSONAL.

Oh, so personal.

One read, *How do you like my gift to you? If you pay attention, you'll get the meaning.* Followed by the Mercury sign.

Caitlin's heart was beating too fast. Memories swam up. The day the newlyweds and Detective Saunders died. Riding her bike home from school to find a patrol car parked at the curb, and even at age nine she knew what it meant when a black-and-white came to an officer's house. *Something happened.* She ditched the bike and pounded inside. *Something happened something happened.* In the kitchen, two uniformed officers stood with their hands clasped. *When the sun comes up he's going to kill again.* Her mom was leaning against the counter in yellow light, a hand over her face.

"Dad. Where's Dad?" *The cuts the cuts. Devilman.*

Sandy dropped her hand, and heartbreaking compassion came over her. Pity. Anger. She swept Caitlin into a hug.

"Dad's okay," Sandy said, and though that

was a lie, it was what Caitlin needed to hear to keep from disintegrating. "He had a car accident. He's going to be fine."

Trembling, Caitlin buried her face in her mom's chest. "Truth?"

"Truth."

Of course it was anything but. Sandy held Caitlin and choked back tears, refusing to cry. Cop's wife. Standing tall. And Caitlin's world fell apart anyhow. She didn't see her father for six months.

Now she stood and walked down the hall to the vending machine, wanting to clear her head. While her coffee cup filled, she paced.

The messages. What did they mean? What did they *reveal* about the killer?

Caitlin could still recite the Prophet's profile from memory, almost word for word. Organized killer. Regards the murders as his mission. Extrovert. Has social skills and may be regarded as charming and outgoing. Incredible anger at women. He will show the dark tetrad of personality traits: Machiavellianism, narcissism, psychopathy, and sadism. Posing of victims' bodies and use of mercury are manifestations of a paraphilic fetish rooted in fantasy.

But how did that help solve the hidden meanings in his new messages?

Their creepy tone seemed increasingly religious. They chilled her more than she wanted to admit. And the messages rubbed her wrong. She suspected they contained a code, but it eluded her.

Patterns.

Guthrie thought she could tease them from the Prophet's notes. She'd tried, reading them word by word, syllable by syllable. Searching for the clue behind each reference and metaphor.

But what she saw were breaks in the pattern. New evidence didn't add up. Footprints didn't match; the timbre of the killer's voice varied. Only one victim was shot by arrows, not two.

Granted, by mailing a letter from the Fremont Processing Center, the killer was hollering that he was the Prophet. Maybe too loudly.

Beneath his shouts, in the recesses of her mind, something whispered, *Watch out. He's playing with you.*

9

In the morning, a storm blew in. Caitlin jogged from her SUV to the station door, splashing through puddles under a blustering gray sky. Inside, she found Guthrie in his office, file folders stacked a foot high, Post-it notes stuck on a dozen surfaces — including a photo of Guthrie holding two Jack Russell terriers. Today he was crisply dressed in a suit and tie. But he had sooty circles beneath his eyes. She knocked.

He glanced at her. "Yes, Detective?"

"Sergeant. Things aren't adding up."

She had learned to state her premise clearly, right up front. Not to ask permission, not to hem and haw. Do that, and she'd be regarded as ladylike. And as a pushover, a voice to ignore.

"In what way?" Guthrie picked up his coffee cup.

She approached his desk. "You asked me to look for echoes between the cold cases and the new murders. For patterns."

"And you're not finding them?"

"Some, yes. The extravagant staging of the crime scenes. Grand Guignol, almost. And the sterility of the scenes. No DNA, no fingerprints, almost no trace. He's the same ghost he's always been. But."

Guthrie drank, looking at her over the rim of the cup.

"There's a bunch that doesn't line up." She gestured at the wall in the war room. "The partial shoe print from the cornfield. It's a different size than the boot print found in 1993. And the voiceprint analysis of the new phone recording — Computer Forensics say they can't exclude the caller as the same voice from the cold cases, but it's far from conclusive. The timbre of his voice is different."

She raised a hand, forestalling the objections she sensed Guthrie might raise.

"I know the original cassettes are in poor condition, and the new recording was made through several layers of phones. They're still analyzing the caller's vocabulary, diction, and accent. But the register of the voice sounds lower. And yes, I know voices change over the course of decades. Smoking, drinking, aging. But."

"You keep saying that. Your point is?"

"Maybe it's age. Maybe it's design. Maybe the killer is merely toying with us. Or maybe not," she said. "Could this actually be a copycat?"

Guthrie put down his coffee cup. "I don't know. What do you think?"

She paused, surprised. "The Prophet has devotees. There are dozens of true-crime books about him. TV movies. And these online forums where amateur sleuths try to solve the case."

"Them. They've been on us like bees pouring out of a hive."

"It's like a cult. Church of the Prophet. Maybe somebody decided to replicate his crimes."

Guthrie rubbed his chin. "I know."

"Now I sense a 'but.' "

"It's been twenty-five years since the Prophet's first known murder."

A sick feeling rolled through her at *first known*.

"He has a fantasy, yes. A core need that drives him — that will never change. But his MO has likely evolved over the years."

"I know he's killed in half a dozen different ways, but . . ."

"Killers learn, Hendrix. They gain experience. This guy is a twisted fuck, but he's a smart, twisted fuck. Don't assume that

101

because things don't line up, it's another guy."

She deflated. Nodded.

"But you were right to bring this to me. I want my team to tell me everything. Don't hold back. You might discard the clue we need."

"Yes, sir."

She turned to go. Guthrie said, "And I understand your point about the forums."

She should have sensed it coming. Shit rolls downhill. But she was an eager puppy this morning. She turned back.

"One of these online people is swamping us with tips. Crazypants, and she knows how to find me."

He turned to his computer and hit a few keys. "I'd ignore her, but she'd probably show up here and run straight into the window like a disoriented bird." He pointed at Caitlin's computer. "Put out the fire. Listen to her but tamp her down. With a pillow over the face if you have to." He looked up. "I don't mean that."

"I keep my pillows at home."

"Good."

She turned to go, and he said, "And talk to your dad again."

Her shoulders rose.

"Hendrix." Guthrie's voice softened. "We

have to pull on every thread. You're the only person who can tease this one out."

"Yes, sir."

As she left the office, she called her father from her cell. Mack didn't answer. Relieved, she left a voice-mail message, vague and harmless and sure to set off his perimeter defenses. She sat down at her desk and looked at the information on the online person Guthrie wanted her to smother.

She was about to ride into a three-ring circus.

"Deralynn Hobbs, please. This is Detective Hendrix from the Alameda Sheriff's Office."

"This is Deralynn." The exclamation mark was implied. "Detective *Hendrix*? His daughter?"

"Yes."

"Oh, my goodness."

Her voice was bright and bouncy. Caitlin's computer screen showed Deralynn's driver's license photo. Caucasian, thirty-one, a full-moon face with a smile that must have burned out the camera at the DMV. Through the phone came the noise of traffic, sounded like the freeway. Kids' voices. Cartoon music.

Caitlin said, "You contacted Sergeant Guthrie. I'm following up."

"Did he tell you about the missing pendant?"

Deralynn had sent a dozen e-mails in the last two days. Plus links to the site she ran, FindtheProphet.com. Caitlin scrolled through the messages to Guthrie.

Re: Barbara Gertz Pendant.

"I have your e-mail. We'll review it."

"Victim number three. March 1995. Next of kin, Barbara's husband, told the medical examiner that when he identified her, her necklace was missing. Made a stink —"

"Yes." Caitlin opened the message. She didn't know about the stink.

"He accused the morgue staff of stealing his wife's jewelry? Before the police realized the killer must have taken it?"

She skimmed the e-mail. *Unique gold & opal hummingbird pendant on Barbara's necklace.* "I'll make a note in the file, Ms. Hobbs."

"Deralynn." Over the phone, the woman's voice went muffled. "Boys, stop. That's for lunch. Well, you should have finished your breakfast. No — Weston, I said . . . don't open that in the car; yogurt will . . ."

From the backseat came shouting.

Caitlin pinched the bridge of her nose.

"Get a towel from your gym bag," Deralynn said. Then, to Caitlin, "You there?"

"Why don't we talk when it's a better time."

"No better time."

In the back of Deralynn's vehicle, which Caitlin was picturing as a minivan with a *Dexter* bobblehead on the dash, a child said, "Mom, the towel just spreads it everywhere."

Deralynn said, "Lick it off."

Caitlin wanted to drop her head to the desk.

Deralynn said, "I found the pendant on eBay."

Caitlin straightened. "You think the victim's missing necklace is for sale on eBay?"

"It was. Four years ago. I got outbid. I contacted the police but never heard back. This week when everything blew up again, I e-mailed Sergeant Guthrie so he could contact the buyer and trace the provenance of the pendant. Find the seller, connect it to the victim."

"Back up and tell me everything from the start."

Deralynn went into a rapid-fire summary of how she'd been on the lookout for this pendant for seven years. "The Prophet didn't always take souvenirs. But on the theory that what came into his possession could always leave again — if he died, say, or was burgled — I had a continuous search alert for this pendant. I spent I don't know how many nights monitoring this. When it popped up, I jumped on it."

"But you don't know if it was actually the victim's."

"Same design, dimensions, same workmanship, and the opal chips for eyes . . . Weston, do not let the dog eat your sandwich."

Caitlin looked again at Deralynn's photo. That smile. The glowing face and Rubens figure. A borderline obsessive, a nocturnal data miner who shopped for case mementos on eBay. A busybody who phoned detectives while carpooling with the kids.

Caitlin said, "Send me any photos and information you have on this pendant."

"Soon as I drop the kids at the factory and hose out the van."

The information arrived half an hour later: screenshots of the eBay listing for the pendant. By then, Caitlin had dug a photo of Barbara Gertz from the cold case files. Gertz had a devilish smile and a martini in her hand. The pendant hung on a gold chain between her breasts.

It looked identical to the pendant Deralynn had found on eBay — down to a crescent scratch in the gold of the hummingbird's wing.

Caitlin took a slow breath. Three months after the martini photo was taken, the Prophet stabbed Barbara Gertz to death. Her body was discovered on the conveyer at an automatic car wash, her clothing blown off by the drying jets.

The longer Caitlin compared the two photos of the pendant, the more she became convinced: They were one and the same. She got the ball rolling to obtain the seller's data from eBay. It would require a court order and could take several days, even with the life-threatening urgency of the case.

She returned to her computer and read Deralynn Hobbs's messages, less dismissively this time. And she opened Findthe Prophet.com.

The site was slapdash but deep. There was a timeline of the killings. Pages of photos taken by law enforcement, the press, and civilians. Pages for each of the victims. Those were thorough and respectful. They included interviews with victims' families.

And the message boards. Caitlin was stunned. The site had forty-five hundred registered users. Plus who knew how many lurkers. There were a hundred and thirty-four topic threads. Caitlin registered under the screen name WarriorFan and dived in.

"Suspects."

"Are the Killings Random or Does the Prophet Know His Victims?"

"Rhymes in the messages. Numerology. Astrology. Satanism."

"Is the Prophet a Zodiac Wannabe?"

"Is the Prophet the BTK Killer?"

"UNSUB Profile. Police Mistakes. Killings that should be attributed to the Prophet."

"Composite Drawings — how accurate?"

"What does the Mercury symbol mean?"

Some threads had hundreds of responses, with links to everything from *New York Times* articles to FBI file numbers.

"Twenty years — where has he been?" The moderator for that thread: D. Hobbs.

She sat back. Some of these threads were batshit. But many posts were thoughtful and intelligent. Intense, yes. Lord, yes. But well documented.

This website went so far down the rabbit hole that it might actually be a repository of information that individual law enforcement agencies had never collated. It might even have photos of evidence that had been destroyed or stolen. Deralynn might have a key to the lost world of the case.

Caitlin saw another discussion topic: "Copycats?" It ran to seven hundred contentious comments.

She picked up the phone and called Dera-lynn. "I need to include or exclude the possibility that the new killings are the work of a copycat. You might be able to help."

"Oh, my gosh. Of course," Deralynn said. She sounded like she was in the car again, or still. Caitlin heard music and a laugh track. *SpongeBob.*

"Could you flag compelling arguments in that discussion thread for me? And if Find the Prophet has pertinent information that's not online yet, send it."

"You got it. And I'll keep this to myself."

"Glad I don't have to ask."

Caitlin heard the sound of a blinker, kids gathering their things, saying, "Bye," and "Thanks." Deralynn said, "Be good. I love you." Doors slammed. Then tires squealed as Deralynn accelerated furiously back into traffic.

"I'm on it," she said, and hung up. Caitlin felt like she'd just climbed off a Tilt-A-Whirl.

She thought of Deralynn and her carload of kids and her bloodhound hunger to find a killer. Laughter and *I love you.*

She thought of calling her dad again. For about a nanosecond. After a moment, she picked up the desk phone and called Child

Welfare Services.

"I'm calling about the baby found abandoned during a police raid two nights ago. This is the officer who brought her out of the house."

A minute later she felt lighter. Relieved and with a loosening in her chest. The little girl, Baby Doe, had gotten a clean bill of health and was in temporary placement with a foster family.

The little fighter was safe and warm and being cared for. Yes, she was in psychological peril. Abandoned. But she was in hands that wouldn't leave her in a crank house full of drugs and knives and gunfire. Caitlin pictured her wondrous wide eyes, held close to her own shoulder.

"Thank you. That's good news."

Take it when you can get it.

Behind Sequoia High School, past the football practice field, down the hill beyond the avocado orchard, was the concrete flood-control channel that skateboarders called the Drain. The cyclone fence didn't keep them out, not even on a blustery afternoon after a sad day, the weird vibe. Mr. Ackerman dead. Half a dozen kids were hanging there now that the sky had cleared, taking advantage of the slopes and curves, the culverts and bends — not as good as a half-pipe or empty swimming pool, but their spot — skating and sitting and talking about the freakiness of it all. Substitute teacher in trigonometry, looking like a rabbit in the headlights. Like the classroom was poisoned. News vans on the street outside.

The Prophet. The actual, no-shit serial killer who carved devil's horns into his victims.

They usually liked to take a run from the top of the sloping concrete ramp, ollie onto the bed of the channel, and sweep into the culvert like they were dropping into a wave at Mavericks. Not today. Today they mostly sat and one or two smoked and they all wished they'd worn warmer clothes. The wind made them jumpy.

Then Kyle Perez climbed to the top of the slope and casually headed down on his board, a long goofy-foot turn to the left. Distracted, or he wouldn't have hit the seam in the concrete at a bad angle and wind-milled off the front. A couple of the guys laughed and clapped as he flailed down the slope. His board slid slick and fast across the bed of the channel and into the culvert.

Kyle regained control of his stork's arms and legs and hitched up his jeans. He bowed to the mocking applause and sidled into the culvert to retrieve the board.

It was dark inside, and dank. His Chuck Taylors squeaked on the concrete. Kyle found his skateboard and kicked the tail so it jumped and he caught it and tucked it under his arm.

He turned to go and stopped.

"Guys," he said.

His friends kept talking. Kyle leaned toward the curving wall of the culvert and his heart seemed to be talking loudly and the skin on the back of his head went tight like somebody had threaded it with string and pulled.

"Guys, come see this."

Tony and Jaden roused themselves and walked over, shadowed in the culvert entrance.

"What?" Jaden said.

Kyle aimed his smartphone's flashlight at the wall. The black writing jumped out.

37.644827, − 121.781943

"Boring graffiti," Jaden said.

Kyle arced the flashlight up the curved wall of the culvert so they could see the rest.

The cops can't find it. Think you can?

"It's coordinates. Longitude and latitude,"

Kyle said. He Google mapped it. "And it's right near here."

A bite of wind rushed through the culvert. At the far end, where the light turned milky, a shadow passed the exit. Tony shuddered and backed toward the daylight.

"Dude. Chill. It was just a bird." Suddenly, Kyle wasn't the freshman. He was the discoverer. "We have to check this out."

"No way."

Kyle showed the map on his phone to Jaden, who pulled down his watch cap, breathing heavily.

"It's in Silver Creek Park. Tony — you drive."

Jaden grabbed his arm. "Don't you see it?"

He grabbed Kyle's phone and aimed the flashlight at the wall. High on the concrete, there it was.

Kyle stared hard for a second. "We gotta get to the park."

10

Caitlin had her eyes closed and her hands pressed over her earbuds. She had the Prophet's voice in her head. The voice from twenty-five years back. The original, no-doubt, no-shit voice of Mercury. Talking to the daughter of a victim, spitting venom as she sobbed and begged him to leave her family alone. "But she was a slut. She got what she deserved," he said.

She hit PAUSE, acid in her throat. After a second, when her pulse stopped thumping, she heard her desk phone ringing. She pulled out her earbuds like they were electrified.

When she answered the phone, the clerk said, "You have a visitor."

She took a second to gather herself, walked toward the front desk, and heard the excited voice of Deralynn Hobbs. She pulled open the door to the lobby. Deralynn bounded up and grabbed her hand.

"Detective. It's so good to meet you."

She was short, blocky, and as light on her feet as a beach ball. Her blond hair was sprayed into a messy headful of hedgehog spikes. She wore capris and a sweater the color of a Day-Glo traffic cone. Her eyes were sky-blue, her smile welcoming.

"This copycat thing. I found suspicious cold cases," Deralynn said. "One in Miami, ten years ago, and one in Houston, eighteen months back."

Caitlin had asked her to flag comments and forward information, not start her own investigation. "Suspicious how?"

"Couples killed near an equinox." She raised excited, clenched fists.

"How near? Dates? Victims' names? Case numbers and investigating officers?"

"Got all that. And get this. The victims met through an online dating outfit. Maybe the killer signs up for dating services."

Caitlin tried not to sound overtly skeptical. "And does what?"

Outside, a horn honked. Deralynn leaned toward the door. "Hang on. Or come with."

She bustled outside. Caitlin hung back, then thought: Get Deralynn back in her car, and she could leave that much quicker.

A dusty minivan was parked in a visitors slot. A bumper sticker read, WARNING: I

115

BRAKE FOR *OH GOD WHAT DID I JUST RUN OVER?* Caitlin felt glad that her instincts had been verified.

"Maybe he finds out people's profiles," Deralynn said. "And their fantasies. We're talking about a killer whose deepest meaning is found in a fantasy. Then maybe when women reject him, he kills them."

"Maybe."

It was difficult to hear Deralynn's voice over the sound of the car horn. In the driver's seat, a Siberian husky stood with its paws on the wheel. Deralynn opened the door and lugged him off. The horn went silent.

"Send me the information," Caitlin said.

"Right away." Deralynn held on to the car door. "I know coming here is irregular. But anything I can do to help. Really."

She shook hands again, climbed in, and drove away, waving vigorously.

Glinda, the Good Witch of the Web.

When Caitlin walked back into the lobby, Paige was biting her thumbnail. She had a FedEx envelope in her hand.

"For you."

"Thanks."

Caitlin buzzed through and took it. Paige spun off her chair and followed her as she walked toward her desk, like a guest who's

116

handed a gift to the birthday girl. Was it really that slow today? Or did Paige just want to hang out in the war room?

"Is there something else?" Caitlin said.

"No. Just . . ." Paige shrugged. "You gonna open it?"

"Yes. Thanks."

Paige slowly backed up.

The envelope was addressed to DETECTIVE HENDRIX. PERSONAL. The station's address was also written in block capital letters. Caitlin didn't recognize the sender's name or address. Caution twitched through her.

She opened the envelope and a flash drive slid out. There was nothing else inside.

"Martinez."

The other detective glanced up, bald head shining. He shot her the look he might give an annoying little sister who'd interrupted him. Then he saw her face. He came when she beckoned.

She pointed at the flash drive. "I'm not expecting anything and I don't recognize the sender. I don't want to seem skittish, but . . ."

"You're not overreacting."

She pulled a pair of latex gloves from her desk drawer and snapped them on. Martinez leaned over her keyboard, asked permission, and typed the sender's address in a search.

Not found.

They exchanged a look. She picked up the flash drive. Martinez walked with her to the station's IT department — a desk in a corner of the main office space — where she logged her credentials into the station's sterile computer, the machine designated to test unverified files and drives. It wasn't networked to the rest of the computers in the building or in the sheriff's office.

She inserted the drive. The computer scanned it and found no malware. Caitlin opened it.

A video played.

The view was dark, unrecognizable. Then came a sound, and it oriented everything.

It was a moan.

The image resolved into a moonlit gravel parking lot. Hills were silvery in the background. Oak trees dark and looming. The camera panned, smoothly, like a Hollywood tracking shot.

"Get Guthrie," Caitlin said.

"Yeah." Martinez watched a second longer, and hustled away.

Caitlin sat rigid, her hands pressed flat to the desk. On-screen, the moan rose to a cry.

She saw Stuart Ackerman on the ground,

on all fours. He was twenty yards from the camera, dragging himself away from whoever was shooting the video. His feet clicked against the gravel. Arrows protruded from his back.

The moans were coming from him. "No . . . no, Jesus . . ."

The camera followed. The cameraman's pace was calm.

A band tightened around Caitlin's chest. Her blood rushed in her ears. Behind her she heard Martinez return with Guthrie, but she couldn't pull her eyes from the screen.

"Help."

Ackerman's voice was thin and beyond desperate. The camera lingered, patiently, seeming to frame the scene.

Then it rushed across the ground toward Ackerman. A crossbow swung into view and as Caitlin realized the camera was a GoPro, probably mounted on the killer's shoulder, the crossbow aimed at its target. And fired.

Caitlin jumped. Her gasp was involuntary.

Martinez said, "Mother of God."

The video abruptly jump-cut to an alley. The unseen cameraman's breathing was slow and heavy. There was street noise. Graffiti was spray-painted on a brick wall: *dripping blood o*

The breathing was a presence. It expanded beyond the computer, suffusing the room. A voice whispered coarsely, "You're lost, Hendrix. Gone astray in a dark wood. You'll never find the path." The screen went black. "But someone will, for punishment awaits . . ."

Caitlin couldn't move. Couldn't turn her head from the screen. But in her peripheral vision, she saw. The entire room was staring. At her.

11

From the bus stop, walking through Potrero Hill to the boardinghouse, Mack Hendrix saw his daughter's weather-beaten SUV roll down the street. Shadows were settling over the neighborhood. The sky was golden edged behind the city's hills. On the bay, whitecaps churned the water. Caitlin parked, got out, and climbed the steps, not yet seeing him.

He slowed. He had a newspaper tucked under his arm. Mud-spattered Carhartt boots, sweat-stained cap. Dirt under his nails. Day labor, knocking out forms after a concrete pour for a millionaire's new house in Pacific Heights.

Honest labor. Clean sweat. Yet, for a moment, he wanted to turn and walk away. She would eye him, and judge him, and find him worthy. And he wanted none of that.

He stopped on the sidewalk and watched

her climb the long flight of steps to the front door.

She was lithe and athletic, with height she got from her mother's people. Her red hair was a fiery crown, tonight pulled back in some messy half ponytail, like she was still eight years old and coming home from soccer practice red cheeked and buzzing. Her steps were urgent.

That was Caitlin: urgent. Even when she stood bone still and guarded her thoughts and hopes — which was far too much of the time — she was racing inside, heart pumping, mind turning over like a high-revving engine, eyes gulping a scene.

How had he created something so beautiful and driven?

The wind bit him. He knew her too well: She was spiky but had a huge heart buried deep. And beneath it all, she was a hunter.

That part, he knew exactly how he had created. She loved playing games. She loved to win. The hunt thrilled her.

Winning gave her a goal, a target. Aiming for targets kept her from wandering into her own head, into the thicket of obsession and depression. It kept her from diving into the pit he had dug for her.

Caitlin reached the porch and knocked on the door. He watched a second longer. She was so like her mother — impulsive. Intuitive, seeing connections where others found only fog. Tough, but somehow not cynical. She had been disillusioned young, in terrible ways. But she remained passionate.

Passionate to right the wrong that befell his life. To redeem the Hendrix name. She tried to take everything on, singlehandedly. That was her trip wire — the can of emotional gasoline that could light in a flash and burn her up.

That, and the secret compassion that she tried to bury in front of strangers. Mack walked toward her.

She was at the door, talking to the landlady. "Do you know when he'll be back?"

He climbed the steps. "I'm here."

She turned. Strands of her hair swirled around her face in the wind. She gave him the look, saw the dirt and the paper and the mud on his boots, took measure of how steady his steps were, and kept her face flat. But he sensed the relief, the *Oh, thank God he's sober.* He had a long way to go to earn more than that. Even after twenty years.

"Just you?" he said. "Sergeant Guthrie decided it works better as a solo act?"

She pressed her lips together. He led her down the hall into the kitchen. "Glass of water?"

"No, thank you."

She stopped at the kitchen island, hands deep in her jacket pockets. "He sent me a message."

Mack stopped, his hand on the faucet. Caitlin rounded the island and approached him.

"I can't understand what he's saying."

He closed his eyes.

"You say you've given up. I don't believe it."

He lowered his head. She took his arm and pushed up his sleeve to reveal his tattoo.

"It's under your skin," she said.

The heat in her eyes seemed to scorch the ink. The pain of the needle returned.

I said the Prophet's symbol. Do it. Drunk in the Tenderloin, yelling at a tat artist. He hadn't wanted argument. He wanted a brand, punishment, a gate to the darkness. A reminder that the Prophet wasn't finished.

"Dad."

He read the second tattoo. *Caitlin.* Years later, he got that one sober. Because she was the light.

She said, "This is the second time he's made a remark that could refer to me. And I —"

"Second. What else?"

"The message he sent to the TV station. 'Old and young into the pit.' I think he knew I was assigned to the investigation from the start. And his message today . . ." She inhaled. "He calls me out by name."

"You don't think he's trying to drive you away from the case."

"He didn't try to drive you away, did he?"

"The opposite," Mack said.

"Like he wants me there. Like he . . ."

"Lured you in."

She looked pensive. "Like he chose me to pursue him."

Mack's pulse hit harder. He didn't dare say it, but he thought: The killer *selected* Caitlin. Every bit as much as he selected his victims. Caitlin didn't get assigned the investigation — she was *part* of the case. And the killer wanted her working on it. He put her on the playing field of one of the biggest unsolved serial murder cases in America.

His heart clutched. "Quit. Get out of town."

But he saw her desperation. Fear for her swept through him. He wanted to pull her close and whisper, *Run from this case.* But her voice was full of fury and determination.

"If he's taunting you directly, he has

125

something in the pipeline." He breathed. "Show me."

It was dusk when the skateboarders turned into Silver Creek Park. Kyle, Tony, and Jaden were silent as Tony drove the old Civic along the puddle-splashed gravel drive. Kyle's eyes darted between his phone, with the geographic coordinates, the hills, and the trees blowing in the wind. Nobody else was around.

Tony said, "This place is creepy."

Jaden said, "You think he was going to send us to Dairy Queen?"

Kyle thought: *He.* A weird quiver pulled at his lips. He bit down to stop it.

They bounced around a curve, into an empty parking lot. Kyle checked the co-ordinates. "It's close. Park here."

When Tony turned off the engine, the wind whistled through the door panels. They sat. Finally, Kyle got out.

He followed the map on his phone across the parking lot to a fire road. The chain was up, but there were tire tracks on both sides. He hopped over and headed up the road, into the trees. Tony and Jaden caught up.

They closed ranks and walked silently in the wind. After five minutes of climbing, they rounded a corner and found themselves

126

at the crest of a hill, looking down a ravine.

There were torn branches and bushes ripped out by the roots, in a fat path that fell deep into the ravine. It looked like a herd of dinosaurs had crashed through the brush.

Tony pointed. "What the hell is that?"

Kyle raised his phone to snap a photo. The camera flashed. Then he was running, and the sounds coming from his mouth and Jaden's and Tony's mouths were long, high screams.

Caitlin opened her laptop on a coffee table in the boardinghouse living room. The bay window was filled with charcoal darkness. She jacked in a flash drive with a copy of the FedEx video. She looked at her father.

"It's rough," she said.

Mack leaned forward, hands clasped between his knees. "Play it."

She hit a key.

Mack didn't move. He didn't blink. His eyes swept the screen. On the video, Stuart Ackerman's plaintive cries stretched on and on. Caitlin's stomach hollowed once more.

When the video jump-cut to the alley with the graffiti, Mack leaned in.

The voice on the video whispered, "You're lost, Hendrix. Gone astray in a dark wood.

127

You'll never find the path. But someone will, for punishment awaits . . ."

The video ended. Mack was as still as a gargoyle.

Quietly, he said, "Play it again."

Caitlin replayed it. Mack watched without moving. When it ended, he said, "Again."

He watched the third time with something hawklike in his face. When the video went black, he said, "You're releasing the graffiti footage?"

"Once Command signs off on it." Caitlin ran her fingers through her hair. "Somebody has to have seen that graffiti."

"Maybe." Mack's voice turned pensive. "The Prophet never chooses victims on the spur of the moment. He researches and scouts his targets. That's one thing he's telling you."

The knot in her stomach tightened. "He has somebody in the pipeline."

" 'Punishment awaits.' "

The air settled heavily around them.

She said, "He likes that word."

From her satchel she pulled out a photocopy of the map the Prophet had drawn of the first crime scene. *PUNISHMENT* was prominent.

Mack nodded at the map. "I found that in

a storm drain a quarter mile from the crime scene."

She leaned back. "I thought — wait. I thought he mailed this to the station. That the water damage happened when the evidence room flooded."

Mack shook his head.

She held the map up. "He dropped the original of this? But everything else has been flawless. He leaves no DNA, no fingerprints, no useful trace . . ."

"This was twenty-five years ago. He was still a novice."

"And making rookie errors?"

"An offender's first crime is often the most revealing," Mack said. "That's why you focus on it when you evaluate a series of crimes. It'll show you where the inexperienced offender is comfortable. That crime is close to where he lives or works, and his behavior is most natural because he hasn't yet perfected his techniques."

"So you're saying I should go back to where it started. With the wasps."

"I'm not saying anything. I told you, I don't want this to touch you."

"Stop that. I'm doing this."

"And you have to hear what I'm saying. Today, he *has* perfected his techniques. He's extremely skillful."

129

His eyes were melancholy, roiling with an emotion she couldn't identify.

"Is that why the first murder was in the fall, and all the others in the spring?" she said.

"Maybe. Counting these new killings, six murders have taken place on an equinox. But the first killing is the only one in the autumn."

She digested it. He scratched at his arms. His jittering energy suffused the room.

"You asked what his message is. But there isn't simply one message," he said. "Yes, there's a reason he addresses himself directly to you in that archaic way. 'Gone astray.' It has meaning to him, and you need to crack it." He caught himself. "Somebody should crack it. But his other 'message' might not be a code."

"It might be a lure."

"Don't let yourself get sucked into his world."

"Understood."

Mack hooked her gaze. He held it for a long moment. "It seeps into you. The truth about what human beings can do to each other. Eventually, to stop him, you'll do anything." He paused to make sure she was paying attention. "We needed a break in the case. We started thinking . . . give us the evidence. *Keep working.*"

She inhaled sharply. He stood and walked to the window.

She sat, hands hanging loose. After a minute she followed him to the window. Though she neared his side he stared vacantly, as though she were invisible.

She curved around until she was right in front of him. "Dad."

He turned his head and finally acknowledged her. His jaw was tight.

"I . . ." Her voice trailed off.

Mack's expression turned rueful. "There's nothing you need to say."

She stared at the floor for a minute, then nodded and turned to go. He caught her by the wrist.

"You have a good life. Don't let him ruin it."

Outside, Caitlin walked to her Highlander in the fading purple dusk. The wind brought the sound of traffic on 280.

Mack had just made an act of contrition. *We needed a break in the case. We started thinking . . . give us the evidence. Keep working.*

It was a confession: that he and Saunders became so obsessed with catching the Prophet, they missed the chance to save the newlyweds at the cemetery. She felt queasy.

The bay window of the boardinghouse blazed with light. She could see her father in the living room. He stood facing the wall, motionless, staring seemingly at nothing.

Her phone rang. It was Guthrie.

"Hendrix. Silver Creek Park. It may be our primary crime scene, where Stuart Ackerman was killed. I'll meet you there."

She jumped in the car. "Rolling. It'll be half an hour. I'm in the city."

"Move. There're high school kids involved."

12

Caitlin pulled into Silver Creek Park and immediately saw a problem. Flashing lights spangled the oak trees, but nobody had defined or secured the crime scene. She stopped beside a sheriff's office Charger and got out. A uniformed officer approached.

"Marston?" she said.

The young officer, who'd been with her on the crank-house raid, raised his chin in greeting. "They're all up this way."

They crossed the gravel parking lot toward a second patrol car. In its headlights stood another uniformed deputy, several civilians in their forties, and three teenage boys. A station wagon, a Lexus, and a Civic with a Sequoia High School parking sticker were parked nearby.

"Is this part of the crime scene?" Caitlin said.

Marston pointed at the far end of the parking lot. "Ravine up the fire road about a quarter mile. That's where the kids found the car."

"Is that the only road that provides vehicle access to the ravine?"

"As far as I know."

A dull annoyance, and a sense of missed opportunity, grew in her. "So the car in the ravine had to drive through this parking lot. The killer could have passed right by here."

Control the scene. That was a cardinal rule in detective work. Gravel ground under her boots. She wondered if they were walking on already trampled evidence.

She nodded at the people huddled ahead. "You spoke to the kids?"

Marston nodded. "Each of them, separately. They seem straight-up scared. Thought they would have some fun, and ended up in something freaky."

Headlights rose, coming from the main road. A brown beater stopped behind the patrol cars and a man got out. Drawn, gray, wearing a worn tweed jacket and Western shirt. He had a notebook in his hand.

He cupped a hand to his mouth and called out, "Detective Hendrix. Bart Fletcher, *East Bay Herald.*"

Fletcher. The hack who'd written the story about Caitlin trying to overcome her father's failures.

"Has the Prophet committed another murder?" he shouted.

Caitlin looked to the second uniformed deputy. Lyle. "Get him out of here. Shut the park entrance. Put out cones. Nobody gets in but Sergeant Guthrie or Crime Scene."

Lyle nodded and headed toward Fletcher. Caitlin heard grumbling conversation, and Fletcher's engine starting. She kept walking.

How did Fletcher know? "What went out over the scanner?"

"Not sure," Marston said.

She approached the group. Parents hovered, hawkeyed and anxious. She made eye contact with them all but addressed herself to the boys. "I'm Detective Hendrix. Are you okay?"

The three teens nodded. They looked at her with shiny fear. Boys in sagging jeans and one with a watch cap, biting his nails. These weren't kids used to encountering the cops. The youngest, Kyle Perez, looked about fourteen and sounded like his voice had broken only yesterday. He explained about finding the geographic coordinates in the culvert behind the high school.

"So we decided to check it out. I thought it could be a joke and didn't want to call

135

the police over nothing. You know?"

His dad set a hand on Kyle's shoulder. "You didn't do anything wrong."

But he squeezed Kyle's shoulder like, *We're going to have a talk about doing something stupid, though.*

Kyle went on. "So we got here and headed for the coordinates up that fire road . . ." He looked again at his friends. They offered no help. "That's when we saw the car. And we . . ."

Jaden, the kid with the hat, said, "Freaked."

Tony, the driver, said, "We were all, get the hell out of here —"

"Fast," Jaden said. "We booked. Ran."

Kyle wiped his nose and swallowed. "You don't want us to go back up there, do you?"

"No."

The boys all relaxed.

Caitlin said, "Marston, with me. Everybody else, stay put."

Kyle said, "And so you know . . . it smells horrible."

Caitlin and Marston walked toward the fire road. As they did, Guthrie pulled in. He parked and joined them. The road climbed into the woods. At the crest of the hill, it turned and ran along a ridge above a ravine.

The fall line ran through torn bushes and

tree limbs. The car was about sixty feet down, grille buried against a boulder. An arrow protruded from the left front tire.

They smelled it. Death. Then they heard it. A buzz, frantic. Flies.

Marston coughed. Guthrie swept the beam of his flashlight across the scene. Caitlin battled the urge to back away. Though she breathed shallowly through her nose, the smell filled her sinuses and throat. If she breathed through her nose long enough, her olfactory nerves would go numb. An old cop had told her that, at the morgue. He also told her that smells are particulate. She clamped her teeth together and fought the gag reflex.

They edged over the lip of the ravine and sidestepped down the fall line, flashlights sweeping the brush. The smell worsened. Ten yards down, they got a better vantage point.

"What the hell?" Guthrie said.

They aimed their flashlights at the wrecked car. Its tail faced toward them. It was a blue Nissan Sentra, the same model and color as Stuart Ackerman's missing vehicle. Guthrie called in the tag number, but the license plate wasn't what they were staring at. And a new smell mixed with death. Gasoline.

Marston said, "Ruptured gas tank or fuel line?"

Guthrie continued to train his flashlight on the car. "Call the fire department."

Marston leaned into his shoulder-mounted radio and called for fire response to a wilderness car wreck. A voice replied.

Marston said, "Detective, it's getting crazy back at the parking lot."

"What's going on?" Caitlin said.

"Media's here in force. The park entrance is closed, but they may come straight through the woods on foot."

"Tell Deputy Lyle to contain it," she said.

Standing halfway down the ravine, Caitlin and the two men tried to get their heads around what they were seeing. They were close enough to discern the source of the stench.

The car was full of dead crows.

The windows were cracked just enough to let the smell pour out and flies swarm in, while keeping bigger wildlife from pillaging the scene.

The installation. The Prophet's exhibit.

A pair of vultures squatted on the roof. Alive.

When Marston swung the beam of his flashlight across them, they cawed and spread their huge wings and leaped into the air, lumbering away into the night.

Crows. Dozens of them. They were stiff and mangled and obviously decaying. Their glittering black feathers covered flattened and drooping flesh. Caitlin didn't know how, but they seemed to all be standing upright, like a choir. They covered the dashboard and the shelf behind the backseat. They covered the steering wheel and the gearshift and the seats.

Every single bird had the head of a doll.

She tried to keep breathing.

Doll heads jammed down over the birds' own. Baby dolls. Plastic toys with clicky, blank eyes. Some with hair, some bald. Barbies, Bratz. Infants. Some pink and shiny, some fuzzed with black mold. Tiny mouths pursed as though seeking to suckle.

One of them had a cell phone clamped between its teeth.

"Sergeant," Caitlin said. "Did San Joaquin find Ackerman's phone?"

"No."

"But his body — that word carved in his chest."

" 'Answer.' " Guthrie cut a glance at her. "Think somebody might call?"

In the back pocket of her jeans, Caitlin's own phone buzzed with an incoming text. She ignored it. Then her phone chimed with voice mail.

Guthrie pulled gloves on. "Check it."

He edged down to the Sentra, tested the window, and snaked his hand through.

Caitlin pulled out her phone and saw a crazy list of messages and missed calls. Texts from her mom and Sean. Calls from Sean. And a text from Deralynn Hobbs.

You're on camera.

Cold sweat broke out on Caitlin's back. She pressed CALL. Deralynn picked up immediately.

"Detective, there's a camera live streaming from that wrecked car. He's watching. Everybody's watching."

Caitlin glanced at the car. Guthrie was reaching into it, arm outstretched, trying to get the cell phone.

The night tilted. The phone. The camera. The smell of gasoline.

She yelled, "Sergeant — get out of there. *Now.*"

Guthrie turned his head, alarmed. She ran down the slope, waving him back.

In the doll's mouth, the screen of the cell phone lit up with an incoming call.

Guthrie yanked his arm out of the car. And with a white flash, the interior of the

140

Sentra ignited.

Yellow light bloomed. The birds, the dolls' heads, abruptly turned flame lit, stark and bright. A blast of heat poured from the car. Guthrie threw himself back, arms raised in front of his face. Caitlin ran toward him.

He waved her off. "Back."

Flames engulfed the interior of the car. As Guthrie spun away from it and pushed through the brush, the windows exploded. Glass spewed across his back. Fire shot from the windows, roiling with black smoke. Guthrie reached Caitlin and they scrambled up the hill.

"You okay?" she said.

He was coughing, his face was bright red, and glass spall littered his hair and jacket. "Fine."

"The phone," she said. "It looked like the trigger."

"This was a goddamned IED."

In the darkening evening, the car in the bottom of the ravine was a small hell. The wings of the dead birds flared randomly. The doll heads melted. The car raged with flame and smoke.

With a sharp *bang,* a tire exploded from the heat.

Marston waved away the greasy, stinking smoke. "Sergeant, you all right?"

Guthrie nodded.

"I have a fire extinguisher in my unit."

He ran down the road. The heat of the fire was a rippling wall.

Guthrie said, "He wanted us to approach the phone."

"He waited until we mentioned it to set the fire." Caitlin raised her own phone to her ear. "Deralynn?"

"Oh, my God. This is awful," Deralynn said.

"It's still live?"

"The camera fritzed out."

The flames rose higher, and smoke poured from beneath the car. Guthrie said, "It's going up."

They retreated to the fire road. A second later a hard *boom* pounded the air, and a swirl of red flame and smoke rose over the lip of the ravine. Sparks littered the air. Heat radiated against Caitlin's face. In the distance came the wail of sirens.

Whatever had been in the car was gone.

Guthrie shook his head. "He played us. The son of a bitch."

13

The car blaze died under the blast of the firefighters' hoses. After they extinguished the brush burning in the ravine, and pried open the car like a charred carcass, they rolled up their gear and climbed in the pumper truck and backed down the fire road. Caitlin approached the burned-out Sentra gingerly, flashlight scanning every inch of dirt, every millimeter of metal and glass. The entire scene was scorched, charred, exploded, wet, and stinking.

Back at the entrance to Silver Creek Park, it was a scrum of news vans and lookie-loos. Starting with the high school boys' initial approach to the car, every moment had been captured on video and posted online. That's why the press was there, and the Internet was going crazy, and ghouls with a jones for the Prophet case were arriving like pilgrims, swarming the scene.

The murder of Stuart Ackerman now

involved perhaps three crime scenes: the ranch where his body was found, the storm drain behind Sequoia High School, and this ravine. Caitlin pointed her flashlight at the arrow protruding from the front tire of the car. That tire, already flat when the car caught fire, had melted.

Guthrie came down the hill. He had removed his jacket and brushed most of the glass from his hair. "Once that arrow punctured the tire, Ackerman didn't drive far. If that's how the killer ambushed him, the initial crime scene is nearby."

Caitlin crept around the car in the burned brush. Both the hood and the trunk were up, pried open by the fire crew. Under the hood was a ruined engine. In the trunk was an exploded spare tire. She angled her Maglite at the car's interior. It was a mess, a charnel, four hundred and twenty blackbirds baked in a pie.

There was no body.

She felt immensely relieved and strangely uneasy. Maybe there was no second victim in the Ackerman slaying. Maybe this — the clue at the high school, the freakish setting with the car, the video — was all a mind job, meant to embarrass law enforcement and terrify the public. Or maybe the killer was still waiting for his moment to reveal another murder.

Here we are now. Entertain us.

"There's something about this. It's so . . ."

"What?" Guthrie said.

She stared at the car. Listened to the wind. "It's so eager," she said. "It's . . . avid."

He eyed her, in much the same manner he'd appraised her the first night at the cornfield crime scene. "What do you mean?"

"The Prophet was always relentless. He killed, and then he extended the . . . *after-glow* of the killing . . . by tormenting the families of his victims. Phoning, playing tapes. And taunting law enforcement. The messages to the media — that braggadocio — were about keeping himself in the spot-light, but also about whipping up fear."

Her Maglite rested on the half-burned face of a baby doll, one eye gone, one gleaming. "But . . . this is over the top."

"Serial murder is by definition over the top."

"This feels different," she said, and checked herself.

Who was she to expound on the nature of the Prophet? She was a homicide rookie standing in muck, with her boots and jeans blackened by soot.

"Go on," Guthrie said.

145

In the deep cut of the ravine, cocooned by brush and oaks that climbed its slopes, under the cover of night, she felt safe to speak. She worked the thought around in her head, trying to put smoke into solid form and turn it into words.

"He was originally so patient. Killing in March and April, basically once a year."

"Then he accelerated."

"Viciously. One murder on the spring equinox, three more a few weeks later," she said. "Then he disappeared for *twenty years.*"

"If he really stopped killing during that period," Guthrie said.

"True." She thought another moment. "But this — his return, the two victims in the cornfield, the call to the family, the note to us, the second killing not even seventy-two hours later, video to the media, and now this . . . *spectacle.* There's no cooling-off period. It's an explosion. It's greedy."

"His glorious return. Bigger than ever. A stadium rock tour," Guthrie said.

"Maybe twenty years of pent-up rage is erupting in a burst of violence. But this . . ."

She gestured at the car. "This takes the game to a new level. It's even more narcissistic than his previous killings. This is all about showing off. It's all about his superiority. He's shoving it in our face, but bragging to the wider world. 'Are you not entertained?' "

"I'm not. Bread and circuses and death."

"He's competing to top himself." She mulled her next words. "Would the FBI update the killer's psychological profile for us?"

He didn't answer immediately. "After twenty years, maybe."

"Because there's something new this time around. Something worse. An open need, an element of . . ."

"What?"

"Frenzy."

14

Caitlin spun the wheel and turned onto her street just after midnight. She ached with fatigue and stank of smoke and sweat and burned feathers and plastic. But she pulled into the driveway and something loosened in her chest. Sean's Tundra pickup was parked there. The kitchen light was on.

She locked her Highlander, went through the gate into the backyard, and trooped to the kitchen door. She fought with the wet laces of her boots and pried them off. In the morning she'd have to scrub out the stench with soap and a boot brush. She yanked off her socks and glanced around. It was dark and the yard was bordered by six-foot-tall red oleander. She didn't know why she was checking for unwanted eyes, because nobody could see in. Unless they were hiding behind the garage or in the bushes or had a camera planted under the eaves.

Shut down the paranoid voice. Just for the

next few minutes.

She unhooked her badge, removed her duty belt, took off her holster and SIG, and peeled off her jeans. They were filthy to the knees with soot and mud and combustion by-products. She fought them down to her ankles, kicked them off, and heard the door open behind her. She turned. Sean stood in the kitchen doorway, backlit by low light, watching.

"Don't let me stop you," he said.

Her shoulders dropped. His face was in silhouette, but his voice was patient. He wouldn't push for details. He knew she'd tell him everything when she was ready.

"Favor?" she said.

He straightened. "Sure."

"Turn on the shower?"

"You got it."

He headed into the house, throwing a look at her over his shoulder. She rewarded him by pulling her T-shirt over her head. Even though she felt chilled and filthy.

A second later, Shadow burst through the open door, all paws and yips and glorious welcome.

Caitlin crouched and let Shadow lick her face. Then she scooped up her dirty clothes, stuffed them in the washer, and padded through the house. The shower was going full blast.

Sean stood outside the door. She gave him a look of abject gratitude. "Thank you."

As she passed him, he brushed the back of his hand along her arm. His expression was neutral — calm, but underlaid with curiosity and concern.

Caitlin stripped off, climbed into the shower, and tilted her face up to meet the spray. It was stinging hot, a blessed welcome. She scrubbed away the soot and shampooed her hair, then stood under the needling water, leaning on her arms against the tile, until her skin turned pink.

The scars stood out on her wrists and forearms. White and ribbed, parallel stripes, self-inflicted with a razor blade.

She hadn't cut herself since she was fifteen. She had tattooed her skin to swallow the slash marks. A coral snake wound around her left arm. A quote ran up her right:

the whole sky

Her ink was reclamation. But tonight the scars seemed to sting.

When she turned off the tap the room was white with steam. She dried off and pulled on sweats and a cami. In the living room, Sean had lit a fire in the fireplace. Gary Clark Jr. was on the stereo. Caitlin dropped beside him on the sofa. Her mind was buzzing.

"How did you find out about the video?" she said.

"Another ATF agent. His daughter's in high school. She saw it and told him."

He got his phone and showed her a link to a streaming site. She shook her head.

"How'd this get traction? Somebody spread the word. High school kids?"

"It was crawling in the social media underbrush by the time you reached the scene."

"Computer Forensics will try to trace the video's source, but I don't hold out much hope that we'll get an IP address. This guy is too slick," she said.

"Who's the woman who alerted you?"

"Loopy amateur sleuth. Only now I'm thinking she isn't so loopy. She was on it like that." She snapped her fingers.

Sean nodded at the kitchen. "You want ice cream? Calming music? Doggy downers?"

"I'm good."

"You're talking at the speed of sound. You need to slow down, flash."

She tipped her head back against the couch. She was still amped, but the frantic edge felt like it had been buffed down to mere excitement.

"The bomb squad ran the scene?" Sean said.

"With the dogs. Arson will get out there in the morning."

"You want me to look at the evidence from that car?"

She and Sean talked often about their work, sometimes on a high, sometimes in sorrow. They were each other's sounding board. They discussed tactics and politics. But neither of them had ever asked for help with a case. This would open a gate to something different.

Cop to cop. Caitlin knew, in a hard and rational part of her brain, that straight female cops gravitated to men in the same line of work, at a sky-high rate. Conventional wisdom said: Socially, female police officers are screwed. Not many men are secure enough to date a woman who carries a gun and represents capital-A Authority. Date a civilian, you can expect it to melt down in less than a year.

Caitlin thought the conventional wisdom sucked. At the same time, she couldn't deny that Cop World spun around its own axis. Getting off night shift at six A.M. Telling a date about your workday — *I arrested a repeat violent felon. I drove a hundred and thirty-five miles per hour down I-580.* Some guys heard it, felt their masculinity threatened, and parachuted back to the regular world.

Maybe it was inevitable: Here she was, with a cop. And not just any cop, but a fed. A special agent with an expertise in explosives.

Sean had trained as a bomb squad expert with the FBI at Quantico, and with ATF's Certified Explosive Specialist program. He dealt with C4 and ammonium nitrate, with fuses and timing mechanisms and everything that could destroy flesh and blood at thirty-four hundred feet per second. He spent his time tracking people who wanted to freelance fiery destruction. Narcos. Terrorists. Sovereign citizens and wannabe jihadis and corporate saboteurs.

Tonight, if she showed him the photos of the burned-out Sentra, he would analyze the device that sent it up in flames. He might confirm her guess: that it was a Molotov cocktail, rigged to ignite when the phone rang.

Sean knew his stuff. But Caitlin didn't want to pull him into this. Not here. Not now. *Job stays at the station.*

"Thank you. But no," she said.

"I'm not getting any rest until you put

153

your mind at ease," he said. "And I know you've heard my spiel about arsonists and bomb makers, and how they love to go after first responders."

She rested a hand on his thigh. Sean eyed her for a moment, his face half shadowed, hands hanging between his knees.

"You okay?" he said.

"Copacetic."

"I know you want to keep it out. Close the door on it emotionally."

She stood up and headed to the kitchen. "We still have that tequila."

He caught up as she reached the bottle. "That's not what we need."

He spun her around. For a second she held on to the tequila. Then she stepped into his embrace.

He gave her a lingering kiss, looking her in the eye. Sean was big into doing things with his eyes open. He slipped his hand around her waist and walked backward, tugging her with him, sliding the strap of her cami off her shoulder. After a few steps she put her hands to his chest and pushed.

"Go."

Her clothes hit the floor in the bedroom. Then she was pulling his work shirt off his shoulders and his T-shirt over his head. Sean tried to stop, to kick off his boots, his hands being otherwise engaged on her back, on her hips, running up her ribs. She kissed him and shoved him backward. He let himself fall onto the bed. She kicked the door closed. Her dog was asleep at the other end of the house, but she did not want to hear whimpers or barking coming from anybody besides her or her man.

On the bed, Sean wrangled his boots off. Caitlin climbed on top of him and pressed his shoulders flat.

"You first," she said.

With Sean Rawlins, sex was a full-contact sport. It was all his tension and excitement and enthusiasm and anxiety and goddamn gratefulness at being alive, pouring out in unfettered physicality. It was how he expressed himself, how he showed her who he was and what she meant to him. It was play and release and deep sharing.

Which was everything that Caitlin struggled with.

The bedroom was dark. Though she was sitting on top of him, working off his belt, Sean reached for the nightstand and turned on the lamp.

"Too bright," Caitlin said.

He tossed his shirt at it. The room dimmed. Caitlin unzipped his jeans. "Blue plaid. My favorite fantasy."

She adored Sean for what he'd done for her. Not just in matching her intellectually, and respecting her mind, and making her laugh. Not just because he loved the same bad movies she did, and because he had a sense of humor, and smarts, and was an adult. But because Sean saw the walls she put up and had given her time. And then he had pounced, full force.

She knew he needed something primal to ground himself, to connect with life when the work he did took him to scenes of destruction. Sex, giving everything, was affirmation. It was him saying, *I'm here. With you.*

He ran his hands up and down her thighs as she sat across his hips, his jeans still on. She said, "Raise your hands over your head and hold still. Don't move until I tell you to."

He was smiling, his eyes bright. When he stretched his arms overhead she lay down on top of him and reached up to circle his wrists like handcuffs.

She wanted to tell him to close his eyes but he never would.

He was the one who knew she fought to keep herself in the world, that even if she closed her eyes she couldn't stop her emotions. He was the one who finally made a connection with her.

There was violence at the heart of his life, as there was in hers. He knew her history. He acknowledged her anger, that corrosive force that she tried desperately to rid herself of.

She held his hands down and pressed herself against him. She felt his pulse against hers.

Sean was the one who'd urged her to tattoo the scars she'd cut with the razor blade. The serpent — sign of transformation and healing. The quote, from Rita Dove's poem "Dawn Revisited." About second chances.

The whole sky is yours
to write on, blown open

She hadn't truly wanted to die. That day when she was fifteen, when the blade cut too deep. But she had been desperate for release. It had taken half her life to deal with it. The pain of the tattoo needle had brightened her, let her integrate the truth into her still-living body.

Sean was a cop. But she didn't think he was inevitable. She thought he was a miracle.

She released his hands. "Now," she said.

He swept them around her and rolled over

and let her fight his jeans off, and then he was wild, and wide-eyed, and smiling at her.

15

The morning broke clear, with the wind rushing through the trees. The alarm woke Caitlin at six. Sean was deep asleep in a jumping-jack pose. She slipped out of bed, dressed in running gear, and headed out.

By the time she reached the meeting point, her running group, the Rockridge Ragers, was already halfway down the street. Caitlin pounded down the hill, pulling the watch cap lower on her forehead. The sky was deep blue, brightening to orange behind the Berkeley Hills. A lone figure waited at the corner, clapping and beckoning, *Come on.*

Caitlin's knee felt stiff and was still the color of an eggplant. She would have liked a slow solo run. But twice a week this group met to hit the hills. Workdays, they did 5K on city streets. Weekends, they hashed, setting a hare-and-hound chase through parks and trails.

"Move it, Red," called the woman at the corner. "Tomorrow's lone-wolf day. Today we run with the pack."

Caitlin reached her and they fell into stride together. "You're feisty this morning."

"Then let's go sub twenty-three."

"Bitch."

Michele Ferreira laughed.

Caitlin matched her pace to Michele's, though she was six inches taller. They aimed for the group, about two hundred yards ahead.

"Big crowd this morning," she said.

Michele gave her a look.

"I know. Nobody wants to run alone," Caitlin said.

Michele had dark eyes and wore her hair in a pixie faux-hawk. She was a mighty mite, warm but edgy. "How much of what I hear on the news is true?"

"Every bit. UFOs are behind it. And the Illuminati. The Jesuits. Major League Baseball."

"Fine, smart-ass. Don't talk about it."

Leave the case at the station, she thought. But it was boiling in her head. If she talked about it with Sean, she would let slip her old obsessions. Michele wouldn't judge. And even though Caitlin had met Michele

160

through Sean, she trusted that her friend would never let their conversations get back to him.

"No, it's okay," she said. "Running in groups is smart right now. And not talking to strangers. I mean not at all. Keeping distance from them. Locking your car doors."

"Saint Peter on a fucking pony. You dealing with this?" Michele said.

Piece of cake, Caitlin nearly said. Her instinct was to keep her gloves up.

"It's a nightmare." Her feet pounded the sidewalk. "But it's been a nightmare for twenty-five years. If I can do anything to stop it . . ."

"Then maybe you can finally wake up?" Michele said.

She felt like she'd been given a shove. "Something like that." She looked at Michele. "Damned ER nurses. Seeing what's really going on."

"Yeah. You have a hickey on your neck."

Caitlin didn't, but she smiled. They were gaining on the rest of the group, warming up and falling into rhythm.

"Can I ask you something, as a nosy civilian?" Michele said. "The symbol. Why does he mark his victims with it?"

"It's how he signs his work."

"You mean it's his signature."

"Literally," she said.

"What does that *mean*?"

It had baffled investigators from the start. Mercury was one of astrology's ruling planets. Did the killer use it as homage to the Zodiac? In her early teens, Caitlin had become obsessed with Mercury's astrological portents. She had learned to spot Mercury in the sky, low on the horizon after sunset or before dawn. She had ached to know if it had a true pull over the Earth, and over the killer who had destroyed so many.

"It depends on what *mercury* means to him," she said. "Mercury, the planet closest to the sun? Or Mercury, the winged messenger — Roman god, guide of souls to the underworld. Or maybe mercury the chemical element. Symbol Hg. Atomic number eighty. The only metal that's liquid at room temperature."

She was gradually picking up her pace. They were reeling in the group ahead.

"It also has astrological power," Michele said.

"If you believe in that."

"Honey, you haven't met my mother."

They reached a corner, checked for traffic, and ran across. The sun was brightening.

"Mom never planned a trip without knowing the state of the planets. She didn't want me to take the SAT in November because my chart looked bad," Michele said.

"So you know Mercury's astrological meaning?"

"It's about communication. You've heard of being mercurial."

"Unpredictable. Capricious, volatile. Fickle."

"When's your birthday?" Michele said.

"September fourth."

"Virgo. Mercury rules Virgo."

They started up a hill, the group only twenty yards ahead.

"But the symbol itself," Michele said. "You know how people see it."

"As a devil's head."

For too many millennia, humanity had given Satan cloven hooves and curved horns. The image was stuck in deep. Nobody who grew up in a society inflected by Judaism, Christianity, or Islam could keep themselves from the involuntary shudder. Hell, she'd read *Childhood's End*.

Michele said. "Before he kills them, does he . . ."

"No," Caitlin said. "None of the victims

163

has been sexually assaulted."

"I thought serial killers did it to get off."

Caitlin measured her words. "You're not wrong. But sometimes their sexual thrill comes from carrying out their fantasy. And reliving it afterward."

"Fuck me with a telephone pole."

"Serial killers are, almost without exception, sexual sadists. But . . ."

"Some get off on death and torture."

"And power. Possession."

Michele glanced her way, breathing hard now.

Caitlin nodded at the runners ahead. "Time to put them in the dust."

"Aren't you freaked out? I am," Michele said.

Caitlin accelerated on the uneven sidewalk. "I can't let that happen."

When she got home, hot and out of breath, Sean was in the kitchen. He was dressed, Glock on his hip, phone to his ear.

"I'll be there before eight," he said. "Siefert has the warrant. The trucking firm parks thirty trailers at that depot, and we search every one."

She got a mug from the cabinet, poured herself a cup of coffee, and refilled Sean's. He ended the call, thanked her, and downed half his coffee, black, in one go. It was less ritual than start-up procedure.

"Hot," he said. "Good. Gotta go."

He kissed her. Shadow padded into the room, ears pricking.

Sean pulled on his ATF windbreaker and hung his badge around his neck. He cocked his head at Shadow. "You go to doggy day care while Mommy scours a crime scene?"

Shadow barked. Caitlin smiled and walked past him. He stopped her.

"I know I wound you up about the arsonist angle last night. I don't want it to get under your skin. Don't let this guy into your head."

"Don't worry."

He held on.

"Seriously," he said. "But watch out."

"Seriously. I hear you loud and clear." She kissed him again. "Be safe."

In the crisp March daylight, the burned-out car stood vivid and dismal. A creek trickled at the bottom of the ravine, descending through the brush until it flowed through a drainage pipe under a road. Caitlin logged in to the scene and met the arson investigator down the slope. Carvalho was a neat man who had a thirty-five-millimeter camera on a strap around his neck and a clipboard with a sketch pad. He was drawing

165

all pertinent features of the scene.

"First thing, no casualties except a Toys 'R'Us somewhere that's missing several dozen dolls' heads," he said. "The birds were already dead, your initial report says."

"Definitely," she said.

"Basic phone-triggered incendiary device." Carvalho showed her the burned cell phone in an evidence bag. "The other components were a beer bottle filled with gasoline, a sparkler — probably twenty-inch, ninety-second burn time — and maybe five bucks of electronic components and model rocket fuses. Stripped USB cable, thyristor, alligator clips. Calling the cell phone completed the circuit."

The crime scene techs had set up a table and a sifting screen to sieve evidence from bird bones and charred seat fabric. There were bits of wire and shattered brown glass, the remains of the beer bottle.

"How much technical know-how did this take?" she said.

"Science-fair proficiency. It's not a nuclear trigger."

He looked over the scene. "This is a hell of a lot of trouble to go to, just to burn a car. Has kind of a pagan sacrifice feel to it."

"Yeah."

"This guy's set fires before?"

Caitlin's throat felt dry. "Once. Twenty years ago." The day in the cemetery. "He killed two people. And he stayed long enough to watch."

"Arsonists love to watch. It's part of their thrill," he said.

Caitlin looked morosely at the phone. "Can anything be recovered from that?"

"The fire eliminated any fingerprints, DNA, trace. The techs may be able to pull some data off the device."

"It's going straight to Computer Forensics?"

He nodded. She texted Eugene Chao at the lab to tell him it would be coming.

Carvalho said, "With luck, what was on the phone is stored in the cloud."

"We're checking that, and his online accounts."

"And his laptop," he said.

"All computers he had known access to," she said, and stopped. A mental lightbulb went off. She knew where she needed to head next. "Thanks, Carvalho. I've got to go."

She jogged up the hill, squinting against the morning sun.

The woman who met her at Sequoia High was wizened, five feet tall, with Jackie O glasses and hair dyed the color of motor oil. She emerged stooped and scowling from the vice principal's office.

Caitlin extended her hand. "Mrs. Lovado?"

The woman examined the badge on Caitlin's belt. "You sounded older on the phone."

"Thank you for making time to meet with me."

Mrs. Lovado made fish lips, expressing her displeasure. "This way."

She led Caitlin across campus to the math quad.

"I would have contacted the sheriff earlier if I'd known," Mrs. Lovado said. "We're all in such shock. We didn't make the connection. Mr. Ackerman's . . . his . . ."

She blanched.

"Ma'am?"

"What happened to him had no connection to the school," Mrs. Lovado said.

Morning classes were in session, the halls quiet. Metal lockers were painted Nutella brown. The linoleum floor coolly reflected morning light from the doors at the end of the building.

Mrs. Lovado stopped at a classroom door, lifted a heavy set of keys, and paused. "After you phoned, I decided it would be wise to examine the computer in his classroom. So I could help your department. It's school property. And that's when I . . ."

Her face was pinched. So was Caitlin's. On the phone, Mrs. Lovado had assured her that the computer had been untouched since Stuart Ackerman last used it. Caitlin had asked her to keep it that way.

"What did you do, Mrs. Lovado?"

"Nothing. The machine is fine. I didn't delete anything. But . . . you'll see."

The woman unlocked the door, led Caitlin in, and headed to the teacher's desk. Caitlin took in the big windows, the half-erased whiteboard, the posters for MATH! High school never changed.

With every step, Mrs. Lovado seemed to grow drier and more toughened, like a shrunken orange. She sat down at the desk and grimly tapped the keyboard. The desktop monitor came awake.

She looked over her shoulder at Caitlin. "Using school computers for personal reasons is strictly against district policy. It seems Mr. Ackerman disregarded that rule."

Caitlin felt a buzz. "Please, show me."

Mrs. Lovado hunched forward and ran bony fingers over the keys. "The day before he . . ."

She continued typing. Caitlin realized that

the woman couldn't say *died* for anything.

"He logged in to a website that is absolutely *not* appropriate for official use."

Mrs. Lovado brought up the site. Caitlin leaned in.

"Zodiac Match?" Caitlin said.

Mrs. Lovado lifted her fingers from the keyboard as though a bad odor leaked from the screen. Caitlin felt an electric scratch along her arms.

The stars have your love match waiting.

The home page was blingy, cheesy, retro. Kaleidoscopic colors throbbed from the circle of the zodiac. At the center of the circle a couple smiled with lust.

Astro-Science: The TRUE way to find your soul mate.

Zodiac Match looked as sketchy as hell.

Your natal chart will reveal . . . Mars and Venus help to determine how a person behaves in romance . . . Mercury can provide information on how a person thinks . . .

Zodiac.

Mercury.

And all the killers in the deep blue sea.

Then she saw it: the blinking cursor on the log-in panel. *No way.* Stuart Ackerman's username and password were pre-entered.

He had apparently logged in to this site so often that he had set up the *Remember me*

170

feature. Even on his school computer.

Mrs. Lovado raised an eyebrow. Caitlin nodded. The woman logged in.

Welcome, Wild Sagittarius 23.

Caitlin held bolt still. Stuart Ackerman's sign was listed as Sagittarius. A drawing depicted a centaur drawing a bow, about to fire an arrow. Zodiac symbol: archer. Element: fire. Sign ruler: Jupiter. Detriment: Mercury.

Her excitement tried to gallop ahead of her. The department would subpoena all this information, but time was scarce. "Can you print this page?"

Mrs. Lovado hit a key.

Caitlin said, "Check messages."

Mrs. Lovado went to the page.

"That one," Caitlin said.

She opened a message thread dated three days before Ackerman's body was found. It was from Starshine69.

Caitlin's eyes widened. Mrs. Lovado sat screwed into the chair, hands folded primly, which told Caitlin she had already seen this photo.

Starshine69 [Thursday 1:26PM] Brace for impact.

Starshine69 was in her midthirties. Her

head was coquettishly tipped to one side, index finger inserted in her plump, pursed lips. She was dressed as a lion. Full-on furry cosplay. Faux-fur bikini top. In a second photo, she was licking the back of her hand, as a cat does with its paw before it grooms itself. Caitlin didn't think Starshine planned to rub her forehead with that hand.

A little profile avatar at the corner of Starshine's message showed the astrological sign for Leo. Yeah, she was a real cat.

Mrs. Lovado said, "This is more than I ever cared to know about one of our teachers or indeed the world."

Starshine69 [Friday 1:27PM] Silver Creek Park tomorrow 9PM.
Wild Sagittarius 23 [Friday 4:06PM] Ready to rumble.

The park. Caitlin kept scrolling. Ackerman's final messages grabbed her breath.

Wild Sagittarius 23 [Saturday 8:24PM] On my way.
Wild Sagittarius 23 [Saturday 9:03PM] Pulling into the park. Are you here?
Wild Sagittarius 23 [Saturday 9:08PM] Here. Where are you?

Two minutes later, Caitlin rushed toward

172

her car, printouts in hand, and phoned Guthrie.

"He had a date. A woman. We have to find her."

16

Caitlin walked into the war room, to phones ringing, Guthrie huddled with Shanklin and Martinez, jangling energy. Guthrie whistled at her to join them.

"We still haven't identified Starshine69," he said.

Martinez had a phone to his ear. He was wearing the ugliest bowling shirt ever conceived. She thought the puke-yellow lightning bolts might cause seizures.

"On hold," he said. "Zodiac Match is running us through the hoops."

Caitlin said, "You searching for that name on sites other than Zodiac Match?"

"Twitter, Tinder . . . you'd be surprised how many people use 'Starshine69' as their screen name."

Shanklin jammed her thumbs beneath her belt. "I wouldn't be."

They all gave her the side-eye. Shanklin turned her head and gave it back, ponytail

174

swinging tightly.

"What? Know your public. This is California," she said.

Caitlin handed Guthrie the printouts of Ackerman's messages. "He arranged to meet her at Silver Creek Park. That has to be the primary crime scene."

"Good chance."

He headed to his office. Martinez remained on hold.

Caitlin said, "Other dating sites? Astrology chat rooms? E-mail addresses at major companies starting with 'Starshine69 at such and such'?"

Martinez nodded. Gave her a look: *Don't backseat drive.*

She backed off. For five seconds. "Other variations with 'Starshine' in the name?"

Martinez raised an eyebrow and pulled up Facebook. "Caucasian female. Midthirties." He examined Starshine69's Zodiac Match photo. "Brown eyes, brown hair. Guessing her weight's one forty-five?"

"One sixty," Caitlin said. "She's got muscle under there."

"One sixty. Presuming that this isn't a catfish . . ."

Martinez typed, and paused.

The profile photo showed a round-faced white woman with brown eyes and brown

175

hair, midthirties, posed coquettishly.

StarshineKitten (Stacy Crawford).

A red straight pin showed her hometown as Daly City, California.

Martinez was already pulling her address from the DMV.

Stacy Crawford's apartment building overlooked a freeway interchange in Daly City, south of San Francisco. Caitlin and Martinez climbed the stairs behind a uniformed Daly City officer and the apartment super. Crawford wasn't answering her phone, and her car wasn't in the building's parking lot. They walked along a breezeway to her unit.

The Daly City cop rapped on the door. "Police. Is anybody home?"

Nobody answered. On the freeway, traffic droned past. The cop pounded again.

After thirty seconds of silence, he gave the super the go-ahead. Caitlin tamped down her anxiety.

The super pulled out a clinking key ring and opened the door. "Ms. Stacy, knock, knock."

The three cops followed the super into a small apartment, dimmed to greenish light by the closed curtains. The kitchen counter was covered with dirty dishes. It was dead silent.

Caitlin's anxiety spread. Martinez looked around the living room.

At the back of a hallway, a door opened.

"What the fuck?"

They turned. Outside the bathroom, naked, wet hair wrapped in a towel turban, stood Stacy Crawford. She made no move to cover her pink and well-tattooed flesh.

"Get out of my apartment."

Caitlin and Martinez raised their badges. The Daly City cop let his right hand linger near his telescoping baton.

Martinez said, "Ma'am, you may want to put on some clothes. We need to talk to you about Stuart Ackerman."

Crawford set her hands on her hips. "Who?"

Caitlin said, "Wild Sagittarius."

Crawford frowned. "What about him?"

"He's dead."

She dropped to the floor.

Five minutes later, dressed, sitting on the sofa in the greenish light, Stacy Crawford dabbed at her eyes. Her face was splotchy from crying.

"My car broke down on the way to Silver Creek Park. Then my phone battery crapped out. It took me two hours to get the car towed, three before I could call my sister from the garage for a ride home. I never made it to the rendezvous." She looked back and forth between the cops. "You didn't come here to tell me Sagittarius is dead, did you? Oh, my God, you came here because you thought *I* was dead."

"We wanted to make sure you're okay," Martinez said. The warmth of his voice couldn't disguise the cold truth.

"You're sure about this. The man shot up with arrows. *That* was Sagittarius?"

"We're positive."

"Oh, God. Did he suffer?"

Martinez said, "I'm sorry, ma'am."

Tears ballooned and fell onto her cheeks.

Caitlin said, "You never replied to the messages he sent from the park, asking where you were."

"No — because he sent that final message, slamming me."

"What message? Sent when?"

"After I got home Saturday night I logged in to explain why I didn't show." She got her phone. "This was waiting for me."

Wild Sagittarius 23 [Saturday 11:47PM]
Bitch.

Caitlin and Martinez exchanged a look. That message wasn't in Stuart Ackerman's

SENT folder. Somebody had deleted it.

"I was royally *pissed.* Then I saw that online video, about the crazy stuff that happened up at Silver Creek Park last night. I thought, what a weird coincidence, and . . ." She stopped, lips parted, and pointed at Caitlin. "You're the one on the video."

Caitlin wished her fifteen minutes was up.

Stacy wrung her hands. "Do you think our date had something to do with what happened to Sagittarius — to . . . Stuart?"

"We're retracing his steps on Saturday night," Martinez said.

The Daly City officer stood near the door, arms crossed. "You didn't know his name?"

She looked at him like, *What the hell?* "Screen names only. That's how Zodiac Match works. It's part of the magic."

"Had you met Mr. Ackerman before?" Martinez said.

"No. First date." She shivered. "Really? The Prophet killed him? *Really?*"

Caitlin said, "Really."

She put a hand to her forehead. "If my car hadn't broken down, I would have been at the park. Oh, my God, I'm lucky, aren't I?"

Caitlin said, "Ms. Crawford, when you signed up for Zodiac Match, did you give them any personal information?"

179

"Dating preferences." Her eyes grew wary. "But everything's consensual. It's play."

"What is?"

"IK." When they didn't respond, she expanded. "On my profile? IK. Impact kink." She looked at them like they were naive. "Slapping, scratching, biting, hitting with a crop. *Tamakeri* if the guy asks. You know — the Japanese fetish? For getting kicked in the balls?"

"You and Wild Sagittarius made a date for violent sex?" Caitlin said.

"Rough body play. *Consensual* S and M. Primal energy. Dynamic empowerment." She spread her hands. "Fight club."

Caitlin thought of the line in the Prophet's note. *Violence sought violence.*

She said, "Did you provide Zodiac Match with any other personal information?"

"Like what? My e-mail." Her brown eyes widened. "Like my address and phone number? No. Never. No. But . . ."

"What?"

"But I linked my Zodiac Match profile to my other social media accounts, and those do have my phone number and address. Oh, God." She stood up. "The Prophet. What if he knows where I live?"

17

Brooding, Caitlin and Martinez jogged silently down the stairs outside Stacy Crawford's apartment. Despite the sunshine, the sky seemed to bear down with portentous weight. They started across the asphalt to their vehicle and a lemon-yellow Volkswagen Beetle squealed past them into the parking lot.

At the wheel was a young woman who looked just like Stacy. A second later, Stacy ran down the stairs with a duffel bag over her shoulder, barefoot, shoes in her hand. She sprinted toward the car, shouting, "Out, out, let me drive."

Martinez said, "Can't blame her."

"Not at all."

Stacy flung her duffel in the car. Martinez pulled the brim of his hat low on his forehead.

Caitlin said, "I'm not commenting on impact kink. Ever."

"Good plan." But he said, "Empowerment. This is what the Prophet does to that idea."

Caitlin hoped Stacy would be safe. The way she scrambled behind the wheel told her plenty about the fear the Prophet provoked.

It was spreading like an oil slick.

They got in their car and Martinez pulled out in the Beetle's exhaust. He readjusted his hat. "I don't think Stuart Ackerman sent those final messages to Stacy."

"The Prophet did," she said.

"Yeah. Did he get possession of Ackerman's phone? Or hack his account?"

"I don't know. But the Prophet's the one who called Stacy a bitch. Because he was angry she didn't turn up for her own murder."

When Caitlin and Martinez arrived at the station, a man was sitting on a bench in the hall outside the war room. He was Caitlin's age, heavyset, African American, wearing khakis and a Best Buy employee shirt. His broad shoulders looked laden. His eyes were warm but weary, with a low, scudding darkness.

Unless they worked there, people didn't enjoy visiting a police station. For most citizens, this was some version of hell. The man checked out the badge hooked on her belt, and the gun on Martinez's hip.

"Excuse me. You're homicide detectives?" he said.

Martinez had a laid-back demeanor, but a presence. "May we help you?"

"Gerald James. I have an appointment with Sergeant Guthrie."

It took Caitlin a second. James. He was the husband of Melody James. The woman the Prophet killed and left in the cornfield.

She extended her hand. "Mr. James, I'm Detective Hendrix. I'm sorry for your loss."

His jaw tightened. He pressed his lips together but they quivered anyway.

Talking to next of kin was one of the most painful things she did in this job. Be up-front, she'd learned. Be direct.

Compartmentalize it. Bar their grief, so it doesn't burrow into you.

But Gerald James stood up, and the physical aura of loss rolled off him in waves. She saw again the lively face of his wife in her driver's license photo, and the destruction visited on her by the Prophet.

James was so close to the ragged edge that he looked like he was about to fly apart. "I'm here for an update on the investigation."

"Let me get Sergeant Guthrie."

"I'll get him," Martinez said, and headed down the hall.

She'd wanted Martinez to wait with James. But she gestured at the bench.

James shook his head. "I can't sit anymore. I need to know. All of it. What happened to her." He stared unblinking. "I don't care how ugly it is. And I'm not talking about her seeing another man. I don't care about that. I care about her. I have to know."

"Sergeant Guthrie will tell you what he can."

"I've talked to him already. Told him everything *I* know. What I need now is to hear everything the *police* know. I just want you all to tell me. Imagining's worse than knowing." He crossed his arms and began to rock back and forth. "Were you there? Where they found her?"

"Yes."

His gaze sharpened and latched on to her. "They wouldn't let me see her. I got to the scene after the first cops did. He . . . he called me. At home . . ." A breath. "And I wanted to get out there so fast, but I had to call my mom to babysit, so I phoned nine-one-one and got out to that field after you all did, and . . ." He looked at her. "They kept me out, sent me home in a patrol car.

Then called me to come to the morgue . . ."

The word *morgue* seemed to loosen his hinges. Caitlin could sense the bolts rattling, the engine overheating.

"It's okay," she said.

He felt like he'd failed his wife. He hadn't even been able to reach the cornfield before the prying machine of law enforcement arrived and began treating Melody as an object to be processed.

His lip quivered again. "I wasn't there with her." James gulped a breath and got it back. "I was with her when our daughter was born. But I wasn't there at the end."

Caitlin's stomach tightened.

"I need to know," James said. "I need to walk with her through those last moments."

No, you don't.

"If I don't know, she'll always be alone. I can't let it be that way. I can't let her last hours be . . . the property of the Prophet. I have to take that away from him."

Caitlin took his hand. It was warm and rough and he squeezed hard against her fingers.

"He took her," James whispered. "But I can't let him have her."

Caitlin held on to his hand. Her eyes were burning.

"Help her," James said. "Help me."

"I will." She gripped his hand, hard.

A figure appeared at the end of the hall. Guthrie's voice.

"Mr. James. Please. Come back to my office."

Gerald James held on to Caitlin's hand.

"You have my word," she said.

James's hand slipped from hers and he headed down the hall.

Caitlin stood there. Phones were ringing. Traffic outside went by in a glare of sunlight. Her hand was warm where James had gripped it. She curled her fingers into a fist, clutching the heat. Then she walked to the war room.

On her desk was a phone message slip from Deralynn Hobbs. It said: *Crows.*

She hesitated only briefly before returning Deralynn's call. She owed her. "Thank you for warning me about the camera in the car."

"Oh, you're welcome." The relief in Deralynn's bubbly voice was palpable.

"Your message."

"I don't mean to hassle you. It's just, the symbolism unsettles me. *Crows,* plural — they're a murder."

And baboons are a troop. "I'll keep my eyes open." For a cackle of hyenas. And a mob of kangaroos. "Don't worry about the crows."

But as she said it, Caitlin looked across the room at the wall where crime scene photos were tacked up. Crows were not the only animals connected to the Prophet's crime scenes.

The bodies of the first couple killed were found mauled by dogs. April 12, 1996. The dogs, three fighting dogs stolen from a shelter, were found at the crime scene, butchered and tied together at the neck.

Stuart Ackerman had been left floating facedown in a water trough, surrounded by spooked horses. Wild Sagittarius, the Centaur.

She remembered what Mack had said the previous night: that an UNSUB's first crime is often the most revealing.

"What do you think of the wasps at the first crime scene?" she said.

Deralynn inhaled. "That scene is the one that freaks me out."

"Why?"

"The location, the time of day, the nerve it took to stage the scene when it was merely dusk, not dark. The patience and exactitude . . . there's a tree line forty-five yards from the equipment shack where Giselle was found, but the killer had to have made his approach in the open. The wasp nest — that was a feat of both engineering and bravery. Or insanity."

Caitlin tapped her fingers on her desk. What she was thinking probably violated department protocol. But Guthrie had asked her to deal with Deralynn.

"What are you doing this evening?" she said.

18

The light was failing when Caitlin pulled the departmental car to the curb across the street from Peñasquitos Park in San Leandro. The neighborhood's ranch homes and apartment buildings were battened down for a chilly March evening. The sky hung, painted indigo. The hills beyond the park, green and dotted with live oaks, caught the last glow of the sun. She and Deralynn got out. Going to the park to view the crime scene turned them solemn.

And Deralynn Hobbs was not a solemn person.

Caitlin had picked her up at her house in San Ramon, where bikes lay on the lawn, a homemade skateboard ramp dominated the driveway, and dozens of green plastic army men dotted the front walk. When she arrived, Deralynn was waiting on the front porch, wearing lime-green jeans and a bedazzled sweatshirt, talking excitedly to a man Caitlin took to be her husband. In his late thirties, he wore a checked button-down shirt and a patient, bemused expression.

"Detective. Walter Hobbs." He smiled at Caitlin but shook her hand awkwardly, seemingly unsure what to make of his wife's expedition.

Two boys bolted from the backyard, firing Nerf guns at each other, and ran laughing up the street. Deralynn blew kisses at their backs. She stood on tiptoe to kiss her husband, said, "Bye, pumpkin," and bounded to Caitlin's car. She was a casting-call PTA mom, bubbling with excitement at a field trip to the site of a serial killer's first murder.

But now Deralynn was silent as she crossed the street at Caitlin's side. At the park entrance, flags hung heavily, hasps clattering against the flagpole in the wind. Caitlin slowed to get her bearings.

Deralynn looked up at her. "This your first time here?"

"Yes."

Caitlin knew all about Peñasquitos Park. It was a place that seemed freighted with bad magic. A site to avoid. Until now.

She had a file folder with maps, photos, crime scene reconstructions. She'd built a mental three-hundred-and-sixty-degree map without ever setting foot on this spot. But now that she stood at the park entrance, she needed a minute to mentally prepare to place herself inside it.

Live oaks lined the street. Jacarandas, flowering purple, surrounded the empty playground. At the back of the park a grove of redwoods stood formidable against the deepening sky. It was dusk, the time of the killing.

"Trees are taller. Noticeably," she said.

After a moment's uncertainty, she sent a text to her father. What should we look for at Peñasquitos Park?

They walked through the gate. It was chilly, too late for sports, too dark for picnics. The only sounds were distant traffic from the freeway and the dull roar of a jet taking off from Oakland Airport. Deralynn knew the way.

"You've been here," Caitlin said.

"Never with a cop."

The crime scene was an equipment shack on a trail beyond the playground. They followed a bark path. The trees closed in.

"This trail was the victim's regular jogging route. We presume the killer ambushed Giselle Fraser along here," Caitlin said. "She lived alone. Nobody knew she was missing until the park maintenance crew

191

unlocked the door to the equipment shack."

Deralynn clenched and unclenched her fists. Her lime-green jeans were the brightest beacon in the park. The bark crunched softly beneath their feet. If Giselle Fraser had run along this path that night, her footfalls would have been audible to anyone waiting in the shadows.

Giselle ran religiously, every evening when she got home from her job as a teller at a nearby bank. A two-and-a-half-mile loop through the neighborhood, with a dogleg through Peñasquitos. The killer had to have known that. Giselle was not a random target.

Deralynn exhaled hard, with excitement — or maybe nerves. "I have to thank you."

"Why?"

"Most cops roll their eyes at me." She shrugged. "I know it. Less-than-amateur sleuth. Not even self-taught. No qualifications. A *mom.*"

"You trying to get me to knock moms? No way," Caitlin said. "This is your own private deal, but you're as organized and thoughtful as some investigative reports I've read."

Deralynn's lips parted and she pressed her hands to her cheeks. "Really? I'm blushing. Thank you. Jeez."

Caitlin smiled, hoping it would encourage Deralynn to keep talking. It was always better that way. It felt less like an interrogation. And Caitlin well knew that when people saw her badge, a part of them always expected her to read them their rights.

Forget it. She *was* a cop. At a crime scene. "What does your husband think about your . . . dedication to this case?"

"He says it's no surprise *you* ended up carrying a gun. But me, *I'm* a nut." Deralynn turned to her. "I remember your dad. He came to my school to talk to us about Lisa Chu."

Lisa Chu was the Prophet's teenage victim. The sixteen-year-old high school junior was drowned in a water treatment pond, chained to the concrete block that weighed her down. It was Chu's arm on which the killer wrote the message: *Infinite wrath and infinite despair.*

Lisa Chu's death terrified every parent, and every young woman, every girl child, in a way that killing middle-aged couples hadn't. It cast the killer's scythe in a horrifying gyre.

"I didn't know the department sent my dad — or anyone — to speak to the public about it."

"Lisa babysat me," Deralynn said.

That was it. The link. Or, at least, *a* link — the personal connection that helped to explain Deralynn's obsession with the case.

"She was like a big sister."

Deralynn said it without hesitation. The cut was hardly fresh. But her cheeks flushed a deeper red. And even in the failing light, Caitlin saw a glimmer in her eyes.

"I'm sorry," Caitlin said.

"Your dad talked to us about personal safety. To always tell somebody where we were going. To walk in groups, stay to well-lit streets. We were majorly freaked out. But he was so calm and reassuring."

Mack, calm. The image jarred. And, at the edges, it tugged at her.

"I remember it like it was yesterday. He seemed larger than life," Deralynn said. "Like you. Now."

Oh, honey. "I get paid to do this. You're the volunteer."

"We all talk about catching the killer. But you actually put yourself on the line."

"This case got to both of us." Caitlin's breath frosted the air. "You handle it with insomniac web sessions. Me, I just . . ." As she stopped herself, she could practically feel the scars burning on her wrists. "I found a different way."

She thought she'd said it coolly. Offhandedly. But Deralynn seemed to sense that Caitlin's wounds were not far beneath the surface, and could still be fatal.

"But you're doing it anyway. You're damned well doing it." She squeezed Caitlin's hand. "You okay?"

"Yeah."

"I mean, of course you're okay. You're here. But, you have a support system? Friends? A church? You have kids?"

"Dog."

Deralynn pulled out a photo. "My family. You met my husband, Walt. And William and Weston."

Caitlin smiled. "Love the matching bow ties."

They kept walking. Caitlin was glad that the dusk shaded her face, that the wind caught her hair and blew it across her eyes. They rounded a bend and came upon an open field. The equipment shack was ten feet off the path, weathered wood, its roof green with moss.

She paused, getting a look at it. No windows. Redwoods behind it.

She turned to see the view from the shack outward. The field, the path. Open, but screened by trees on three sides.

He could have stood to the side of the shack, just off the trail, mere feet from the door, waiting invisibly for Giselle Fraser to run past. Or he could have listened for her footsteps, then sauntered toward her. Whistling, or listening to music through headphones, or limping like he'd sprained his ankle. He was patient and cagey. He had social skills. He could probably lure people into his orbit with charming talk, before he isolated and killed them. He didn't blitz attack in a fit, like psychotics or disorganized killers.

He drew maps of the entire neighborhood, with concealment spaces highlighted and escape routes plotted in detail. And with his goal inscribed in hard capital letters. *PUNISHMENT.*

Caitlin took out the key the parks department had loaned her. The night of the murder, the killer had jimmied the lock with a screwdriver. Now there was a stronger door, with heavier hinges, and a Yale dead bolt. Caitlin opened it.

The smell of wood and dust and fertilizer hung heavy inside. She got her Maglite.

Deralynn said, "It would have been this dark, wouldn't it?"

"He wanted concealment. He was daring, but uncertain of himself and the environment."

"I'd think they would have torn this shack

down. I would have. Holy jeez. The exposed rafters are still there."

He had to have brought all his gear ahead of time and stashed it inside the shack. When he gained control over Giselle, all he had to do was kick the door shut.

Giselle had been strangled with a silk scarf. And she had multiple bruises around her head and face. He had punched her with a closed fist, possibly knocking her unconscious, before he killed her.

But he didn't hang her from the neck. He stripped off her socks and shoes, her running shorts and T-shirt. He left her in her bra and panties. He bound her hands with sturdy rope and threw it over the exposed rafters. Then he hauled her up and left her hanging by her wrists with her head thrown back, as though weeping in anguish.

How long did he work to raise her? How long did he stay in the shack, admiring his work? Did he touch her as she swung, dangling, her body slowly beginning to cool?

What do you want, you bastard?

And then the killer booby-trapped the building. That was the vicious detail. He brought an entire mud-dauber wasp nest in a Hefty bag, and he left it inside the door, so that when the maintenance crew arrived in the morning, they knocked it over and set loose an enraged hive.

Caitlin stepped outside. The scene was fading to gray. She had an unsettling feeling that the play of the shadows in the wind was less than random. Sounds moved within the brush.

"From the start, he set up a secondary ambush. A way to hurt people when his crime was discovered," she said.

"From his first kill, you mean."

Caitlin nodded. It was presumed that Giselle Fraser's death was not the Prophet's first crime. He would have worked up to murder. Peeping Tom. Flasher. And earlier: Animal torture. Arson.

The wind swirled Caitlin's hair. Deralynn's hedgehog spikes remained unbowed.

"Think she knew him?" Deralynn said.

"I think there's a good chance she at least recognized him. Somebody she'd seen in the neighborhood. Maybe another jogger. A dog walker."

"Somebody who didn't arouse immediate distrust."

"This park is a place where he felt comfortable. He knew it. Knew the neighborhood."

"So did Giselle, unfortunately."

Did Giselle Fraser sense danger as she rounded the bend? Did she feel eyes watching her, sense any threat as the killer lunged in? Caitlin nodded at the grove of redwoods.

"Let's walk the park the way it would have happened that night."

Deralynn looked troubled, but she followed. "Coming in the way Giselle did, going to where it happened, and following the killer's probable path out? You mean we're putting ourselves in the footsteps of both the victim and the killer."

"If there's something to find, we have to look at it from every angle. And from both outside and in."

Across the park, screened by trees and the deepening twilight, a man watched.

Look at her. Detective Hendrix, here to relive the opening chapter.

19

On the park playground, the swings hung empty. The slide caught the last embers of sunset. Beyond the oaks, out on the road, streetlights came on. The moon was rising, the scene falling into chiaroscuro. Deralynn stuck close by Caitlin's side.

The killer had walked this path. He had come into the park from the back, on foot, from at least a mile away — over the hill, along the creek, through the storm drain. Silently, through the empty grove of redwoods that stood tall under the rising moon.

"Have you heard of geographic profiling?" Caitlin said.

"Analyzing the location of connected crimes to determine where the offender most likely lives." Deralynn looked around. She still seemed eager, but less bouncy — more jumpy, like a small woodland creature sniffing the air for hawks. "You think the killer lives around here? That we're headed in the direction of his home?"

"I think this park is probably the crime scene closest to where he lived at the time," Caitlin said. "And we're heading the way he did after he killed Giselle Fraser."

Deralynn didn't know about the hand-drawn map. That wasn't public knowledge. They followed the trail beneath the towering redwoods. The bark dwindled to dirt.

Deralynn said, "You think he came this way because . . ."

You're lost, Hendrix. Gone astray in a dark wood.

They topped a rise in the path and looked downhill. The path ran alongside a creek. It headed perhaps two hundred yards to a picket fence and then a quiet road.

"You think he parked there?" Deralynn said.

"No. I think he was more careful than that. He didn't want anyone to recognize a car parked outside the park entrance, or remember a man coming through this gate. Especially not a man carrying a coil of rope, though he might have hidden that in a backpack. And I think he might have had a flashlight, because he knew it would be dark when he left again."

You'll never find the path. But someone will . . .

Maybe this was the dark path the Prophet meant. Maybe he wanted her to follow it.

"Come on," she said.

She cut off the trail, down to the creek, and aimed her Maglite along the creek bed. It was wide but contained only a trickle of water. Ahead, it ran beneath the road, through a square concrete storm drain. That was where her father found the Prophet's map.

Deralynn hurried along beside her. "How much farther do you think we should go?"

They reached the storm drain. Caitlin stepped inside. It was about forty yards long, with mud along the bottom, the creek running in a channel choked with weeds and trash.

"He came this way," Caitlin said.

"You're sure?"

"Yes. He either walked from his home, or drove and parked his car another half mile up the creek. There's a shopping center over the next hill. It's been there for forty years. He could have left his car there without being noticed."

"He planned."

"Like a mofo. But he wasn't perfect."

Something had spooked him, or at least distracted him. He had been in a hurry here — finished with his deed, eager to get away.

202

What led him to lose the map in this storm drain? Had he pulled it out to check that he was moving in the right direction? Was he careless about shoving it back in his pocket? Did he hear something, see someone, and impulsively take off?

Or was he distracted by his own joy?

"As killers gain confidence, they expand their hunting grounds," she said. "But this was his first."

She turned her flashlight on the walls. Skater graffiti. Slowly she panned it.

"You think he might have come back? Left a message?" Deralynn's words rushed out, sounding somewhere between eager and terrified.

"I think he's always followed the investigation obsessively. And that he's picked up where he left off, maybe because he found inspiration in revisiting the site of his early work." She continued looking around. "Whether he's taking a victory tour, I can't say."

She mentally pictured the map the Prophet had drawn. The entire thing was exacting. But the only feature marked for scale was the storm drain. *125 ft.*

The killer liked to go off road. But more than that, he liked to go *underground.*

At Sequoia High, he had placed the geo-

203

graphic coordinates in a culvert. At Silver
Creek Park, the ravine where Stuart Ackerman's car was set ablaze had a creek at the
bottom that disappeared beneath a road
into a corrugated steel pipe. The killer might
not have used it that night, but Caitlin was
sure he knew it was there, and available as
an escape route.

The night sharpened. She let the sensation soak into her.

"He likes tunnels. He used them then.
He'll use them now."

Her phone buzzed. The screen showed a
text from her father. HIM.

She stared, disconcerted. What was he saying?

Deralynn said, "Okay, I'm just going to
admit it. This place is creepy."

Caitlin entered her password to unlock
the screen. As she did, the phone rang.
Guthrie. She answered the call.

"Hendrix. We're monitoring the forums.
FindtheProphet.com. Deralynn and her
crime-geek friends." He sounded harried.
"Traffic's been going crazy — we're keeping an eye on it."

"Is something . . ."

"Your father posted a rant. Directly calling out the Prophet."

The heat seemed to leach from Caitlin's

hands. "What?"

"He posted it on the open forum. Publicly. Where anybody can read it."

Caitlin turned to Deralynn. "Pull up a post on the public forum. It's —" *Hell.* "It'll be from my father. Mack Hendrix."

Deralynn grabbed her phone. She bent over it, face lit by the screen, and brought up the site. After a second, reading, she inhaled.

Her eyes were wide and anxious when she showed Caitlin the screen.

To the Prophet. You SICK LOSER — you've left a stink every place you stepped. It's not 1993 anymore. Forensics can peel your thoughts from the earth. From that bloody water trough to the shack in the park, the cops are closing in on you. This very second.

Any remaining heat seemed to drain from Caitlin's body. Son of a bitch. Mack's text. It was his answer to the question she had sent him — what she should look for.

Him.

She heard the wind through the storm drain and felt the shadows shifting around her. She grabbed Deralynn's arm. "Out of the park. *Now.*"

They hurried from the storm drain and along the creek bed until they could scurry up the bank. They reached the footpath and Caitlin pulled Deralynn into a run.

Ahead she saw a dark form, nothing but a shadow, moving at sharp angles and speed. Right at them. She pulled up.

From the trees directly ahead, a man burst onto the path.

Shoving Deralynn back, Caitlin reached toward her gun. *"Sheriff. Don't move."*

He jerked to a stop and raised his hands. "Don't shoot! I'm press!"

Breathing like a rabbit, Caitlin raised her Maglite in her left hand. Her right rested on her holstered SIG.

In the beam of the flashlight the man squinted and turned his head away. His hands stayed up, one blocking the light and obscuring his face. They were empty.

"Keep your hands up," Caitlin said. "Who are you?"

"Bart Fletcher, *East Bay Herald.*"

Fletcher. Supposedly. Squinting under the light, he looked vampirish, shadows turning one side of him dark. He wore a bomber jacket over a Giants T-shirt. He was gaunt, aside from a middle-aged paunch. His

206

knuckles looked arthritic.

He stepped toward her. "I'm . . ."

"Don't move," she said.

He stopped, frowning.

"ID," she said. "Put your right hand behind your head. Get your ID with your left. Very slowly."

"It's in my wallet. Which is in my inside jacket pocket. I'm going to reach for it. Very slowly." Gingerly he reached into his jacket.

"Careful," she said. Eyes on him, focused, but trying to keep a sense of what was happening behind her. Fortunately, Deralynn was still there, a fizzing presence at her back.

With two fingers he lifted a wallet from the pocket. "Well. You're every bit the Valkyrie I heard you were."

"Toss it here."

He flipped the wallet across the ten feet between them. Caitlin caught it. Opened it. In a window inside was a California driver's license. Bartholomew Fletcher. His photo.

Her rabbit pulse eased off, but her anger built. She crossed the distance to him, Maglite trained on his face. "You can lower your hands. What are you doing here?"

"I'm covering the story." He took the wallet, still squinting. "Including you."

"You're following me?"

"No."

"Bullshit." She felt flushed. She hadn't noticed anyone tailing her.

He raised his hands again and put one across his heart. "Not following you, Detective. Though if I were, that's not illegal. We all have our sources. And I'd like you to be one of them."

"You covered the story earlier in the week without bothering to contact me for comment."

"And here I am." He smiled, a toothy grin that stopped halfway up his face.

"Let's leave things the way they were."

She put a hand on Deralynn's back and urged her along the path.

"You done here? I don't want to cut your trip short," Fletcher said.

Caitlin kept walking. Deralynn shot a glance at her, then at Fletcher, then at the bark on the ground.

Fletcher caught up and leaned inquisitively toward Deralynn. "You are? Ma'am, your name?"

Caitlin didn't say anything to stop her, but the raging black stare on her face might have kept Deralynn's lips sealed. They crunched along the trail toward the park exit. Caitlin wanted nothing but to drive away from Fletcher at light speed.

He skipped ahead and turned to walk

backward, crowding them. He smelled of beer and breath mints. "What was it like growing up in a home overshadowed by the Prophet?"

Caitlin ignored him and led Deralynn to the car.

"How did you cope when your father was committed?" he said.

She reached the car and turned to him. "No goddamned comment."

He hovered, just inside her comfort zone. "It must have been a searing experience. Is that why you became a police officer?"

She urged Deralynn around to the passenger side and opened her own door. "And if you ever hinder an ongoing police investigation again . . ."

"I hear you got a message today," he said.

What? How did he know that? She turned the death stare on him.

He held up a yellowed notepad. "Look familiar?"

Under the streetlight, writing was visible on the notepad. Fletcher held it up until Caitlin turned the Maglite on it.

In faded ink was scrawled, *Dripping blood our only drink.*

It was the Prophet's FedEx message — plus more. Caitlin said, "Where did you . . ."

"Heard it in 1998, when I spoke to the

survivor." His toothy grin returned. His eyes stayed dark and fervent. Seeking her response.

She tried to speak in a neutral tone. "We have the survivor's statement."

"Call me to set up your interview. You're going to want the rest of my notes." He dropped the smile and walked away. "Because she didn't tell you everything, did she?"

20

Joe Guthrie hurried up the flight of stairs outside the San Francisco boardinghouse where Mack Hendrix lived. Through the heavy wooden front door he could hear a voice raised. Caitlin's voice. He rang the bell. How she'd beaten him here he didn't know. Familial rage was a powerful thing, bending even time and space.

The landlady let him in. He followed Caitlin's voice along the hall to the kitchen.

"No. It wasn't a stupid mistake," she said. "It was calculated. And dangerous."

Guthrie walked in. Caitlin had her back to him, arms spread wide. Across the kitchen, with the island between them, Mack Hendrix paced, head down, as though keeping a barricade between himself and his daughter. The guy might be a nutcase, but he wasn't dumb.

"Look at me, goddammit. I asked for your

advice, and instead you set me up at the park."

Mack mumbled something Guthrie didn't catch, raising his hand, seemingly trying to placate her. He stared at the floor. He seemed to be talking to himself more than to her, shaking his head.

She slapped a hand down on the countertop. "You called the Prophet out. To a scene you told me to investigate."

"I didn't know you were there," he said.

"The hell you didn't."

"I did not." He glanced at her, shoulders drawn up like a boxer in a defensive crouch. "You said, 'What should we look for?' We. *We.* Like Homicide was planning a trip to the park."

"Are you fucking kidding me? You used me as bait."

Open horror filled his expression. "Never."

The apparent depth of his shock seemed to take Caitlin aback. "Then what the hell did you think you were doing?"

"Drawing out the poison," Mack said.

"It didn't work," Guthrie said. "She nearly drew her weapon on a reporter."

Mack turned his head in surprise, as if only now seeing that he was there. Caitlin half glanced at him over her shoulder, and turned back to her father with barely contained fury.

"You put me in jeopardy," she said. "I was with a civilian."

That jarred Mack to a stop. "You're the one who came to me. With that *video*. Begging me to help you stop him."

"Dad, I was *nine years old* when you spread those case files across the workbench in the garage and asked me to organize them. You're the one who brought this into the family."

Mack's shoulders slumped. He took a breath and sat down at the kitchen table.

Caitlin took a second to get her emotions under control. When she spoke again, though her voice still sounded sharp, she talked at conversational volume.

"How did you even think he would —"

"Because he monitors the forums," Mack said, looking up at her. "Just like I do."

Caitlin stared at her father. Her pulse pounded in her ears. She pressed the heels of her hands to her eyes. *Say nothing else. Not in front of Guthrie. Hold your shit together. Don't kill Mack.*

She left the kitchen and stalked along the hall and strode out to the front porch of the boardinghouse. She breathed in the cold air.

Of course her father was still invested in the Prophet case. Of course he hadn't cut himself free from it. He never had. He'd *told* her. He never would, never could.

She stood on the porch. The night was colder in San Francisco, sharper, more ragged.

Guthrie's gaunt form appeared as a shadow beside her. "For a guy who —"

"I know."

"We ripped open a wound, but we needed his input. Can you contain him?"

She was glad for the night. It hid her sour smile. "When you open a wound, can you control the flow of blood?" She shook her head. "He's like quicksilver. Liquid and changeable and poisonous."

Guthrie didn't respond. She knew her words were too harsh. She was angry and confused. And felt used.

"I love him, but this is what happens."

She did not say, *I told you so.* Guthrie looked at her in the dark. She wondered if she was just a tool to him, the sharp stick he was using to pry open all her father's thoughts. If so, it was working out in the worst way. She didn't tell him that he was the one who had brought both her and Mack into this case.

She forced herself to speak levelly. "I got

this. He's going to back off. I'll see to it."

Guthrie held her gaze and nodded. "I'll see you in the morning." He walked down the steps.

She stood on the porch, waiting for him to start the car and pull away. The night sounds of the city came to her, traffic and a distant siren and hip-hop thumping from a window up the street.

Behind her, the door creaked open. Her father's voice was soft.

"Caitlin."

She stared at the city.

"I didn't think," Mack said.

She exhaled and shook her head.

He was a vibrating presence behind her. She waited for him to retreat into the house. Instead, he walked out and came to her side.

"I read your message wrong. I . . ." He cleared his throat. "I saw what I wanted to see in it. And got carried away. All I could think was to rattle his cage. Flush him out. Do *something*. Then I lost track of time in the forum." He stared at the street, and at her. "I should have called you right away. Should have called you first, even before I posted the comment."

"Got that straight."

"Caitlin, look at me. I would never use you as bait. Never."

She gazed down the hill to the bay and across its black surface to the lights ringing the far shore. Berkeley, Oakland, the hills, seven and a half million people in danger.

Her father grew up in San Francisco, went to high school here, but had lived his adult life in the East Bay. And though he was back in the city now, Mack hadn't come home. This wasn't a place to make his life, this boardinghouse. It was a lonely way station.

It was exile.

And it had this view. From this house, her father spent his days and nights staring at his former home.

But it was more than that. Mack had placed himself at a vantage point that overlooked the Prophet's killing grounds. Every time he opened his eyes, every time he looked out the window, every time he stepped out the door, he was seeking the killer. Endlessly.

She turned to him. The pain in his eyes could have stripped the light from the stars.

"I would never deliberately put you in harm's way," he said.

Her voice went quiet. "I can see that."

"I'm sorry."

A band seemed to cinch around her chest. He held her gaze.

She nodded. "You have to stand down."

He pressed his lips tight, maybe to keep his chin from trembling.

"You do nothing. Zero. You don't post in the forum, you don't talk to people on the street, you don't say the Prophet's name out loud. You don't speak about this case to anybody but me. You tell me everything. But you take no action. Period."

He nodded.

"You can't screw this up," she said.

"I know."

"Say it."

"I'll stand down."

He sounded sincere — but his sincerity could, famously, erode in an instant. A car drove past. Its headlights caught a sheen in his eyes. It must have caught the doubts in hers.

"Wait here," he said.

He strode inside. When he returned he was carrying a canvas duffel bag. He dropped it on the porch and unzipped it.

"Oh, Dad."

Inside were his personal case diaries, notes, and crime scene maps. Copies of case photos, dozens of files. A photocopied message the killer had sent him: *The more beautiful and pure a thing is, the more satisfying it is to corrupt.* Cassettes that could only be recordings of victims begging for their lives.

It was accumulated tragedy, and her dad was dragging it around like Marley's chains.

"You never let it go," she said.

"Every year, I've watched the equinox, waiting to hear if he's come back. I could never make myself believe he stopped forever."

She stared at everything, distressed. This stuff wasn't supposed to exist.

"I'll back off. I swear it to you." He nodded at the duffel. "Take it."

Mack had told her mother he'd destroyed it all.

That bad summer, when she was fifteen. Her mom had held her close when she came home from the hospital.

It's gone. He burned it, Sandy had said. *Don't think about it anymore.*

Now Mack took a breath and touched her arm. "Use it. Or torch it. But take it."

She held still. Here were the ghosts that crowded her father's life. They seemed to whisper, to extend spectral hands, imploring. She crouched down, peering in.

She zipped the bag shut. When she stood, she hoisted it over her shoulder.

"I got it," she said.

21

Thursday

Wishing that blustery March mornings didn't make her feel so stiff, J. T. Wilcox turned up the thermostat in the café and bustled past her aches. It was 6:08 A.M. Coffee, Tea & Tarot opened at seven.

The coffeehouse sat on a side street off Shattuck Avenue in Berkeley. The shop was cozy, with hardwood floors and wicker baskets that held exotic teas. The walls boasted posters of several of the tarot's major arcana — the Magician, the High Priestess, and the Moon. J.T. brewed the coffees of the day. Sumatra, Guatemala, and Empress Blend. Knuckles throbbing, she wrote the morning's selections on a chalkboard. She pulled upside-down chairs from tables and set them upright, preparing for the early birds. Her dangling red earrings, which depicted the Wheel of Fortune, swung as she worked.

Gaia Hill, her partner, came out of the broom closet they used as an office. Gaia was the morning person. J.T. called her Steel-Cut: She was sturdy and small and wore her gray hair razored short on the back and sides, with a marine's crew cut on the top. Even though she'd been out of the corps for thirty-five years. Gaia's T-shirt read, I'M JUST A POE BOY FROM A POE FAMILY, with a drawing of a nineteenth-century group, all Edgar Allan Poe. Dad, mom, sons, and daughters. Even the dog. Gaia would never give up her dream of expanding the shop into a bookstore. But for now, she made do with the tiny free library she'd built from a dollhouse outside the front window.

Gaia bustled behind the counter, shaking her head. "Computer's glitchy again."

"You sure it's not your eyes?" J.T. said.

"Just because I'm five years older than you, doesn't mean I'm going blind. The screen keeps flashing. It'll strobe for a few seconds, then stop."

"You tried hitting it?"

"Of course. Now I'll try calling the repair people."

She glanced outside. A black pickup was parked across the street.

"You see that truck before?" Gaia said.

J.T. set a pink bakery box of croissants on the counter. She glanced out the window. "Sure. That truck's all over the place. I've seen it everywhere a guy wants to feel bigger than he is." She smiled. "Why? Have you?"

"Seems like I might have. Those rims — not exactly Berkeley style. So shiny. I thought maybe it was parked on the side street yesterday?"

"You think . . . ?"

"Wondering if Mr. Pickup's the one who spray-painted the graffiti on the wall outside."

J.T. harrumphed. "That was more likely some poser. Goth asshole or teenage vampire fan. 'Dripping blood . . .' " She rolled her eyes. "I'll get the paint later and white it out."

"At least it's low, and on the side of the building away from the street. With the Jeep parked there you can't even see it."

"You worried?"

"Just wondering if it's a hate message. Against our spirituality, or us."

"If so, it's obscure and indirect. Sweetie, it's graffiti."

There wasn't a sound, not even a disturbance in the air. But at the back of the shop, the light shifted. A shadow crossed the hallway. It caught the edge of J.T.'s vision.

"It isn't graffiti."

Without seeming to move, or breathe, a man slid into view. One second the hall was empty. The next he was there.

J.T. froze. She and Gaia traded a look, brief and full of meaning. The back door was locked.

The stranger stood in half shadow, staring.

Gaia grabbed for the phone. And like a whip, he unfurled in motion, flying at her.

Late morning, Caitlin stood in the war room, feeling bruised and jumpy. Guthrie was the only one who knew that Bart Fletcher had surprised her at the park the previous night. Guthrie had no love for the reporter. And he hadn't berated her for getting surprised at a notorious crime scene.

Fletcher had claimed that he didn't follow her. She was tempted to buy his denial. She was ninety percent certain he'd ferreted out her plans from the Find the Prophet forums. That he got the location thanks to Mack's post.

But that last ten percent of uncertainty nagged at her.

She ran a criminal background check. Fletcher had a misdemeanor arrest for drunk and disorderly and was on probation for driving while intoxicated. He was required to wear an electronic ankle monitor and to install an ignition interlock device — a Breathalyzer — in his vehicle. She recalled the smell of beer on his breath, and the breath mints that didn't cover it. She wondered whose car he had borrowed so he could drive to the park without having to blow into the ignition lock.

Fletcher had covered the original Prophet murders, and it didn't take long to unearth his archive and biography. His earliest byline for the *East Bay Herald* was 1995 — two years after the Prophet began killing. Caitlin found earlier articles he'd filed as a staff writer for *The Des Moines Register.* The night Giselle Fraser was murdered at Peñasquitos Park, Fletcher had covered a flood and looting at an Iowa strip mall.

She rubbed her eyes. Guthrie had called it. Fletcher was a washed-up drunk writing venomous articles. Still, she wanted to kick herself for letting him get that close.

She downed the last of her coffee. It burned her tongue. She threw the take-out cup in the recycling bin like a dart, and headed to her desk with an eight-by-ten photo she'd printed earlier.

Because damned if Bart Fletcher, asshole

supreme, hadn't given her a lead.

The survivor. *She didn't tell you everything, did she?*

Caitlin felt certain that there were people in the Bay Area who had narrowly escaped being targeted by the Prophet — people living their lives unaware how close they came to death. People, maybe women like Giselle Fraser, who drew his eye but escaped disaster when a bystander walked into view at the right moment.

But there was only one person who had faced the Prophet head-on and lived to tell. Caitlin studied the photo.

March 20, 1998. Kelly Smolenski. Age sixteen. Eyes wild with fear. Duct tape in her hair. Face cut by branches as she ran for her life.

She had given the police a bare-bones statement. Now Fletcher claimed that Smolenski knew more than she had ever let on.

The sheriff's office had been trying to reach her since the Prophet's return. They were still trying, harder now. Smolenski had a current California driver's license but no longer lived at the address listed on it. While another police department checked on her purported job, Caitlin sat at the conference table and read through Kelly's file. A couple of speeding tickets within the past ten years. For going extremely fast. No major criminal record. No next of kin.

The statement Kelly gave to the police when she was sixteen sounded like snapshot observations, recounted by a young girl a breath away from complete breakdown.

UNSUB was a white male, witness thinks. Because he was masked and wore gloves, she cannot be sure. Average height, average weight.

At his desk, Martinez ended a phone call, tore a piece of paper from a notepad, and swiveled in his desk chair.

"Found her."

"Where?"

"She lives outside Tassajara, in Contra Costa County."

"You spoke to her?" Caitlin said.

"For about fifteen seconds. She's terse."

"What does that mean?"

He handed her the piece of paper. "It means she agreed to talk about the Prophet. But only to a woman. Call her."

22

Dusty's was a wooden shack in the coastal hills between Palo Alto and Half Moon Bay. A neon MILLER BEER sign winked crazily in the front window. Outside the entrance a rank of motorcycles gleamed in the afternoon sun, mostly Harley-Davidsons. Caitlin pulled into the packed-dirt parking lot and dust blew from beneath her tires.

This was the only place Kelly Smolenski would agree to meet.

Caitlin parked and got out. Her jacket was buttoned over her holster and badge. She didn't need to hide who she was. The boots and jeans and long-sleeve black Henley T-shirt weren't camouflage. They were her. She didn't wear them to fit in at a biker bar, but they didn't hurt. She pushed through the door.

The bar was dark, the sunlight browned by windows that might not have been washed since the seventies. Stevie Ray

Vaughan on the jukebox. As she stood in a square of light in the doorway, a dozen men, feet on the brass rail at the bar, turned from their drinks to stare at her.

She let the door swing closed behind her and strolled in. Beneath the music came the percussive sound of billiard balls striking one another. The bartender paused, both hands on the counter, watching her as she walked. She raised her chin in greeting.

Kelly was sitting in a wooden-backed booth, picking at her nails. Foot jittering. Caitlin slid in across from her and extended her hand.

"Thanks for meeting me."

Kelly's handshake was brief, her fingers icy. "This is the only time. I'm gonna talk today, and that's it."

Tattoos rode her bare arms. A weeping rose, a savage angel, a sharp-winged butterfly. Her hair was dyed scorpion black. With her ink and Marlboro voice, Kelly was hard years from her teenage photo.

Caitlin said, "I want to take notes."

"No notes." Kelly didn't look around. "The people who matter know why I'm talking to a cop. Nobody else needs to think you're taking down names."

"Then I'll record it." She set her phone on the table and casually touched buttons, as though checking her messages.

Kelly didn't object. "Did you read the police report before you came?"

"Yes."

A caustic smile came and went. "Want to tell me what's in it?"

At the back of the room, under hanging lamps, men in bandannas eyed them from the pool tables. At the bar, eyes watched them in the mirror.

Kelly said, "I talked to the cops that day, and I figure I signed the report, but I don't remember doing it. Maybe you can fill me in."

"The report was very brief. You managed to give the investigating officers a basic description of your attacker."

At the word *attacker* Kelly's gaze flicked away. She took a pack of cigarettes from a slumping purse on the bench seat. She started to tap one out, caught herself, and instead began turning the pack in her hands, over and over.

"Whatever you can tell me — that's all I want," Caitlin said softly.

Kelly shut her eyes. She set down the cigarettes, spread her hands flat on the table, and seemed to turn off a light inside. She opened her eyes and looked evenly at Caitlin.

"I was late for choir. Home alone, rushing. I didn't see him in the garage, bolt still against the wall, wearing a plastic face mask," she said. "Then he breathed. And was *on* me. Like a rattler striking."

Her flat tone unsettled Caitlin. "Did he say anything?"

" 'Sullen bitch.' And head-punched me."

She said it dully. Removed. The disconnect, Caitlin suspected, had taken a massive toll.

"That's the word he used?" she said.

"Yeah. 'Sullen.' Like I was a character in a Regency romance."

Caitlin thought, *Yet another archaic literary term used by the Prophet.* "What did his voice sound like?"

"White boy. Young, I mean. A man, but hadn't been for long. Hoarse. Don't know if he always sounded that way, or he was putting on a disguise to impress me. Which he did."

"Did you see any part of his face?"

Kelly shook her head. "Mask, with sports sunglasses over the eye holes. Wearing a hoodie cinched tight so I couldn't tell what color hair he had, if he had any. Gloves. I didn't see any scars or tats or other distinguishing marks."

"His teeth?"

229

"The mask covered his mouth. He was there, but not a recognizable person. Like I said, blending into the wall. He was an *it.*"

Caitlin gave her a second. "You said you were home alone. After school?"

"My dad worked at a semiconductor factory. Mom was secretary at our church." She toyed with the cigarette pack. "The punch knocked me out. I woke up in the back of a pickup with a camper shell, duct-taped. Ankles, wrists, mouth. He was outside at the pond, prepping. I heard a chain rattling. But I knew a trick — slam your arms against your hips, duct tape snaps off." She shrugged. "Church camp game. I got free and ran. If I hadn't, I would have gone in the water with Lisa Chu."

The smooth surface of her voice couldn't eliminate the glass horror at the back of her gaze.

"Did you know Lisa?" Caitlin said.

"No. No connection except we spent an hour lying beside each other unconscious in the bed of a pickup truck driven by a serial killer, and I've spent two decades being the one who got to keep on breathing."

Kelly's hands lay flat on the table. Her foot started to jitter again. The music switched from blues to shitkicker country. Jerry Jeff Walker, "Up Against the Wall, Redneck Mother."

"Can you tell me about the inside of his camper?" Caitlin said.

"Dark. No windows. Plastic cargo-bed liner. The kind you can hose off if you need to."

"Did you see him after you escaped?"

"No."

"Did you hear his voice?"

A pause. "Yeah. The pond was through some trees. I heard him grunting. Dragging the parking bumper to the water, I guess."

"Did you see Lisa?"

Kelly shook her head. "Never saw her. Never heard her. Maybe she was unconscious when he rolled her into the pond. Maybe she never knew what was happening."

Behind the flat affect of her voice, the glass shards in her gaze sharpened.

This was what hope looked like, when it dealt with the Prophet. Wishing desperately that a girl she'd never met, who had literally touched her at the last moments of her life — wishing that the long-lost teenage babysitter died without pain or fear, oblivious.

Caitlin had read Lisa Chu's autopsy report. She suffered a subdural hematoma, evidence of being battered in the head. Possibly hard enough to cause loss of conscious-

231

ness. But the medical examiner found water in her lungs. She had drowned. She was alive when she went into the water.

Caitlin said, "You were close enough to hear him. If Lisa was conscious, you would have heard her too. She wouldn't have gone quietly."

Kelly licked her lips. Looked at the pool tables, and at her hands. Tossed her black hair over her shoulder.

"She could have been whispering in my ear the whole drive. Sometimes I wonder that. In my nightmares she talks to me. From under the water. Her voice is a whisper that's coming from *inside* me." She put a clawed hand to her chest. "But I never saw her."

Her eyes welled. She blinked furiously, refusing to let tears fall.

"Afterward I smelled her perfume. Lavender and vanilla. It was Love's Baby Soft. I could smell it on my clothes. Because she'd been lying beside me. We were curled together on that ride. And I didn't put two and two together. I didn't figure it out."

The flat tone was rising, the edges fraying. This was not part of the script Kelly had planed to a monotone over the years.

"The cops took my clothes," she said. "When I got to the police station, they took

232

my shirt for forensic tests. I still didn't add it up. It was only when they told me there was another girl missing . . . that's when it hit me. That the scent didn't come from the camper, but from another girl. But I didn't tell them before that, because I . . ."

"You were in shock."

Kelly looked at her like, *Yeah, right.*

Caitlin saw her as she must have been that day: sixteen, badly injured, *kidnapped.* Yet she'd managed to free herself and flee to safety, in utter fight-or-flight mode. There was no way, physically or cognitively, she could have had any space left over in her head.

"That day you couldn't have put two and two together," Caitlin said. "Now? It sounds like it. But then? It was life or death and a fleeting scent in the air."

Kelly stared at her. Her foot jittered like a jackhammer.

"How far did you run?" Caitlin said.

"Two miles."

"How long did it take for the police to arrive at the gas station after you got there?"

"Maybe twenty minutes."

Caitlin's shoulders dropped. "Lisa was gone before the cops rolled. You couldn't have saved her. God's honest shitty truth."

Kelly's chest rose and fell. After a minute,

she stood up.

"I'll be right back."

She walked briskly on stacked-heel boots to the women's room, her T-shirt sliding off one shoulder to reveal a red bra strap. Caitlin didn't know if what she'd said was the God's honest shitty truth, but it was the best approximation she could assemble at short notice. She looked at her hands. When she held her fingers out, they were shaking. She pressed them against the table.

Chill. Compartmentalize. For God's sake, keep it under control.

The toilets at a biker bar were one of the last places on earth Caitlin ever wanted to enter, but Kelly came out looking better. She'd splashed water on her face and pulled her hair back into a ponytail. She leaned on the bar, spoke to the bartender, and a minute later returned to the booth carrying two shot glasses shining with whiskey. She set them on the table and slid into the booth.

"If you're on duty, I'll drink on your behalf," she said.

"I'm on duty."

Kelly hoisted her glass. "Na zdrowie." *Naz-droh-vee-ay.* She downed the shot, pulled the second glass close, and said, "What else?"

Caitlin considered her words. "After you escaped from the truck. Did he pursue you?"

"No idea. At the time, I thought he was right on my heels. I pissed myself running. I ran through the woods until I came out on a road and saw the gas station. I went inside the mini-mart screaming and didn't stop for about an hour."

Caitlin was grave. "You asked to speak to a woman. Because . . ."

"I don't need another leering male cop imagining what the Prophet did," she said. "But he didn't touch me. Not sexually. He seemed — repelled by contact. He stank of lye soap. I still smell it."

Caitlin's pulse ticked up. That detail was not in the police report.

A man sauntered past the booth. "Ladies. Or should I say, lady and narc."

His voice had a crack at the edge, like he'd once been punched or cut in the throat. Caitlin glared coolly. He gave her the side-eye, skinny young guy, heels of his boots scuffing on the wood. Kelly ignored him.

Caitlin said, "The message. *Dripping blood* . . ."

Kelly glanced after the man. He strolled to the bar, looking like he had a wad of spit

235

in his mouth he wanted to hawk at Caitlin's feet.

Kelly said, "Did you park an unmarked Caprice outside?"

"Dodge."

"My friends know why I'm talking to you. Some random asshole won't be a problem."

The skinny young heckler watched her in the mirror behind the bar, then — to Caitlin's relief — paid for his beer and headed out the door.

She leaned forward, gently. "Kelly, tell me about the message."

Kelly downed the second shot of whiskey. "He wrote that on my arm." She turned her left hand over on the table, exposing the inside of her forearm. She ran a finger along it. The skin was covered by a sinuous tattoo of a tigress. "Didn't have this then."

Both her arms were covered with images. Bright, dark, big. Caitlin understood that she wanted to claim her body for herself.

"I washed it off before the cops saw it," Kelly said.

Caitlin nodded. That explained a major gap in the record. Nothing in the files mentioned a message written on Kelly's arm.

"I had to get rid of it. Had to. The old couple who ran the gas station tried to calm

236

me down; I was drooling and screaming, shaking like a broken washing machine. And it took forever for the cops to get there," she said. "I didn't know about preserving forensic evidence. It's not like now, when every five minutes there's a new TV crime show about collecting pubic hairs with tweezers. Nobody stopped me."

She was rolling now. "I went in the gas station bathroom and scrubbed my skin raw. My face, my neck, my hands, my arms. I had to."

Caitlin simply nodded.

"The cops, the uniforms who came, they never asked me about it. At the hospital where they took me, a CSI woman did ask about my hands. I told her I'd washed them, but she didn't ask about anything else," she said. "Then . . ." She leaned back. "That reporter showed up."

"Bart Fletcher," Caitlin said.

"He caught me in the parking lot at the high school."

"It felt like an ambush?"

"I guess. I just froze. It was my first day back at school after . . . maybe a week? He totally surprised me. Very forward, confident man. He talked like he was my best friend, with my best interests at heart. He smelled like beer."

237

"And . . ."

"I said I didn't want to talk. When I backed away, he said I was unique. I had escaped. And I could save others. I was a miracle and I had no right to hold back on how I'd done it."

"He guilt-tripped you into talking."

"I tried to walk away. That's when he dropped the news that a message was inked on Lisa Chu's arm." She shook her head. "I think I peed myself again, in the school parking lot. And man, did he pick up on it. 'What's wrong? You look so frightened. Please let me help you. What do you know about the writing?' " she said. "I got scared and told him. He didn't print it, but . . . There was more to the message." She shut her eyes. " 'The dripping blood our only drink, the bloody flesh our only food.' "

Caitlin held perfectly still. She checked that her phone was still recording.

Kelly turned her forearms over again. "The first line was written on my left arm, the second on my right. I didn't tell anybody else. I don't know why the reporter never printed it. Maybe because there was no evidence. I mean . . ."

"I believe you."

Kelly nodded. Leaned back. "I gotta go."

"Thank you. You've made a big difference." Caitlin got out her card. On the back she wrote the number for Victim Witness Assistance. She handed it to Kelly.

"You won't hear from me again. And I won't be around for a while. Road trip," Kelly said.

"Still, if you need me, or to talk to someone, call." Rising to leave, she glanced around Dusty's. "Can I ask you something?"

"What's a choirgirl doing in a biker bar?" Caitlin raised an eyebrow. "Yeah."

Kelly's eyes were dark. She glanced at the men who stood at the bar. A bearded guy with a ponytail, wearing his leather cut, caught her gaze. She raised her chin in acknowledgment and looked back at Caitlin.

"Because I'm safe. Nobody's gonna get through them to me."

Outside in the dusty lot, with a lineup of bikes shining chrome in her eyes, Caitlin hurriedly searched online. When she found it, she phoned Guthrie.

"It's a poem. 'East Coker' by T. S. Eliot," she said. " 'The dripping blood our only drink, the bloody flesh our only food.' "

"Sounds right up his alley," he said.

"There's more. 'The bloody flesh our only food, in spite of which we like to think that

we are sound, substantial flesh and blood
—' " She took a breath. " 'Again, in spite of
that, we call this Friday good.' "

Guthrie was silent. She squeezed the
phone.

"It's about Good Friday. The poem's talking about tomorrow."

23

The war room hummed with anxious energy, like a poorly grounded electrical cable. The team gathered in front of the wall of photos. Guthrie strode in, eyes darting.

"Where are we?"

Shanklin rocked up and down on her toes, arms crossed. "Nobody's found the location of the 'dripping blood' graffiti. Photo's been on the news. But the zoom on the camera is so tight. There's traffic noise, but we haven't been able to isolate any background sounds." Her red lips tightened. "We've received a dozen crank calls. Six morons spray-painted 'dripping blood' on their own property and called the media. The usual."

Guthrie ran his palm across his face. His five-o'clock shadow made him look like a wiry Nixon impersonator. "It's like sifting information fired from a confetti cannon."

"I half expect my mother to call in a tip, and she has Alzheimer's," Shanklin said.

"She can't remember eating lunch, but sees the Prophet on the news and starts reciting details from the early cases."

Caitlin felt a small pang. Martinez gave Shanklin a consoling look. Shanklin shrugged.

Caitlin leaned against a wall, shoulders tight. For the Prophet murders, no multi-agency task force had ever been assembled. That's why the files were scattered. Now, with the Ackerman crime scenes spread between Alameda and San Joaquin counties, the pattern was repeating.

But nobody wanted to hear that from the rookie. She kept her mouth shut.

Guthrie turned to her. "The survivor. The message she says the killer wrote on her arms."

Caitlin tacked up the T. S. Eliot poem. "This is the first explicit link between the Prophet's original murders and his return. This binds the old and new cases together."

"But what does it mean?" Martinez said.

"I think he's revived a plan that was interrupted or abandoned twenty years ago. He wants us to know that he's back on track and proceeding with something big." She paused. "Kelly — the survivor — is an emotional grenade. I gave her the number for Victim Witness Assistance, but could we have someone call her?"

Guthrie said, "We?"

She heard the rebuke. "Me. Of course. I'll ask. Sergeant."

Shanklin said, "The last time. When the Prophet accelerated his cycle, he sent a cryptic message your father deciphered. 'Mercury rises with the sun,' that mumbo jumbo."

Caitlin didn't respond to *mumbo jumbo.* Shanklin scowled. Maybe her sensible shoes were pinching. Or the bondage paddle she had jammed up her ass.

"Now he's posted a message about Good Friday — supposedly," Shanklin said.

Guthrie said, "Let's take it as read that the message is about Good Friday."

Shanklin raised her hands, placatingly. "I'm just playing devil's advocate."

The hell she was. She was challenging Caitlin, and they all knew it.

"What if the poem is a con?" Shanklin said.

Heat rose in Caitlin's neck. "It's not a con."

"We have only Kelly Smolenski's word that the killer wrote this message on her arms. No physical evidence, no photos, just the word of a biker's old lady drinking in a bar. This reporter, Fletcher — he could have set it up with her. He could have paid her to act like a poor little emotional grenade and convince you a message was written on her skin."

Now Guthrie scowled.

"Fletcher's supposedly had this secret message under wraps for the last twenty years. Why didn't he print it at the time, when it would have been a sensational scoop?"

Caitlin parsed her answer. "Kelly didn't know why. I'd guess it's because he interviewed a minor, on school property, without permission and without her parents present — and without corroboration. And when Fletcher's editors found out, they killed the story."

Guthrie stroked his chin.

Caitlin said, "But I'm going to find out."

Shanklin looked at her. "Did the Prophet ever kill someone on Good Friday?"

"No. But the message was never distributed. And his would-be victim escaped. Maybe that ruined his plan," she said.

"Maybe." Shanklin gestured at the poem. "And maybe there's no connection to his earlier cases. I mean, the 'Mercury rising' message was about a planet with astrological meaning. This one's supposedly about a religious holiday. What's the link?" She shook her head. "The message he sent to KDPX News talked about a young cop stumbling into a pit. Maybe he's trying to shove you off the cliff. Maybe the message is meant to make you crazy."

At the word *crazy,* the room seemed to flash with liquid light. Caitlin gave Shanklin a flat stare. "Maybe. Maybe not."

Martinez, standing in front of the wall with his feet planted wide, spoke pensively. "Both messages talk about celestial events."

Shanklin said, "Astrology and the Crucifixion are nowhere close to the same thing."

Martinez turned. "Not celestial in the sense of heaven. Celestial in the sense of astronomy."

"Don't go hippie-dippy on me, Martinez."

"Easter is tied to the start of spring. Holy Week — Palm Sunday, Holy Thursday, Good Friday — goes back to the Last Supper, which was a Passover Seder. Right? Which is why those two holidays almost always align. You know how Easter is not celebrated on a particular date?"

Guthrie nodded. Shanklin still looked skeptical. The light in the room wavered and flared in Caitlin's vision. *Make you crazy.* Their voices seemed to come from underwater.

Get it together.

She forced herself to concentrate. The light settled. Their voices swam closer.

She said, "The date of Easter changes from year to year."

"That's because Easter is based around the rising of the full moon after the start of spring," Martinez said. "Easter is celebrated on the first Sunday after the first full moon after —"

"The vernal equinox," Caitlin said.

Martinez nodded.

Shanklin said, "I'm impressed."

"Altar boy. Plus twelve years of Jesuit education," Martinez said. "Both the 'Mercury rising' message and the Good Friday message refer to astronomical events."

Shanklin said nothing for a minute. "Say it's legit. What does it matter?"

Lieutenant Kogara strode in. "It means we add patrols. It means the first item at roll call for every shift at every station is to be alert to signs of any activity that might relate to the Prophet."

The team all turned to acknowledge the commander. Kogara looked intense but unruffled. His white dress shirt could have been ironed in the last five minutes. Possibly while he was wearing it. He nodded at the board.

"What do we have on the evidence from

that burned-out car at Silver Creek Park?"

Caitlin opened a report. "The phone in the car belonged to the victim, Stuart Ackerman. Arson confirms that it triggered the incendiary device. The phone itself was toast. We accessed his cloud data but found nothing connected to the crime scene or the case."

Kogara walked along the wall of photos. When he came to the shot of Stuart Ackerman, with information below it, he stopped and tapped a list of points.

Zodiac Match. Starshine69. Wild Sagittarius.

"The astrological angle. How important is it?" he said.

Caitlin said, "It's too obvious to ignore. But it doesn't completely fit with the literary tone of the Prophet's most recent message, or the religious overtones of the new ones."

Kogara looked at her, seemingly surprised that she had offered analysis. She went quiet.

Martinez said, "Maybe we're making him out to be a genius when he's not. He's just random. Like music videos." He shrugged. "Right? You watch, and think, Why am I not getting this? But it's because they don't make sense. There's no meaning. The images are random, meant for shock and sensation."

Shanklin said, "Wow. When did you become a cultural critic?"

Guthrie said, "I get Martinez's point. The forums, the obsessives, may be overthinking this. We shouldn't fall into the same trap."

Caitlin thought: *The Prophet is a genius. Because he's managed to stay ten steps ahead of law enforcement for twenty-five years.*

Kogara said, "Keep at it. We're increasing patrols tomorrow."

He glanced at Guthrie and then at Caitlin. He was increasing patrols on the strength of their belief that Good Friday was a threat. She kept her expression flat and her hands clasped behind her back. Where he couldn't see her nails digging into her skin.

"I'm going to issue a public safety bulletin telling people to be alert and aware of anything out of the ordinary tomorrow," he said. "Okay, people. Keep it up. We're counting on you."

He strode away. The detectives gathered their notes.

As Shanklin walked past, Caitlin said, "Kelly Smolenski's the real deal. She's telling the truth."

Shanklin's glance was cutting. "You'd better hope so. We'd all better."

24

Ana Maria Garcia walked from the Berkeley BART station to Coffee, Tea & Tarot, her disquiet building with every step. Evening traffic was desultory, the sidewalks empty. The brick-fronted shop was dark.

Though her back ached from standing all day at work at the thrift shop, she huffed and sped up. The blinds were down. The sign on the door read, CLOSED.

Okay, she thought; *not to worry.* The windows weren't broken, and when she cupped her hands and put her face to the glass, things inside looked orderly.

Except she couldn't get hold of her friends. Neither J. T. Wilcox nor Gaia Hill was answering the phone or responding to texts. A fluttering bird began beating its wings in her chest.

She knocked. "Hello? Gaia? J.T.?"

She heard footsteps coming around the side of the building. She hustled toward the sound. "J.T.?"

A man turned the corner. She put a hand on her chest and said, "Oh."

He was lanky and skittish. The look in his eyes took her aback, so intense.

"Are they home?" she said.

"No." He looked over his shoulder. "Back door's locked. Lights off."

"You went in?"

"I don't have a key. If they're upstairs, they're not answering the bell."

J.T. and Gaia lived in an apartment above the café. Ana Maria frowned and put a hand on the young man's arm. "Daniel, I don't want to alarm you, but . . . I'm worried."

Daniel Wilcox looked at her from under his heavy fall of black hair. His frayed jeans sagged on his hips. The horned-devil tattoo on his neck and his skull-and-crossbones ear studs gave him a dark mien, from a distance. Up close, with dismay filling his eyes, Daniel looked like the little boy Ana Maria had known since he was four years old. She knew that his death-metal heart was twisted in knots. His mother was nowhere to be found.

He walked to the café door and tried to see in past the glare of the evening sun. "No broken glass, no signs of robbery. I mean, look — everything seems okay inside," he said. "Except they never opened up, apparently. And . . ." He hesitated. "Aunt Ana, the chairs."

She peered past the glare. "What?"

"Half of them are upended on the tables. But half are down. Mom and Gaia were here this morning. Had to be."

She tried to calm the frantic beating in her chest, the sparrow trying to crash through her ribs. Her friends were easygoing but diligent. They wouldn't simply shutter their business and take off with no notice. Certainly wouldn't go dark when friends and J.T.'s boy were becoming increasingly concerned about them.

Daniel bent over his phone, sent yet another text to his mom, and checked the café's social media.

"The Coffee, Tea and Tarot Facebook page has no posts by Mom or Gaia today. Just messages from disappointed customers asking why the place is closed," he said.

Ana Maria was looking at the counter inside the café. A pink box of croissants sat beside the cash register. And the lights on the coffeepots were on.

A young woman came along the sidewalk, pushing a stroller. Ana Maria said, "Excuse me. Have you seen the women who run this coffeehouse?"

The woman barely slowed. "Sorry." She shook her head and continued down the street.

"Come on," Ana Maria said to Daniel.

They found an open store three doors down, a clothing boutique about to shut for the day.

"Excuse me. Do you know the women who run Coffee, Tea and Tarot?" she said.

The woman behind the counter nodded.

"Have you seen them today?"

"No. They never opened. Had to go to Star-yucks for my fix."

"Have you seen anything unusual?"

"Like what?"

Daniel said, "Strange people in the neighborhood. Anything."

She shook her head. "Sorry. Something wrong?"

They left, Ana Maria's anxieties spinning faster and faster. Daniel's mouth had tightened to a white line.

He said, "Let's check the alley."

Behind the row of stores a broken beer bottle glinted on the concrete next to a Dumpster. The parking space beside the back entrance to the café, where Gaia usually squeezed her Jeep, was empty. Daniel turned in a full circle, eyeing the ground, the windows, the rooftops.

Ana Maria walked toward the brick wall that abutted the parking space. On the brickwork, about three feet off the ground, fresh white paint had been applied in a strip with a roller.

"What's this?" she said.

"Looks like they painted over some graffiti." Daniel approached, crouched, and lightly touched his fingers to the wall. "It's still tacky."

Ana Maria stepped back. Trying to get a big picture. She saw the tire tracks on the ground. Maybe eighteen inches long. Somebody had driven over a splotch of the wet white paint on the ground, smearing it into a tread pattern.

Daniel's face, beneath his heavy bangs, was white. "Somebody was here today. They did this. Today."

They looked at each other in the glare of the setting sun.

Ana Maria said, "Daniel, we need to call the police."

25

Through the smoked-glass windows of the Briarwood Sheriff's Station, the western sun shone dull red as Caitlin turned to the task she'd been putting off. She picked up the phone and called the *East Bay Herald.*

"Bart Fletcher, please," she said.

She leaned on her elbows and closed her eyes as the switchboard transferred the call. Fletcher's extension rang. It went to voice mail. A part of her was relieved.

"Mr. Fletcher, it's Detective Hendrix." She asked him to return her call, even if it was after hours. She said, "Thanks," and hung up, proud that she hadn't mentioned how much she wanted to boot him in the balls.

Maturity. Also — the ball booting would be battery. She headed for the car, waving good night to Paige at the front desk.

Her phone chimed. She looked, but it wasn't a call from Bart Fletcher. It was a public alert about the Prophet.

The Alameda County Sheriff's Office has issued a threat advisory urging citizens to be alert to possible activity by the suspect known as the Prophet.

She stopped. Wow. Kogara had done it.

Based on credible evidence, the sheriff's office asks citizens to . . .

The alert system posted threat advisories at least twice a week. Caitlin monitored it but wondered how many citizens paid attention beyond news that I-880 was shut down or a riot had broken out at a Cal football game, instigated by the Stanford marching band.

Out of an abundance of caution, we ask . . .

But this would jab folks like a poke from a cattle prod. Watch out. Freak out. Stay locked and loaded. *Remember: If you see something, say something.*

Halfway across the parking lot, her phone chimed again. But it still wasn't from Bart Fletcher. She checked the screen and slowed. A text from her father.

We okay?

It looked innocuous, and poignant. Almost thirsting for connection. He knew he'd screwed up.

256

He probably wanted something. Wanted to keep abreast of things. Well, she didn't have to give him that, did she?

She thought: *jerk. That's what I'm being.*

Of course Mack wanted connection. Of course he wanted to know what was going on. He also wanted things to be okay with her. And *that* was a step in the right direction. That was the promised land in her book. She replied to his message.

It's good.

It was a lie, but if she kept it up, maybe she could turn it true.

Half an hour later she pulled up in front of Sean's house in a crowded Berkeley neighborhood. She glimpsed the bay, gold and whitecapped. The sun was sinking into the Pacific beyond the Marin Headlands and Mount Tamalpais.

The house was a Victorian the size of some pool cabanas in rich neighborhoods. Sean's pickup filled the driveway. He commuted half the time to the ATF's San Francisco Field Division office but didn't want to leave the East Bay. The reason was visible in the crew cab of the truck: Sadie's booster car seat.

The radio news came on as she parked. "The Alameda County Sheriff's Office has issued a threat advisory asking citizens to be alert to the possibility that the Prophet may intend to strike again. They . . ."

She turned off the engine and the radio hushed. She got out. The whole street was silent. Usually kids would be out, shooting hoops and riding bikes. It was empty.

Inside the front window, Sadie stood on an easy chair, watching the street. When she saw Caitlin she waved, put her face to the window, and blew a raspberry. In reply, Caitlin crossed her eyes.

As she climbed the steps to the door, a Subaru Outback pulled to the curb. Inside, Sadie jumped up and down and banged on the window.

"Mommy!"

Caitlin paused on the porch. Michele Ferreira parked the Subaru and got out.

She came around the car and climbed the steps. "You in the eye of the hurricane?"

"Dead center."

Sean opened the door. The look on his face when he saw them speaking was fleeting but blatant: *Are you talking about me?*

Michele and Caitlin both looked at him.

"No," Caitlin said.

"Never," Michele said.

Caitlin didn't talk to Michele about Sean Rawlins. Michele knew all she wanted to about him. She'd flushed him from her system, willingly, after their brief marriage. She had a rare ability to forgive and forget, a skill Caitlin longed to learn. How she and Sean's ex-wife ended up running together with the Rockridge Ragers, and became friends, was a mystery none of them wanted to explore.

Sadie zoomed out the door past Sean and leaped into Michele's arms. *"Mommy."*

"How's my girl?" Michele kissed her, and asked Sean, "Everything go okay?"

"All good," he said.

She set Sadie down. "Get your things."

The little girl dashed back into the hall. Michele lowered her voice.

"Sunday runs are canceled until further notice. Nobody wants to go off trail in the hills."

"Yeah."

Sadie returned, lugging her backpack. Sean pulled her into his arms, let her plant a soft kiss on his lips, and set her down to take Michele's hand.

Michele pecked him on the cheek, then did the same to Caitlin. "You take care."

"You too," Caitlin said.

Michele walked Sadie down the steps to

the car. As always, Sean had to will himself to smile while he waved good-bye. He had Sadie half the time, but that didn't matter at moments like this.

Michele beeped the horn as she pulled away, with Sadie waving from the backseat. Sean watched them go and draped an arm over Caitlin's shoulder.

She continued looking up the street, watching Michele's taillights recede to red pinpricks.

"What?" Sean said.

"Everybody needs to have eyes in the back of their heads right now."

He followed her gaze. After a second he said, "Michele's townhouse complex has a secure garage, and a second, locked gate to get to their building." His hand tightened on her shoulder. "But I'll text her to keep a heads-up."

"Thank you."

She looked at the darkening sky, the lights sparkling on the distant Berkeley Hills. There were seven million lives around her. And a ghost was loose among them, hunting.

26

Good Friday

Crowded roads, clattering radio, flawless blue sky — the morning looked and sounded like a thousand others, but Caitlin kept her eyes open for signs that its normality was a lie. Public schools from San Jose to Santa Rosa were holding their final day of class before spring break. Parochial schools were already closed for the Easter weekend. A chill ocean wind blew through the Golden Gate. A few churches, mostly Catholic, had open doors in preparation for afternoon services. Others, mostly Protestant, had banners welcoming all comers to Easter sunrise services on Sunday. The early commuter traffic was as sluggish as always.

Police patrols were noticeable to Caitlin's eye, but not overwhelming. How could the sheriff's office power up overnight? Not easily, and not without authorizing massive overtime.

Threat advisories were an easier call. But they had to be backed up by at least some show of presence on the street.

At Northside Joe, a neighborhood coffeehouse in Berkeley, Caitlin stood at the counter. Outside, Sean waited in his truck, talking on the phone with a fellow agent about stolen blasting materials. Acoustic jazz played on the coffeehouse speakers. A television showed the morning news, a San Francisco station. The sound was muted but the closed captioning expressed alarm.

. . . ISSUED A THREAT ADVISORY LAST NIGHT, BASED ON EVIDENCE THAT THE PROPHET HAS MENTIONED GOOD FRIDAY IN HIS MESSAGES TO POLICE . . .

The woman standing beside Caitlin shook her head at the TV. "Crazy times."

A man in a suit, armored with aftershave, said, "Think it's real?"

"Why wouldn't it be?" the woman said.

"This feels like the weeks after 9/11. Everybody jumping at their own shadows, thinking a sprinkle of powdered sugar on a tabletop was anthrax. It seems like fearmongering."

Behind the counter, the cappuccino maker hissed and the barista banged the espresso filter against the sink to empty the grounds.

"I'd rather get fearmongered than get

262

killed," the woman said. "This shit is for real. There wasn't an anthrax killer around here, but the Prophet sure is."

The barista handed the woman her espresso. "I didn't even take the dog out last night. The sun goes down, I dead bolt the door. I'm asking the landlord to install bars on the windows."

The man said, "This guy isn't a vampire. He can't flit in like a bat. And what are the odds? The cops are covering their butts in the remote event that something happens. They don't want to look slow on the uptick, like last time."

The barista gave the woman her change and turned to Caitlin.

Caitlin raised two fingers. "Two brews of the day. Large. To go."

The barista grabbed cups and continued talking to the man. "You're not a woman living alone. It doesn't feel so remote when you're lying in bed at two A.M., and you hear strange sounds in the dark outside, and you know he's out there. Because he is. And he's waiting, and looking. It doesn't feel remote in the least."

Caitlin felt it. The atmosphere was beyond jittery. People weren't just nervous. They were full of dread.

So was she. But nothing had happened

overnight. No calls, no emergencies. The barista poured two large coffees in takeout cups. On the TV, the morning hosts had moved on to the weekend weather. The forecast for Easter sunrise services looked good.

The barista set down Caitlin's order. "Five seventy-five."

As Caitlin got her wallet, a horn honked outside. The barista frowned. The honk sounded again. And didn't stop.

Caitlin turned. Sean was standing on the horn hard, his left arm out the window, waving at her.

She threw bills on the counter, grabbed her coffees, and ran out. As she approached the pickup, she heard the radio. It was the drive-time show they'd been listening to on the way over, Chaz and T-Bone.

Sean propped his sunglasses on top of his head. His expression mixed incredulity and alarm. Caitlin leaned in.

One of the deejays said, "Yes, you're on the air. You're live. We're listening."

"No. You hear, but you don't listen. You ignore my message. This city, feeding on its selfish panic. Eating itself alive."

The voice belonged to a phone-in caller. But that wasn't why it sounded so strange. It was a mechanical drone. The caller was using an electronic voice changer.

"You challenge me. The police dare to goad me. But it's futile. You can't stop me."

Caitlin said, "Jesus Christ."

It was the Prophet.

265

27

Caitlin stood rigid in the parking lot outside Northside Joe, coffees hot in her hands, sunlight spearing through the leaves of the maples. The radio blared from Sean's Tundra. The deejay was tripping over his words.

Sean said, "The show's doing a segment on the Prophet, and this guy called in. He gave out details of one of the murders that the police haven't released."

She eyed him.

"Nails driven into the victims' chests at the cornfield." Sean was grim. "Chaz and T-Bone are just keeping him on the line. They believe he's the real thing."

"He is," she said.

On the air, Chaz said, "But I don't want to goad you, man. I want to talk. I want to understand what's going on." His voice sounded strained. He cleared his throat. "Can you tell me what you want?"

Caitlin said, "Don't ask him that — he

266

will tell you."

She shoved Sean's coffee through the open window at him and grabbed her phone. She called the war room as she ran around to the passenger side.

Nearby, a Subaru pulled into the parking lot with its windows down. The radio was playing Chaz and T-Bone. The driver looked at her, openmouthed.

"Are you listening to this?"

Caitlin hopped into the truck. From inside the coffeehouse, people pushed through the door to the parking lot, curious. Chaz and T-Bone was the biggest drive-time show in the Bay Area, broadcasting out of San Francisco. A couple of hundred thousand people were listening to this.

The war room phone was picked up. Martinez. Caitlin said, "Turn on the FM radio."

Traffic was congested on the main road. Caitlin knew that many of those drivers were listening.

Which was just what the Prophet loved: an audience. What the hell was he doing? Was this his Good Friday act — a live call-in performance?

No. He never called just to talk. Her stomach knotted.

At the Berkeley Police Department, Detective Keith Warnaker approached the middle-aged woman and the young man who were waiting anxiously in the lobby. Ana Maria Garcia and Daniel Wilcox introduced themselves.

Daniel said, "I know we were here last night, but Mom and Gaia didn't come home."

Daniel tossed his heavy black bangs from his face. Above the devil tattoo on his neck, he had the face of a scared kid.

"They haven't responded to any of our messages, and the coffeehouse is still locked up. Something is way wrong."

Warnaker was heavyset and highly experienced. "I just got in. The report you filed is on my desk, but I haven't had a chance to look at it in detail."

"Something happened yesterday morning at their place. Coffee, Tea and Tarot — it's two blocks from here. It's like they were getting ready to open and just vanished."

Daniel told him in a rush of words about the half-prepped café, the coffeepots with the lights on, the pastries on the countertop. And about the fresh paint in the alley.

The detective's radar warmed up.

"Fresh paint? What kind of wall?" he said.

Daniel looked baffled. "Redbrick."

The detective inhaled. He thought of the

alert regarding the graffiti the Prophet had painted.

"Daniel, do you know if your mom saw the televised request for information about some graffiti painted on a brick wall the other day?"

Daniel shook his head. "Televised? She and Gaia don't own a TV." He looked like he was about to cry, or to throttle somebody. "We have to do something. Go to the café. I'll break down the door or you bring a crowbar. We need to find out what's happened to them."

Warnaker nodded. "Yeah. Let's go."

Around the Bay Area, in bumper-to-bumper traffic, drivers turned up their radios. On air, the deejays worked to keep the Prophet talking.

"You called me, man," Chaz said. "I want to know what's on your mind. This is — I mean, this is your chance. You have the air. Talk to me."

" *'Talk to me.' Do you think you're my confessor?*"

"Not at all. Of course not." Chaz's voice rose in pitch, half an octave. He *sounded* like he was sweating. "I just . . ."

"*Stop babbling.*"

Caitlin and Sean stared at the radio. She

269

knew that at the radio station, a dozen frantic people would be in contact with the police and the phone company, trying to trace the caller's number and location. The Prophet wouldn't make it easy for them.

On the street behind her, a horn blared. A moment later came the crunch of a collision. She and Sean swiveled to look out the back window. At the stop sign, a car had been rear-ended. When the driver got out, they heard the radio show. The driver who hit her opened his door. The same voices poured from his car radio.

The Prophet was everywhere.

In the alley behind Coffee, Tea & Tarot, Detective Warnaker followed Daniel Wilcox and Ana Maria Garcia to the parking spot where white paint covered a stretch of brick wall. Warnaker's radar was pinging louder. Returning to his car, he pulled up the bulletin issued by the Alameda Sheriff's Office about the graffiti painted by the Prophet.

He saw the photo. "Damn."

He grabbed the radio. "Dispatch. Request backup at my location." He rattled off the address and jogged to the front door of the café. Daniel followed, his face fraught.

"I have reason to believe this is an emergent situation," the detective said. "So I'm going to effect entry into the premises."

Ana Maria said, "Oh, my God."

Daniel said, "Do it."

Detective Warnaker looked at the glass in the door, and at the lock, and at the alarm company sign beneath the roofline.

Daniel said, "If something happened to them and the alarm hasn't rung yet, it isn't going to."

"Stand back," the detective said.

Daniel put an arm around Ana Maria's shoulder and they pulled back. Warnaker took a telescoping baton from his belt and whacked the safety glass in the door. It cracked. He hit it again and it sagged. A third blow shattered the entire pane. It collapsed with a loud crunch. He covered his hand with a handkerchief, reached inside the frame, and flipped the lock. No alarm sounded.

Daniel pushed forward, but the detective raised an arm. "Stay here."

"No, I —"

"Son, the situation may be dangerous. And a crime may have been committed. Do not come inside. I'll let you know if it's okay."

Warnaker was stern, but Daniel was like a dog straining at the leash. Ana Maria set a restraining hand against his chest. "Please,

Daniel."

The detective stepped across the threshold, shoes crushing the fallen glass. His jacket lapel was pulled back, his right hand resting against the butt of his gun.

"Police. Is anybody here?"

Daniel pushed against Ana Maria's hand. *"Mom,"* he yelled through the door. *"Mom!"*

The only sound from the café was the detective's shoes, crunching on broken glass as he cautiously stepped deeper inside. On the street, cars at the traffic light had turned up their radios. Some call-in show, weird voices. Ana Maria kept her hand against Daniel's chest to calm him, but her own heart was racing like a hummingbird's.

In the café, shadows fell heavily across the floor. The detective peered over the counter and walked toward the back, hand never leaving the butt of his gun.

"Berkeley Police. Is anyone here?"

Reaching the back hall, he slowed at the door to Gaia's office. He nudged it open, creaking. Ana Maria held her breath. Daniel's heart thudded beneath her palm.

The cop stepped into the office and back out. He continued down the hall to the stockroom and pantry. He jogged up the stairs to the apartment. A minute later he returned, shaking his head.

"Nobody's here."

"But they were," Daniel said. "I know it."

Warnaker stood in the middle of the café, slowly scanning the premises. From the sidewalk, Ana Maria did too.

It was Daniel who said, "What's that thing?"

He pointed through the door at a white plastic gizmo sitting on a table. It was about the size of a credit card.

Warnaker took a quick step toward it, and caught himself. He slowed down, as though it might be dangerous.

He stopped three feet from the table, scowling.

"What is it?" Ana Maria said.

He looked perplexed. "It's a timer. A cheap digital timer." He kept his feet planted where they were but leaned forward, squinting. "It's . . ."

He stopped, lips parted.

"What?" Daniel said. "What's wrong?"

Abruptly, Warnaker got his handheld radio and put it to his face. "There's a timer here. And it's counting down."

Daniel lunged for the door. The detective raised his hand to straight-arm him like a halfback.

"What's going on?" Daniel cried.

The detective turned toward the timer and

spoke into the handheld radio.

"It's down to twelve minutes and forty-two seconds."

28

In Sean's truck, Caitlin gripped the dashboard with one hand, staring at the radio as if doing so could conjure the Prophet to appear before her.

"Stop staring at the second hand on the wall clock. And at your producer, who's twirling his hand, signaling you to keep me talking," the caller said.

Inside Northside Joe, people were looking at their phones. Someone pointed at the television. The barista changed the channel. A fresh newsroom appeared, anchor in a red suit, red headline behind her. BREAKING: PROPHET CALLS LIVE TO KZED RADIO.

"We have to do something," Caitlin said.

"What? How?" Sean said.

On the air, Chaz said, "All right. Okay. Hey, I'll chill. Please, go ahead and talk. Talk about whatever you want. The air is yours."

"I know the police are attempting to trace

275

my location."

A cold finger ran up Caitlin's spine. The mechanical voice was creepy beyond belief, but also weirdly seductive. Mechanical smoke.

Chaz coughed and again cleared his throat. "Okay. You called. You talk . . ."

"I'll save the police the trouble." The voice paused. *"Write this down."*

Caitlin said, "No way."

Sean grabbed a pen from his shirt pocket. She pulled one from the glove box.

"Thirty-seven point eight six eight eight seven four, negative one twenty-two point two six four eight two nine."

Caitlin scrawled on her palm. "Did you get it?"

Sean had a piece of scrap paper in his hand. "Yeah. Map coordinates. Latitude and longitude in decimal degrees."

On the radio, the mechanical voice said, *"They should hurry."*

Sean grabbed his phone. He typed in the coordinates.

"Berkeley." He zoomed in. "Whoa, they're — it's Fulton Street. On campus."

Caitlin looked at the phone. "It's Edwards Stadium. The track and soccer field."

Sean zoomed out. "It's just over two miles away."

They looked at each other. Sean squealed the tires backing out of the parking spot, spun the wheel, and floored it.

29

Sean slewed out of the coffeehouse parking lot, the heavy pickup bouncing onto the street. Caitlin fought to buckle her seat belt as he swung toward the traffic light at the corner. He gunned it as the light turned yellow and hit a hard left, heading south toward the UC Berkeley campus.

On the radio, the flat mechanical voice said, *"Time is ticking, ticking."*

"Got it, yeah, got it," the deejay said in a rush.

"You got nothing. But you're going to."

Caitlin still had the call to the sheriff's station open on her phone. She put it to her ear. "Martinez? You get those coordinates?"

Martinez said, "We're recording. Yeah. Soccer stadium on the Berkeley campus." He paused. "You sound like you're in a vehicle moving at high speed."

Sean passed the fender bender at the intersection. The drivers were talking but pointing at their radios. Everybody was listening.

Sean swung around a Prius and accelerated. The coffee in Caitlin's hand sloshed as the cup hit her in the chest. The lid popped and half of it slurped onto her T-shirt. She flinched from the heat. With her elbow she put the window down and poured the rest of the cup out.

Traffic was slowing ahead, backed up from the morning rush. Sean said, "Shit."

Caitlin wished she had a light strip to flip on, and a siren. But this wasn't even her jurisdiction.

"Hendrix?" Martinez said.

"I'm with Sean. We're a mile and a half from the coordinates. We're on our way."

"Berkeley PD —"

"Of course. But we're on our way."

Guthrie's voice came on. "Hendrix."

She waited for him to tell her to back off and let the local police handle it.

"Just got a call from a Berkeley detective."

"Sergeant, I . . ."

"He thinks he found the location of the Prophet's graffiti. The Prophet may have taken two more people. And he left a timer at the kidnapping site, counting down."

"Where?"

"That's not the point. The timer was at

twelve minutes, and that was six minutes ago. Haul ass."

"Sean, we have six minutes."

He cut a glance at her. He was gripping the wheel, muscles in his forearms corded. Traffic ahead was backed up at the next light.

"We need to get off the main roads," he said.

"Side streets will have stop signs but much less traffic." She leaned out the window to check the gutter along the sidewalk. "Bike lane's clear. Go."

He braked hard, swerved into the bike lane, and accelerated along the curb. Bits of paper and discarded Taco Bell wrappers blew into the air.

"Set your own timer," he said. "Count it down for me minute by minute."

Caitlin swiped through her phone. The engine gunned. Sean screeched to a stop at the corner and checked cross traffic before swinging right and racing down the street to the next block. He turned left into a leafy urban neighborhood. Tall Spanish-style homes. Redbud in bloom, ivy marching over fences. The road was narrow and cars were parked along the curbs. The school run was just getting started. Sean saw a couple of kids coming out of a gate and heading toward the corner. He braked sharply.

"School bus stop ahead. Can't use this street."

At the stop sign he headed left, spinning the tires, back toward the way they'd come.

"Five minutes," Caitlin said.

The light at the main road turned green when they were halfway up the block. The speed limit was thirty.

"Hang your badge out the window," Sean said. He had his own badge in his left hand.

That could normally get her in big trouble, but she figured if the Berkeley police had called Alameda for information, she was damn near deputized on this. This was an ad hoc emergency task force. Sean raced across the intersection as the light turned red again.

Two blocks up he took the right-hand turn without even tapping the brakes.

"Four minutes. We're point seven miles out," she said.

"Berkeley PD has to have units in the area."

"The stadium's on campus. It'll be campus police."

Another stop sign, and another, and another.

"Three minutes," she said.

The homes broke out into a row of shops

along the street. Coffee bars and boutiques. They were still half a mile away. Through another stop sign. Over a hill and down toward campus.

Caitlin said. "There's gonna be traffic on University and . . ."

Sean hit the brakes hard. Caitlin lurched forward against the seat belt.

A delivery truck was parked outside a bakery. It took up the entire lane. Sean laid on the horn and swung around the truck. The street was narrow, lined on both curbs with parked cars. The Tundra barely fit.

A UPS truck was coming straight at him. He had nowhere to go.

He and the oncoming UPS truck both hit the brakes. Sean's pickup slid toward it. Caitlin inhaled. The pickup screeched to a stop. The brown UPS truck kept coming, looming, cab swinging down as the driver stood on the brakes. It filled Sean's windshield.

It stopped five feet away. Its grille was right in front of Caitlin's face. The driver, in his brown uniform, was feet from her, shaking his head, arms spread wide, implying, *What the hell?*

Caitlin and Sean both raised their badges. Sean leaned out his window. "Back it up,"

282

he shouted. "Federal agent. It's an emergency."

The guy ground the long gearshift into reverse. Slowly, with the inertia of a lumbering beast, he backed the truck up the street and angled to the curb.

Sean spun the wheel, squeaked past it, and poured on the gas again.

"We need a police scanner," he said.

"Two minutes," Caitlin said. "Quarter of a mile."

The radio was filled with Chaz's chatter. The Prophet had gone silent, the mechanical voice quiet, but there was a buzz-like sound that Caitlin realized was the caller breathing. The hair on her arms stood up.

"He's still on the line," she said. "He wants to see what happens when people get to the coordinates. He wants to be live on the air when the results come in. Jesus Christ."

They reached a T junction. Sean turned right, downhill, toward central Berkeley. The sun was up, cresting the green hills. The view ran all the way to the bay. The water gleamed in the morning sun, blue flashing to molten pewter. The Golden Gate Bridge, San Francisco white on the hills across the water — where the SFPD was surely going balls to the wall to trace the Prophet's call.

283

But she couldn't imagine he would do anything less than play with the cops. With everybody.

With the people he'd taken.

Sean raced along, his face fierce with concentration, leaves of low-hanging trees brushing the windshield, birches and willows. He snagged the corner of a blue recycling bin with a hollow *whack*. It spun and flew onto the sidewalk.

"Ninety seconds."

They squealed out of the residential neighborhood onto a broad street at the border of the campus. Tall university buildings formed a wall along the far side of the street. Sean screamed down the road. The stadium was still a couple of hundred yards away. Tall fir trees swept by, a picket fence of green. They swung onto Oxford Street, which ran along the front entrance to the campus. Horn blaring.

"Sixty seconds," Caitlin said.

They reached an intersection. The traffic was backed up in all directions.

She pointed. "I can see the stadium."

"There's a damn traffic jam of people trying to get there," Sean said.

He laid on the horn again.

Everybody was laying on their horns.

Sean screeched to a stop. All lanes, in all

directions, were jammed.

"We can make it," Caitlin said.

"We can't." He looked at her. "Not in the truck."

He jammed the transmission in park and put on his flashers. They jumped out and ran.

"Forty-five seconds," Caitlin said.

She was fast, but Sean had longer legs and was damned fit.

"Go," she said. "I'm right behind you."

Sirens were coming from several directions. She ran down the middle of the street, around stopped cars. Bicyclists eyed her, perplexed. She looked down a side street. Two police cars were stuck behind a line of traffic, lights flashing, sirens wailing.

In the distance, she heard the *blatt* of a helicopter. She kept running. Sean was outdistancing her. The stadium, about twenty thousand seats, was on a corner of the campus, right up against the road. In every car she passed, she heard Chaz and T-Bone. In stores along the street, TVs were on. Local stations had broken in with coverage. Overhead, a news chopper swept past. Students were everywhere. Some were following Sean, running toward the corner.

Caitlin ran along the sidewalk behind him, ivy on a wall greening against the sun, hair falling from her clip into her eyes, breathing hard.

"Guthrie, we're there," she said.

The timer chimed.

"Sean, we're out of time," she yelled.

She heard the radio from a dozen cars stopped in the street, people jumping out and running after Sean. She heard the Prophet's weird mechanical voice.

"Time's up."

From car speakers, a repeating buzz sounded. Like the buzzer at a basketball game.

"Fuck." Caitlin ran harder.

The buzzer faded in the background, but it seemed to drill into Caitlin's head, deep, reverberating. Something was off-key and looming.

Sean reached a gate, a six-foot cyclone fence outside the stadium. It was locked. He leaped for the top, jammed his boot into the latch, and hauled himself up.

A bright fear shot through her. "Sean — be careful."

He kept going, rolling over the top and dropping to the other side.

Campus police cars snaked around the corner, sirens shrieking. So did Berkeley PD units. They pulled up at all angles, and officers poured out. Caitlin felt a surge of support. A blue wave. She ran to the gate. She held her badge out and passed a dozen people who were running in her direction, all holding up cell phones, already recording the scene.

The Prophet's voice poured from cars on the street. *"Do I hear sirens?"*

Caitlin leaped at the fence and scrabbled hard to pull herself up and get a foot on the chain.

"Where are the sirens? Is that what I hear?"

What the hell was the Prophet talking about? Sirens were everywhere.

"No. I hear something different."

She hoisted herself to the top of the gate and paused. Sean was halfway to the field. Nobody else was there.

From the radio came the clicking of a computer keyboard.

What was the Prophet doing? Caitlin scrambled over the top of the gate and dropped to the pavement on the other side. Ahead, Sean pounded down the stadium steps and jumped from the bleachers onto the track. He ran onto the field. She sprinted after him.

On the radio, there was a pause. Then came the sound of a final, heavy key being hit.

She hurried down the bleacher stairs,

dropped to the track, and ran onto the soccer field behind Sean.

Sean reached midfield and stopped, turning in a circle. Caitlin ran toward him.

A cry fell from her lips.

The stadium scoreboard lit up.

Caitlin spoke into her own phone. "Guthrie. It's a ruse. They're not here."

On the scoreboard, a video feed came on. It showed two middle-aged women sitting in front of a wall hung with a white sheet. They were swaddled in white sheets as well. The camera was tight on their faces. One had a gray crew cut. The other wore dangling red earrings.

Sick fear raced through Caitlin. White sheets. *Shrouds.*

The two women watched someone off camera. Their eyes were hot. Simultaneously they shrank back. Someone was approaching them.

The woman with the earrings looked at her friend. "I love you."

Fast as a bullet, she turned toward the unseen figure and lunged, teeth bared.

Someone stepped in front of the camera, obscuring the view. A gut-splitting scream poured from the screen.

Caitlin ran toward the scoreboard. *"No."*

The scream intensified. The sound rolled

288

out of cars and from cell phones tuned online and from open windows all along the street. It poured over Caitlin, Sean, and two hundred thousand horrified radio listeners from Berkeley to Santa Cruz.

Caitlin swept past Sean, running raggedly toward the scoreboard. He grabbed her arm but she shook him off.

"No. *No.*"

The news chopper swooped overhead and turned in the sky to hover over the stadium. Its engine couldn't block out the agonizing screaming. Caitlin slowed, helpless, beneath the scoreboard. Sean's arm went around her from behind. She struggled, then sank back against him, chest heaving.

The scoreboard went dark. The voice on the radio spoke confidently, with vicious delight.

"I am the way, the proof, and the strife. Those who defy me will suffer."

The call went dead.

The news came twenty minutes later. Caitlin was stalking up and down the soccer field. Sean was talking to the Berkeley cops.

"Construction site at the Oakland airport," Guthrie said. "Double homicide."

She looked at Sean. He was prowling, frustrated and angry. The light in the sky seemed too brilliant.

"On my way."

Guthrie paused, and a crack entered his voice. "Hendrix. This one's bad."

30

Caitlin walked with flickering dread toward the construction site, a half-built operations building at the edge of the Oakland airport. Bulldozers belched black exhaust, and sparks cascaded from arc welders. The airport stuck into the bay, and the sea breeze blew strong and salty. Beyond the Bay Bridge, San Francisco's Financial District seemed close enough to touch. A heavy jet accelerated down a nearby runway and roared into the air.

Eleven million passengers a year, and it seemed not one of them had witnessed the Prophet leave his latest two victims here.

Sidestepping a fat roll of rebar, Caitlin logged in to the scene and ducked under the yellow tape. Construction had been halted in this building. Ahead, Guthrie was waiting for her.

His face looked more gaunt than it had even a day ago. His eyes burned. This time he didn't seem to be taking her measure so obviously. He looked like he'd been struck across the forehead with a two-by-four.

That wasn't good.

"Sergeant?" she said.

He led her deeper into the building, his jacket flapping in the wind. His voice echoed against the bare concrete walls.

"Construction foreman found the victims when he arrived at eight thirty. He called it in."

He jerked his thumb at a man wearing a high-visibility vest and heavy boots, a hard hat in his hand, sitting on a pallet of plywood just beyond the yellow tape. The man's eyes looked someplace beyond vacant, like he'd seen something that had wiped his brain.

They walked to a corner of the building. The walls and ceiling closed in and the wind died.

"Any other witnesses?" she said.

"No." There was bite in Guthrie's voice. "The site is secured overnight and a guard makes rounds, but the killer got in and out unnoticed."

Caitlin saw it like a photo under the camera flash. "He's showing off."

Ahead, a forensics team was working. They wore white Tyvek suits. Their collection cases were open on the concrete floor. A photographer circled the area, snapping the scene. Guthrie and Caitlin stopped six feet from what they were working on.

"Doc," Guthrie said.

The medical examiner stood from a crouch.

Zachary Azir was gray bearded and stout. "Joe," he said. "We're just getting started. Don't have anything for you yet."

Caitlin faced the scene on the concrete and braced herself. The bodies were draped in the white sheets that had been visible in the scoreboard video. The victims' heads were now shrouded. They lay on their backs and were both barefoot.

The Prophet's symbol was cut into the soles of their feet.

There was little blood. *Postmortem,* Caitlin thought. Hoped.

Guthrie's hands hung at his sides. "He killed them here."

Caitlin seemed to see the video again. *I love you.* A heartbreaking good-bye. A battle cry.

Don't lock your knees. If she was going to work Homicide, if she was going to work this case, she had to keep herself upright.

"They were found this way?" she said.

293

"The construction crew didn't drape them?"

"Not according to the foreman," Guthrie said. "But he did pull back the sheets. When he saw the bodies, he covered them again. Then ran."

The photographer finished shooting. Dr. Azir stepped to the nearest figure on the floor. Delicately, he lifted the white sheet.

Caitlin first saw the faded jeans and the bra strap showing where the woman's shirt had slipped from her shoulder. She saw hands that looked like they'd worked with the soil and kneaded bread. She saw the dangling red earrings. The ME went still for a discernible beat. He said absolutely nothing. He stepped around to the second draped form and pulled that sheet back as well.

Caitlin saw the black T-shirt, twisted over a middle-aged belly. It read, I'M JUST A POE BOY FROM A POE FAMILY. She saw the buzz-cut salt-and-pepper hair. She saw all of it, and her brain rebelled, trying to put it together, to make it fit. Nausea hit her like a breaking wave. *Don't lock your knees.*

The ME looked at Guthrie. His face was gray.

The victims both lay on their backs. But their necks had been twisted so hard that their skulls faced the floor.

A high-pitched hum rose in Caitlin's head. It sounded like the buzzer she'd heard over the radio call-in show when the Prophet said, *Time's up.*

She squeezed her eyes shut, hard, and opened them again. She had to fight down the fear and the rolling noise in her head. She breathed. Her vision cleared. The ME and the techs and even Guthrie were holding still, maybe in shock.

The ME finally spoke. "Dislocation of the skull at C1. Both victims." He stared. "Though dislocation doesn't really cover it."

Guthrie took a long time to speak. "Have you ever seen anything like this?"

Azir shook his head. He crouched again beside the body of the woman with the gray buzz cut. "Evidence of head trauma. It looks like a depressed skull fracture."

He stood and stepped around to the other body. Bruises ringed the woman's neck. Her skin was grotesquely swollen where it met her skull.

"Rigor hasn't set in," Azir said. "Death probably occurred less than twelve hours ago."

Guthrie's piano-wire posture tightened further.

Caitlin said, "He killed them live on the air."

"No way to know that from what I see here," the ME said.

"Can you establish time of death and determine that?"

"Not with the degree of specificity you're asking for."

She wanted him to tell her that she and Sean could not possibly have saved them. That the victims had already been murdered by the time she and Sean took off for the fake coordinates in Berkeley. That if they'd reached the stadium before the buzzer, it wouldn't have mattered. But Azir couldn't do that.

She looked at Guthrie. "Where'd he set up the camera? How'd he stream it to the stadium? A hack, or a splice into the wiring? We have to find out."

He gave her a sharp look: *Lower the temperature.* She clenched and unclenched her fists. Unspoken was the torturing thought that somehow, somebody could have saved these women.

That she could have.

The ME motioned to the photographer, who neared with body language that seemed to want to flee. She photographed the bodies from several angles. When she was done, the ME got a thermometer and took liver temperatures for both victims. He read the results.

"Preliminarily — they likely died less than two hours ago." He called to the forensic tech. "Let's turn them over."

Azir and the tech knelt and gently turned the crew-cut woman onto her stomach.

Caitlin's vision swam. "Holy Christ."

The ME stepped back abruptly. He signaled the tech and, quickly this time, they rolled the second body.

"Goddammit," the photographer said.

The ME raised his arms. "Out. Everybody clear the scene."

On the concrete, the two women lay grotesquely twisted on their stomachs, faces turned to the ceiling. Their eye sockets were stuffed with CFL spiral lightbulbs.

Azir barked, "Out of the building."

Guthrie stepped back. "What?"

Caitlin backed up but couldn't stop staring at the women's faces. Eyes gone, giant spiral bulbs protruding. Two of the bulbs were shattered.

The techs scrambled to close their kits and hurry with the photographer for the exits. Caitlin and Guthrie followed.

"CFL bulbs contain mercury. When they break they release toxic vapor." The ME hustled them out. "Call the fire department. I'm declaring this a hazmat site."

31

When Alameda County Fire's Hazardous Material Response team arrived, they scoured everybody's clothes, shoes, and belongings for traces of mercury. They took the photographer's camera bag for decontamination. And, though Dr. Azir had worn paper booties over his shoes, they took his oxfords and his socks, leaving the medical examiner standing barefoot in the morning air. Jet engines roared in the background. Outside the construction site, a paramedic unit and an ambulance waited to transport the victims' bodies to the morgue.

A firefighter gave Caitlin the all clear. A news van rolled up as she headed to her car. A TV crew hopped out. She studiously avoided looking at them. The wind poured off the bay, chapping her face.

Then she saw that the van had parked behind a brown beater. Bart Fletcher was already there.

As soon as she got within shouting distance, he jumped from the car. "Detective
Hendrix."

"Not now."

"What's in that construction site? The
missing women? Are they dead?"

She kept walking.

"Caitlin."

Oh, no, you don't. She turned her head.
"Why didn't you ever print what Kelly Smolenski told you?"

"Whoa." Fletcher's eyes lit up like a
pinball machine. "Where's this coming
from?"

She angled toward him. "You sat on
evidence for twenty years. Why?"

The TV news crew eyed them, curious.
Fletcher smiled. It looked cold.

"You finally ready for your interview,
Detective? To go on record?" he said.

She walked at him. "No. I'm asking the
questions."

Fletcher's smile widened but didn't reach
his eyes. "What happened in the construction site? Did you see the results of the
Prophet's scavenger hunt? The victims —
those women were together for fifteen years.
Gaia Hill was a veteran. J. T. Wilcox has a
son. What do you have to say to their
families?" He waved his notepad. "Why'd

you lose it at the stadium in Berkeley?"

She felt her jaw tighten and a burst of words rush toward her lips. Then Guthrie swept in, put a hand on her back, and urged her to keep walking.

"The sheriff's office will have a statement for the press soon." He leaned close to her ear. "Go."

She screeched out of the airport, vision pulsing, hands cold on the wheel. She was angry at herself for letting Fletcher get under her skin. She was aghast that the news chopper had broadcast her loss of emotional control at the stadium.

She saw the women on the scoreboard screen again. *I love you.*

Screw it all.

She sped along the road and called Sean. Across the bay, the skyscrapers that included the ATF's San Francisco Field Division flashed in and out of view.

"It was a mind job," she said.

"This is beyond that," he said, voice low. "This is . . ."

"I know."

She gripped the wheel. She understood how it felt to deal personally with the Prophet for the first time. It was a hot knife through the center of your head.

"This cocksucker," he said.

She frowned. Sean didn't swear like that around the carpeted halls of the ATF's city headquarters. Not usually. Not anywhere in front of other people. Rarely in front of her.

She drove, and his silence stretched. "Let it go," she said. "It's not your case."

"You're not going to let it go."

"It is my case."

Again he paused. "I don't like that sound in your voice."

"There's no sound in my voice."

"Like you're grabbing on to a runaway train, thinking you have to stop it single-handedly."

Her face heated. She headed for the freeway. Traffic slewed past in a blur.

Sean's voice softened. "Sorry. It's been a miserable morning." He seemed to take a breath. "This is your introduction to Homicide, and it's a monster. Don't let it have you."

Sunlight flashed off the hood of the car.

"Cat?"

"I'm here." Her throat was tight. "You're right." Though he couldn't see her, she shook her head. "You're right, Rawlins. Bastard."

The tension unwound. He laughed. It sounded melancholy but relieved.

"We'll do something when this is over,"· he said. "Wash this out of our systems."

"Yeah. That needlepoint class? Or hunt Bigfoot?"

"I'll think of something good."

You're something good. "Surprise me."

"On it."

When she reached the station, she headed to the women's locker room. She stripped off her shirt. It was wet and clinging, from the coffee that had spilled on it in Sean's truck. She dampened a gym towel and washed her chest. Her bra was wet but she didn't have a spare. She sponged it as best she could, pulled on a spare navy-blue T, and slammed her locker.

In the war room, the other detectives were gathered near the wall. Guthrie was pinning up photos from the airport building site.

Martinez said, "Holy mother."

Caitlin sat at her desk and tried to get her head back in the game. She moved pencils around and straightened a stack of papers and brought up her computer screen and wanted to upend the whole thing and kick it into splinters.

Her desk phone rang. She picked up. "Hendrix."

"Detective, there's a delivery for you at the front counter," the desk clerk said.

Caitlin spun, phone to her ear. "What is it?"

The other detectives turned. She set the phone in its cradle and strode across the station to the front desk through air that felt bright with trepidation.

Paige swiveled on her chair, smiling. She gestured at a long, narrow cardboard box on the counter like a game-show hostess revealing a prize. The box had a blue bow around it and a sticker that read, SWEET-NESS & LIGHT FLORAL.

Paige clasped her hands under her chin in anticipation. "Who's it from?"

Caitlin's question exactly. She untied the bow and lifted the lid.

She inhaled. After a stark moment, still staring into the box, she said, "Who delivered this?"

"Florist shop guy. I signed for it." Paige leaned over the box. "Whoa."

"Where'd he go?"

Paige pointed out the door. "He just left."

Caitlin bolted through the door into the lobby and out onto the front walk. A van detailed with roses was about to pull onto the street. She whistled and ran up to the driver's window. The young man inside looked at her with surprise.

"Park and come inside with me," she said.

304

"Is something wrong?"

Understatement of the morning.

She jogged back inside. At the desk, Paige looked half afraid, half eager to be part of whatever action had sprung up.

"Call Guthrie." Caitlin got a pair of latex gloves.

Guthrie came to the desk just as Caitlin lifted an envelope from the box. The flap was unsealed. She pulled out the note inside, computer printed on high-quality stationery.

All your hunger to bring me down
will come to nothing.

Inside the box, wrapped in cellophane, was a bouquet of a dozen flowers. Black lilies.

Howl away. Your desperation only
visits grief upon multitudes
and your savagery is repaid threefold.
Day upon day upon day.

Guthrie said, "Who delivered —"

"Him." Paige pointed at the front windows.

The delivery guy came through the door, looking alarmed. Caitlin's pulse throbbed in her ears. She read, trying to keep her vision from swimming.

You ran like dogs when I called,
but were as blind as those
wretched hags. Fortune-tellers, but
they couldn't foresee this.

The son of a bitch. Her hand shook as she clutched the note.

Eventually they paid for their fraud.
Horrible that everyone else
will pay for your failure.

She turned the note over. In tiny, scratchy print was a postscript.

And, caitlin: How does it feel? All your fears are coming true. You're losing everything. When this ends, you'll be locked in the psych ward with your father. Electroshock . . . then you and mack can cut out paper dolls in the shape of Mercury. He'll wipe the drool from your face — you'll be daddy's little girl again, forever.

The deliveryman answered questions for half an hour and left severely spooked. Craig Leffers had worked for Sweetness & Light for eighteen months. He had no criminal record. The delivery to Caitlin was one of a dozen on his morning run.

His boss, the owner of the florist shop, talked to Caitlin on the phone. The order for the black lilies had been called in yesterday. A man. No discernible accent, no speech impediments, no verbal quirks that the woman could recall. Didn't sound young, didn't sound old. Maybe a bit curt. To the point.

Caitlin knew now that the pitch of the Prophet's voice would be an unreliable indicator. He had a voice changer.

The florist said the man who ordered the lilies paid by credit card. Was there a problem . . . ?

There damn well was. The name on the card was J. T. Wilcox. The Prophet had paid using his latest victim's account.

But. But: the note.

That was the weird bit. The florist explained: The man who ordered the flowers didn't dictate the note to her over the phone. Not like most people. You know — *Happy Birthday, Mom.* Instead, the man said his son was going to drop it by the shop. And a kid showed up, with the envelope, and left it at the counter.

The florist had not opened the note. She

insisted on that. Hadn't looked inside.

The kid was just a kid. Chinese, or Korean maybe. But American. Maybe twelve years old? No, she didn't get his name. She didn't see if he got in a car outside or talked to anybody after he left. The shop didn't have a working surveillance camera, but the shopping center must — maybe, the florist said, Caitlin could talk to the security people and see if they had pictures of the kid. Though . . . he was just a kid. There were hundreds of kids around. Thousands. Lots of schools were out.

The florist was in San Jose. Thirty-five miles from the sheriff's station. And yes, that was an uncommon distance to travel for delivery, but Sweetness & Light specialized in unique floral arrangements, things you couldn't get most places. Deliveries to the East Bay weren't that strange. And the order? She did think that was slightly out of the ordinary. Most orders for black lilies came in around Halloween. But the arrangement was pictured on their website. And they had plenty of fresh lilies in stock, this being Easter weekend. They just needed the time to dye them properly.

The call to the florist was traced to a phone that had connected via a cell tower near the Muni bus station at the Civic

Center in San Francisco. That phone, of course, was now dead.

Martinez said, "Burner."

Caitlin thought about the locations involved with this crime. "Berkeley, Oakland Airport, San Jose, San Francisco. The Prophet pissed everywhere on this one."

The note had been sent to the criminalistics lab, with orders to expedite it. No fingerprints. No DNA on the flap — of course the Prophet had not licked the envelope. The stationery was a standard size, heavy bond, sold in a thousand locations in the Bay Area and everywhere online. The printed note was in a calligraphy font common to multiple word-processing programs.

Caitlin slouched in her desk chair.

When this ends, you'll be locked in the psych ward with your father. Pressure built behind her eyes, a stinging sensation. *You'll be daddy's little girl again, forever.*

Her skin prickled, an adrenaline spike. She closed her eyes. That feeling, at her desk, was a ticket to rage and an ulcer.

But she couldn't help it. She stared again at the note. This bastard, the Prophet, had destroyed her father. He knew he'd done it. Now he was digging the needle into her.

And telling her that he wanted to destroy her too.

All your fears are coming true. You're losing everything.

She couldn't let him. Had to stop this. Had to . . . "What?"

She looked up. Martinez was waving at her. He looked like he might have been waving for a while.

"You were talking to yourself," he said. "Anything interesting?"

Her cheeks went hot. She straightened. "The Prophet ordered the flowers yesterday."

"He did."

"How did he know I would attend the crime scene at the airport?"

"Maybe he didn't. But he knows you're working the case."

"Martinez, he ordered the flowers from a pay phone in San Francisco during business hours. That was after he attacked Gaia Hill and J. T. Wilcox at the café in Berkeley."

"He's been a busy boy."

She ran and reran the lines of the note through her head. "Even for him, this is splashy. The graffiti, the timer, the radio call-in, tormenting the entire freaking Bay Area with . . ."

The sound of the women's cries rose in

her head. *Stop it.*

"The staging of the victims' bodies, and now this . . . this flourish, this coda, sending me the flowers and the note."

"He's worked up."

"He's putting on the Broadway show of shows." And he wanted her to know it.

But he wouldn't just want her to recognize his brilliance. He wanted to draw her along.

"He has something else planned," she said.

"He always does. This is his revival. His spring tour."

"He's showing himself to us. The airport — that's like saying he can come and go anywhere. This note. All of this. The lilies."

Lilies. Signifying spring. Common at funerals.

Your desperation only visits grief upon multitudes and your savagery is repaid threefold. Day upon day upon day.

An image popped into her mind — the church she and Sean had passed on their way to get coffee that morning. It seemed a millennium ago. The colorful banner hoisted across the church facade, advertising an Easter sunrise service. Traditional images: a cross, a golden dawn, and lush, almost gushing bunches of flowers. Easter lilies.

Day upon day upon day.

"Martinez. It sounds like a schedule."

"What does?"

She was already out of her seat, crossing the war room to Guthrie's office. " 'Day upon day upon day.' Good Friday, Holy Saturday, Easter Sunday."

32

Caitlin rapped hard on Guthrie's office door and didn't wait for him to respond, just went straight in and told him.

"Today, tomorrow, Sunday. If that's the Prophet's schedule, this morning was just the start," she said. "And we're in for hell."

He leaned on his elbows.

"We have to do something," she said. "Put out another bulletin telling people to be alert."

"After this morning, I think they are."

"He's been building up to something for twenty-five years. This is it."

"Serial killers never reach 'it.' That's why they keep killing."

"But he has an elaborate fantasy. This ties in with the cold cases. Somehow. He's working up to something and we need to figure out what it is."

He thought for a long moment, his face shadowed. "You have the cold case files. You have everything we can get. You have stuff *only* you can get." Eyebrows raised. "Use it."

He was talking about her father. She returned to her desk. Sat down and told herself to focus.

She had to analyze the evidence. To do that, she had to calm down. Because she knew she was good at finding connections. The links she sometimes saw were blinding, instant, as clear as glass. She didn't think that was mysterious. Some people thought she relied on freaky intuition. But to her, it added up. Almost mathematically. The evidence was being run through some equation, some algorithm, that operated deep beneath the surface.

She got that from Mack.

His duffel bag was on the floor beneath her desk. Though she'd had it more than a day, she'd barely had time to catalogue its contents, much less dig deeply into them. In truth, unzipping it felt like tearing open a wound. But she pulled it out, opened it, and unloaded everything. Bracing herself, she began to read. The notepads, scrawled with first impressions from crime scenes. The notes he wrote while interviewing suspects. The journal.

March 21. At scene, words scratched in fence with a nail. "The soul falls headlong."
What the GODDAMNED hell?
This soul didn't fall. He STABBED her and called her KIDS to tell them where to find her. FUCK.

She tried to read further, but closed her eyes. She saw it. But what she saw wasn't the Prophet's next move.

She saw what had shattered her dad.

For the first time, it was clear to her. What ruined him wasn't simply his failure to capture the Prophet. It was the pain of the victims and their families.

She rested her hand on the passage in his journal. His anguish was still there, scrawled deep into the page. Five years working this case, nonstop — the relentless exposure to sadistic violence had stripped him of all joy and driven him to despair.

She knew he wasn't the only cop who buckled under such sustained assault. Long-term work on serial murders could cause PTSD in the most dedicated officers. She'd known that, intellectually, but hadn't felt it viscerally. As a kid, she had felt its effects — in his rages, his wanderings, his hallucinatory diatribes. She'd glimpsed the truth late one night in the garage, and had been swallowed by her own screams. But she hadn't seen what the case looked like from the inside of Mack's head and his tormented heart.

She ran her fingers over his furious words. Mack had taken on the horror. And in the Prophet case, the horror was too much for one man to bear.

But the message he'd transcribed — had that appeared anywhere else in the evidence? *The soul falls headlong.* She started going through her inventory sheets.

Movement at the corner of her eye brought her back. Shanklin was walking toward the photo wall. Guthrie beckoned.

"Everyone," he said.

Shanklin's eyes sparkled darkly. "We have a suspect."

Caitlin and Martinez approached. Shanklin held an eight-and-a-half-by-eleven sheet of paper. She grabbed a thumbtack and jammed the sheet against the corkboard with her thumb.

Caitlin stilled. She stared at the driver's license blowup, inhaling every detail.

Shanklin planted her feet wide and spoke briskly. The iron Brownie troop leader.

"Caucasian male, age fifty-four. He's a customer of Zodiac Match. That's how we first clocked him."

Caitlin turned sharply to her.

Shanklin returned the look. "Your friend Deralynn Hobbs? Maybe her theory that the Prophet kills women he profiles on dating sites isn't nuts after all."

Caitlin stared again at the photo. A suspect.

There had been more than two thousand suspects over the last twenty-five years. She'd seen the endless names in the files. They included people fingered through anonymous tip lines. Men whose neighbors or coworkers or friends or enemies had contacted the police. People whose license plates had been captured near crime scenes. None of them had proved sufficiently compelling to arrest, much less to prosecute.

This man wasn't one of them.

"I thought of geographical profiling," Shanklin said, "but it's inexact. It gives us a cross-reference when we have potential suspects' addresses. It predicts but can't pull a suspect out of the blue, especially in a dense urban zone like the Bay Area." She nodded at the photo. "But we could cross-reference the Zodiac Match data with something else."

It was her moment, and nobody stopped her.

She stabbed the suspect's photo with her finger. "He's on probation for DWI. He wears a GPS ankle bracelet. And that bracelet has been clocked at every recent crime scene."

Martinez said, "You're shitting me."

Shanklin smiled a grim smile of triumph. The man in the photo was Bart Fletcher.

33

Caitlin approached the photo of Bart Fletcher, desperately trying not to shake her head. This was their suspect? The reporter?

Shanklin said, "He's been under our noses the whole time."

Martinez said, "The sneaky shit."

"All the evidence fits. He's the right age bracket."

He's at the top end, Caitlin thought. Fighting it.

"He's got the perfect cover. A press pass. He's a *crime* reporter. And look at the Prophet's new messages. Flawless grammar and spelling. The killer obviously styles himself a writer. Plus, Fletcher's intimately familiar with the case." Shanklin looked at Caitlin. "He covered the story from the time your father worked it."

"But . . ." Caitlin shook her head. "I checked his background. Fletcher came to the Bay Area from Iowa, in the middle of the original murders. He wasn't here when the Prophet started killing."

Shanklin simply tilted her head at Caitlin. "Fletcher has a dating profile. And the ankle bracelet confirms his presence at every new murder scene — even those he was not assigned to cover."

"What?"

"He's the copycat," Guthrie said.

And Caitlin saw deeper into Fletcher's photo. The morose eyes, the not-quite-clean hair. *A washed-up drunk.* Or not.

A career marooned in the shallows for years, until the story of his lifetime called to him again. Was that it? Fletcher had decided to imitate the Prophet for the sake of glory? It seemed impossible — the violence, the frenzy.

The dramatic story line. The starring role. The Pulitzer Prize.

Caitlin said, "He has to know his location can be tracked. That's the whole point of the ankle monitor."

Guthrie rubbed the side of his nose. "Fletcher's probation imposes a curfew. That's why he wears the monitor. But it only alerts if he removes or disables it. And unless it alerts, let's be honest. Nobody tracks the GPS records of these things in real time. Most monitors will never have their travel history examined."

"Every. Single. Crime scene," Shanklin said.

Caitlin's fingers felt cold. The cornfield. Silver Creek Park. Fletcher had been there. Been there *first.* Always seeming to know about the crime before the other news organizations.

Shanklin said, "Sequoia High School. That Arabian horse ranch. He was there."

Caitlin ran a hand through her hair. "No. Something's off. All those locations can be explained — at least on first glance — by a reporter doing his job. And they're all public record."

"Hendrix," Guthrie said. "Look."

On the conference table, Shanklin opened a ream of GPS printouts from Fletcher's monitor. She pointed to a time stamp and coordinates. "This location is in Union City. It's the Olive Garden where Melody James worked as a waitress."

Caitlin leaned over the printout. "March nineteenth."

"Yeah. *Before* Melody and Richard Sanchez were kidnapped. He was there that night."

Shit. The cold spread along Caitlin's arms.

"What about San Francisco?" she said. "The call to Sweetness and Light Floral, ordering the black lilies, was made near the Civic Center bus station."

Shanklin flipped through the GPS data. "What time?"

Caitlin told her. Shanklin ran her finger down the page. Stopped, and pointed. "Is this it?"

Caitlin entered the coordinates in her phone. On the map screen, a red pin dropped near the bus station. The chill sank through her.

"Yes," she said.

Guthrie nodded at Shanklin. "Excellent."

Caitlin's stomach felt hollow. She had dismissed Fletcher too quickly.

"I'll prepare the warrant application," Shanklin said.

Caitlin thought: *the Oakland airport.* Fletcher had been there too, ahead of the TV news crew. Energized. Breath mints but no beer. Freshly showered.

Like he'd scrubbed off any trace evidence.

She realized that she'd had him at the park, two days before the latest killings. She'd had him there, with him shoving the words *dripping blood* in her face. With him giving her the link to Kelly Smolenski and the entire message, to the graffiti on the wall outside Coffee, Tea & Tarot.

She'd had him, and she'd let him go.

■ ■ ■ ■

At a crumbling asphalt lot along the Alameda waterfront, Bart Fletcher hunched against the wind. His lank hair flattened across his face. Rain clouds were boiling in from the Pacific across the San Francisco hills. The bay was scalloped with chop.

He paced. When his phone finally rang, he answered it with cold fingers.

"You said you could mask the ankle monitor signal without alerting the cops," he said.

A couple of cars passed on the nearly empty street. He turned his back to them. The cars were headed in the direction of the USS *Hornet* Museum. At the end of the road, beyond aging warehouses and bent Monterey pines, the decommissioned aircraft carrier's conning tower bristled against the sky. Its flight deck cut the horizon, as flat and sharp as a razor blade.

Fletcher listened and pressed the phone to his ear. "Yeah, I'm having doubts . . . You . . ."

He ran a hand across his jaw.

"Of course what you've provided is valuable. I'm not saying . . . I would never do that. But if I'm going to take it to the next level, I need absolute assurance that the

323

GPS and cell signals are being spoofed. If they aren't, I'm compromised. You've . . ."

He shook his head, calmed himself, and walked toward the water. "Listen. I'm about to use what you've given me to get deep inside the sheriff's office. I need to be positive I don't leave a trail. For both our sakes."

He listened some more. "Yeah, I will . . . Yeah, immediately's good."

He hung up. The road had emptied. Nobody was on the running path along the bay. He was alone. A gust of wind scoured the waterfront. For a while Fletcher paused and breathed it all in: the hills that ringed the Bay Area and turned it into a vast amphitheater; the turbulent sky; the deep cold waters of the bay, which went dark and deadly with silent currents below. Nobody could see him, yet he felt center stage.

Big things were happening. Once he took care of this technical issue, his path would be clear. This source was gold — and was about to help him unlock the vault. Of all his dreams.

He sent a text to his boss at the *Herald,* saying he would be in to the office in an hour. He looked up from his phone and hustled to the black pickup that was pouring exhaust at the far end of the lot.

34

The judge signed the arrest warrant at three forty-five P.M. Five minutes after that, with Shanklin and Guthrie hovering beside her desk, Caitlin phoned the *East Bay Herald.*

"Bart Fletcher, please."

Muzak came over the speaker as the call was transferred. Caitlin tattooed the tip of a pen against the desktop. *Don't go to voice mail.* Then, with a clatter, the call was picked up.

"Detective Hendrix. Well."

She squeezed the pen in her hand. She had to make it convincing. "Mr. Fletcher. Sorry for getting so hot at the airport this morning."

There was a pause. "Is your sergeant standing by your desk to confirm that you actually make this call?"

"That would be a big, fat yes." She eyed Guthrie. "But he's right. I was out of line." She cleared her throat. "And he thinks we

325

should talk."

"What do you know. You ready to go on the record?"

"If you bring all your interview notes."

Fletcher took a second. "There's a place on Franklin. The Emerald. Five o'clock?"

Caitlin knew it. A dive bar. Shanklin shot her thumbs-up.

"That'll do. See you then."

Caitlin hung up and got a nod from Guthrie. She clenched the pen so he wouldn't see her nerves. Shanklin was already at her desk, holstering her gun.

Half an hour later, they rolled for Oakland. Shanklin led, loaded for bear. Guthrie rode shotgun for Caitlin, coordinating with the Oakland PD, which insisted on sending officers to assist in executing the warrant.

Nobody wanted to be left out when the killer was captured.

Caitlin drove silently, weaving through the sluggish traffic, getting her head in the space. If Fletcher came quietly, fine. If not, she had a ballistic vest beneath her zipped jacket.

Shanklin's voice buzzed from the radio. "No movement on the ankle monitor. He's still in the twelve hundred block on Franklin."

Guthrie said, "Get the monitoring company to narrow that location down. Way down."

A minute later, Shanklin came back. "They confirm it's the Emerald."

They swung into downtown Oakland and reached the rally point, a corner gas station two blocks from the bar. Oakland PD was going full bore: A four-man tactical squad was waiting for them. Caitlin recognized Sergeant Rios, who had led the raid on the crank house for the Narcotics Task Force.

Shanklin strode up, ponytail bobbing, lips as red as an alarm, and shook his hand. Rios spread a map on the hood of his vehicle. The wind tried to lift it. The clouds had lowered, gray obliterating the hills. Cars and buses had their headlights on. At the gas pumps, customers filling their cars stared at them.

Rios pointed at the map. "Corner building with doors on Franklin and a rear exit on the alley behind."

Shanklin said, "I know it well. And GPS confirms he's there."

"What's the time lag on the data?"

"Ten minutes. But he's been there an hour. Looks like he's settled in."

Guthrie cocked a thumb at Caitlin. "Detective Hendrix will enter and identify Fletcher. He's expecting her. It will keep his guard low."

Rios shook his head. "TAC leads and is first through the door."

Caitlin pursed her lips. Guthrie shifted his weight.

Rios said, "You're serving a high-risk warrant. That's one of TAC's specific operational responsibilities. And if this guy's the Prophet, he's already a cop killer."

Guthrie nodded. He thought Fletcher was a copycat, but they were in Oakland. Their show.

Shanklin said, "I'll make the arrest."

At the pumps, a man snapped a photo.

This operation hadn't been on the police scanner. The media wasn't aware of the impending action — yet. They got in their vehicles and convoyed to the corner where the Emerald sat, garish and dispirited, its buzzing green lights the only sign of vitality.

Caitlin got out, adrenaline popping. Shanklin looked ready to strip Fletcher's skin from him an inch at a time, with her bare hands.

Rios pointed at his men. "Front and back. Go."

They crossed the street. Guthrie accompanied the team going in the back. Caitlin and Shanklin followed Rios to the front door. Thirty seconds later they were in position. Rios gave the signal.

They went through the door into gloom and Irish music. Rios and his team swept through the room with Shanklin on their heels. The bartender raised his hands. Patrons turned, shocked. A waitress squealed with fright. At the rear, TAC and Guthrie came through the back door and along the hall.

Caitlin didn't see Fletcher.

"Where is he?" Shanklin said.

Caitlin turned three-sixty. He wasn't sitting at the bar or at any of the tables.

Shanklin charged into the hall and slammed open the door to the men's room. Caitlin heard stall doors being kicked open.

She ran after Shanklin. When she shoved through the men's room door, Shanklin had her phone to her ear. She was talking to the alarm monitoring company.

"I said, he's *not here.*"

She pulled the lid off the trash can and peered in. "Dammit."

Shanklin put on gloves and lifted the ankle monitor from the garbage. The strap was sliced in half.

Rios came in, followed by Guthrie. Shanklin stared at the monitor.

"Goddammit," she said.

Rios spoke into his shoulder-mounted

329

radio, calling in a BOLO.

Shanklin visibly gritted her teeth. Then turned to Guthrie, her gaze scorching. "He lives half a mile from here. That's our best shot."

She slid around him and ran for the car.

Fletcher lived in a 1950s vintage apartment building a block off a main road. A scattering of lights shone from apartment windows. The rain descended as they pulled up, blowing cold in their faces. At the corner a bus rumbled past.

Fletcher's brown beater was parked along the curb.

Guthrie knocked on the super's apartment door. It opened to a square of yellow light. A minute later, Guthrie came back with a key.

"Third-floor apartment with external stairway access via the balcony walkway. One door. No rear exit, no fire escape. Fletcher lives alone. Super hasn't seen him today." He pointed at the third-floor apartment. "Door opens directly into the living room. Kitchen on the left. One bedroom down a hall at the back."

A light was on in the apartment behind closed blinds. Rios took his rifle in his hands.

"Noise discipline unless I signal other-wise," he said.

They drew their weapons. He looked at them one by one. Each gave thumbs-up. He pointed, driving his arm forward. *Go.*

They ascended the stairs in a single column, TAC leading. Rios's team moved with a heavy silence, smooth, thrumming with energy. On the third-floor walkway, they stacked up on Fletcher's door.

Rios pounded his fist against it. "Police."

Nobody answered. Watching Rios, with his assurance and presence, Caitlin had a sense of déjà vu. The rain picked up. Downstairs, the super closed his apartment door. The yellow square of light vanished.

Rios pounded again. "Police. Open up."

No response, no footsteps inside. But, holding poised, they heard music within the apartment. Rios pounded again. Something clattered inside.

The tension on the walkway tightened. Rios tried the key. The lock wouldn't turn. He raised his hand in a C. *Crisis entry.* He signaled the fourth man in the stack.

Today they'd brought the small battering ram. The fourth man stepped up to the door and swung it. The lock splintered and the door banged open.

He stepped aside and Rios swept in with

the rest of them close behind.

As Caitlin crossed the threshold a fresh clatter came from the kitchen. A cat scrambled past her out the door and disappeared along the walkway. Rios sighted on it, then swung back to the living room.

"Right clear," he said.

The number two man moved past him. "Left clear."

"All clear," Rios said.

The living room was empty. Sagging sofa, nicked coffee table. Faded posters on the wall. The Dead at Fillmore East.

Shanklin, Caitlin, and Guthrie held inside the front door. TAC entered the kitchen.

"Left clear."

"All clear."

They turned to the hallway. It was dark. The door at the end was closed.

Rios told one of his men to return to the walkway and another to remain in the living room. The rest of them closed up again. Rios pointed down the hall. *Go.*

They walked quickly. Rios and his second man cleared the bathroom. Then they approached the bedroom.

Caitlin focused on the door, left hand on Shanklin's shoulder, right hand on her SIG. Behind her, Guthrie's left hand on her shoulder was solid. Rios raised a fist. They

332

stopped.

Rios examined the door and ran a gloved hand around the frame. He held his hand close to the knob, testing for heat. He looked over his shoulder, got nods from everyone, and leveled his rifle on the door. He began a countdown on his fingers. *Five. Four.*

For a second, the only sound was the rain outside. Then, in the kitchen, a phone rang.

They froze. Rios halted the countdown and raised a closed fist. *Hold.* The phone continued to ring. It was a black house phone that sat in a cradle on the kitchen counter.

Rios pointed again at the bedroom door and restarted the countdown. *Five. Four. Three.*

Voice mail clicked in. On speaker, a voice hissed. "The door's unlocked. Drop the battering ram and turn the knob."

It was the voice Caitlin had heard on calls to victims' families. The hoarse rasp of the Prophet. Not the cajoling slur of Fletcher in the park, but a darker version. In performance.

Her heart hit overdrive, thudding against her chest. He was watching.

From where?

The TAC officer in the living room peered

out into the rain. Rios signaled him to shut the splintered front door. Caitlin scanned the apartment. Saw no cameras, bugs, nothing. From the phone came slow, harsh breathing.

Rios eyed them. One by one they shook their heads. How the hell was he watching?

Rios made a decision. He gave the go signal. Caitlin squeezed Shanklin's shoulder. Shanklin nodded.

Rios turned the knob and swept into the bedroom. The second man was close behind. From the hallway, the bedroom yawned into view. It was dark. The beam of a streetlight fell through the window. There were bookshelves. A double bed. In the middle of it, waiting, was Bart Fletcher.

Dead.

He lay on his back, palms up, penitent, face garishly lit by the streetlight. Even six feet outside the door, Caitlin could see horrific bruising on his throat. Strangulation.

"Right clear," Rios said.

"Left clear."

Rios continued to sweep the barrel of his rifle around the room. Shanklin entered. The room was as still as the grave. Every inch of Rios's posture blared, *Red alert*. Caitlin thought of wasps, and the wired-up cell phone in a car packed with dead birds.

334

Her heart pounded.

Shanklin pointed at the bed. "What's that?"

They all turned. Shanklin stepped to the wall and flipped the light switch. Even as Rios turned sharply toward her, harsh overhead light blanched the room.

Shanklin said, "Damn, something's taped to his —"

Click.

Rios shouted, *"Bomb."*

He grabbed Shanklin and dived for the doorway. Caitlin just had time to turn away and throw her arms over her head.

The flash bleached the walls white.

Dead, we're all dead —

But there was no explosion. No blast wave, no shrapnel, no fiery light. Gasping like she'd run ten miles, Caitlin lowered her arms. Rios stood near the door, his face a storm, pressing Shanklin to the wall.

From the bed came hissing. The sound of the click had been a controller tripping a switch. Caitlin's hair stood on end.

Taped to Fletcher's chest was some kind of pyrotechnic pack. The hissing increased.

The Prophet had strapped him with fireworks.

The paper wrapping on the fireworks burned away. Inside it was a rusty orange powder, like iron dust, on a bed of aluminum foil. The pyrotechnics fizzed and burned like sparklers. Popping, jumping, orange-red sparks. Stretching to shoots of flame, burning too fast. Brilliant. Like a volcano erupting on his chest. Black soot falling all around him, shrouding his arms, his neck and face. Then they flared. Tendrils erupted, like charred snakes flailing from a nest. Glowing red, curling, growing, two feet, three feet long, they entwined the body.

"Shit," one of the TAC guys said. "Holy mother of — *fuck.*"

Eight tentacles. Ten. Curling like horns, cooling to four-foot-long fingers of bone, flailing, rocking, probing. One slid across his face and curled into his gaping mouth. The TAC officer stumbled back, retching. Thick stinking smoke filled the room.

"It was a radio-controlled switch," Guthrie said. "Whoever triggered it is close."

Coughing, Caitlin ran to the window. On the street below, in the rain, a man in a hooded jacket slipped an object into his pocket. His face was invisible. He had a phone to his ear.

From the phone in the kitchen, the voice said, "Ten steps behind, Hendrix."

Breath gone from the caustic bite of the smoke, she said, "There."

The TAC team charged out the door. The hooded man stared at the window a second longer, then began to walk, backward, faceless, headlights backlighting him in the rain. He stuck the phone in his pocket, turned, and melted into street traffic. Caitlin watched until the TAC team appeared on the sidewalk, running, then hacked and doubled over and ran from the bedroom.

She heard a radio transmission, rushed and staticky. *"He headed into the BART station."*

She lurched out the front door onto the walkway and leaned over the railing, gulping air. Shanklin stumbled out and grabbed the rail next to her. She retched and spat a long string of drool over the side onto the courtyard far below.

The rain blew in cold gusts against Caitlin's face. Guthrie came out of the apartment and asked if they were okay. Caitlin nodded. She looked through the splintered door. A slippery sensation crawled across her. Those flailing snakes. Like tentacles. Like the Thing. Alien, erupting from Fletcher's body.

"Goddammit," Guthrie said.

A full-body shiver ran through her. She stared hard through the door.

She pulled a pair of latex gloves and a

bandanna from her jacket. She tied the bandanna over her nose and mouth, bank-robber style.

She gave Guthrie a look. He took a hand-kerchief from his pocket and covered his nose. When she walked back into the apart-ment, he followed.

In the bedroom, the smoke had ebbed. Fletcher remained on the bed, hands still penitent. The horrifying snakelike tendrils had cooled from red to gray white and were now frozen in place, a wreath that had writhed and fossilized. They had flailed around Fletcher's face, across the bed, between his legs, settling near his crotch. The stench of chemicals and burning flesh was overwhelming, even through the bandanna.

For a second her stomach tried to empty itself. She held still and forced herself not to breathe.

Then she saw the message scrawled on the wall.

And there great coils of vipers swarm hideous amid that nest he writhes terrified Yelling Whimpering his confession Endlessly —
  THIEF.
Hell awaits you all.

35

Afterward, shuddering against the car outside the apartment complex in the thickening dusk, Caitlin took off her jacket and let the rain pelt her shoulders. A festival of flashing lights spun around her, cop cars and a fire truck and an ambulance. She didn't care that it was cold and that the wind would draw all the heat from her. She needed to get rid of the smell.

The hooded man had vanished in the Friday rush at the BART station. Four train lines ran through the station, and despite TAC's vehement pursuit, he had evaporated.

She took out her phone, hesitated a second, and called Sean.

He said, "Hey, what's —"

"I'm at a crime scene," she said. "One eighty-seven."

The California Penal Code designation for murder.

"Oakland's Fire Investigation unit is on its way. I could use a set of eyes that knows pyrotechnics. Will you look at a photo?" she said.

"Send it."

She ended the call and pulled up a photo she'd snapped of the damage done to Bart Fletcher's body. The charred snakes were front and center. She cropped it so Fletcher's face wasn't visible.

Guthrie came over as she worked with the photo. "What are you doing?"

"Sending this to Sean Rawlins. He's an ATF certified explosives specialist. I'll tell him to delete it as soon as he gives me his opinion."

Guthrie shook his head. She looked up from under her plastered hair.

"This is a countdown, I know it," she said. "This won't be the last victim this weekend. We need every minute we can get and the arson team isn't here yet."

Guthrie pulled up the collar of his coat. "Very well."

She sent the photo. Sean phoned back almost immediately. She put it on speaker.

Sean said, "Those pyrotechnics are called pharaoh's serpents."

Great coils of vipers swarm. A shiver passed through her.

340

"They were banned in the U.S. in the forties. Still available overseas, former Eastern Bloc mostly, Russia. It's a combination of mercury thiocyanate and ammonium dichromate."

Caitlin looked at Guthrie. "Mercury. There's your signature."

Guthrie leaned toward the phone. "Agent Rawlins, you're positive?"

"One hundred percent," Sean said. "And even if I didn't recognize them myself, I'm looking at a photo database of exactly this kind of display."

"You said it was banned in the U.S.," Guthrie said.

Caitlin nodded. Importing it would be difficult — maybe they could get a line on that.

Sean said, "Because it's a poisonous combination. The thing is frickin' toxic. They used to market it to kids. Nuts."

"Thank you," Guthrie said. "Please delete the photo Detective Hendrix sent."

"Done," Sean said.

Caitlin said, "Thank you. I gotta go. Talk later."

She hung up.

Guthrie said, "This is insane."

"I know." The rain pelted her face. "But there's a method to it."

"Then we'd better find it." He turned to

go. "Put your damn coat on, Hendrix, and figure it out."

36

It was dark when Caitlin returned to the station. In the locker room she peeled off her wet T-shirt and pulled back on the coffee-stained shirt she'd started out wearing that morning. The station was busy, but the darkness outside, the fluorescents reflecting back from the windows, made the place feel close, isolated, exposed.

Guthrie tacked two new photos to the wall. The serpents. And the message.

Everybody felt drained. Even Martinez, who hadn't been there. Shanklin wouldn't meet anyone's gaze. Guthrie's eyes seemed, if possible, even more deeply sunk in his gaunt face.

In the corner of the room, a television silently played the news. THE PROPHET CLAIMS CREDIT FOR NEW KILLINGS. BAY AREA TERROR. CHURCH SERVICES POSTPONED. WARRIORS CANCEL TONIGHT'S GAME.

The Prophet had beaten them again. It burned. It burned and stank and felt like it would eat through her, corrosive and erupting with white fire.

Now, removed from the scene, she saw it again. Fletcher, motionless on the bed as the fireworks ignited, hotter than a furnace, hotter than a forge. He couldn't feel anything. His eyes didn't blink as flecks of molten metal hit his face and scalded his corneas.

Death. Beyond death. The Prophet wanted them to inhale it, to crawl from it, to know he was inflicting it on all of them.

Guthrie stood in front of Fletcher's photo. "Why did the Prophet choose this guy?"

Nobody answered. Guthrie turned.

"He picked Fletcher for a reason. What was it?"

Martinez said, "We sure that Fletcher's the one who set up the Zodiac Match profile?"

"Check it out."

"The ankle bracelet," Caitlin said. "How was it removed without triggering a tamper alert?"

"Don't know yet."

He looked at her, but Shanklin stirred. "I'll check."

He nodded. Caitlin said nothing. Shanklin's hair was falling from her ponytail. She looked like a whipped dog.

Guthrie's original question hung in the air. Caitlin said, "I don't know why he chose Fletcher. But I think he chose Melody James and Richard Sanchez because they were at the Union City Olive Garden the night Fletcher stopped in."

It was a horrible thought — that they'd been taken and killed because they could help throw suspicion on the reporter. She rubbed her eyes.

The Oakland Police Department was in charge of the crime scene. Until they completed their investigation, and wrote their report, and volunteered any information, all the war room could do was wait. And attack on other fronts.

"Back to work," Guthrie said.

Martinez and Shanklin trudged to their desks. Caitlin stared at the wall of photos. Her hair was tangled. Her shirt was crusty with coffee. Her jeans stuck damply to her. And the smell was lodged in her sinuses. Greasy, chemical, stinking of smoke and burned flesh. She wanted to throw her clothes away and stand under a hot shower for an hour. Maybe a shower of cleansing lava. Anything to dispel the sense that Bart Fletcher had been transfigured to smoke

that was lodged in her lungs and blood-
stream.

Shanklin dropped into her desk chair and
tented her fingers over her eyes. For a
second, Caitlin took satisfaction in looking
down at the top of her head. A shameful
second.

"Mary. Coffee?" she said.

Shanklin glanced up. Caitlin dug change
from her pocket. Shanklin nodded.

Caitlin returned with a cup for each of
them. Shanklin thanked her. Caitlin walked
to the photo wall.

She stared at the blowup of the message
written in spray paint on the wall of the
bedroom where Fletcher lay dead.

*And there great coils of vipers swarm hideous
amid that nest he writhes terrified Yelling
Whimpering his confession Endlessly —
THIEF.*
Hell awaits you all.

It mocked her.

There was a pattern in it. In all the messages. She knew so.

But nothing she'd come up with made
sense.

Yet.

She returned to her desk and typed the

lines into a search engine. Nothing. It wasn't a published poem like the line from *Paradise Lost* or the T. S. Eliot verse written on Kelly Smolenski's arms. It wasn't song lyrics or gang mottos, not even the lines individually. At least not in English.

She pressed her fingers to the corners of her eyes. *Take it in another direction.*

Poetry. The messages the Prophet had sent this time seemed related to poetry. And poetry had form — meter, rhythm, rhyme. She compared the number of syllables in each line of this latest one, wondering if it translated into a mathematical pattern.

Nothing.

She stopped looking at the words then, and told herself to free-associate. Back up a few steps.

Why were the words in the message so spread out? Because he was rushed as he wrote? Because of the difficulty of spray-painting on a vertical surface?

She didn't think so. She sat up straight.

The Prophet had written dozens of notes and messages over the years. On paper, in marker, in paint. The written messages were all perfect grammatically. The handwritten ones were neat and clear. Even the map her father had found showed deliberate, well-articulated penmanship.

The breaks in the line had to mean some-thing.

At least, she wanted them to mean some-thing.

She grabbed a pad of paper and a pen. Wrote out the message. First with an ap-proximation of the spaces. Then with nor-mal spacing. She didn't think the extra spaces — ten inches between *Yelling* and *Whimpering* — were to indicate where punctuation should go. Maybe they were caesuras, to indicate pauses in spoken speech. She read the message aloud.

It wouldn't come. Nothing would come. She stabbed the pen into the notepad, hard, and harder.

"Speak to me."

Breaks. They were breaks.

She rewrote the message, this time giving each segment of text its own line.

Deep in her mind, a worm of recognition uncurled. A hint, intangible, just out of reach.

She held her breath, almost touching it, fearing to move or blink lest the thought blow away before she could grasp it.

And there great coils of vipers swarm hideous
amid that nest he writhes terrified

Yelling
Whimpering his confession
Endlessly — THIEF.
Hell awaits you all.

She scrabbled through the files on her desk for a folder. Flipped it open. Found a copy of the Prophet's message that had accompanied the black lilies.

She pulled up another message on the computer screen. From the cornfield. Still not breathing. She found the one sent to KDPX News after Stuart Ackerman was found floating in the water trough. She pulled out every written communication the Prophet had sent since he returned.

Only one was publicly available — the message to KDPX. The rest were in the hands of the Alameda Sheriff's Office and had not been made public. She picked up the notepad. Her hands were starting to shake.

The cornfield note. *All these years you thought I was gone. But . . . hell . . . Angels . . . your . . . wail . . . Equinox . . . hurricane . . .*

The video message sent to KDPX after the math teacher's murder. *Arrows pierced him when he ran . . . hunted . . . Alameda . . . Yet . . . without . . . Expect . . . here . . .*

The note that came with the black lilies.

All your hunger . . . Howl . . . and . . . You . . .
wretched . . . Eventually . . . Horrible . . .

The postscript scribbled on the back of that note. *And, caitlin: How does it feel? All . . . You're . . . When . . . Electroshock . . . He'll . . .*

She said, "Jesus."

The first letter of each line was the same in every one. Except for the personal postscript. And in that note, the capitalized letters matched the first letters in the other messages.

A H A Y W E H.

37

Caitlin's pen hovered above the sheet of paper. She didn't want to move an inch or the letters in front of her might disappear.

A H A Y W E H.

She checked all the Prophet's messages again. No doubt. Those were the first letters in the lines of every one he'd sent to the police since his return. Same order every time. It was an acrostic puzzle.

"Damn." She hadn't seen it before. Noise-to-signal ratio. *Focus.*

She shoved files off her computer keyboard and brought up Search. *A H A Y W E H.*

Did you mean: YAHWEH.

Did she? What did the letters signify?

She scrolled down the page of search results.

Descent: Ahayweh Gate. Level 1, Level 2, Level 3.

Ahayweh on Game Jam.

Ahayweh Art and Music, Omaha.
ACRONYM DEFINITIONS. WHAT DOES AHAYWEH STAND FOR?

She clicked.

"Fuck me."

There it was, staring her in the face.

Abandon Hope, All Ye Who Enter Here.

She read further, her mouth going dry, palms tingling.

That was the common phrase in English. Seven words, well-known, though inaccurately translated. They didn't originate from fire-and-brimstone sermons, or from *Pirates of the Caribbean.* They weren't modern.

The phrase came from Dante's *Inferno.*

Caitlin read on, the room seeming to focus and brighten. She found a university site that summarized the *Inferno.* She knew only the barest bit about it. The title, basically. Shortcomings of a criminal justice degree — you didn't study medieval Italian literature.

She tried to absorb it, racing through the text.

Lasciate ogne speranza, voi ch'intrate.

Canto III, Line 9.

In the *Inferno,* Caitlin read, the phrase is

carved in stone above the gate to the underworld. It greets lost souls as they pass
forever into the world of the damned. *All
hope abandon.* Because every soul that
reads those words is condemned to eternal
torment. They're entering a world of cries
and suffering from which they will never be
released.

Welcome to hell.

She thought of the message written on
Lisa Chu's arm. *Infinite wrath and infinite
despair.* The line, she knew, was from
Satan's soliloquy in *Paradise Lost.* Even
twenty years back, the Prophet's messages
had been pointing at hell.

She grabbed her phone and went to an
online bookstore. Her fingers trembled with
excitement. This was the track. This had to
be. Her search pulled up a dozen versions
of the *Inferno.* The Longfellow translation.
The Ciardi translation, the Pinsky bilingual
edition, in English and the original Italian.
She could buy it separately, or as part of the
trilogy — *Inferno, Purgatorio, Paradiso* —
Hell, Purgatory, Paradise. *The Divine Comedy.*

She bought the trilogy, downloaded the
Inferno, and turned to Canto III. Its opening lines read:

I am the way into the city of woes.
I am the way into the forsaken people.
I am the way into eternal sorrow.

Her head throbbed. *I am the way . . .*
That's what the Prophet had said on the
drive-time radio show, just before he hung
up. *I am the way, the proof, and the strife.*

She'd thought he was perverting the
words of Jesus: I am the way, the truth, and
the life. But no. Way, proof, strife. Woes.
People. Sorrow. W. P. S. The same letters in
both cases.

"Son of a bitch."

Then she remembered something else.
She tossed aside papers on her desk and
found her father's journal. *March 21 . . . "The
soul falls headlong."*

She searched online.

The Divine Comedy of Dante Alighieri.
Hell, Canto XXXIII. "When a soul betrays
as I have done . . . the soul falls headlong
into this cistern . . ."

All at once, Caitlin understood. She saw
it. She saw through the years, and the
deaths, and the grotesque crime scenes, into
the Prophet's secret fantasy. She read on,
frantic, finding confirmation. She ripped a

page from a notebook and in bold, big letters wrote *ALL HOPE ABANDON, YE WHO ENTER HERE.*

"Sergeant Guthrie," she called across the war room.

She stood and strode toward the wall. People looked up. Martinez spun in his chair and stood up to follow her. Guthrie emerged from his office. She stabbed the torn sheet of paper onto the center of the board.

Guthrie approached, fists on his hips. "Yes, Detective?"

She turned. When Guthrie caught the heat of her glare, he stepped back.

"I know what he's doing," she said. "The Prophet. He's staging the murders to portray the Nine Circles of Hell."

38

"Dante," Guthrie said.

"It's all here. I'm positive. I have no doubt," Caitlin said.

"Slow down. Take me through it."

"Every move the Prophet makes comes straight out of the *Inferno*. Even speed-reading, it's there. References to wasps, wild dogs, vipers — it's all there."

Martinez approached. Guthrie raised his hands as though trying to calm a stampeding horse. "Back up."

"The book. It's about a journey through hell. Which Dante imagines as a cave beneath the earth. Like a funnel. With nine concentric circles descending deeper and deeper, punishing different levels of sin."

She bent over her phone, peering at the text. "Look. In the Seventh Circle, violent people are scalded in a river of boiling blood. If they try to escape they're shot down with arrows."

Another connection hit her. She raised her head, ran to her desk, and grabbed the Prophet's new messages. She scanned them with increasing excitement.

"It's here. He's been telling us. It's right here." She read from the message sent after Stuart Ackerman's murder. " *'Violence sought violence. So he was hunted into a river of blood.'* "

"Mother Mary," Martinez said.

Guthrie was looking at a crime scene photo. Stuart Ackerman's body in the bloody water trough. "What about the Mercury symbol? Does that play into it?"

She searched the text. "It's . . ."

She stopped the fast scroll and looked at a footnote. The hairs rose on the back of her neck.

"Hendrix."

"Hold on."

"Come on."

"This is one of the greatest works in Western literature and I've had half an hour to skim it on a phone. Give me a second." She shot him a look, and regretted it. "Sorry, Sergeant."

He set his face and nodded at her screen. "Continue."

She paraphrased the footnote. "In the *Inferno,* the Messenger of heaven strides through hell, raging at the damned. He lashes it like a hurricane and scatters demons. The footnote says, 'The Messenger is sometimes identified with the god Mercury.' "

She turned to the board, to the photo of the Prophet's symbol.

"The killer isn't a disciple of Satan. He thinks he's on the side of the angels. The messenger of death, punishing a world that heaven hates."

Electricity seemed to charge the air, a subliminal hum.

"How does this relate to the T. S. Eliot poem? Does it?" Guthrie said. "And the equinox?"

"The *Inferno* takes place over the Easter Triduum. Dante descends to hell on the night of Maundy Thursday. The story ends on Easter Sunday."

"What time?"

"I don't know." She looked again at the cramped text of the book on her phone.

He thought a second. "Take a car. Get to the nearest bookstore and buy all the copies they have." He looked around the war room. "Everybody reads tonight. The Prophet has a twenty-five-year head start and we need to run like hell to catch up."

39

Saturday

Caitlin marched into the war room at seven thirty A.M., sleep-deprived and wired. She dropped her satchel on her desk and pulled out the *Inferno* Sparknotes Literature Guide she'd nabbed at the bookstore overnight. Pages were dog-eared. Multicolored Post-it notes protruded from the book like paper tongues. When she looked around, everybody's desk had a paperback on it. Dante was everywhere.

Shanklin was freshly put together, her hair slicked back into a bun. She held up her copy. "Aren't we intellectual?" She read the back cover. " 'A poem of wild and interesting images. — Samuel Taylor Coleridge.' No kidding."

"That must be the best blurb in history."

"Good for Dante. But we get to clean up after his mess."

She dropped the book. Caitlin felt oddly

relieved that Shanklin was back to her sharp-tongued self.

Martinez walked past, trilby cocked back on his gleaming skull. "There is some crazy shit in that book. Literally — people covered in it as punishment. Or dunked in boiling pitch. Or cannibalizing each other alive. Guy had a whack imagination."

"Which still has power."

"Spooked the crap out of me, man."

Caitlin noticed that today, along with the aloha shirt covered in screaming green pineapples, Martinez wore a crucifix.

He touched the cross and pointed at her. "Wouldn't hurt you either."

She had just a few minutes before roll call. She phoned her father, excitement putting a quaver in her fingers. He deserved to know what she'd discovered. He might have insights to add. Voice mail.

"Dad, call me. It's important. I have news."

Hanging up, she texted Sean.

MUCH news. Working today. Will fill you in when I see you.

Thirty seconds later, Sean called. "You okay?"

"Yeah. Slammed. But, Sean, I broke the code."

"Holy — Cat. What is it?"

Guthrie walked past. He nodded her toward the roll call room.

"I have to go," she said.

"Call if you have time. I want to hear."

"Will do." She hung up. She started after Guthrie but lifted her phone again. She texted Sean: Send mojo. She silenced her ringer and headed after the sergeant.

Twenty minutes later, the Prophet team assembled in the war room. Lieutenant Kogara stood at the back. Guthrie nodded at Caitlin. "You have the floor."

She walked to the wall. When she turned to face the entire team, nerves shot through her. Then her certainty kicked back in. This was a real breakthrough. She had it right. Her pulse was racing.

"Every murder committed by the Prophet, going back to the killing of Giselle Fraser in the shack at Peñasquitos Park, matches a scene in the *Inferno.*"

She held up the book. "This was written seven hundred years ago. An epic poem about a journey to the center of hell. And it's the Prophet's playbook."

Everyone was silent.

"The story takes place from the evening

before Good Friday to Easter Sunday. Dante descends to hell on the spring equinox."

Martinez pushed his hat back. Guthrie straightened. She pointed at a crime scene photo.

"The first murder, September 23, 1993, was the *autumn* equinox," she said. "The crime scene matches one of the first scenes in the *Inferno*. The entrance to hell. Damned souls are blown around the circle by a dark wind. These are the waverers — people who never took sides in life, and angels who stayed neutral in the heavenly battle between good and evil, when Lucifer fell. They fly through the air, wailing as they're stung by wasps."

Martinez whistled. Guthrie paced.

"This is the only murder that's out of season. I think it's because the UNSUB knew the victim, and took her when his need to kill overcame him. But once he started on his — *project* — he lined up the killings with the chronology in the *Inferno*."

She walked along the wall. "David Wehner. Professor of Eastern religions, killed on the 1994 spring equinox. He was suffocated with a plastic bag and left on a carnival Ferris wheel."

She tacked up a photo: fun house, cotton

candy stand. Wild Mouse, Limbo, Skee-Ball.

"The First Circle contains virtuous pagans — souls who didn't know the light of Christ. They exist in endless sighing and sadness." She checked that they were following. "It's Limbo."

Shanklin was nodding.

Caitlin moved to the next photo. "Barbara Gertz, left under the drying jets in a car wash. The Second Circle punishes the carnal, and Barbara was married five times. These souls surrender to the storm of their passions. In death, they're swept through the storm of hell."

She put up a photo of Helen and Barry Kim at a banquet. "Third Circle. Cerberus, the three-headed dog from Roman mythology, rips apart the gluttonous in a garbage pile."

Kogara leaned against the back wall, suit sharply creased, arms crossed. "They were found April twelfth. That's not an equinox. Was it Easter?"

"We can't confirm the exact date they died. Their bodies had been in the landfill for days. But that year, April seventh was Easter — in the Eastern rite calendar."

He nodded thoughtfully. She moved on.

"Fourth Circle. Justine and Colin Spencer. Holy Saturday in the Orthodox calendar. Their bodies rolled out of a dump truck."

She tacked up a photo from a Bay Area lifestyle magazine. Justine Spencer was pictured smiling in front of a walk-in closet built for her designer shoes.

"The greedy haul rocks around hell, eternally fighting for possession of them."

Caitlin reached the photo of Lisa Chu. "The Fifth Circle is Styx — a swamp. It punishes anger. The wrathful attack each other in the muck. The sullen are sunk in it, gargling slime."

Guthrie said, " 'Infinite wrath and infinite despair.' "

Caitlin took a breath and moved on. "Tim and Tammy Moulitsas." She touched the young couple's wedding portrait. "That's the Sixth Circle. Heresy."

Kogara said, "And Detective Saunders?"

"Pure murder, committed by a fleeing UNSUB."

His eyes were hard and worldly-wise. "What about the new murders?"

"Every one of them." She paused. "His messages confirm it."

She tapped a photo from the cornfield. "Another scene from the Sixth Circle. Fallen angels bar the gate to lower hell. The

Furies shriek and flay their breasts with their nails. Then the Messenger tears through them all. The note says, '*Angels fall, the messenger descends, your insolence is harrowed, defiance ends. You wail in fury, but the Equinox delivers pain.*' "

Guthrie said, "Fallen angels — a young wife fooling around?"

"Possibly. With a man who had an angel tattoo."

Kogara's expression hardened. "He stayed on the Sixth Circle?"

"Yes. In the book, the scene marks a shift — the journey into the deepest parts of hell."

His expression remained hard.

She moved on to Stuart Ackerman. "The Seventh Circle punishes violence. The night he died, Ackerman went to the park expecting bare-knuckle sex."

Guthrie said, "What about Ackerman's car — the dead crows with dolls' heads?"

"Harpies," Caitlin said. "Monsters with the body of a bird and the face of a woman. They infest the Wood of the Suicides, tearing souls to shreds."

Martinez said, "Frickin' Catholicism. That's the head game that scared me into daily mass."

Shanklin folded her arms. "The dolls'

heads were mostly baby dolls. Sounds like anger toward all women, starting in the cradle."

Caitlin looked at her. "Absolutely."

She turned back to the crime scene photos. "The Eighth Circle punishes fraud. Sorcerers, astrologers, and false prophets have their heads twisted backward, so that they can never see what's coming. His note read, *'Fortune-tellers, but they couldn't foresee this. Eventually they paid for their fraud.'* "

She paused. "The *Inferno* is about ironic punishment — poetic justice. And that's what the Prophet thinks he's delivering."

Kogara sauntered toward the wall. "What about Bart Fletcher? Those . . . tentacles."

"Thieves are thrown in a viper pit. They stole in life, so their identities are stolen in hell. Snake attacks transform them into horrifying, mutant reptiles." Her own skin threatened to start crawling again. "I don't know what the Prophet thinks Bart Fletcher stole. Yet."

Kogara now looked convinced. "This has been a long time coming. The question is, how do we use this information to identify the Prophet?"

Guthrie said, "We're going to look for suspects with any interest in Dante. People who have these books on their shelves."

Caitlin said, "He's getting bolder. Broadcasting his message."

Kogara turned to her. "I want a written report on my desk by the end of the day. Detailing every murder. Explaining how each killing matches the book. Analyzing where he's been and where he's going next. What else he might try."

Caitlin swallowed. "Yes, Lieutenant."

"We need to try to get ahead of him."

40

Night had fallen, clear and endless, when Caitlin walked through the door of the San Francisco watering hole. She was keyed up like a wind chime in a gale.

She'd stopped by the boardinghouse first. When the landlady said, "He's down the road," Caitlin said, "What's the name of the bar?"

But the landlady shook her head. "Coffee place. Strange Brew. Has a computer."

Strange Brew also had a shabby charm. But tonight it was almost empty. The barista glanced up from beneath his man bun with faux languor. She saw the way he sized her up — as someone he didn't need to handle with the baseball bat he kept beneath the counter.

"Large Americano," she said.

Mack sat in the back, at a terminal against the brick wall. She walked toward him.

Her report to Lieutenant Kogara was half

369

written. She hoped this field trip would let her fill in some blanks.

And she needed to deliver her father the news.

She took Mack in. He leaned forward, close to the screen. He probably needed reading glasses but didn't have them. He filled out the Pendleton work shirt but looked bent. His hair was so white. She remembered when he'd host barbecues, the house and backyard filled with friends, laughter, music, the smell of burgers on the grill. Mack gregarious, drawing people to him, reaching out, welcoming.

Not this: alone. Always, now. Dealing with people seemed almost physically painful for him.

When she sat down beside him, Mack didn't even react. She leaned forward until she was directly in his gaze. His guard went straight up. Then he saw it was her. The guard remained up.

On the screen was FindtheProphet.com. He was surfing the forums.

"Log out," she said.

He considered it, and typed. The screen reverted to the coffeehouse's home page.

She leaned toward him, elbows on her knees. "I know what he's doing."

He didn't move or change expression. He

looked like a dog ready to bite, or bolt.

"What I'm about to tell you stays between us." She looked pointedly at the computer. "Not a word, to anyone."

He still didn't move. "Understood."

"He's depicting the Nine Circles of Hell in Dante's *Inferno.*"

She told him. He listened, face dark, almost motionless, for several minutes. When she finally stopped to catch her breath, he began to nod. Softly. And to rock. He closed his eyes.

"He's not psychotic. Not even close," he said.

"No."

"All the crime scenes?" He looked at her. She nodded.

"Giselle Fraser?"

"It's one of the first scenes in the *Inferno.* Right after the gate where 'All hope abandon, ye who enter here' is carved."

She explained the canto in detail. He let out the slowest breath. She couldn't tell how he was processing it.

"Wavering. Staying neutral. That sent these people to hell?" he said.

"It's medieval, Dad. Literally."

He nodded. "Known associates of the victim. There's a list in the files."

"You think he knew Giselle Fraser?"

371

"If there was any victim he knew, or had contact with, it was early on. Maybe she wouldn't go out with him, or couldn't decide whether he was 'just a friend.' "

Caitlin nodded.

"The Kims," he said.

"Cerberus," she explained. "The three-headed dog."

He rubbed his fingers across his forehead. "Lisa Chu."

"The Fifth Circle. Styx. It's a swamp. That's why Lisa was drowned in a water-treatment pond."

He gave her a look when she said *Lisa*. She knew why: It meant she'd started thinking of the victims as people she knew, people close enough to call by their first names. That could be a boon to an investigator. It could also be psychologically dangerous.

"I met the woman who escaped from him that day," she said.

"Kelly Smolenski."

She nodded. "Kelly told me what the Prophet said when he attacked her in her family's garage."

" 'Sullen bitch.' "

She explained. He leaned back in his chair. "That poor child."

A heavy sense of grief pressed on her, killing the energy she'd come in with. Mack's gaze had retreated inward.

The barista called to her. "Here you go."

She brought back the coffee. "Are you surprised? Does this make sense to you, help any pieces fall into place?"

Her excitement was returning, but fear underlay it. Mack was calmly intense, but that could be a precursor to any kind of outburst.

His voice was low. "Tim and Tammy Moulitsas."

Caitlin drank the coffee, orienting herself. If he wanted to talk about the newlyweds, that would lead down a dark road. One he'd never spoken about with her. With anyone, maybe. She wondered if they should move to a different table, away from a computer he could easily smash.

He said, "Please."

She put down her cup. "Yeah."

His eyes were dark. They were so deep set, she thought, deeper than she'd realized. He looked like someone who was being slowly ablated by a blowtorch, all the excess blown away, leaving a heated, hurting core.

He said, "They were bludgeoned unconscious in their home, trussed with duct tape, and taken to the cemetery. He dragged them into the mausoleum and then . . . the

373

gasoline. I could never understand that. The horror it inflicted on them. They may have been unconscious when he threw the match. We'll never know. If Tim and Tammy felt that pain . . ." He swiped a palm across his face. "They were both twenty-four. Kids. Seeing that . . ."

"The Sixth Circle is a vast graveyard of red-hot tombs. Dante thought heretics denied the immortality of the soul, so their punishment was to spend eternity in a grave, burning from God's wrath."

Mack closed his eyes. "Tim and Tammy were not religious. If we'd —"

She set her hand on his. "You'd what, protect every atheist in California? You couldn't have known his victimology ahead of time. He chose them because he's a murderer." She held on. "The urge to kill is what drives him in the end."

He looked at her. "And a fantasy that can never be perfected."

"So he'll keep trying."

He nodded. His hand trembled beneath hers. He leaned back, maybe planning to stand, but she stopped him.

"Dad."

"Whatever you're going to ask, I don't like that tone. But it's not like I'm going to stop you."

"That day, at the cemetery, after you and Saunders got there . . ."

He pulled back. She held on.

She lowered her voice to a murmur. "Please. You're the only living person who's seen the Prophet without a mask. Please."

He looked at her without blinking, for what seemed an endless time. Then he said, "It was blind luck Saunders and I got to the cemetery so fast. We were two blocks away when the call came in. Pulled up and saw the truck."

"Parked outside the mausoleum?"

"Camper. Stolen. He used it to transport Tim and Tammy to the cemetery."

She nodded, encouraging him to continue.

"He'd backed it up to the mausoleum. From our angle we couldn't see past the mausoleum door, and he wasn't behaving in an overtly suspicious manner. We didn't know . . ."

He looked away. He tried to speak, but no words came.

She spoke as gently as she could. "Did he stay to watch?"

Mack nodded. "He wanted to enjoy his work." He blew out a breath and scratched at his arms. "He watched for at least five seconds after we floored it toward him. Just stood there. He was so consumed with it, he didn't see our car coming. He . . . he was *entranced*."

He shook himself. "Then he fled. Jumped in the camper. But he'd hot-wired it. When he tried to leave, it died. He couldn't restart it. So he had to run."

He paused and gathered himself. Seemed to pull back from the edge. "Today, it's much harder to hot-wire a vehicle. New electronics mean you can't rip out the wiring and just spark the ignition. May mean he drives his own vehicle now."

"Right."

"Huge cemetery. He took off over a hill through the graves. Only way to go after him was on foot."

"I know."

Mack stopped, seeming lost in memory. Caitlin leaned toward him.

"What did he look like?"

"We were two hundred yards away when we spotted him. Dark sweatshirt, navy blue or black. Jeans. Sneakers. The soles of his shoes as he ran — they were white. He was lanky. Caucasian. Brown hair, well groomed. And he could motor."

"How did he move?"

Mack's gaze lengthened. "Like a scalded cat. Like he was scared shitless to be confronted with capture. He was young, and he moved easily, but he was pumping his arms wildly . . ." He swallowed. "He knew he'd made a mistake. And he made another one. He didn't know alternate exits from the cemetery. That's why he went over the hill — he didn't know it led straight to the freeway."

"But he didn't stop."

"Hell, no. He . . ." Mack looked at her. "That's when he looked over his shoulder. When he saw the freeway dead ahead, he looked back. And saw us coming."

"You saw his face?"

"It was as lean as the rest of him. All I saw from a hundred yards away was eyes and a wide-open mouth. Then he turned and leaped the fence. And I mean leaped. He was strong."

She leaned closer, and pressed. "When you got across the freeway, after you got sideswiped . . ."

"Did Saunders say anything? That's what you want to know, right? Because he saw the Prophet up close and lived long enough for me to get to him."

"Did he?"

Mack shook his head. "Two shots penetrated his lung. Sucking chest wound. He couldn't talk. He was . . ." He closed his eyes. "He was close to death. Seconds away.

He didn't say anything. He mouthed . . ."

She leaned forward.

"He mouthed his wife's name. Bella. Clear as day. I . . ."

Mack stood and shoved the chair back. It toppled. The clatter startled the barista. Mack backed away, hands raised, and headed for the restroom.

"Dad . . ."

He shook his head and slammed the men's room door behind him.

The barista gave Caitlin the side-eye. She said, "It's okay," and picked up the chair.

She sat back down to wait, and turned from the man's stare.

Always the stares. Growing up, she had hated the pity, the furtive glances, the nods . . . *Yes, that's her, the poor girl . . .* the smiles, the shunning, the refusal of some people to talk about it, shutting down like a falling guillotine if she mentioned her dad's name. She felt like she'd been branded, that an aura glowed around her, alerting people that she was a pariah. She especially hated the ones who said that her dad needed to repent or he'd go to hell. She knew now: Suicide was her dad's dream of escaping from hell.

The men's room door opened. Mack returned and sat down heavily. He'd splashed water on his face. It beaded on his forehead in the amber light.

Caitlin opened her mouth, but he held up a hand.

"There was blood on the floor of the warehouse. Drops trailing away. It belonged to Saunders," he said. "The Prophet first shot him from at least ten feet away. But the fatal shots were fired from less than a yard." He looked at her. "Do you understand? The Prophet ambushed him, hit him with a two-by-four, and got Saunders's gun. He backed out of reach and shot him, and when Saunders was down and dying, he approached close enough to touch him. There were swipe marks on Saunders's shirt. The Prophet got the man's blood on his hands and wiped it off as Ellis lay there choking and gasping. He got enough blood on him that it dripped after he fired the final shots and fled. That's what I know."

Caitlin's throat was dry. This wasn't in any file that she had read.

Mack said, "Even though he had Ellis down, he moved in close to finish the job. He wanted the personal touch. He savored it. He reveled in it." His eyes were hot.

"And then he ran away. He ran, Dad."

Mack nodded tightly.

She felt another touch of something just

379

out of reach. "Why did he run? You were closing on him? Is that it?"

"Maybe."

"But he'd ambushed one cop. He could have . . ." Her voice gave out.

"He could have ambushed me too. He had a handgun at that point. But he didn't. He fled." The heat in his eyes seemed to be spreading to her. "You think I haven't wondered why? Think I don't ask myself that, every goddamned night?"

"What's your answer?"

"I don't have one."

"Think back. Picture yourself there."

"I am."

"Really, really put yourself in the moment. What did the warehouse smell like? Where was the light coming from? What sounds did you hear?"

"Caitlin."

"Dad, you saw him. Let go and go back. Please. It has to be there. *Think.*"

"Caitlin, stop."

She turned her palms up in supplication, leaning far over the table. "You may not know what you know. But it's there."

He grabbed her hands. "Caitlin. I didn't see him. Not well enough."

She felt like a flywheel, racing at ten thousand rpm. She wanted to press him.

380

But she understood, and it fell through her hard. He couldn't give her more. Not on this.

She slowly brought herself back down, fighting frustration. Mack let go of her hands.

"Except I think Saunders tried to stop him, even though he was dying. Even though he ended up getting shot from close range. He was a stand-up guy," Mack said.

The look in her father's eyes, the way his shoulders bent, nearly broke Caitlin right then. She set a hand on his, gently this time.

"I'm glad to know it," she said.

Mack pressed his lips tight together. She stood up.

"Let me drive you home," she said.

The barista was wiping the counters, preparing to close. Caitlin said, "We can wait and walk with you to your car."

He shook his head. "I'm staying here tonight, sofa bed upstairs. But thanks. I'll bolt the door behind you."

When they got outside, the street was empty. A heavy quiet suffused the city. Mack shoved his hands into the pockets of his jean jacket as they walked to her SUV.

"Your mom texted me," he said. "She's worried."

"Everybody's worried. I'm working on it."

"So's she. Putting together a ride-share program for her neighborhood, so women don't have to take the bus or drive alone, especially if they work nights."

"That's so damn smart." She smiled. "God bless Typhoon Sandy."

"Mainly she's worried about you," he said.

She looked past the streetlights into the night. "I'm fine."

"She worries that you're fine like I'm fine."

Their boots scuffed on the sidewalk. Caitlin remembered what her mother had once told her: Most homicide detectives stop taking their worst cases home at night, but Mack never did. Eventually, he lived in the mental house that created.

She thought about the dingy boarding-house, the creaking halls, strangers living side by side in shells of suspicion and hurt. Loneliness.

"Dad. The Prophet is working his way deeper into hell. What's the end game? What happens when he reaches the Ninth Circle?"

"What does the Ninth Circle punish?" Mack said.

"Betrayal."

His eyes couldn't have darkened, because there was nowhere darker for them to go. But his voice settled into calm depths.

"The world betrays us all. He could do

anything."

He slowed on the sidewalk and pulled Caitlin into a hug. "He's close to the end. He's nearing the heart of his fantasy. And you're a part of it. Caitlin, you have to get away from this."

For a moment she wanted to pull away. He held on tight. She let out a breath, wrapped her arms around him, and pressed her head to his chest.

"It's too late," she said.

41

Miles away, in a hillside house above San Francisco Bay, a man read the latest news. He sat at a desk by the windows. The light from the screen was a blue portal reflecting on the darkened walls. Outside, city lights spilled to the bay and ringed the water.

He saw her name — Caitlin Hendrix. It was so fitting. It was poetic.

It ain't poetry, his mother would say. *It's fate.*

But fate was a myth constructed by fools — people who gamble or follow horoscopes, who believe the stars rule their lives. Who think you have to *take it.*

Fate was bunk. There was no fate, only sin and recompense. And he was delivering it. He, Mercury, was sending the message.

He was punishing humanity with all the contempt and creativity that poetic justice required. Every sentence fitting the crime, exactly as the book prescribed.

The *Inferno.* The first horror novel. The epic tale of a journey to the depths of hell. The book that invented the very idea of the "depths" of hell — of a pit where descending levels punish increasingly monstrous sins.

He had now reached the Eighth Circle, where sorcerers and astrologers — who try to see the future through magic — have their heads wrenched backward, so that they can never look ahead. Where thieves have their very identities stolen by writhing vipers, like the dead reporter engulfed by pharaoh's serpents.

They have no clue, he thought. Not the taken. Not the police, the press, the public — nobody was close to understanding Mercury, much less capturing him. But it was no surprise that they failed to understand. In hell, the damned rage in confusion.

He stood and walked to the window. He spread his arms, inhaled, and beheld the stage.

Titus Rhone was forty-seven, fit, well maintained, well turned out, well-spoken — if he said so himself. Well financed too: a valuable manager for the conglomerate where he worked. Bunk paid. Bunk made sinners pay too.

385

The moving boxes were mostly unpacked. He had settled back into the East Bay as though he'd never left. This place fit him like a warm latex glove.

He made a mental note to restock his supply.

He returned to the computer and admired Caitlin Hendrix on the screen. His heart beat faster. *At last.* Mack Hendrix's own daughter — poetic indeed.

A shiver swept through him. Caitlin Hendrix would need to be crushed, as he had crushed her father. She could not be allowed to derail him. He turned to his bookshelf and selected one of the translations, a newer one, though after all these years, he knew each line of the poem verbatim, in the original language. *"Through every city shall he hunt her down, Until he shall have driven her back to Hell."*

His heart beat harder. Soon would come the next epiphany. The next manifestation of Mercury and his poetic justice.

His mother's hiss again filled his mind. *Caitlin Hendrix is a she-wolf. Look at her: Something's witchy in her eyes. She'll put a curse on you, Titus. Take a fork and a rusty nail and cross them and stick them in the ground to break the spell.*

He ignored his mother's whispers. Growing up in West Virginia, his ma said *he* brought a curse on the family. She took his emotional irregularities as a sign that he was hexed. She refused to believe the family's poisoned luck had anything to do with her own ignorance and bad habits. How many days did she drag him down the hollow to the library so she could check out movies and stand outside smoking and gossiping?

Never mind. The library was where he discovered the books, the ones with illustrations of torments and the damned. He found beauty and purpose. He became a student, of literature and source code and pain. He got out. So, *thanks, Ma.*

Black magic was bunk. Yet the people getting hysterical about the Prophet thought *he* was an astrologer, or even satanic? The irony.

He looked at the news story. His palms itched with anticipation. The hours were counting down to the next outpouring of poetic vengeance.

The anger, the heat, the expectant thrill, began to build.

But his masterwork remained obscure to the public. He might need to be bolder. To clarify to the bumblers in law enforcement and the media what his grand plan entailed.

What it *showed.* Whom it punished, and why.

Twenty years. After that final day, he'd thought he was done. After he shot Detective Ellis Saunders. After he drew close and knelt over him, waiting for him to die, that moment of possession . . . until Saunders grabbed him by the throat. Saunders's hand held death, a chill from empty eternity. His eyes opened on starless voids. His voice was not Saunders's voice but a hiss from the ceaseless black. *You. Will be. Annihilated.*

He shot Saunders again and fled.

He scrubbed himself clean. Moved away. And he might have stayed away forever. But a new whisper rose in the wind, clearing the fog and fear from his mind. *Your work is incomplete. You haven't evened the score yet.*

So he started again.

He picked up where he left off, amid the Sixth Circle. He began his final descent with a statement of purpose. The Messenger Appears. He scatters the fallen. Nobody can now stand against him in the depths of hell.

You are unstoppable, the whisper had said. *Don't pause for breath. Finish it.*

That same whisper now said to him: *Caitlin.*

Yes. She brought herself into this. The daughter of one of the two men who hunted

388

him, now a cop herself. Trying to redeem her father's failure. So avaricious for glory. Her hunger was a sin. For this, she would pay.

On his laptop, he opened the RAT. After twenty-five years as a programmer, he knew plenty of dirty tech tricks. The RAT — remote administration tool — was spying software. It let him access other people's computers. With the RAT, he could open disk drives. He could track people without their knowledge. He could silently turn on webcams and observe people.

Like the math teacher, and the Coffee, Tea & Tarot women, and the drunken reporter.

The new millennium had opened his world in many ways, and the silent approach via spying software was one of them.

It wasn't like the first time. Not like the jogger in Peñasquitos Park.

The First. She who became the marker of the Vestibule of Hell. Giselle Fraser, the Tease. The jogger who smiled at him, who said hi to him, then ignored him. Hot and cold. Leading him on, then running with another man and never speaking to him again. Whispering with the other guy, and laughing . . . at *him,* undoubtedly.

He was ready by then. He had grown

beyond killing animals. Even though he laughed now, thinking of the stapler and his schoolmate's hamsters. That was goddamned funny. Not as satisfying as the hammer and the rabbits, but funny.

Those things had helped him get through. The verb *slaked* wasn't used often enough these days, but that's what those animals had done. Slaked his rage, slaked his thirst. For a time.

And after he saw a video about the circus freak with the piercings, the nails through her private parts . . . and the report of the nail bombing . . . so frightening, so freakish. So exciting.

Pieces. Ideas. They were all eventually assembled for his vast canvas.

It was as yet incomplete. Unperfected. When he first began, Giselle the Tease had lured him into acting out of season. But since then, he had worked within the confines of the *Inferno*'s chronology. If the Sullen Bitch had not escaped from the water treatment pond and erased the message on her arm, he would have acted on Good Friday that year.

And if Bart Fletcher had not taken information from the Sullen Bitch, and held on to it, he could still have acted. Fletcher had taken what was not his, and kept it. The Thief.

This month it had been frightfully simple to lure Fletcher within his reach. He simply contacted the Thief anonymously, claiming to be a source within the Alameda Sheriff's Office. He fed him juicy tidbits about the investigation. Invented tidbits, yes — but the Thief gobbled them up, and held them quiet, hoping to spin them into a shocking exposé. And when he said he could free the Thief from the constraints of his ankle bracelet . . . the man was on the hook.

Titus Rhone was in the midst of his masterwork. The poetic *beauty* of displaying the damned with their sins so explicitly portrayed. Part of him wanted Caitlin Hendrix to figure it out. To apprehend his blinding genius.

But this yearning was his own sin. His desire to let his light shine — that was his failing. His quest was pure, but he was not. He should scourge himself of it. Rid himself of this competitive urge.

But not yet. He would destroy Caitlin Hendrix before she could stop him. When she fell, he wanted her to die understanding his plan's *perfection.*

So it was time to up the volume.

He had planted malware in one of the sites

that he knew the authorities would access during their investigation — the site he'd given to KPDX News in his letter to the television station. The malware had downloaded to Caitlin's computer and mobile devices.

He looked at the information on his next targets. Circle Eight. *Soon.* He stared at the image of Caitlin Hendrix. Deep in the night, he turned on her webcam. *O lucky day.* Her laptop sat open on her living room coffee table. His heart hammered.

It's time, come round at last, Caitlin.

42

When Caitlin got home, the wind was up. The street was silent, houses dark. She sensed that everybody else had hunkered down behind locked doors. Shadows scraped the sidewalks beneath the street-lights.

She felt frayed. She'd turned in her report to Lieutenant Kogara. Fourteen typed pages that only confirmed everything she'd feared: The Prophet's game was escalating. It was designed to terrorize — and it was succeeding. Because no matter how hard she tried to read through the poetry in the *Inferno,* she couldn't see where in the pit the Prophet planned to drag them.

She parked on the driveway and ducked under the purple wisteria, ghostly in the dark. Beyond the gate, she heard Shadow's tags clink as she raced out of her doghouse, whimpering with joy.

"Hey, girl."

Caitlin opened the gate and knelt to greet her. Shadow yipped, jumped, and put her paws on Caitlin's shoulders. She snagged Caitlin's satchel. It fell and spilled on the walk. Her phone clattered on the concrete. It was silently vibrating with an incoming call.

She'd silenced it at work and hadn't turned the ringer back on. She grabbed it. Deralynn Hobbs. She answered.

"Deralynn? Is something wrong?"

"No. Why?"

"It's midnight."

"And now I know you're a night owl too."

Shadow licked her face, bright-eyed, tail wagging. Caitlin stood up and pushed the gate open, but instead of coming when Caitlin whistled, Shadow bolted for the street in a blur of black fur and white paws.

"Dammit."

"Sorry," Deralynn said.

Caitlin ran down the driveway. "That wasn't for you. My vixen of a dog just made a getaway." She jogged up the street, whistling. "What's going on?"

"Wanted you to have a heads-up. I'm chasing a lead. This Zodiac Match thing. Me and another member of the message board."

"What kind of a lead? Can you give me

details?" She couldn't see Shadow. She whistled again.

Deralynn said, "Got all night. Walt took the boys camping at Mount Diablo Park, so I'll talk to him . . ."

"In person? A guy from the message board? Not a good idea."

"Online. We know each other from the forum."

"Assume that the Prophet monitors the forum."

"This guy's vetted."

"Still, be careful." Caitlin reached the corner. "Hang on." She lowered the phone. "Shadow. Come."

She listened to the wind. For a minute, there was nothing but the shiver of the leaves, and acorns hitting the ground. Then Shadow appeared from the neighbor's bushes and trotted toward her, perky and satisfied.

Caitlin grabbed her collar. "Great escape, you little mutt."

She led Shadow toward her house and returned the phone to her ear. "What exactly is this lead you're following?"

Nothing.

"Deralynn?"

The call had gone dead. Caitlin tried to call Deralynn back but couldn't reconnect.

All she got was a *Call Failed* message.

"Dammit."

She shoved the phone in her pocket and awkwardly led Shadow home. When she shut the gate behind her, the dog bounded up the steps to the back porch while Caitlin fished out her keys. The house was dark. She opened the door and Shadow scurried into the kitchen. A second later, Caitlin heard her slurping from her water bowl.

Caitlin shut the door and flipped the switch for the under-cabinet lighting. She dropped her satchel on the counter. And stopped. On the kitchen island was an envelope.

It was cream colored. Good stationery. Looked like heavy vellum.

She went absolutely still. She listened to the house. Shadow's head popped up. The dog pricked up her ears and ran from the kitchen toward the back of the house.

"Sha—"

Caitlin stopped herself. Heart pounding, she reached under her jacket and drew her gun.

She sidestepped through the kitchen, edged up to the wall, and reached around to flip a light switch in the living room.

Living room clear. Front door locked, dead bolt secure. She opened the coat closet. Clear.

Shadow hadn't come back.

Silently she advanced down the hall, both hands on the gun, half turned to present a smaller target to anyone who might lunge from a doorway. She swung into the guest room and flipped on the light. Nothing. Window secure. Closet clear.

She spun and continued down the hall to her bedroom door. She swept through the doorway, hitting the light switch as she entered. Saw nobody. She threw open the closet and flipped back the duvet and crouched to look under the bed.

A noise clattered in the bathroom. She crept close and threw it open, SIG raised.

On the bath mat Shadow lay with her paws in the air, gnawing a chew toy.

Caitlin holstered her gun and stalked back to the kitchen. Heart thudding, she put on latex gloves and picked up the envelope. It wasn't sealed. Carefully she lifted the flap.

Out fell a note. She unfolded it.

You're going to get this done. Then you can wash it out of your system courtside. Sean

Along with the note were tickets to a late-season Warriors game.

"God. Crap."

She checked her phone — three missed calls from him.

"Goddammit."

She dropped the note and bent over the counter. *Surprise me.* She'd actually told him that. *Can't wait.*

The phone rang. She jumped. Sean. She clamped her jaw tight, trying to calm herself enough to answer.

Outside, the gate creaked open.

Spinning, she drew her SIG and hit the switch to turn off the kitchen lights. Her phone kept ringing. In the dark outside, a shadow passed beneath the wisteria.

She threw the door open and charged onto the porch, weapon aimed at it. "On the ground. *Now.* Do it. *Do it.*"

A man threw himself down, rolling as he landed. "Cat —"

She swung her weapon. He rolled deeper into the darkness and jumped to his feet again, hands spread.

"It's me!"

Her phone kept ringing. So did the cell the shadow held in his right hand. She trained her SIG on him, disbelieving.

Sean shouted louder. *"Caitlin."*

Chest heaving, she lowered her gun. Stared at him.

"What are you doing here? Why'd you call when you were at the gate? The sound . . ."

He continued to stare at the SIG. Though

the barrel was pointed at the ground, she held it two-handed. Her finger was still on the trigger.

"You came into my house and left a *letter?*" she shouted. "Like the Prophet? What were you thinking?"

He took an actual step back.

Her hands were trembling. Her arms. All the heat in her body seemed to have poured out through her palms and evaporated.

"You freaked me *out.*" She heard the corroded panic in her voice. "I almost . . ."

He crossed the yard, long slow strides, and climbed the steps. He looked pointedly at the SIG, held tight in her hands.

"Caitlin, for Christ's sake."

She holstered the gun.

"I forgot my house keys here earlier." His voice had gained a deadly calm. "I came back to get them. I called because I didn't want to bang on the door and scare you."

She turned and went inside. When she flipped the lights back on, she saw his keys by the toaster.

She slumped against the kitchen counter, balled her right hand into a fist, and bumped it repeatedly against her forehead. All the windows bled to the night, to darkness, to a deep and vast hiding space where the monsters crawled. Where they could see her, inside, shaky and huddled under thin pools of light. She strode to the living room, where the blinds were drawn.

"Sean. I'm sorry."

He stepped inside. "Okay."

His tone was ice. She tried to pull herself back down off the ceiling, but her nerves skittered in all directions. She paced.

"Seriously. I'm sorry. But you walked into my backyard in the dark."

"I can't fault you for extreme caution. But you're cranked so tight, you're going to blow."

"You think I should take it down a notch. I get it. I'll be better in the morning."

"And next time?"

"What's your point?"

"You're letting this own you."

"It's twenty-four/seven right now. We're at battle stations."

"You're losing control. There's a blind curve ahead, and you're gunning straight at it."

She stopped and put the heels of her palms to her eyes. "I can't do this right now."

"The case isn't just bleeding into your life. It's bleeding you dry."

"Back off." She put her hands out. *Stop.* "Don't lecture me. Not tonight."

She walked back to the kitchen, picked up his keys, and held them out. After a cold second he took them. The door banged shut behind him when he left.

She stood staring at the walls. Heard his truck pull away, hard. Outside, the trees raked against the roof in the wind.

She was way off-kilter. She couldn't lie to herself about that. The compass was spinning from true north to west and the lands beyond direction.

She opened the cabinet and took out the bottle of tequila. She poured a clattering inch into a tumbler. She eyed it, shining under the lights. Screw it. She poured another inch. She threw it back, coughed, and stood pressing the back of her hand to her lips.

She tried to phone Deralynn, but once again got *Call Failed*. Shadow padded in with her chew toy drooping from her mouth. She dropped it at Caitlin's feet and looked up with guileless eyes.

Caitlin walked to the living room and dropped onto the sofa. What had she done?

43

She wasn't sure at first what woke her. A sound. On the sofa in her living room, Caitlin stirred. She had drifted off sometime after one A.M.

She heard the sound again. Low and guttural. A growl.

It was Shadow, standing on the floor beside the sofa. Caitlin jerked fully awake.

On the coffee table, her phone was jittering in a slow circle. She had turned off the ringer again, but it was vibrating like a rat in a trap. She sat up and grabbed it. *Number Blocked.*

Her head pounded. The phone kept vibrating.

She connected and heard a harsh whisper.

"How can you sleep? After failure upon failure. All those dead bodies, Caitlin. Piling up."

Sparks danced at the corners of her vision.

How the hell. It was him.

Careful. "You can't put this on me."

"I didn't. Your father did. It's in your blood. Catastrophe. Insanity."

Beneath his scorn lay an undertone of rage. Her breath came quick. *Don't blow this. Keep him on the line.* She put the call on speaker, scrambled for her iPad, and hit RECORD on Voice Memo.

"That's not me. It's you," she said.

"You can't save them." He was eerily calm. "You think you can, because you saved the baby. I saw the news, you carrying her out, holding her tight against the chaos."

Her mouth went dry.

"It looked heroic," he said. "But chaos always wins."

Her computer glowed awake. On-screen a dash-cam video played. Suburban street. House with a skateboard ramp and army men on the sidewalk.

Deralynn's place.

"How does it feel to want something you can never have?" the voice said.

Jesus God. Caitlin ran to the kitchen and grabbed the cordless phone from the counter. What was Deralynn's number? *Shit* — she only had it in her cell phone. On the cordless, she hit 911.

403

"This is Detective Caitlin Hendrix of the Alameda Sheriff's Office." She reeled off her badge number and Deralynn's street. She couldn't recall the number but described the house. "Attempted murder in progress. Suspect is armed and extremely dangerous. It's the Prophet. Get units there. *Now.*"

From her cell phone, the voice spoke. "Average law enforcement response time in that neighborhood is twelve minutes, Caitlin."

She ran back to the living room. *Fuck him.* She grabbed the cell phone, put the voice on hold, and scrolled to recent calls, searching for Deralynn's number.

On her computer, the camera light came on. The voice rolled through the laptop's speakers.

"You can't escape. No matter which way you turn, death awaits."

The dash-cam video cross-faded to a new scene. Urban road, four lanes. Headlights caught a red Camry ahead.

Caitlin froze. "Oh, my God."

It was her mother.

On the road, Sandy Hendrix slowed and stopped at a red light. Ten minutes earlier she had dropped a friend at her apartment complex. The woman lived alone and worked swing shift at the Radisson in Concord. Sandy had waited at the curb while she walked to the lobby, and while she unlocked the glass door, went in, securely locked the door again, and gave a thumbs-up.

Now Sandy was half a mile from home. She was tired, but this was worth it.

In the cup holder, her phone flickered. Before she could check it out, a black pickup pulled up on her left and stopped beside her at the red light. The driver honked.

The passenger window of the pickup scrolled down.

The driver shouted something. Sandy turned down the radio and cupped a hand to her ear, indicating, *Say again.*

A man shouted, "Said, your right rear tire's flat."

She couldn't see his face. The truck had jacked-up suspension, the cab a good three feet higher than the driver's seat of her Camry. In the night, with only the dim red illumination from the traffic light, all she could see was the driver's hand, gesturing at her car.

He pointed at a side street. "If you'll pull over, I can take a look at it."

In her living room, Caitlin clutched her phone. Her finger hovered over Deralynn's number.

Shadow stood before the computer, growling at the screen. The dash-cam video showed Sandy's car stopped at a red light beside the vehicle with the camera.

Were these videos both live? Was one recorded? Which?

What did he want?

Barely breathing, she hit CALL.

It rang. Once, twice. Caitlin knelt in front of her laptop. On the dash cam, the vehicles remained stopped at the red light. The phone kept ringing.

The call was picked up. "Caitlin? Sweetheart?"

"Get out of there," Caitlin yelled. "Go. Drive to the nearest police station and —"

"Oh, shit."

Caitlin heard her mother's phone hit the center console as Sandy dropped it. On the dash cam, the Camry floored it through the red light, screeching away.

"Drive, Mom, drive, drive, just go," Caitlin yelled.

Through the phone she heard the engine

rev. On-screen she watched the Camry recede from view. Her chest heaved.

Hands shaking, she ended the call with her mom and dialed Deralynn. The phone rang.

On-screen, the dash cam remained stationary. The vehicle hadn't run the light to chase her mom. The traffic light turned green.

Deralynn's phone continued to ring. Nobody answered.

From the computer speaker, the voice said, "You see? You turn, and turn, until inexorably, you turn on some*one*. It's inevitable."

The dash-cam vehicle slowly pulled away from the light and took a soft turn onto a side street. The view showed nothing. The computer screen went dark.

The voice returned. "When your demons wake you at night, do you hear the dead screaming? Because you'll never make things right. You don't understand that, but they do."

A woman came on. *"Stay back. Don't."*

Her voice was trembling, choked and hoarse. Shadow jumped back from the table, barking, hackles up.

Caitlin said, "What are you doing? You bastard, stop —"

"You don't want to hurt me. I'm too useful to you. You . . . Oh, God." The woman broke into a sob. *"God, no. Don't. Jesus, no, no . . ."*

The woman screamed. And screamed.

The whisper returned. "Every step you take makes it worse. You betray everybody you touch."

Caitlin's legs weakened. The screaming filled her ears. The call went dead.

44

Sunday

They found her at dawn. At a gas station off of I-580, halfway up Altamont Pass, Deralynn's body was stuffed into an outdoor freezer, buried in ice.

Blue and red lights turned the desolate hills into a carnival sideshow. Caitlin's breath frosted the air. The morning star rode the eastern horizon, above a red streak of sky. Its light faded even as Caitlin approached the crime scene tape.

She nodded and approached Guthrie. She didn't think she could speak. The gas station clerk sat in the open door of a patrol car, looking vacant. The Crime Lab team and medical examiner were already there.

The photographer was leaning over a bloody object on the asphalt in front of the freezer. When he took the shot, the flash reflected off a stainless steel blade.

It was a heavy cleaver.

Caitlin stopped at Guthrie's side. "The murder weapon? He left it?"

"Presumptively."

That had to be deliberate. It was a message.

The attending ME was Zachary Azir. He leaned over the freezer and paused, staring down. Caitlin's stomach wrenched and she shut her eyes.

Guthrie walked toward Azir. She heard his footsteps fade. Her feet seemed screwed into the ground. It took every effort to move them, one at a time, and approach the freezer. But she had to. She couldn't look away.

Deralynn deserved her witness.

The dawn light broke across the hills as she reached the freezer, glass and steel glazing red. The ice was heaped on top of Deralynn, bags slit open, burying her like she'd been overcome by an avalanche. Only the tips of her fingers, and her face, were visible. Her skin was a flat gray, her lips blue, half parted. She'd been bled nearly dry somewhere else. Her eyes were closed.

Caitlin's vision seemed pinpoint clear, and pulsing. A high hum rose in her ears. There were voices around her, people moving with purpose. She couldn't hear their words at first.

Dr. Azir leaned over Deralynn. "Something at the corner of her eye."

The ME opened her eyelid. Mercury ran out. The quicksilver tear caught the rays of the sun, swimming gold and orange.

"Damn. Get me something to contain this so it doesn't contaminate everything," Azir said.

Caitlin said, "The cleaver . . ."

The photographer's flash blanched Deralynn's face. Caitlin choked up and had to stop.

Guthrie, ashen, prodded her. "Which scene from hell?"

"More than one. The blade . . ." She cleared her throat. "In the Eighth Circle, the Sowers of Discord are hacked apart by demons. The ice, that's the Ninth Circle. Treachery."

They watched the ME work.

Caitlin said, "She promised she wasn't going to meet anybody."

"Her back door was wide-open and a kitchen trash bag was spilled next to her garbage cans. The dog was shut in the garage, lured in with a hunk of steak. It looks like Deralynn stepped outside to empty the trash and was abducted. Somebody, maybe from that message board, got her home address."

And Caitlin was the one who'd urged De-ralynn to dig into the case via the message board. She was the one who delayed a call that could possibly have warned her. *You betray everybody you touch.*

Guthrie said, "I've taken the gas station clerk's statement. You search the scene."

She couldn't look away from the freezer. "Sergeant, he got into my computer via malware. It's probably infected everybody's. Shanklin's, Martinez's, yours. He may know where all of us live. He got my contacts. If the malware spreads easily, it might be in our contacts' devices too. Like my mother's. Your family's as well."

He looked at her darkly. "We'll get Computer Forensics on it. Get yourself a new phone. But . . ."

"But I have to keep my current number active. So he can call me again."

"Yes. We'll set up a tap on it this morning."

She nodded.

"Your mom all right?" he said.

"Nails. Cop's wife — no way she was going to pull onto some dark street with a stranger. When I called she didn't hesitate, just floored it. She tore into the Walnut Creek police station blasting the horn. I think she pulled a drift and a hand-brake

412

turn," she said. "But she's spooked. Didn't get the plate number of the vehicle but saw a brand logo on the chassis. Dodge."

"Good."

"She's going to stay with my uncle for a few days. In Chicago."

Sandy had begged Caitlin to come with her.

Guthrie turned back to the freezer. Caitlin turned to the parking lot.

The bitter March wind sharpened her senses. *Work the scene.*

The gas station stood on a corner where a country road cut beneath the interstate. On the opposite corner was a diner and beyond it a tire yard. Past that were miles of hills and gullies and trees and the occasional winding farm road. On 580, eighteen-wheelers girned up the climb toward Altamont Pass. The rising sun turned the rain-fed hills a gleaming emerald green.

Which way had he come? Where did he go?

She had a Canon camera in her car. No way could she use her phone now. She got the camera, took photos, and drew a rough map of the scene in her notebook.

The diner was just opening up. Outside it, early-bird customers and a waitress stood talking and pointing. A few wandered toward the crime scene tape, where a deputy stopped them. They were all trying to see past the flashing lights, the cop cars and ambulance, to that freezer. It wouldn't be long before the media gunned out here in their vans. The news helicopter would swoop in behind them.

She couldn't stand the thought of a television camera catching sight of Deralynn. Tears welled in her eyes, and an overwhelming protective instinct rose within her. She wanted to run and haul Deralynn out of that ice and wrap her in her own coat, swaddle her and hold her close and protect her from any more insult. To gentle her, tell her it was all okay now, all okay, all . . .

Outside the gas station, Guthrie was staring at her.

She blinked away the tears and turned into the wind. She walked the parking lot, looking for evidence. On the freeway, traffic was slowing to get a good look at the scene. *Screw off,* she wanted to yell.

Get it together. You're skidding.

She walked the scene in a grid, slowly. Eyes on the ground; eyes on the view; taking in vantage points, ingress, egress.

The freeway provided easy access. And the gas station had a security camera trained on the front door. She hadn't heard anybody yell that they'd found something on it.

She walked the station forecourt. Found nothing. She continued her search along the side of the building, and on to the back. Behind the building was a field, bordered at the far side by a creek lined with oaks. At the edge of the grass, she found the tracks.

They were muddy wheel tracks that led from the grass onto the asphalt. About three inches wide. Beside them were footprints in the dew.

A wheelbarrow.

He hadn't pulled into the gas station. He'd transported Deralynn to the freezer in a wheelbarrow, from beyond the trees and the creek at the far side of the field.

She hollered for the forensics team and photographer.

She crossed the field. The creek wound through heavy oaks, willows dragging their branches in the water. She splashed across, ducked through the trees, and emerged onto a two-lane road.

There was no traffic, but near a bend, a telephone company crew was working on a cell tower. She jogged over.

"Been on-site about an hour," the fore-man said. "Not much traffic. Newspaper delivery guy, just after we got here."

"Anybody on foot?"

They shook their heads.

Another member of the crew descended from the cell tower. "There was that truck."

"What truck?" Caitlin said.

"I saw it from up top. Parked down that way." He pointed around the bend.

"It was here when you arrived?" she said.

"Yeah. Sitting there, dark as hell. I thought it was a strange place to park."

She opened her notebook. "Describe it."

"Black. New. Big truck — Dodge Ram or Chevy Silverado. What caught my eye were the wheels. Those chrome full-throttle warrior rims. Been wanting to get some for my own truck."

Dodge. Like the truck that stopped beside her mother's car.

"Did you see the driver?"

He shook his head. "I was inside the guts of the tower."

None of them had seen it drive away.

Around the bend, she found tire tracks in the damp earth along the shoulder. She snapped photos, setting down a ruler to measure tread width. She took the distance between the tires' front and rear resting points. She radioed Guthrie and the techs.

She turned three hundred and sixty degrees. Farther along the blacktop, the bend sharpened and the road crossed the creek.

The morning sun lit the concrete railing on the side of the bridge.

It was right there. Scrawled in chalk.

When a soul betrays / it falls from flesh / and a demon takes its place.

She got on the radio to Guthrie. "He left a message. It's from the *Inferno.*"

"The actual text?"

"Yes."

"He hasn't done that before."

"He knows we know. Or he wants us to know. It's a slap in the face."

The sun sharpened. The chalk lit bright white. At the far end of the bridge, there was further writing. Smaller. She jogged down the bank so she could read it.

"There's more." It was tiny, jagged, scrawled askew on the railing. " 'Bone of my bones and flesh of my flesh.' "

"That's from the Bible," Guthrie said.

Caitlin pulled up Search and typed in the phrase. "Genesis. The story of Adam's rib."

She read the next line of verse. *Therefore*

shall a man leave his father and his mother, and shall cleave unto his wife: and they shall be one flesh.

"What do you make of it?" he said.

One flesh. Falls from flesh. Cleave unto his wife. Cleaver. "I think it means Deralynn is the first act. Her husband could be the second."

She started running. "Guthrie. We may have an emergency."

45

In the war room, Caitlin tried yet again to reach Walt Hobbs. He didn't pick up on his home phone. The phone company provided his cell number, but he didn't answer either voice calls or texts. At his desk, Guthrie slammed down his own phone.

"Hendrix. You positive Hobbs took the kids camping at Mount Diablo Park? The rangers can't locate them."

"Yes. They should be there."

When she'd spoken to Deralynn overnight, Deralynn told her Walt and the boys had already left. But something felt very wrong.

Everything felt wrong.

Guthrie said, "If the rangers can't locate them ... ." He picked up his phone again. "We'll send a unit."

He made the call, then stormed past her desk. Caitlin said, "They'll have to do a death notification. Walt Hobbs doesn't know

419

about Deralynn."

"Then that's what they'll do."

Her stomach knotted. She followed him toward the front of the station. "I . . ."

He spun. *"What?"*

People turned to look, or pretended not to.

"You want to spend the morning driving around a state park looking for kids and a dad hiking in the woods?" Guthrie said.

"I should." The thought stung her, left her drenched in dread. "I'll go."

"You will not," Guthrie said.

"But I'm the —"

"No, you're not. The Prophet killed Deralynn Hobbs because he's a psychopath. Not because of you. Don't make yourself a martyr."

She shut her mouth.

"The Hobbs home is a crime scene. Cops are crawling all over it. If Walt Hobbs comes home, he'll be notified." Guthrie's face was white. "Focus on the evidence. The Prophet probably has another victim in his sights."

"What if Walt Hobbs *is* the next victim?"

"That's why I'm sending a unit to Mount Diablo Park."

He stalked off. Caitlin stood for a moment, hearing chatter and phones and feeling the heat of the station's gaze.

Across the building at the front desk, a voice said, "Detective?"

Paige looked at her sheepishly. Beyond the glass in the lobby stood Sean.

Caitlin took a calming breath, walked past surreptitious stares, and buzzed through the door. Sean had Sadie's pink backpack slung over his shoulder. He was holding the little girl's hand and had Shadow, on a leash. The space between him and Caitlin felt charged. Paige watched like they were a telenovela.

Sadie jumped, arms wide. "Boo!"

"Hello, Roo." Caitlin smiled weakly and said to Sean, "Let's go outside."

They stepped into the breezy morning. Clouds scudded across the sky.

Sean nodded at the building. "What was all that?"

She looked at Sadie. Sean put Shadow's leash into his daughter's hand, pointed across the lawn, and said, "Walk her to that tree and back. *Walk.*"

Sadie toddled off with Shadow trotting at her side.

Caitlin said, "This latest killing." She clenched her jaw, forcing her voice to stay even. "It was Deralynn Hobbs."

Sean's face dropped. "Jesus God."

"Her name hasn't been released because we can't contact her husband."

He touched a hand to his forehead. "De-ralynn. Christ, that's —"

"He should be camping with the kids at Mount Diablo Park, but the rangers haven't located them." *Breathe. Do not fucking cry.* "Guthrie's sending uniforms. But . . ." She pressed a clawed hand to her heart. "He told me to stay here and work the evidence. But I . . ."

"Caitlin, I'm sorry."

"It was Deralynn. *Deralynn.* How can I just stay here?"

"Because stopping the Prophet is what counts."

"*Finding* the Prophet is what counts. And I'm close." She heard her voice rising. "If I find Walt Hobbs, I'm even closer. And it shouldn't be a choice." *Don't yell.* She held up her hands. "I know how I sound. This is just driving me right to the edge."

"Past that."

His face had the Apache raider stare.

"Last night I screwed up." She touched his arm. He didn't react.

Oh, shit.

"I know I blew it. Bad. Please. I'm sorry." She waited.

He looked at the street. "I understand. I used to say the same stuff to Michele."

Her hand dropped from his arm. "Low blow."

"No, truth. I see it, and I understand where you are." He turned his eyes to Sadie a moment, then to Caitlin. "You think you're doing your job. But the case is consuming you."

"No. I've got this."

"You don't. Deralynn — it's awful. But you cannot hand your life over to the Prophet in response."

She tried to cool down, and failed. "You're kidding, right? Deralynn's dead — and he *watched me.* In my own home."

"You're following his script. The other day you said he was playing a mind game. He is. On you. And you're letting him. You have to stop."

"I have to stop *him.* Any way I can."

"Listen to yourself. Guthrie asked you to work the evidence, and you blew him off? You're such a ball of rage, you don't even see where you are."

"I can't apologize enough for last night."

"Forget last night. I don't care about that. I care that you think it's up to you to single-handedly stop a tsunami."

"I don't know any other way," she said.

"Find one."

She was wound as tight as a kettledrum.

She didn't want to hear any of this, and certainly not from him.

"I don't need life-coaching today. I need DNA and fingerprints and the plate number for the Prophet's truck. Witnesses. A neighbor who saw him take Deralynn. Somebody. Didn't *anybody* see him? It's a friendly neighborhood and *nobody* stopped the abduction . . ."

She pressed a fist to her lips.

Sean's eyes were hot. He looked angry. He looked exasperated and worried. She took a juddering breath and reached out to him again. He stepped back.

Dammit. God*dammit* — what was she doing?

She touched her fingers to the corners of her eyes, battling down tears and the urge to punch a wall and the quiver that threatened to break on her lips.

"You're right," she finally said. "He's in my head, and I need to kick him out." She tipped her head back. "You're right. And do you have any idea how much I hate being called on my bullshit?"

His expression eased. "That's what comes from thinking it's up to you to spin the world back onto its axis."

The wind lifted her hair. She looked at

the ground, and up at him. His eyes softened.

He said, "All we can actually do is keep it from blowing up for one more day."

"Spoken like an explosives expert."

She reached for his hand. After a moment, he took hers. They held on, tentatively. Sadie and Shadow reached the tree and headed back toward them.

Caitlin tightened her grip. "I hate to tell you this. If the Prophet accessed everything in my computer and phone, he has your number. And if he has that . . ."

"You think his RAT malware could have infected my cell?"

"I hope to God not. But . . ." The wind gusted. A shiver overtook her. "You were on the news footage in Berkeley. He might try to put a name to your face."

"I'll be careful." He frowned. "What are you saying?"

Caitlin watched Sadie as she skipped up, cheeks pink in the breeze. She had a dandelion in her hand. She held it up to Caitlin.

Caitlin crouched down. "You blow."

Sadie put the dandelion to her lips and blew. When the seeds swirled into the air, she laughed delightedly. Caitlin stood and turned to Sean. His eyes were hard.

"I'll drop Sadie at Michele's," he said.

"And I'll tell Michele to head up to Eureka, to her mom and dad's place."

Relief washed through her. "Good. I hate this. But that's good."

"I have to work this afternoon anyhow."

"Hell of an Easter weekend."

"CIs don't stick to business hours. It's part of their charm." He scooped Sadie into his arms. "Okay, rug rat. We're going to Mommy's."

She clapped. "Yay!"

He took Shadow's leash. "She can bunk with me until you come up for air."

He leaned in and pressed his forehead against Caitlin's. "Which has to be before you drown."

She closed her eyes. Sean clasped the back of her neck, kissed her hard, and turned away. As he left, he nodded at the station.

"Don't leave here without security. That's not obsessive — it's necessary."

He walked toward his truck. Sadie peered bright-eyed over his shoulder and gave Caitlin a little wave.

Caitlin waved back.

Martinez leaned out the door of the building. "Hendrix. You need to get in here."

An ominous mood pervaded the war room as Caitlin approached her desk. Guthrie,

Shanklin, and Martinez were hovering.

On her computer screen, a bright red window had opened. It was flashing like a warning siren.

"Holy hell." She sat down but didn't touch the keyboard. "You call IT? If he's in our system, past the firewall, then . . ."

"We can't sanitize it." Guthrie picked up the phone and asked for one of their computer experts to come to the war room.

"He's showing off," she said. "He's not hiding anymore."

"Open it," Guthrie said.

Caitlin clicked. The image burst with twinkling stars and flames and a sound like thunder cracking.

The screen faded from stars to a dim room with a white sheet hung on the back wall. Caitlin felt a stabbing sensation between her eyes.

The camera was aimed at Deralynn. She sat gagged with duct tape and bound to a kitchen chair.

Her eyes brimmed with tears.

Martinez muttered, "Jesus, save us."

Caitlin's hands drew tight into fists.

Deralynn, hair matted and bloodied. Mascara streaked. Those eyes, so wide and always hopeful, were focused on the figure behind the camera. She was terrified.

427

But she wasn't panicked.

That was what Caitlin saw. Deralynn was in the throat of the monster, but she wasn't panicking. She couldn't move. She was at his mercy, and knew he would show her none. But she wasn't screaming behind the duct tape. Wasn't kicking or trying to shy back from the killer in front of her.

She was focused. The light bore down on her, third-degree style. She looked directly into the camera. Tears welled. She blinked them away and kept looking at the camera. She blinked and blinked and didn't flinch.

Off camera, the killer spoke in a hoarse whisper. "How far can you fall?"

Deralynn inhaled and seemed to bear down, staring even harder at the camera.

"The Ninth Circle contains room enough for all," the voice said. "More to come."

The video cut away, to footage of people strolling along the Embarcadero outside the Ferry Building on the bay in San Francisco.

Come back, Deralynn, Caitlin thought. An ache throbbed in her chest.

The tourist footage continued. Then, abruptly, it cut from the Ferry Building to photos of a cross-country race in a hillside park with the Rockridge Ragers. Michele's face was visible. Then it jumped to TV footage shot by the news chopper over the stadium on the Berkeley campus, looking down as Caitlin pulled away from Sean and charged at the scoreboard. Then to a dash-cam video — a slow roll past the Briarwood Sheriff's Station.

Caitlin's heart spiked. The video cut again, to a crowded BART train. Then went black.

Gathered around her desk, everyone stood silent. Caitlin's chin was trembling. *Get a grip,* she told herself.

Guthrie said, "Play it again."

She cued it up. Just before she clicked, her phone rang. She jumped.

Number Blocked.

She looked at Guthrie. Her hand hovered over the buzzing phone. She picked up on speaker.

"Your arrogance has dragged you to this chasm," the voice said. "Your pride, daring to challenge me."

"You're no messenger of heaven. You sin like everybody else. You belong in a ditch in the Eighth Circle with the other hypocrites," Caitlin said. "The net is closing."

He hung up.

Caitlin set the phone down. She didn't want to touch it. She wanted to leap through the ceiling and fly away screaming.

Martinez said, "He's rattled. The fucker's

429

rattled."

He clapped her on the shoulder. She was shaking.

"You rattled him, Hendrix. Fuckin' A."

But she knew: He had already targeted his next victims. A crushing weight settled on her. That was the message in the bayside footage, the BART scenes. With scenes from her life sandwiched between. The case was not behind her. His next victims were being watched and tracked. Somebody was marked for death.

46

Amid the war room's cacophony of voices and ringing phones, Caitlin sat before her screen, staring at the frozen image of Deralynn. Beaten, terrorized, knowing she faced horror and death, knowing she would never see her children again.

And yet she refused to flinch. She seemed to strain forward against the duct tape that bound her to the chair. She seemed fierce, and determined.

Just an amateur. A stay-at-home mom. Caitlin had never seen such a look of courage before.

She hit PLAY. The sound of the Prophet's breathing sent a nauseating shudder down her spine. She forced the sound to the background of her mind, and watched Deralynn.

The blinking. It caused tears to fall, but didn't stop when those tears slid down Deralynn's cheeks. It had a purpose, beyond physical reaction. It was patterned.

"It's a code. It has to be," she said under her breath.

Her phone rang. Dad. She declined the call and texted, Call the station. A moment later her desk phone rang. She picked up.

"My cell phone's compromised," she said. "Yours may be too. Until we find out, call from a landline."

Mack paused only a second, as if that news barely surprised him. "Understood. Now — two things. Then I'll let you go. First. You can do this. I know it."

She closed her eyes and pressed her lips together.

"Second. Let me help." His voice throbbed with fury and determination. "Lure him into a trap. Use me as bait."

"Dad."

"You think I'm off my meds. I'm not. But I'll go off to help. Stop sedating a tricky cop like me and I can wreak all kinds of havoc on your behalf. Give me a few hours."

She tried to laugh, then sobered. "Dad . . . thanks. It's not going to happen, but — thank you."

In the call background, the air brakes of a bus hissed. Coins dropped in a slot. There was the rumble of a diesel engine pulling away from the bus stop.

"Where are you going?" she said.

"To your mom's. I'm going to stay with her until it's time for her to go to the airport."

"Thank you."

"Caitlin — what I said . . . this is no joke." He was calm. A long-missing grit had returned to his voice. "Whatever it takes. Call me."

She hung up. Raggedly she watched the video again. Deralynn was desperately trying to tell them something. The intense blinking had to be a code, almost certainly Morse.

She rewound to the start of the video. Deralynn stared. A long, solid stare. Then she began to blink. Caitlin counted. Forty times. Deralynn shut her eyes and dipped her head. When she looked up, she started again. She blinked twenty-two times. And again. Twenty-two.

The same pattern. Dots and dashes. Thinking, *I hear you,* Caitlin found a Morse code chart. She transcribed Deralynn's message and translated it.

P-L-U-S-J-T-P-V-M-G-B-M-M.

It made no sense.

"What?" she said. "God, Deralynn . . . what are you saying?"

Caitlin was no authority on cryptography.

Yes, she'd seen through the metaphor in the Prophet's cornfield message, and spotted the acrostic in his notes. Her father had intuited the killer's cycle from his message about the sky. But they weren't trained to decipher codes.

Could she enlist help from cryptography experts? The CIA and NSA had been called in to analyze the cryptograms in the Zodiac case.

And they'd failed. The only people who'd solved any of the Zodiac's puzzles were a married couple who saw one in the newspaper and tried it on a whim. And even if the sheriff's office got hold of the spooks, it would take a bureaucratic age to get help. That wasn't going to happen on a holiday weekend.

But Deralynn wanted someone to see and understand her. For a second, Caitlin felt paralyzed.

She stood and went to the women's room. She splashed water on her face. Her reflection was pale, eyes spooked beneath stringy hair. The corner of the mirror was cracked.

A sharp edge of the glass shone green. For an instant, an old craving stirred and bared its teeth. *Cut.*

Bring the pain. Take control.

She exhaled. That craving had sold her

lies. Always. She turned her right palm up.
The tattoo was there.

the whole sky

She closed her eyes. When she opened
them, she returned to her desk.

She reminded herself: *Set your feelings
aside and focus on the job. Work the evidence.*

Calming down, forcing herself to concentrate, she started over: with the video.

She played it again. 40 blinks. Then 22.
22. 22. 22. A repeating pattern.

The first iteration, the 40 blinks, had to
include a key.

She played the video once more, this time
in slow motion. She copied down the initial
sequence afresh. She had originally transcribed it as *P-L-U-S-J.* But with Deralynn's
tears, the number of blinks in that last letter
was actually ambiguous. She checked the
Morse code chart for other possibilities. She
came up with *P-L-U-S-1.*

Was Deralynn telling her to take letters
she was blinking and move one letter farther
in the alphabet?

She tried it. *U-Q-W-N-H-C-N-N.* Garbage.

Come on, Caitlin thought. It was here. Deralynn didn't miss this one. Then it fell
across her shoulders like rain: Go one letter
back.

Deralynn had thought of the word she wanted to convey, then blinked it out — plus one step forward in the alphabet for each letter in the word. To decipher the code, Caitlin needed to take the letters Deralynn had blinked and move one step in the other direction, toward the start of the alphabet.

S-O-U-L-F-A-L-L.

She tore through the duffel bag beneath her desk and grabbed her father's journal.

At scene, words scratched in fence with a nail. "The soul falls headlong."

That line from the *Inferno* echoed the message scrawled in chalk on the bridge that morning. *When a soul betrays / it falls from flesh / and a demon takes its place.*

Holding her breath, she checked FindtheProphet.com. Yes. There, on the message board, she found him. A registered member. Screen name: Soulfall.

The Prophet.

Caitlin raised her fists. Her eyes welled. "Deralynn, you did it. You did it, girl."

Across the room, Shanklin frowned at Caitlin. Then her expression softened. She rose at the same time Caitlin did.

"We need Computer Forensics," Caitlin

said. "We've got him. We've got a lead."

It took an hour, but Caitlin managed to get one of the site administrators for Find the Prophet to pick up a phone.

"We can't violate our privacy policy," the man said.

He sounded young and rushed. But then, the object of his obsessions had just reached through the computer screen and interrupted the site's amateur enthusiasm with a meat cleaver.

"We can get a warrant," Caitlin said. "But you can help us get the information we need more quickly."

"Then get a warrant." He sounded overly brave. There was a quaver in his voice.

"Deralynn was a friend of mine," Caitlin said. "I was at the crime scene this morning."

"Don't try to scare me into doing your job for you."

She heard the emotion beneath his words, and backed off.

"I'm not. Before Deralynn died, she left information that might help end this whole thing. She aimed us back to the message board. John — can I call you John?"

A pause. "Sure."

"You have a mole."

A longer pause. "Crap."

"A dangerous mole. Who might already be drawing a target on people. Think about it. Deralynn had administrator privileges, and she gave me this information. She wanted us all to use it."

There was an even longer pause. "Yeah. All right."

"Thank you." Caitlin signaled thumbs-up to Guthrie in his office. "The easiest thing is to give me a log-in and password to your site's back end."

He set her up with a temporary username and password. She thanked him again. "Don't say a word to anyone, John. Don't mention anything on the forum. We're on this."

Going to the site, she logged in. She silently traced Soulfall's activity. It was sparse. He'd been a member for five years, but posted only a few times.

A lurker.

Her desk phone rang. Computer Forensics was calling, about tracking Soulfall's digital footprint. It was Eugene Chao, who had also analyzed the Prophet's early audiocassettes.

"Got him. The IP address he used to log in most recently."

"Location?" she said. "Can you get that?"

"Yeah. Because it's a corporate IP. Daedalus. Headquarters are in San Francisco. Give me a minute; let me see if I can get a little more granular."

She stayed on the line.

Chao came back. "It's a division of Daedalus, housed at their office in the Mission. That IP address belongs to a company called Zodiac Match."

47

Caitlin stood up at her desk. "Sergeant Guthrie." She put the call on speaker. "Say that again."

"The log-in came from the corporate offices of a company called Zodiac Match," Chao said. "It's a division of Daedalus Inc., which in turn is a branch of Aquarius Capital Systems. It's a multinational conglomerate."

Guthrie approached. Caitlin said, "It came physically from that address. It couldn't have been rerouted or masked or . . ."

"Soulfall submitted his comment to the message board from a device logged in to a network in the building that houses Zodiac Match."

She and Guthrie exchanged a look. Guthrie said, "That sounds either sloppy or unbelievably convenient, given the guy we're talking about."

"Let me see what else I can find out. I'll

get back to you."

"Go," Caitlin said, and ended the call.

Guthrie stood hunched in thought. Caitlin said, "Is he still toying with us?"

Chao came back half an hour later. "Have a contact who works for Aquarius. That log-in at Zodiac Match was made from a cell phone that connected to the company's Guest network."

"Tell me it wasn't a burner," Caitlin said.

"It was. No calls before or since."

"Goddammit."

"Hold your horses. Zodiac Match has two networks. One for employees, and one, as the name suggests, for guests. That office in the Mission is their core programming center, and they are paranoid about network security," he said.

"So the guest could have been anybody. Someone off the street."

"No. All guests sign in at the desk. They're logged in to the system. And the morning the comment was posted, no guests were signed in. Soulfall wasn't a guest there. He tried to be slick, and slipped up. He's an employee."

She made a fist. "Names?"

"Got their entire corporate directory. I'll send it. I've flagged a dozen people I consider most promising. Folks with technical

441

know-how, who live in the Bay Area."

"Beautiful."

Chao listed the names he'd flagged. Caitlin scribbled them down. Five were women, whom she discounted. Seven men.

"More info on the men?" she said.

Chao gave her their ages, nationalities, and the length of time they'd worked for the company. Three were in their midtwenties. Three others in their thirties. Two of those — Minsoo Kim and Wei Jian — had come to the United States within the last year on H-1B visas.

"What about the last guy?" Caitlin said.

"Your man Titus. DOB puts him at forty-seven. Programmer. His employee number indicates he's been with the company for a long time. A long, long time."

Her hands were tingling. She saw it now: a forty-seven-year-old core software programmer who had access to every client's dating profile. Phone numbers. Addresses. Passwords. Hell, people's *desires.* He could choose targets, install RAT software on their computers and phones, and remotely scout houses and businesses before he attacked.

"Can you get his employment records?" she said. "Address, phone?"

"Already have them."

"You're a golden god."

442

"Social engineering," he said, without explanation. "This guy just returned to the Bay Area after working overseas. Been an expat for a dozen years. Brussels, Hong Kong, London. I'll send you everything."

It came through a few seconds later. Caitlin leaned forward eagerly, reading, and stopped.

"This is his last name?" she said. "I thought you said 'Rome.'"

"No, Rhone. *R-H-O-N-E.* Like the river."

A sick, prickly feeling spread across her. "Hang on."

She found the sheriff's office personnel directory. Scanned, and her eyes snagged on a name. An address.

Jesus God. "I'll call you back."

She looked around the war room. Shanklin caught her eye. She frowned at Caitlin a long moment. Caitlin walked toward the front of the station, where Guthrie was huddled in intense conversation with Lieutenant Kogara. Caitlin heard Shanklin following her.

She sped up. As she approached Guthrie, he gave her a look that said, *Not now.*

She walked past him. Looking over her shoulder, she urged Shanklin to hurry.

She approached the front desk. The clerk was bent over a doughnut and her phone.

443

"Paige. Can we talk to you for a minute?"

The girl looked up with eager, avid eyes.

"You live in the Berkeley Hills, right?" Caitlin said.

"Yeah, the house I inherited from my mom."

"Alone?"

"No, my . . . why?"

"Your what?"

The happy enthusiasm became guarded. "Why do you want to know?"

"Who's Titus Rhone?" Caitlin said.

"I don't understand. He's only there temporarily, until he gets his own place."

Shanklin stepped closer. "What's this about?"

Caitlin pointed at the girl's name tag. "Paige?"

The clerk touched the tag. M. P. RHONE. "He's my dad."

"It's temporary. I told you," Paige said. "What's the problem?"

In an interview room, Paige hunched over a Formica table, picking at her nails. Caitlin sat across from her. Shanklin leaned against the wall. Mama Badger, ready to lunge.

"What kind of vehicle does your dad drive?" Caitlin said.

"I don't know why you're asking me all

these questions, but I feel kind of intimidated. This is like, microaggression."

"Oh. What kind of vehicle?"

"A hybrid. Chevy Volt."

Shanklin said, "Does he ever drive a pickup truck?"

Paige shook her head, but stopped, lips parted. Shanklin straightened.

"Dodge Ram?" Caitlin said.

Paige's face cleared. "That was Tanner's."

"Who's Tanner?"

"This is about the truck? Why didn't you say so?" Her face brightened.

"Paige."

"My ex-boyfriend. His Ram got stolen last month. Did you find it?"

Shanklin said, "What's Tanner's last name?"

"DeVries. It's a white Ram, pre-owned but like new."

"White?" Caitlin said. "Rims?"

"Oh, God, yes. Those chrome full-throttle warrior rims. He loves those things."

Caitlin nodded. Guthrie was watching the video feed and would now be checking for a stolen Dodge Ram owned by Tanner DeVries.

"Where was it stolen?" she said.

"My street. Tanner went ballistic. Supposed to be a safe neighborhood. And he said the truck couldn't be hot-wired. You need the key fob to start the engine. Is that true? That's one of the things I need to learn if I'm going to apply to the academy." She smiled. "That's why I'm working here. Get a head start on that stuff."

Caitlin nodded. "Good plan. Tanner got mad at you?" she said sympathetically.

"One reason he left. Like *I* made his stupid truck disappear." Paige tossed her hair. "No big loss."

Shanklin, in Caitlin's peripheral vision, looked like she was using every ounce of restraint not to shake the girl. Caitlin heard it all in the interstices of Paige's ramble. If her father was living with her, how hard would it be for him to steal the keys to the truck while Paige's boyfriend was at the house?

Not much harder than getting the truck painted black.

"Did Tanner accuse your dad of losing the fob?" she said.

"Oh, yeah. Ranting and strutting around, pointing his finger. Dad just walked out of the room. That set Tanner off too." She exhaled. "Good riddance."

Caitlin folded her hands. "Are you and your dad close?"

"Course. Working on it. I hadn't seen him,

yeah, since I was little. But he asked, and he's family, so he's staying with me. For now. But we're getting close. He understands me. He's the one who said I should apply for this job. 'You'd be an awesome cop.' Besides, he gave me my real first name." She tapped her name badge. M. P. RHONE. "Myrrha. Myrrha Paige. One of a kind. Because I'm one of a kind. It's too weird to use, but . . ." She looked back and forth between Caitlin and Shanklin. "That's something, right?"

"It sure is." Caitlin stood up. "Hang here a sec. I'll be right back. You want a Coke?"

"Please."

She headed for the door. "Remember a necklace with a hummingbird pendant? You sold it on eBay, right?"

"That was years ago." Paige frowned. "What did Tanner say? I had permission. I mean, Dad forgot it. He never asked for it."

"Sure. Diet?"

Shanklin gave her the eye. Caitlin strolled out calmly. When she shut the door, she pulled out her phone and searched. *Myrrha.*

Greek mythology: Myrrha was the mother of Adonis. She was turned into a myrrh tree after lusting for her father, the king, and having intercourse with him.

"Damn." New search. *Myrrha + Inferno.*

447

Canto XXX. Line 24.

I beheld two shadows pale and naked,
Who, biting, in the manner ran along
That a boar does, when from the sty turned
   loose.

She scrolled. The shades sank tusks into other shades' necks, savagely tearing them apart.

That is the ancient ghost
Of the nefarious Myrrha, who became
Beyond all rightful love her father's lover.
She came to sin with him after this manner,
By counterfeiting of another's form

Caitlin stood chilled in the hall. "One of a kind. No kidding."

Daughter of a vicious, legendary UNSUB. What a legacy.

Guthrie stepped out of the monitoring room. "The pendant."

"That was a shot in the dark. Lucky hit." She shrugged, abashed but excited. "And Myrrha is a character from the *Inferno*. It's him."

Guthrie handed her an eight-by-ten photo, a driver's license blowup.

The photo showed a man in his midforties. Slim, Caucasian, superficially unexceptional. But the very air in the hallway seemed to cool. It was his eyes. Hot under the lights, a heavy brown that let nothing past. Lips parted as though about to say something suggestive to the DMV worker. Conspiratorial. The near smile showed a crowded mouth of crooked teeth. Thinning hair, a few long strands combed straight back. He looked like a road-worn Matthew McConaughey. Chummy expression. With a complete sense of assurance and utter emptiness behind it.

Titus Rhone.

She looked at Guthrie. "That's him."

48

At two P.M. they assembled in the war room: the raid team, readying for the takedown of Titus Rhone. The atmosphere crackled. Guthrie briefed the team on Rhone. The Special Response Unit commander laid out the tactical plan.

"Target residence is a single-family dwelling in the Berkeley Hills." The commander used a laser pointer to indicate Paige Rhone's home on the satellite map projected on a whiteboard. "Our approach will be via Winderaker Road."

Caitlin stood cracking her knuckles. Inside her, a turbine seemed to spin to life, ready to unload energy in an electric flash. Her SIG was holstered. She had two extra clips of ammunition in her left jeans pocket. A folding knife with a drop-point blade in her right. She tightened her ballistic vest.

Nearby, Shanklin looked focused. Martinez stood with his hands at his sides. His beach-bartender demeanor had blown away; he was pure fight. Guthrie looked like he had loaded every bit of information about the operation into his very cell structure. The SRU team stood at parade rest, their dark fatigues monolithic and intimidating.

The commander finished his briefing and turned the floor over to Guthrie.

"This is a suburban neighborhood. Family dwellings to three sides of the target. Sunny afternoon. Presume kids will be playing outside." He clicked to close-up photos of the house. They'd been obtained from Paige's phone, which she had handed over willingly.

Paige remained in the interview room, reluctant to talk now that she realized something bad was going on and she was in the middle of it. Caitlin couldn't believe Paige was as clueless as she presented herself. Not if Titus Rhone had urged her to apply for a job with the sheriff's office. Not if she was encouraged to keep her eyes and ears open and share that information with him. Keenly. Like a friendly kitten, instinctively driven to rip apart small animals without remorse.

Guthrie clicked through photos of the house. "We had a plainclothes officer perform a drive-by of the residence in an

451

unmarked car, fifteen minutes ago." He raised a hand. "The officer's personal vehicle, not anything the suspect could make. He reports the suspect's Chevy Volt is parked in the driveway."

The SRU commander said, "We have eyes on the dwelling. Front and back. The vehicle is still in the driveway and nobody has left the house."

Guthrie squared up to the room. "This man is presumed to be armed. He is exceptionally dangerous." He looked at each member of the team individually. "Let's do this."

With a rustle of gear, they moved. Adrenaline seemed to tingle in the air. As Caitlin turned to go, Guthrie stopped her.

"Walt Hobbs came home. He and the boys are safe."

"Thank God."

Even as relief poured through her, grief welled at the thought of Deralynn, and what her family was now enduring. Guthrie briefly looked drained. She knew he had been the one to notify Walt Hobbs of his wife's murder. She nodded crisply.

As they headed through the door, the medical examiner came down the hall. Azir looked stern.

To Guthrie he said, "News?"

"Yeah." Guthrie nodded at the manila envelope in the ME's hand. "The autopsy results on Gaia Hill and J. T. Wilcox?"

Azir nodded. "I wanted you to have them as soon as possible." He watched the tactical team pass by, and Martinez, ballistic vest tight, badge hanging from a strap around his neck.

The ME said, "I don't need operational details, but — if you're attending another crime scene, or . . ."

Guthrie eyed him. "Or. Yes. And we're on our way."

"I won't keep you. But I will warn you. Take exceptional care with hazardous material exposure when you raid wherever you're going."

"Got it, Doc."

Guthrie started past, but the ME pointed at the manila envelope. "The mercury contamination at the last crime scene was off the scale. It's the vapor. It can be in the air and you won't know you're inhaling it."

Caitlin glanced at the envelope.

The ME frowned at her. "How many of these crime scenes have you attended?"

"Three. Four if you count the burning car."

"Closed environments, incendiary devices — those fireworks were poisonous."

453

Guthrie wanted to get going. So did Caitlin, but a dark worm was burrowing under her skin.

Azir said, "I'm issuing a bulletin about the dangers of mercury vapor. You need to take precautions not to suffer further exposure." He raised a finger to both her and Guthrie. "This could have permanent, catastrophic health consequences."

Guthrie was itching to move.

Azir waved. "Go. Be safe. But make sure your people are safe from mercury too. Not every deadly weapon is a bullet."

"Got it." Guthrie stalked down the hallway, headed for the car pool. Caitlin followed.

She turned and walked backward. "What consequences?"

"Tremors. Memory loss. A sensation that insects are crawling beneath the skin. Insomnia. Emotional volatility. Headaches. Loss of peripheral vision," he said. "Don't mess around with this."

"I understand."

Caitlin followed Guthrie outside into the sun. But a light had already flipped on. *Her father.*

Mack's symptoms. The shaking. The bugs crawling beneath his skin. The insomnia, the rage, the headaches, the gaps in memory.

The way he only saw you when you were right in front of him.

He wasn't rude or obstinate — he'd lost his peripheral vision.

She reached the car. Checked the shotgun in the trunk: broke it, looked down the barrel, snapped it shut, and assured herself that the box of shells was secure and ready. She replaced it, climbed behind the wheel, and fired up the engine with something approaching shock and dread and enlightenment.

Her father had mercury poisoning.

49

They rolled toward Paige Rhone's house under a blinding blue sky, racing past shotgun homes and tired apartment buildings on an overgrown Oakland hillside. The black SRU command vehicle spearheaded the convoy. At the wheel of an unmarked car behind it, Caitlin pressed her foot hard on the gas. A refrain ran in her head. *Come on, get there, do this. Take him.* The moments before had never felt as protracted, or as perilous.

Fifty yards from the driveway, the command vehicle braked to a stop, angling across the street. Two sheriff's office Chargers roared past it, lights flashing. Caitlin swung her car to a stop behind the command vehicle, angled the opposite way across the blacktop, blocking the road.

The Chargers cut off the far end of the road. The SRU team poured out of their vehicle. On the driveway sat Titus Rhone's gold Chevy Volt.

At the house, the curtains were closed. The front door stood in shadow. The place looked unexceptional and menacing. Still and hunched, as if growling at a frequency too low to hear.

Over the radio, Caitlin heard the leader of the SRU team that was staging at the back. *"In position."*

Caitlin drew her SIG. Her heart beat against her vest. Beside her, Guthrie stared at the house as if he could hear it breathing. Shanklin's jaw looked tighter than a guy wire. Nearby, Martinez touched his crucifix. He caught Caitlin's gaze and nodded.

The SRU commander led them to the door, single file. They stacked up, and every second felt like a bottomless age. The commander signaled *Go.* Caitlin put her hand on Shanklin's shoulder and went in behind the battering ram, behind SRU's shouts and Guthrie's animal force.

The light was dingy, the rooms a warren. The house smelled of cigarettes and bleach and old books. Weapons level, they cleared the kitchen, living room, bathroom, bedroom, bedroom, garage. They swept closets, cupboards, cabinets, and the attic.

The house was empty. Rhone was gone.

■ ■ ■ ■

Caitlin stepped outside the Rhone house and walked to the Crime Lab truck. She brushed a strand of hair from her face with her forearm. She wore latex gloves and paper booties over her boots. She ignored the crowd that was gathering at the end of the street behind the sheriff's barricade.

Until she saw her father standing among them. Motionless, silent, watching.

She ducked under the yellow police tape and strode along the street to the barricade. The uniformed deputy doing crowd control was Lyle, who had been at Silver Creek Park the night the crow-filled car burned.

Caitlin pointed at Mack. "He's with me."

Lyle let Mack around the barrier. She drew her father out of the crowd's earshot.

"What are you doing here?" she said.

He wore a heavy work shirt with a frayed collar, jeans, and mud-caked boots. He hadn't shaved. He held up his phone.

"Police scanner app. I heard the code for a tactical op go out as I was heading back to San Francisco. Nobody mentioned the Prophet, but I read between the lines." He looked at the house. "What is it?"

She knew what happened when somebody

458

broke big news to Mack. His circuits fried. He could explode or withdraw, turn turtle. But Lieutenant Kogara had scheduled an imminent press conference. This was going to break in the next few minutes. Mack deserved to hear it from her. She breathed.

"We know who he is," she said.

Mack stilled like a spike driven into the ground.

"His name is Titus Rhone. We know this for sure. It's him."

She waited for him to react. His gaze lengthened beyond the horizon. Then his face crumpled. And his knees.

"Dad." She put a hand beneath his elbow.

He caught himself, straightened, raised a hand. "Titus Rhone." He said it slowly, one syllable at a time. "My God. How?"

She explained how they'd traced him. Then got her phone and pulled up Rhone's driver's license photo. "This is him today."

Mack looked. For long, aching seconds.

"There's something wrong with him. You can see it," he said.

She nodded. He continued staring into the photo. He looked up at her. "You . . ."

Pressed his lips together. Fought back emotion.

"Caitlin." He reached out with a shaking hand and looked like he might squeeze her arm. "Unbelievable." He whispered it. "You found him."

"We still have to *catch* him. But he's on the run now. He can't come back here. BO-LOs, full press, blanket news coverage. He can't hide anymore. We'll get him."

"But his house . . ."

"He just lost his home base."

He whispered something she couldn't make out. A prayer, maybe. A curse. He looked at her with dark eyes and nodded. He didn't need to say anything else. She took his hand and held on. He looked at the house, his expression unreadable.

"There's something else you need to know. It can't wait," she said.

He kept staring at the house. She paused. But there was no way except forward.

"Dad. Everybody working the Prophet crime scenes has been exposed to mercury vapor." She squeezed his hand, trying to capture his attention. "You more than anyone."

His head turned slowly, as though on a swivel.

"You've been poisoned," she said.

His lips parted but he said nothing.

"The ME ran down the symptoms. Tremors. Bugs below the skin. Auditory and visual —"

"Hallucinations." His voice was distant, as if he'd been pulled underwater. "Colors and lights. Snakes at the edge of my eye, slithering around the corner every time I look."

"Your restricted peripheral vision." Her voice was close to cracking. "The depression. Withdrawal. Anger."

He looked catatonic. Caitlin thought she'd made a huge mistake. He stayed silent for a long minute. She waited for an explosion, but when he spoke again, he was calm.

"You're saying this has affected me for twenty years?" he said.

"Heavy-metal poisoning. Yes."

He closed his eyes and shook his head, as though it was unbelievable.

"Tomorrow we hit the doctors. A full workup," she said.

Now he frowned. "You think there's something I can do?"

"There has to be." To relieve his tormented existence. To repair him.

"Most heavy-metal poisoning is permanent." His expression darkened. "The ME's concerned about *you*."

Fear flicked through her. "Now we know to take precautions."

She said it quickly. She couldn't let fear distract her.

Mack stared, seemingly at nothing. "Saunders and I were first on scene at a victim's house where a kitchen trash can was set on fire. It was full of smashed fluorescent bars. We extinguished it and opened the windows — aired the house out before the crime scene team arrived . . ."

"You didn't tell anyone?" Caitlin said.

"At that point, what difference would it have made?"

She felt dismayed. "Maybe all the difference. This changes . . ."

"Everything?" he said.

She felt a pang. "Yes. No."

She told herself to get calm.

She said, "I blamed you. For things that weren't your fault."

He took a beat. "But they were."

She looked at him urgently. "I was still wrong."

"Because of mercury."

"Yes. No."

He almost laughed. For a brief second, the cop's sense of gallows humor lit his face.

She had blamed him for everything. Now she saw a cascade of cause and effect — homicide work, and his dedication beyond the call of duty, and the newlyweds' murder, Saunders dying, and mercury streaming through his veins.

"You didn't jump into the abyss. It

grabbed you and pulled you in." She gripped his hand. "You took on more than one person could carry. I only blame you for trying to shoulder it all."

He held still for a second. A stone. Then he nodded at the house.

"You get back to work."

She kept hold of his hand. "I don't want you to be alone."

"I need to be. When this is over we'll talk." He nodded, seemingly to himself. Then he turned a blistering look on her. "You find this son of a bitch and drag him to the ground."

50

The wind scurried across the asphalt, blowing empty fast-food wrappers along the road. Choke weeds and thistles crept through the chain-link fence. Sean Rawlins eased his truck along the alley, avoiding broken beer bottles that had shattered against the side of a Dumpster.

What a spot for an Easter egg hunt.

But confidential informants didn't generally meet him in the bar at the Fairmont. And in truth, he didn't mind. In fact, he loved this.

Explosives was a funny job. He worked the side of the street that tried to keep explosive materials out of the hands of idiots and maniacs. He wasn't Explosives Enforcement. *Those* guys were crazy. *Cut the blue wire.* Bomb Disposal: full-on nuts.

He went after nitwits who didn't care whether a factory blew up, and moral deficients who wanted jetliners to break up at altitude. He stopped explosions before they ever got to the stage where a detonator could be attached.

The public had little idea how many explosives filled the world around them and, in his experience, didn't appreciate how useful explosives were. In mining and demolition. Avalanche control. Fire extinguishers, air-bag inflators. Fireworks. Special effects.

Better living through chemistry. As long as explosives detonated only at the right time.

Explosives specialists tended to come at the job from either a chemistry or an electronics background. Sean's degree was in chem. He could analyze explosive materials ranging from dynamite and other high explosives to black powder, pellet powder, initiating explosives, detonators, safety fuses, squibs, detonating cord, igniter cord, and igniters. Materials that — despite what some sovereign citizen types thought — it was illegal to ship, transport, or receive without a license or permit.

Of course, organized crime, jihadists, white supremacists, and various wackos disregarded that prohibition. Thus sending him out on Easter Sunday to investigate and interdict.

This tip had come in to the ATF's San Francisco Field Division. The tipster claimed that blasting materials were being diverted from a construction company that did highway work in the Sierras. Couple of guys were selling an ANFO/emulsion blend to an outlaw motorcycle club. Bikers more commonly dealt in guns — ATF was always chasing that — and if they were moving into the big boom, it was bad news.

One of Sean's colleagues had worked the CI for a month, before bringing Sean in. The guy wanted to meet. Today, he said. This afternoon. He wanted to negotiate payment and an immunity agreement.

Sean drove past workshops and warehouses that were shuttered for the weekend. In the distance, the loading cranes of the Port of Oakland rose above the docks, like AT-AT walkers from *The Empire Strikes Back*. He followed the chain-link fence deeper into the complex. He saw a man outside a building on the other side of the fence. The guy was leaning against the wall, smoking. When Sean slowed, the guy tossed the butt and hurried toward him, looking around.

Sean pulled alongside the fence. He texted the supervisory special agent in charge — his boss. At meet. Then he put down the passenger window.

The guy hunched into his shirt and squinted through the fence at Sean. His hair blew across his eyes. He acted like he was on the lookout for the Walking Dead.

"You aren't Peretta," he said.

"Peretta couldn't make it. And she told you I would be coming."

The guy tilted his head thoughtfully. "What, she had her baby last night?"

Sean gave him a neutral look.

The guy cracked a smile. "Huh."

"Rawlins," Sean said.

"Dix."

It was the guy. He looked around again, squirrel style.

There was a gate just ahead, but Dix said, "Can't come in this way. CCTV still works on this side. Go down to the corner of the building and around." He pointed at the long road between warehouses. Beyond it, bright in the afternoon sun, a container ship steamed across the bay.

"I'll meet you there," the man said.

Sean drove to the corner. He checked for tails, for lookouts, for any suspicious activity. It was a vast industrial site, dirty and rundown and empty on a holiday weekend. Which was ordinary. He saw nothing suspicious.

Around the corner, a couple of hundred yards up the road, Dix pushed open a rolling gate. Signs on the fence indicated the property was a teardown. Yeah. The kind of place that was good for hiding stolen materials. And not great for keeping explosives safe. Sean parked outside and walked through the gate.

The building was the size of an airplane hangar, boxy, faceless, and seemingly abandoned. Seagulls circled overhead, screeching. He walked past rusting fifty-five-gallon drums that didn't look OSHA compliant. The CI unlocked the door, looking around like a spooked prairie dog. Sean took off his sunglasses and accompanied him inside.

The space was empty, and echoed like a high school gym. The factory floor had been stripped, but he could still see the bolts and anchor points where machine tools had once stood.

"This where they're going to make the delivery?" Sean said.

"Let's talk about immunity."

"Give me delivery dates, descriptions of the vehicles they're using. Names. Cell phone numbers. Then we can talk about immunity."

Dix ran his hand across his stomach like the idea gave him indigestion. "Okay — but

468

one thing at a time. Next delivery's gonna come in here at the loading dock."

"Show me."

"Other end of the building." He led Sean toward the door at the far side of the factory floor. "But quick. Don't want to hang here a second longer than I have to."

Nobody said following a tip about contraband purchases of bomb-making material was easy. Mostly because you dealt with squirrels. But this was serious. Ammonium nitrate and fuel oil primed with nitroglycerine dynamite, allegedly. Truck-bomb shit.

The screeching of the gulls was dulled by the walls. Outside the high, grimy windows, clouds skimmed past in the acrylic-blue sky. In the next room, Sean saw pallets covered with blue tarps, and more fifty-five-gallon drums stacked along the walls. Pipes and spools of copper wire, possibly stolen from a construction site. When they reached the far end of the room, Dix got his keys to unlock the door to a back hall.

"Hold up," Sean said. He was looking at the drums.

"Forget that shit. Keep moving. I know it's Easter Sunday, but the guys doing this, they ain't pious Christians. They could show up anytime."

The CI unlocked the door. The hallway

was dark. He flipped a light switch but nothing happened.

"Hang on." Dix jogged down the hallway. Sean pulled the door open wide and followed. Dix tried a switch farther down the hall. Still nothing. He rounded a corner into the dim recesses of the building.

"What the fuck?" he said.

Sean pulled his jacket back and set his hand on the butt of his pistol. From around the corner came scuffling sounds and a muffled shout. Empty barrels clanged and toppled to the concrete.

Sean drew his gun. He moved rapidly along the hall and stopped before the corner. He heard nothing.

This was bad. All caps *B-A-D*. It was dark. He was alone. He approached the corner at an angle. He raised his gun and incrementally cleared the intersecting hallway, one vertical slice at a time, stepping gradually closer to the turn. Nothing.

Commit. He swung around the corner. Halfway down the new hallway was a double door. He advanced, gut-checked, yanked open the door, vertically swept it again, and went through. He found barrels knocked over, like they'd been hit with a human bowling ball. Blood on one of them. A phone cracked and abandoned on the concrete. No sign of Dix.

He cleared the room and stopped. The walls were covered with wild drawings.

From floor level to eight feet up, the walls were spray-painted and chalked with psychedelic images. Demons torturing people in pits. Pigs digging their tusks into screaming men. Vultures with women's faces, ripping flesh from weeping trees.

A trail of nails was pounded into the walls. It looked like machine-gun fire.

This was an ambush, and he'd walked directly into it.

Weapon sweeping the room, he put a wall to his back and got his phone to call for backup. He had no signal. He saw that his text to his boss had failed to send.

Back off. Get out, find a signal.

From deeper in the building, Dix cried out. "Fuck, stop, oh, Christ, *don't* . . ."

Forget backing off.

Sean crossed the room, following the trail of nails to the door on the far side. Again he incrementally cleared it, and went. He advanced quickly into the room, sweeping it. Saw nobody. The CI had been dragged away. The wind blew through empty windows, and plastic sheeting flapped against the walls. At the far end of the room, shadows flickered beyond it.

471

The Prophet.

The son of a bitch who had sent him running onto an empty field while he tortured and murdered two women. The killer who wanted to destroy Caitlin.

Sean crossed the floor, gun raised, sweeping the room, and pulled the plastic sheeting back. There was a hole in the concrete floor. Spray-painted in front of it were the words *All Hope Abandon, Ye Who Enter Here.*

The hole in the concrete dropped to a tunnel far below. The wind whistled through it.

The shot came from the dark doorway he'd passed through, and hit him in the back.

51

Outside Rhone's house, Caitlin handed an evidence bag to a forensic tech and signed the chain of custody. Beyond the barricades, the crowd was swelling. TV crews jostled for position. A news helicopter hovered overhead. A second was inbound.

Lieutenant Kogara had made the official announcement that the sheriff's office was seeking a suspect in the Prophet killings. Titus Rhone's photo was everywhere, along with a warning: *Be on the lookout. Do not approach. Rhone is armed and extremely dangerous.*

Caitlin's phone buzzed with an incoming message. She pulled it from her pocket. She saw a number she didn't recognize: 925 area code. Pleasanton prefix. Sheriff's office prefix. She hesitated.

Subject: Re: Mercury.

She opened it. A video played.

Her legs turned to water. "Oh, Christ."

The sunlight seemed to shriek at her. On-screen was Sean. Weapon raised.

A figure swept from the shadows, raised a pneumatic nail gun, and shot him in the back. Twice.

Sean spun. Buckling, pain on his face. He aimed at the figure. Center mass. Fired.

The figure kept coming. Nail gun up. He shot Sean again, in the chest. Again and again.

Sean dropped.

The figure swept across the screen toward him. Kicked Sean's gun from his hand. Kicked him in the head. Sean lay still. The figure grabbed his arm and dragged him across a floor to a hole in the concrete. With the heel of a work boot, he kicked Sean over the edge into it.

The Prophet's voice seeped from the phone. "I heard Rawlins abandoned you when you needed him. Betrayal condemns sinners to the darkness of the pit."

The screen went black.

52

In the war room, Caitlin stalked back and forth in front of a freeze-frame image. It showed light falling from high windows into a room where Sean stood. A concrete floor. Corrugated walls. A warehouse, hangar, or disused factory floor. When she hit PLAY and watched again, shadows passed over the windows and she heard the screech of gulls. He was somewhere near the water.

The entire Bay Area was near the water. The shoreline ran for hundreds of miles. Sean could have been in San Jose, Vallejo, or Suisun Bay.

In the corner, the big-screen TV showed the national news on mute. PROPHET SUSPECT SOUGHT. FEDERAL AGENT MISSING.

Shanklin and Martinez swooped in and out, talking into their phones, writing notes, sticking Post-its to the wall. Guthrie swept in, phone to his ear.

Sean, we're going to find you.

But they needed better video. They needed to find the stolen Dodge Ram truck Rhone was driving. And to locate any storage units, get his phone and credit card records. They had nothing yet.

Patrols were scouring the streets. But they had hardly anything to work with.

"Keep me apprised," Guthrie said, and ended his call. "ATF special agent in charge never received confirmation from Rawlins that he arrived at the meet with his CI."

"Where were they supposed to meet?" Caitlin said.

"East Bay. That's all she has."

"GPS from his phone, his truck?"

"It went down this morning. Long before the meet."

"The Prophet ratted his phone and disabled GPS," she said. "God*dammit.*"

"Highway Patrol has closed the bridges. They're setting up checkpoints. Searching every vehicle," Guthrie said. "The streets were practically empty to begin with, and now the whole area's on near complete lockdown."

Shanklin said, "Who was the CI? Was it a legit meet or a setup?"

Guthrie said, "ATF's looking into that."

Caitlin's stomach churned. An image played in her head. Sean, walking away from the station with Sadie in his arms. His face turned to his daughter, smitten, protective.

Her eyes went to the clock on the wall. Six forty-five P.M.

She turned to the items spread across the conference table — the scant evidence found in the raid. Seven editions of *The Divine Comedy*. A box of sixty-four-color artists' pencils. And a stack of hand-drawn maps.

Rhone's clothing and a pair of hiking boots had been seized and were in the criminalistics lab, undergoing analysis. There was no sign of a laptop, any computer at all, or the black pickup truck with the chrome rims. Rhone seemingly had lived like a day camper in his daughter's spare room: pack it in, pack it out, leave no trace.

But they had found the false space behind the floorboard in the bedroom, where he'd stashed the maps.

Those maps had been rolled up and stored inside a cardboard poster tube. They meant something important to Rhone. They'd been dusted for prints and examined with ultraviolet light for hidden writing. There was none.

They were puzzles nobody could solve.

Caitlin's desk phone rang. Michele Ferreira. Her blood pressure spiked.

She answered, dreading it. "Michele. Where are you?"

Silence. Caitlin heard traffic noise. And a bright little voice in the background. *"Mommy."*

When Michele spoke, her voice was tight. "Just pulled off the freeway at a truck stop south of Eureka. What's happened?"

Caitlin thought she might cry. Michele hadn't heard. She'd probably been driving with a kiddie album on the car stereo. "Stay there. I'm sending a CHP unit to your location."

"Caitlin."

The room had become airless. "It's Sean."

She told it to Michele plain. "Everybody's on this. Alameda, ATF, SFPD, statewide BOLO. We're going to find him if we have to tear the Bay Area apart."

Michele took a shuddering breath.

"Wait for the CHP," Caitlin said. "Then check into a motel. They'll escort you. Call your parents and have them meet you there. Get them a room too. Once you check in, don't open the door."

"Got it."

Michele went quiet. In that pause, Caitlin heard fears and accusations. If Caitlin hadn't brought Sean into her cracked orbit, this wouldn't be happening . . .

Michele said, "Do you pray?"

"I will."

"Let me. You find this cocksucker and bring Sean home."

In the background, Sadie gasped. *"Mommy, you said a swear."*

Caitlin lowered her voice. "Motherfucking right I will."

She ended the call, more alone than she'd ever felt, and again looked desperately at the clock.

"The Prophet never keeps his victims alive for long. Sean left here at twelve thirty. The video was sent at four thirty-seven P.M."

The sound of the nail gun drilled through her. Time was ticking down. Briefly she felt like she'd been shoved off the roof of a skyscraper.

"He has a showstopper planned," she said. "And we have no leads."

She turned and booted a wastebasket across the room. It bounced off the wall and clattered across the floor. Everyone stared at her.

"Take a turn. It helps," she said. Then she scraped her hair back from her face and returned to the conference table. "These maps tell a story. We have to find it."

Guthrie approached. "Like you said, everybody's on this."

"We can't add time. We have to add eyes."

"This is all we've got."

She turned. "No, it's not."

Caitlin saw him through the glass: her father, standing at the front counter, coiled with energy. He clipped on a visitor's badge and was buzzed through. His hands balled into fists but she could see the tremor.

He was her last throw of the dice.

She wanted to toss her arms around him. His look, the glittering heat in his eyes, told her he knew she wouldn't, not here. Not now. The disquiet that washed his expression told her how she looked: half unspooled with fear and rage.

He put an arm around her as they walked through the station. "Channel it. Channel it all."

She nodded. "We have to strip this bastard's mind bare."

They walked into the war room and conversation stopped. Shanklin and Martinez eyed Mack warily. Guthrie approached and extended his hand.

"Detective Hendrix. Thanks for coming."

Mack gave him a handshake. "Show me what you've got."

Guthrie led him to Rhone's maps. Mack leaned over the table.

"Most of these are old," he said. "He's tried to protect them, but the paper's yellowed at the edges and the pencil work is smudged."

Caitlin handed him a pair of latex gloves. "They mean something. Let's find it."

He snapped the gloves on as he circled the table. For a couple of minutes, he absorbed it all. Then he said, "Some of these are operational maps. Some are fantasy."

He indicated one drawn in black and white. "This looks like a pit mine. The hills, the winding roads, the little figures with pickaxes. And that machine, with the spinning teeth at the front."

"It looks like a thresher," Shanklin said.

"It's a continuous miner. For digging coal."

Guthrie said, "We got an image of Rhone's passport from his employer. He was born in West Virginia."

Mack said, "The machine is pursuing the miners. It's about to drive them into a pit and chew them to bits."

"Hell," Caitlin said.

Mack picked up the next map. "This is the Bay Area. The peninsula, San Francisco, the bridges. But it's highly . . ."

"Freaky?" Martinez said.

"Allegorical."

481

Caitlin saw. "It's another rendering of hell."

"He sees Earth as an immense abyss. All these maps show the world as a surface that's hollowed out. That's filthy and undermined with evil. And he's sending people to the depths for punishment."

He moved down the table to a map that consisted of lines, circles, and text. The two lines of text formed an X.

The bottom of all the universe
Deep in the darkness of the pit

The first line started at the top left corner and ran diagonally down to the bottom right. The second started at the bottom left and ran to the top right. The lines of text crossed at the letter *a*.

"From Dante?" Mack said.

"Canto thirty-two. The Ninth Circle," Caitlin said. "The Prophet used part of the second line in his video message. 'Betrayal condemns sinners to the darkness of the pit.' "

Mack pulsed with energy. He rounded the table, slowly, deep in thought. Then turned back. He shoved maps around and grabbed one that had been half covered by the others. It too was an X. The arms of the X were

482

stringy and misshapen, and drawn in vibrant colors: red, orange, yellow, green, and blue. It looked vaguely like a chromosome.

Mack stabbed at it. "That's the BART system."

Caitlin and Guthrie rounded the table.

Mack held it up. "It's not simply an X. There are multiple threads within each branch. Those are train lines."

He nodded at Shanklin. "Can you put up a BART map on the projector?"

Shanklin found one. Put it up. "He's right."

Martinez said, "Does it mean anything?"

Caitlin felt a sensation deep in her brain, nibbling at her conscious mind. She tried to turn it into a concrete image. It wouldn't solidify. *Come on, come on.*

Mack was snapping his fingers, staring at the maps, like he had the same sensation.

"Why would he draw the BART system? What does it mean to him?" she said.

Guthrie said, "He used it to escape after the raid on Bart Fletcher's apartment."

"Ingress, egress," Shanklin said. "He can be faceless and move anywhere."

"But why draw his own map of the system?" Caitlin said.

Mack said, "He wouldn't have carried it with him around the world if it didn't mean something. He wouldn't have hidden it."

She stepped back and ran her fingers through her hair. X. X marks the spot. X it out. *Come on.*

She picked up the small abstract map with the X design. Did it relate?

Always. This was the Prophet. His fantasy was a grand design.

Caitlin stepped back from the table, closed her eyes, and cleared her mind. She stood still until all she could hear was her own breathing, all she could feel was her heart-beat in her throat. She opened her eyes and looked at the maps.

The crossed X of the text that described the Ninth Circle, the center of hell. The X of the train lines. They meant the same thing to him.

She thought about the video the Prophet had sent of the attack on Sean.

"On the video, the phrase 'All hope abandon, ye who enter here' is spray-painted in front of a hole in the floor. That's the sign that it's the portal. It's the gate to the underworld. And from what we can tell from the video, the hole drops to an abandoned tunnel. A subway tunnel?"

Caitlin stared at the BART map. Mack neared her, nodding.

Guthrie said, "Most BART lines run

484

aboveground. Tunnels are mainly in downtown San Francisco and Oakland."

"Where does the X cross?" Caitlin walked to the projected BART map. "Eastern edge of the bay." She turned to Guthrie. "We need a schematic of the system."

Shanklin made calls and unearthed BART blueprints. The clock read 7:17 P.M.

The grainy video of Sean strongly suggested he'd been attacked at an industrial site. There were few clues beyond the construction of the building, its seemingly abandoned character, and the hint that pallets and barrels were at the corner of the frame. It wasn't much. But when they identified East Bay industrial corridors that overlay underground BART lines, they managed to narrow their search area — to a stretch from the Port of Oakland to the oil refineries in Richmond, a strip of land approximately twenty miles long.

They identified twenty-one specific sites to start with. Lieutenant Kogara arrived and coordinated with the ATF and law enforcement agencies from Oakland, Richmond, and Contra Costa County.

Guthrie alerted Alameda's Special Response Unit. Six of the likely sites lay in the sheriff's office's jurisdiction. Caitlin eyed the clock.

485

Guthrie assembled his people. "Three teams. Detectives accompanied by uniforms."

"Tactical?" Shanklin said.

"Are on alert, ready to roll if one of us gets a hit on Rawlins. They won't deploy unless we confirm we've found him. They can't risk being caught out of range if they're needed."

He pointed around the room. "Martinez, you lead the team to Lake Merritt. I'll take Twelfth Street."

He turned to Caitlin. His eyes welled with misgiving.

She stepped toward him. "I'm going. You're not pulling me out of the field."

"Hendrix. It's Sean."

"That's why you need me. I put two and two together. I know this case better than anybody. I know *Sean*. I can recognize his voice, I can —"

Guthrie held up a hand. "Okay. You take the waterfront."

Caitlin nodded. Adrenaline ran through her.

Shanklin said, "What about me?"

"You're with Hendrix," Guthrie said. "The Prophet has put a target on her back. You're —"

"A bodyguard?" Shanklin said.

"Reinforcement. Nobody has eyes in the back of their head."

Mack was crouched against the wall, hands hanging off his knees. He stood up. "I'm going too."

"No."

"You need extra eyes, extra hands, and someone who understands what to look for. That's me."

Guthrie paused. His expression said, *I should have seen this coming.* "Very well." He shot a look at Mack's shaking hands. "But unarmed."

"Understood."

Guthrie looked at each of them. "Saddle up."

Caitlin's heart thundered. She headed for the door. Her father fell in at her side. As they passed the windows, he slowed. The sun was low on the western horizon, sinking toward a golden sunset.

Mack stared at it. "Is Mercury visible in the sky tonight?"

"No idea."

Martinez and Guthrie went past them. Guthrie said, "Mack, you'll wear a vest. Come to the locker room. Martinez, Caitlin — patrol units will accompany you."

Caitlin gestured for Mack to head for the locker room. Mack continued to stare at the western sky.

"Is it visible?"

He turned to her. Alarm filled his eyes. She stopped. At the door, Guthrie and Martinez turned back.

"Hang on," she said.

She grabbed a laptop and bent over the keyboard. A minute later she found the information. It felt like the blood had drained from her limbs.

"Mercury's visible tonight at dusk. We'll be able to see it after sunset," she said.

"For how long?"

"It sets at eight thirty-four P.M.," she said.

She and Mack looked at each other, and out the window.

"Holy God," she said, and ran for the door. "It's a countdown."

53

They swung off the freeway near the Port of Oakland and raced along a surface street toward an industrial park built above the BART lines. Caitlin drove the first car. Mack sat in the passenger seat. Behind them were the headlights of a Charger driven by a uniformed deputy, with Shanklin riding shotgun.

Caitlin's watch pinged: 8:04 P.M.

Half an hour and counting down.

She pressed her foot on the gas. Streetlights swept past. The radio chattered. Mack glared out the windshield, a dark coil of energy. He adjusted the department-issue ballistic vest again.

"Never gone into a potential firefight unarmed." He clenched his fists to stop the noticeable tremor.

Caitlin cut a glance at him. "You're my eyes and ears, not my gun."

"So you're not going to let me cover you

489

with that Remington in the trunk?"

"I'll cover you. So will they." She nodded at the car behind them. "Got it?"

"Drive," he said.

They rounded a corner into an alley, a dim and dusty wasteland where broken glass clicked beneath their tires. They rolled past darkened warehouses and factories — two cars, lights on, side spotlights sweeping the street and buildings. Night was falling, sunset a crimson smear of light evaporating on the western horizon.

Between buildings, Caitlin caught sight of stars in the sky. Low, and sinking toward the ocean, was a single white point. Mercury.

Mack had a copy of the BART map and the subterranean tunnel blueprints. "The train line runs at an angle below us — another hundred yards, approximately."

"Approximately?" she said.

"Best I can do."

Caitlin drove the hundred yards, to a darkened warehouse. "High windows. Let's go."

They stopped and got out. The patrol car pulled up behind them. Shanklin and Deputy Lyle emerged. Earlier that day at the barricade outside Rhone's house, Lyle had been calm and low-key. Tonight he moved like a firecracker about to go off.

"I lead," Caitlin said. "Single column. Me, Lyle, my dad, then Shanklin. Observe noise discipline."

She and the two officers checked their shoulder-mounted radios. Mack grabbed a flashlight. Caitlin chambered a round in her SIG Sauer, reholstered it, opened the trunk of the car, and pulled out the shotgun.

She mounted her Maglite on top of the Remington 870. She eyed them each and got nods in turn. She signaled *Go*.

They found the door to the warehouse broken open and partially torn from its hinges. Caitlin swung inside. The Maglite swept the space.

"Right clear."

"Left clear," Lyle said.

Caitlin's heart hammered. The warehouse was empty.

There was no hole in the concrete, no message from the Prophet.

"All clear." Her mouth went dry. "This isn't it."

Her watch pinged. Twenty-five minutes.

Rage and helplessness splintered in her chest. She radioed Guthrie. "Nothing. It's a bust."

"Proceed to the next site," he said.

That meant nobody had found any sign of Sean.

"Where's air support?" she said.

"Inbound."

She gritted her teeth and signaled the team out the door. "We move on."

The next site on their list was three miles away, near the Oakland Coliseum. Back in their cars, they gunned it. Caitlin's stomach was knotted. Mack's expression was iron. Her watch pinged. Twenty minutes.

The alley was narrow, a cracked asphalt path bisected by cross alleys, driveways, even footpaths leading down to the bay. Telephone poles stood like barren trees.

I found myself within a forest dark / For the straightforward pathway had been lost.

"What?" Mack said.

"Nothing. This is a maze."

"That's the point."

They swept along a chain-link fence outside an abandoned factory. Caitlin's knuckles were white on the wheel.

She stomped on the brake.

"Caitlin?" Mack said.

They screeched to a halt, with Lyle's Charger inches behind them.

"What?" Mack said.

She was staring at the cyclone fence

outside the abandoned factory. A sign hung
from it.

CONDEMNED.

54

Condemned. The sign hung crookedly in the diamonds of the cyclone fence.

"This is it," Caitlin said.

"Are you —"

"Come on." She jumped out and stalked toward the fence.

The doors of the Charger clacked shut. Shanklin jogged to catch up with her.

"The message on the video said, 'Betrayal condemns sinners to the darkness of the pit,' " she said.

The rolling gate to the property was open several feet.

"And that," Caitlin said, "is an invitation."

She brought up a satellite zoom of the alley and property. "It's an abandoned machine-tool factory. Cyclone fence completely encloses the property. Railroad tracks run along the western side. Two buildings, each approximately a hundred yards long, joined by offices in an H configuration." She looked through the rolling gate. "Door immediately ahead. Loading docks on the far side of both buildings, so exits there too." She looked at them. "No intelligence on the interior layout, so we'll be each other's eyes."

Lyle was wound tight. "Yes, ma'am."

"Radio Dispatch."

He nodded and jogged to the car.

They formed up and crossed an empty asphalt lot. The moon was rising, cold light frosting the edges of the building. Caitlin scanned the perimeter and the roof line and saw no shapes, no movement. No blinking lights, no obvious cameras. But the Prophet could lurk in the shadows, crouched like a vampire, waiting. They reached the building and stacked up on the door. Caitlin aimed her weapon-mounted Maglite at the crease between the door and the jamb. She saw no trip wires, no sign of explosives.

Still, she took no chances. She pulled out her telescoping baton. She wrapped a latex glove around the end for gripping power. She signaled the others: *Go.* They all nodded.

She used the baton to turn the knob and pull open the door. She waited for the click, the blast, the sound of machine-gun fire. Nothing.

Lyle's hand squeezed her shoulder. She swung inside, gun and flashlight sweeping the interior.

It was an enormous factory floor. The building was dark, the moonlight dimmed by the grubby windows. They crossed the room, clearing it as they went, shining their lights around the pallets and fifty-five-gallon drums.

"All clear," Caitlin said. Behind her she heard Mack's breathing.

Her watch pinged. Fifteen minutes.

At the far end of the room, they reached a door. They swept through and cleared the next room. They then found themselves confronted with a dark hallway.

Bad stuff. No way around it. Again they stacked up. *Commit,* Caitlin told herself. She swung through the doorway and entered the hall with the others close behind.

At a T junction, Caitlin raised a fist. *Stop.* She signaled Shanklin to go around her and clear the end of the hall.

Shanklin swept past, gun held in both hands. A few seconds later she said, "Clear."

Caitlin looked back at the rooms they'd come through. They'd cleared them, but their back felt completely exposed. She pointed at Lyle.

496

"Cover and surveillance. Hold at this corner."

He nodded. He too had a Remington shotgun in his hands.

Caitlin pointed down the intersecting hallway. She led Shanklin and Mack deeper into the building.

Sean's here. He has to be.

Halfway down the hallway was a door. They stacked up, Caitlin opened it, and they swung through.

Her breathing tightened. Inside was a long factory floor space. High windows. Dingy moonlight.

Mack swept his flashlight across the walls. Shanklin inhaled.

The walls seemed to leap at them, grasping, shrieking. Psychedelic nightmare, screaming mouths, claws, heads ripped open, bloodred paint splattered across a darkened pit. Caitlin advanced.

"Right clear."

"Left clear." Shanklin's voice was dry.

"All clear."

Mack swept his flashlight around. The beam caught a sinuous trail of stainless steel nails, pneumatically hammered into the wall. It led to the door at the far end of the room.

There, an open door showed moonlight.

A heavy flapping sound came through. Caitlin raised her weapon light to the ceiling. She saw no cameras, no microphones. But electronics could be hidden in a pinhole at the end of a piece of glass fiber. Holding the Remington tight, she led Mack and Shanklin to the doorway.

She heard only the sound of wind batting plastic sheeting. She swung through the doorway, shotgun leveled. The ragged plastic fluttered in the night wind like ghostly wings. The room was long, with a concrete floor.

She cleared her sector, as did Shanklin. Then she stopped breathing.

Dead center on the floor were bloody drag marks. They led to a gaping hole in the concrete.

The words were painted before it. *All Hope Abandon, Ye Who Enter Here.*

She inched toward the hole. A sense of space opened beneath her. Of endless depth. A strange breeze swirled up from within it. Humid, sour, dense with chemicals and stagnant water. She peered down.

Beneath the broken concrete, a vertical tunnel dropped about twelve feet. A ladder was propped against its dirt wall. At the bottom, support beams and metal struts gave way to another hole, cut with a blowtorch into the roof of another space — a subway tunnel.

Caitlin leaned into her shoulder-mounted radio. "Guthrie. It's Hendrix. We found it."

She released the TRANSMIT button, heard only static.

"Guthrie."

More static. She looked around. The walls were sheetrock and corrugated metal, not anything that should block radio transmission.

She got out her cell phone. Fingers shaking, she punched Guthrie's number.

Call Failed.

She pulled the radio from her shoulder and switched frequencies. Static.

Dread descended on her. "Shanklin. Call for backup from the Charger. Get SRU here ASAP."

Shanklin hesitated. "I hate to split up."

"Same. But we need to keep eyes on this room, and that hole, until backup gets here."

"Roger." Shanklin took off.

Caitlin leaned over the hole. The wind rushed through it. She tried her phone again, calling the main switchboard at the station. Couldn't get through.

"Dammit."

She stilled. Dialed 911.

Call Failed.

499

That should have been impossible. She turned up the boost on her radio and still got nothing. Mack checked his phone too. Shook his head.

"No signal."

The phone signal was one thing. The police radio was another.

All at once she remembered how often calls had dropped.

She remembered the phone company crew working on the cell tower where Deralynn's body was found — and where the Prophet had parked the black pickup.

"He has a radio frequency jammer."

She and Mack looked at each other.

"He's here," she said.

They turned back-to-back and scanned the room. It was black, deeper than black, the dusty white light from the windows stopping halfway down the walls. The floor lay in shadow.

Mack spoke in a low murmur. "Retreat, wait for backup. Even with Lyle and Shanklin, we're undermanned."

Ping. Ten minutes.

"We can't." She turned back to the hole in the concrete. "Sean's down there."

"You want me to be your eyes? I'm also your second opinion. You're not thinking tactically. We need more firepower."

She leaned over, crouched down, aimed the Maglite into the hole again. She started to swing around to climb down the ladder.

"No." Mack grabbed her arm and hauled her back. The strength and swiftness with which he moved surprised her.

"We'll find him. But we're going in with every gun we can get. Don't get yourself killed, Caitlin. Listen to me."

He had to drag her with him as they backtracked out of the room. She fought, staring at the hole, feeling her very life seem to ebb with every step they retreated.

"Caitlin." Mack's voice was commanding.

He pulled her back through the cathedral of paintings and nails. Fuming, she shook him off and jogged to the far door. When they entered the hallway, she looked for Lyle at the corner where she'd posted him. He wasn't there.

She stopped.

"Behind me," she said to Mack.

They advanced to the T junction. Stopped, listened, heard nothing. No radio static, no shuffling feet, no breathing. Cold, heart pumping, Caitlin slid around the corner.

Moonlight dribbled into the hall. It illuminated the two shapes slumped on the floor. One sat against the wall, legs splayed. The second was spread-eagled across the first, arms flung overhead. The shimmering light baptized the tableau like snow.

Caitlin advanced toward them, shotgun leveled on the far doorway. Nobody came through it. The building was utterly still.

She crouched, adrenaline jacking through her. Lyle sat limp, back against the wall, hands at his sides, upturned like a beggar. His throat had been cut. His eyes stared past her, unseeing. She put two fingers to his neck, trying to find a pulse. He was dead.

"Jesus, no."

She scrambled around him and kneeled at Shanklin's side. She'd been stabbed in the neck, above her vest. So many times.

Caitlin stifled a scream. She grabbed Shanklin's vest, to yank her up, slap her, scream her awake. Shake her alive. Blistering reality seemed to turn the empty hallway garish white.

Get up.

It was in her head, distant at first. Then she felt it, and heard it, in her father's voice.

"Get up," Mack said.

She stood, looking up and down the hallway, shotgun leveled on the exit.

Ping. Nine minutes.

"Come on," he said. "We need backup. Right now. But before that, we need to get out. Go. Fast."

502

She knew he was right. Knew that staying was suicidal. An ache, a horror, bled through her. *Sean.*

Mack put a hand to her back and pushed her toward the exit.

Then a sound echoed in the hallway. It came from beyond the walls, beyond the paintings and the nails. It echoed from the tunnel.

It was unmistakable. A cry of pain.

They exchanged a look. She unholstered her SIG and handed it to her father.

They ran back to the hole in the concrete. And descended into Hell's Gate.

55

Caitlin slung the Remington across her back by its strap, swung her legs over the edge of the pit, and lowered herself to the rickety ladder propped against the side of the well. Above her, Mack aimed his flashlight down the hole while she climbed down the flimsy steps. The muggy air grew heavy as she descended.

The sound came again — a keening, beyond a moan, high-pitched, twisted by walls and echoes. Caitlin's throat felt as dry as paper.

Mack followed her down, taking care to place his feet carefully and grip the ladder with both hands. Caitlin needed him to hurry but saw that he had to focus on every step. Her heart tightened further.

He stepped off the ladder. Caitlin crouched, peered down through the hole blowtorched in the roof of the subway tunnel, into a darkness where it was impossible to see. She listened.

The moaning had stopped.

Mack swung the beam of the flashlight through the hole. On the struts and beams surrounding it, blood had dried. Her head thudded. She took a baseball-size chunk of broken concrete and dropped it through. It hit bottom with a clop. The drop was do-able, and at the bottom of it lay wood and rocks.

Her watch pinged. Eight minutes.

"I'm going," she said.

She squirmed through the hole, dangled exposed, and dropped.

She hit the bed of a train track. Crossties, gravel heaped along the bed. She stood and raised the shotgun. The Maglite reflected darkly from the tracks.

"Come on," she said.

Mack wrangled through the hole and dropped awkwardly, landing on one of the tracks and tumbling. He got up, jeans ripped, knee bleeding. Breathing hard, he checked the SIG and nodded.

"I'm fine. Eyes on the tunnel," he said.

Caitlin swung the shotgun both ways along the tracks.

To her right the tunnel ended fifty yards away, against a concrete wall.

"This is a spur," she said.

They sent their lights the opposite way down the tracks. The walls were close, covered with moss and dripping water. The tunnel scoped to darkness.

"And it's abandoned. Looks like it has been since construction ended."

They ran along the track. The ceiling seemed to press down with the weight of all the earth above it. Caitlin eyed the concrete over their heads, the brown stains that crept from cracks. Earthquake country, and this spur might not have been inspected for decades. The lightless, clammy air carried a fetid undertone.

Soon the tunnel curved and joined another track. They stopped at the fork.

"Damn," Caitlin said.

The junction in the tracks spread to a vast subterranean world — miles of abandoned, crisscrossing subway tunnels and access corridors. It must have been a construction hub. The wind whistled and keened.

"Which way?" Mack said.

Ping. Seven minutes.

Caitlin's stomach clenched. The tunnels branched and extended beyond the hot scope of the Maglite.

"It has to be near. We heard the voice from the surface."

The wind keened again.

506

Mack said, "Did we?"

It couldn't have been the wind. She couldn't let herself believe that. She ran along the main track. Her flashlight hit bright-red paint on the wall of the tunnel.

"Dad."

Painted on the wall was a crimson face. Its eyes were the size of Caitlin's head, with serpents' slit pupils. Horns extended black and sharp from the creature's forehead.

It surrounded a rusted door in the wall.

Mack approached. "The devil."

"No. One of the giants that guards the deepest circle of hell. This is the way in."

Mack reached for the door.

"Wait."

She picked up one of the rocks that lined the bed of the tracks, and scratched an arrow on the wall, indicating the path.

They slipped through the door, went through an access corridor, and emerged into another abandoned tunnel. She swept the barrel of the shotgun up and down the tracks. Nothing. She marked the wall with another arrow.

They rushed along rusting tracks in the echoing dark. Despite the shotgun, Caitlin felt vulnerable. Heavy cables were bolted to the walls. She eyed the third rail.

"We're sure the power's off?" she said.

"Just don't touch it," Mack said.

They rounded a bend. The sense of space opened up.

Ping. Six minutes.

Mack swung his flashlight around. It caught an abandoned platform. He inhaled. On the wall was the name of the station. MERCURY.

It was the killer's lair.

56

Their flashlights illuminated a cold and dripping dark. Chaos and decay. They climbed up onto the long train platform. Caitlin swept her gun-mounted flashlight ahead of her, inch by inch, illuminating ovals of dusty light a foot at a time. Anybody sighting on her had a pinpoint target. But she wasn't going to stumble around the echoing platform in pitch dark.

Mack stood on her right flank, a step behind, SIG in a two-handed grip, covering the tracks.

Her flashlight scanned the platform. The walls were dense with paintings. A Hieronymus Bosch dystopia, rendered in Day-Glo and spray paint, unskilled and vicious. The images seemed to squirm and fight with one another.

Where was Sean?

The Maglite illuminated a plastic chair. A wooden cabinet. And a cinder-block bookshelf. It was packed with books and tools, spools of copper wire and jars full of a bright silvery liquid. Caitlin felt a draft. To her left, an exit from the platform loomed in the dark, stairs visible to a ticket hall that never went into service.

She swept the Maglite overhead. A disturbing crack ran like lightning across the ceiling.

Ahead, parked carelessly near the wall, was a wheelbarrow. Beyond it were tarps, humped and crumpled. A boom box furred with dust. She crept forward. Felt Mack right behind, matching her step for step.

After ten yards, the light from the Maglite caught the farthest reaches of the platform. Another carelessly tossed form lay on the concrete. Twisted, rag-like, motionless.

It was Sean.

Adrenaline spiked through her, a prickling sensation that opened her pores and vision and set her ready to charge, screaming. But she kept herself from bolting for him.

He was so still. His plaid flannel shirt lay half off his shoulder. His white T-shirt was stiff with blood. Red darkening to black. He hadn't been wearing a ballistic vest.

The blood spread beneath him on the concrete but didn't glisten in the beam of the flashlight. It had stopped flowing. She was too far away, and her heart was thundering too hard, to tell if his chest was rising and falling. But he was so still. His face was partially turned away, but the light reflected from his eyes. She let out a breath like she'd been hit with a battering ram.

No. No not Sean not now not like this Christ in heaven please no —

Mack took a step toward him.

Caitlin grabbed her father's arm. "Don't move."

There was always a second phase. An incendiary device, a trip wire, a decoy.

She held Mack back and choked down the urge to yell Sean's name. She tried to see where the trap lay, where it was loaded, how they would walk into it if they crossed the platform.

She shut off the Maglite. Mack did the same. The darkness didn't envelop them; it simply was. Absence, total, and no shadows rose even as her eyes adjusted. She heard her father's hard breathing beside her.

Ping. Five minutes.

"Wait," she whispered.

From deep in the gloom came a harsh whisper, amplified by echoes. "As Mercury descends, here you are. Hendrix. In stereo."

Caitlin tightened her grip on the Remington. Slowly, she inched the barrel toward

511

the sound of the voice. A few inches to the right. Off the platform. Farther down the tunnel in the direction they'd been heading.

The Prophet. Live. Here. Out of sight, invisible, a specter, not even a breath. But nearby, taking them in, hungrily. Mack was breathing like he'd just run up a mountain.

The voice rose. "At last you come to the Ninth Circle."

A heavy switch flipped, an electrical hum filled the air, and an icy light shone on them from the end of the tunnel. Every hair on Caitlin's head stood up.

"Dad. The track's live."

Squinting, turning her face aslant from the light, she snugged the shotgun against her shoulder. Mack raised the SIG.

The voice came again, distant, disembodied. " 'And then it was I could have wished to go some other way. But lightly in the abyss, which swallows up Judas with Lucifer, he put us down.' "

Caitlin held steady, shotgun level, her eyes adjusting to the light, seeing the shadows of the tracks themselves. Nothing else. No movement, no shadows shifting down the tunnel. She hardened her stance, listening. Mack shifted beside her.

"By your own actions you've brought yourselves here," the voice said.

She felt a sense of dislocation. The voice was harsh, was *his*. The echoes couldn't disguise it, couldn't keep it from infiltrating the air from the tunnel, behind the light.

Mack's hand was shaking, the SIG heavy, his senses seemingly overwhelmed. He focused hard on the source of the light and sound. Briefly, Caitlin thought — *he's focusing* too hard *on it.* Because that was all he could see. His peripheral vision was bad.

Then she saw, beyond Sean, a flashing red light. She heard a new beeping tone.

She stopped breathing. It was a timer.

She inched forward, vision pulsing. The flashing numbers matched those on her watch.

The voice said, " ' 'Tis no enterprise to take in jest, to sketch the bottom of all the universe.' "

Something was wrong. The timbre of the Prophet's voice. Its flatness, a thickness, radio static. The voice from the deep distance of the tunnel wasn't . . . right. Wasn't . . .

He's not there. What they were hearing — the Prophet's voice, the moans and cries, all of it, wasn't there. It was a recording.

She barely had time to turn her head before the pneumatic whir and spit of a shot came through the air.

513

Mack lurched.

Caitlin whirled to fire, Remington leveled, gaze swinging from the spotlight brightness to corners and blackness where she could see nothing.

Another shot came, and another, hitting Mack in the legs. He buckled.

The killer was behind them, nail gun in hand, firing. Titus Rhone, the Prophet, shooting from the dark like a wraith.

Mack went down, hit hard, twisting his hand toward his arched back, trying to reach the four-inch nails that had been fired deep into him. Caitlin continued turning, flipping on the Maglite again, barrel coming around.

Mack shouted. "Cat — he's . . ."

The blow hit her from the shadows.

Hard, heavy, fast. A baseball bat or two-by-four. Flat to the side of her head. Stars flew across her vision. She felt the air tilt, felt a shove and tackle.

The smell of lye soap.

She hit the platform. Searing pain in her head, the dark and white gone to fractals, spinning, thick tongue, iron taste of blood in her mouth. Hot trickle running down the side of her head, into her ear. Dusty smell, face hitting the concrete, dirt on her lips.

Near her father, the nail gun spit again,

twice, three times. Mack roared in pain.

A dark form swept over her, shadow or sail, unfurling. A hand grabbed her wrist, hot flesh, calloused. Yanked her right arm and dragged her across the platform.

Right arm, *right arm.* Something wrong. Empty hand. *Dammit* — shotgun.

She flailed her left hand, found the strap of the Remington, tried to grab it. A foot kicked the gun away. She tried to roll, to grab the shadow's leg. Her vision was broken, screaming white-black, pulsing with shadows and lights like strobes. Her face fell again to the concrete, dragging. A noise in her ears, ringing, like a fire alarm, deep in her head, and she couldn't seem to lift her free arm. Too heavy, numb, fingers wouldn't close. She was in a dream, unable to run, and her head had burst into a shrieking ball of pain.

Her right arm was being pulled hard against her shoulder socket. She felt the stars recede, the hum ebb and swell and ebb. Double vision, but a form above her, breathing, human. She tried to bunch herself to resist the force with which he was dragging her.

He shoved her against the wall. A corner, concrete, the smell of wood. The heavy cabinet. Hand grasped firmly, raised over

515

her head.

The pneumatic blast of the nail gun. He fired it through her palm. Once, twice, three times, pinning her there.

She screamed and tried to fight free. For a millisecond, the nerve signals from her hand had yet to reach her brain. She could tell that the nails had driven hard, all the way through her hand, nail heads counter-sunk into her flesh.

Then the signals hit. The pain hammered her, sharp, deep, a broken ache.

It woke her up. She was screaming and knew it was her hand, couldn't move it, felt her arm, raised her head, felt her legs splayed in front of her. *Like Shanklin in the hall.*

She opened her eyes, saw white light, black walls, shadows. The stars tried to fight her, but she shook her head. Raised her left hand. Numb, heavy, but moving. She bent her legs, tried to bunch them under her, to balance herself. The black sail fled to the periphery of her vision. Lye soap again, harsh, too present, a scrubby smell, trying to erase skin and dirt and existence beneath it.

She raised her head against the spiking pain and light. A man passed in front of her. Tall, wiry, backlit to silhouette. *Prophet.*

Messenger. Mercury.

No. Call him by his name. *Titus Rhone.*

Long gun on the concrete. At her feet. Black barrel, walnut stock. Rhone kicked the shotgun away from her. It spun, scraping. Just a couple of feet away, but out of her reach.

Near the edge of the platform, facedown, crawling, was her father. Rhone turned toward him. Lanky, long arms, scarecrow smile, eyes black holes, strings of hair slipping in front of his face. He raised the nail gun again.

Dad, look out.

Aloud, say it aloud.

"Dad."

She couldn't tell if he heard her. Couldn't tell if her words carried or were even actually words. But Mack got to one knee. In the white-black light, stripped of color, she could see that he was bleeding heavily. Rhone was a photo negative, slim and strong, stalking across the platform toward him, nail gun gleaming in his hand.

Mack gathered himself. Like a sprinter from the starting blocks, he bellowed and launched himself at Rhone.

The nail gun spit. Bright streaks. But Mack was in midflight, momentum and twenty-five years of rage propelling him, and

517

hit Rhone with his shoulder, solid, in the diaphragm. The collision sounded like bone and meat.

Caught above his center of gravity, Rhone tumbled backward. Mack tackled him. They hit the platform, and the back of Rhone's head smacked the concrete. The nail gun clattered off the platform to the tracks.

They rolled toward the edge of the platform. Fighting ugly. Punching, grabbing, elbows, fingers scrabbling for each other's eyes. Knees to the stomach. Rhone on his back, feet kicking, seeking purchase, Mack on top of him, trying to get a hand around Rhone's throat. Whites of his eyes. Wild. On the edge of death.

Caitlin heard the hum in her head recede. The stars faded. For a moment, she felt *there.*

The Remington.

The shotgun had spun away from her feet. To her left. Toward her free hand.

She forced her muscles to work. The effort to send her thoughts down her arm to her hand seemed superhuman, like pushing her way through putty.

The shotgun was three feet away. With her free hand Caitlin clawed for it.

Couldn't reach it.

Beyond the gun, the red light flashed. The

518

timer beeped. *4:19. 4:18. 4:17.*

She closed one eye, squinted, and saw the mechanism — timer, dry-cell batteries, wires attached to a red-and-yellow cord that ran off the edge of the platform and up the track. It was a blasting circuit.

She inhaled, breathed hard, in-out-in-out, huffing. She slid herself along the concrete, ass scratching, feet scrabbling, trying to get closer to the Remington. Reached again. Six inches short. Stretched. Same. She couldn't possibly grab the gun.

No.

She knew: The Prophet had killed Sean, he was going to kill Mack, and then he would kill her. And when she was gone, he would complete his master plan.

She knew it now. He'd told her — he'd sent video footage of a crowded BART train, had said, *The Ninth Circle contains room enough for all.* He thought the entire world had betrayed him. He wanted to send that world to the depths for punishment.

3:44. 3:43. The Prophet planned to detonate the stolen explosives in an abandoned BART tunnel. He was going to blow open a pit to swallow the people of the city above.

She had to get the shotgun.

She turned her head to look at the mess that was nailed to the cabinet. Her vision spun up a fresh handful of stars. Across the platform came grunts, punches, cries. Mack could hold out only so long. The nails had buried themselves deep.

Focus. She stilled her head, tried to get her double vision to coalesce. Couldn't. Looked at her right hand. Throbbing, stabbing, blood chugging from around the nail heads, already grotesquely swollen, fingers white, claws. She had to get loose.

She gritted her teeth and bunched her biceps and pulled, trying to wrench her hand free from the nails. The pain deepened and leaped, teeth and claws, shooting up her arm and deep into her brain. The stars shattered across her field of vision and turned yellow and dusty red and her head rolled back, hitting the wall.

Then the throbbing hum returned, and the sound of her father shouting.

She couldn't black out from the pain. She had to take it. Even if she ripped her hand in half, pulling it free. She yelled to clear her head. Hunched, trying to get the best leverage. Counted in her head. *One, two . . .*

And she heard a whisper, barely there.

Fear rippled across her. The black sail, was it returning, a shadow that could separate itself from the Prophet and smother

her? She turned toward the source of the sound.

Steel scraped across concrete. She gasped. Sean was looking at her.

He lay on his back, arm outstretched toward her. He tried to lift his hand, pursed his lips. His hand fell back. She knew what he meant. *Shh.*

With anguished effort, Sean rolled over. He tried to crawl, and couldn't. He was tangled in — no, tied up with cabling. His free hand lay near the Remington's stock. *3:12. 3:11.*

Across the platform, Rhone punched Mack in the face, broke free, and scrambled for the shadows.

Mack can get the shotgun. Mack can get the gun.

Still clawing for it, Caitlin shouted, *"Dad."*

Mack groaned, stood, and staggered up the platform in her direction. Behind him in the tortured light Rhone appeared. He was holding the SIG.

"Enough," Rhone barked. "Don't move."

He racked the slide on the pistol. A cartridge ejected and the sound did the work. The magazine was full. Mack froze.

Rhone took a step closer, limping. He held the SIG straight out from his shoulder, aimed at Mack's back. "Turn around."

521

Caitlin held still, head throbbing, her vision swerving in and out of double. She heard a bare scraping sound to her left. Sean had inched the Remington closer. She tried to see him without turning her head. He was motionless. She didn't think Rhone could see him.

2:50. 2:49. She touched her fingertips to the end of the barrel.

Mack stood fifteen feet from her, silhouetted. The Prophet stood another fifteen feet behind him, near the edge of the platform. They were all lined up, she thought.

She tried to grip the barrel of the Remington. Sean's fingers were near the light — if he moved any more, the Prophet would see him. But he was no longer moving. His hand looked lifeless.

Her heart seemed to slide off axis, pain and fear an electric force, building, building. The Remington had a twenty-inch barrel, blued steel, with a sight on the end. But it weighed . . . her mind swam. More than seven pounds. Her fingertips couldn't pull that, not at this angle. She tried to stretch, tried to dislocate her shoulder to reach. Took a breath and told herself, *Don't scream,* and leaned toward it, hanging on her crucified hand. The world went a shrieking yellow.

The Prophet's voice came through the pain. Talking to her father. He sounded rushed. Not the calm of his phone messages, not the needling, teasing sound of the radio call. It was a naked beatdown.

"You think you can get away," he said. "You can't. Even if you ran for the exit, I'd shoot you down. And a second after that, I'd shoot your daughter."

Mack was straining to hold himself together; Caitlin could see it. He was vibrating. She tried to signal him. Mouthed, *Don't move.*

"*Bang bang.* Right in the forehead." Rhone's voice took on relish. "What an utter failure your life has been. And now you've destroyed the one thing that could have outlived the catastrophe that you've become. *Boom.* Lights out."

Mack shut his eyes.

"And everyone will know," Rhone said. "I control the airwaves, the Internet, the papers, the way people piss themselves and see me in their sleep. I bring the message. I am Mercury."

He shifted his weight forward. "The public will know that Mack and Caitlin Hendrix brought death on the sheriff's office, brought death on their comrades, brought death on the city, and finally, on themselves.

You'll be the detritus of the case. Eternal losers."

Caitlin struggled to grip the barrel of the gun. She didn't have it.

"Or," the Prophet said.

Caitlin looked up. She could see only a shadow behind her father, voice from the white hole of light. And, peripherally, the flashing red timer. *1:55. 1:54.*

"Or?" Mack opened his eyes again.

He faced her, fighting to hold absolutely still. But he was swaying. Blood dripped heavily from his jeans and spattered on the concrete. Worse, it ran from beneath his ballistic vest. Rhone had managed to shoot him with the nail gun where the vest gapped on his side. He was struggling to breathe. The nails may have been driven into his lungs.

His shadow fell across her left hand, and across the Remington. She searched within herself for the fraction of an inch that would let her get a secure grip on the end of the barrel. It wasn't working.

"If . . . ," the Prophet said, drawing out the syllable.

Good Christ, the bastard loved to talk. He talked to his victims. Talked to their families. He used words like a Ka-Bar knife. Every syllable from his lips repulsed her. *Keep talking, asshole.*

1:32. 1:31. Get the Remington. Neutralize Rhone. Pull the firing wire from the circuit. *Sean . . .* She wanted to scream to him, but instead kept reaching.

"Spit it out," Mack said.

"Caitlin."

The word hissed over her. His voice was velvet, rust, probing.

Caitlin tried to pull the shotgun. Her fingers slipped. Mack's expression swam from sharp to confused to desperate. She mouthed, *Dad.*

"I deliver justice. But I understand mercy," Rhone said. "So tell me, Caitlin. Who deserves clemency? Your loved ones, or the city above?"

She couldn't see his face but heard the vicious joy in his voice. Mack was rigid, trying to stop swaying. He kept his eyes on her. *1:17. 1:16.*

Rhone said, "The last time, you chose your family over your friend. Who matters now? The men who brought you to these depths, or the community you swore an oath to protect?" He paused. "Tell me true, and you can leave here alive."

Mack held still.

Caitlin shook her head, tightly. "No."

Rhone's voice rose. "Tell me, Caitlin. Which? You think climbing out of the Ninth

Circle is *easy*? That it's *painless*? Come on. *Tell me.*"

She stretched, in agony. *"No."*

"Coward."

He took a step back and picked up something from the platform. It was a spool of copper wire, like those on the cinder-block bookshelf. The wire trailed from the reel to the shadows where Sean lay. That was what he was tied up with.

Rhone held it up. "Stop dithering and *tell me.* Or once I shoot Mack, I toss this on the third rail."

Caitlin's heart hammered. *:58. :57.*

Mack looked at her. "He's a fool to think this is a hard choice. Don't hesitate."

Caitlin clawed two fingertips around the gun sight at the tip of the Remington's barrel. Mack saw her struggling. She thought, *Not enough time.*

"Dad, I'm sorry," she said.

"Yes," Rhone said. "*Yes.* Mack, turn around."

"No."

Mack locked eyes with Caitlin. He swayed, almost tottering, but kept his balance, standing between her and Rhone. His gaze was piercing. It seemed to hold everything. His life, hers, Deralynn's, all the dead and those marked for death.

"Macklin Hendrix. I said, *turn around*." The SIG wavered in Rhone's hand. He locked his elbow and centered his aim.

A whisper came from Caitlin's left. "You're done. Dead."

Rhone swiveled toward Sean. Mack held Caitlin's gaze a moment longer. Resolve filled his eyes.

He spun and charged at Rhone. Roaring, leaping.

Rhone's eyes widened and his arm swung around. The shot was deafening. Mack doubled over, keeling as he ran. Rhone fired again, and again. Mack dropped at his feet.

On the platform before Caitlin, Rhone stood over her father, silhouetted by white light. She screamed. Raising the shotgun with her left hand, she fired.

The blast hit Rhone in the right shoulder. He corkscrewed, screaming like a banshee, right arm flailing. Then he caught himself.

He straightened, savagery in his eyes. His right arm hung bloody and useless. The SIG was gone. But he had a direct run at her. He dropped the copper spool and staggered forward, left hand a claw, to grab the shotgun. She frantically fought to brace the stock of the Remington against her leg so she could pump the action and load a new shell into the chamber. The gun slipped.

She grabbed it again. Rammed it against the concrete.

:07. :06. One shot — that's all she'd get.

She swung the shotgun toward the timer and fired. The gun roared. Chunks of concrete exploded from the wall.

Rhone shouted, "Wolfen *bitch.*"

The timer continued ticking. *:04. :03.*

She'd missed. *:02. :01.* She let out a cry. *:00.*

She braced for the explosion, the shock wave, for flames and shrapnel.

Nothing happened.

Rhone stared at the timer in disbelief. *:00.* He shrieked, *"No."*

He stepped toward it, face wild with confusion. Then he stopped himself and spun toward her. His eyes went to the shotgun and he lurched at her, hand grasping.

But, as if hitting a wall, he stopped. His gaze lengthened into the darkness beyond her, and a revelation seemed to overtake him. Some truth, hideous and inevitable. His expression veered between rage and perverse satisfaction. His voice dropped to a rasp.

"So advance the banners of the king of hell." He glanced at her, backed across the platform, and grabbed the spool of copper wire.

"No!"

Caitlin slammed the butt of the shotgun against the concrete, hand on the action. She jacked the shell into the chamber. Rhone swung his arm, winding up to throw the spool across the third rail.

Caitlin raised the shotgun, stars filling her field of view, and squeezed the trigger.

The shot blew Rhone back off the platform. He hit the tracks. Sparks flew. There was a snap and buzz, then darkness.

57

The echo of the shotgun blast rolled down the tunnel. The dark swallowed all. Caitlin tried to hold the Remington up, aimed where she'd last seen Rhone. Her arm shook wildly. She waited for him to appear, to crawl over the lip of the platform, scrabbling, ravenous, returning for her. A smell crept to her nose, like cloth scorched under an iron. And worse. Burned flesh. Her arm wavered.

"Dad," she cried. No response. *"Sean."*

Somewhere in the dark, beyond her vision, beneath the searing hum in her head, came sliding, skittering sounds. Rats running. Bats unwrapping their wings. Something treacherous, scuttling away, retreating from the barrel of her gun, into the deeper dark. Something that wasn't really there, or wasn't anymore.

"Dad!"

She turned again toward Sean.

They were both out of reach. She pulled the shotgun onto her lap and put her finger on the trigger again. The Maglite lit shadows and corners.

Mack lay on his side near the edge of the platform. His hand was stretched in her direction. He moved his fingers.

"Dad. Hang on."

He was wheezing. His shirt was sopping with blood, dark, low on his right side. Massive internal bleeding; that's all she could think.

He couldn't get to her. She had to get to him.

"Hold on. I'm coming."

She wriggled her phone from her left pocket. Still no bars. Rhone might be gone, but his frequency jammer seemed to still be active. Either that, or she was too far underground to get a signal. She hesitated before trying her police radio, but thought: If a massive electrical surge didn't detonate the explosives, nothing would. She pressed TRANSMIT. Dead air.

"Sean," she called.

No answer.

The only way to get help was to get herself loose. She tried to reach the knife in her right back pocket, but, pinned, couldn't stretch her left arm far enough to get it. She swept the beam of the flashlight in a jerking loop around her, looking for anything to use as a tool.

Near Sean, on the Prophet's bookshelf, were a screwdriver, a chisel, and a crowbar. They were too far away.

She looked at the barrel of the shotgun. Looked long and hard. Tried again to get the knife. No way. She leaned her head back against the wall. Turned the barrel, estimating.

She raised the gun and tried to see how to position it.

"No."

Sean dragged himself to her side. He was as pale as ice. Lips nearly blue, eyes too wide, even in the dark. He lay a hand across her leg.

"Give me," he said.

"The gun?"

He nodded.

"Did Rhone hit you with the SIG?" she said.

"Doesn't matter."

His hand was cold. She didn't think he had much time left. He tried to hoist himself up and managed to kneel against the cabinet. He couldn't possibly get across the platform to help Mack, much less get out of the tunnel to summon help. He looked at the barrel of the gun, as Caitlin had.

"What's the plan? Blow your hand off?" he said.

She swallowed.

He braced himself. "Scream all you want. This is going to hurt like a mother."

He held up the screwdriver from the bookshelf.

He roughly jammed the screwdriver under her hand, against the wood where the nails were lodged. He pried, using his shoulder, and she screamed, and kept screaming. Everything was pain, bright red, heat and fear and Christ make it stop —

With a final lunge against the handle of the screwdriver, he pried her loose. Her hand fell to the concrete, the nails sticking out of it.

"Thank you. Jesus." She shakily looked at it, bleeding, throbbing, three nails protruding, long and sharp, crazy claws. She reached toward it, thinking to try to push them out, and couldn't manage. Sean put a hand on her wrist and shook his head.

"They'll bleed."

She nodded and tried to stand. Couldn't. Got to her knees and balanced on her left hand. She tried to give him the Remington. He nodded and sank back against the wall.

She crawled across the platform, cradling her right hand to her chest. Heard Sean topple over, the gun clatter to the ground. She kept going. The beam of the Maglite cut across the platform, throwing her shadow ahead. She reached Mack. Under the flashlight, she saw that he was desperately injured.

She collapsed at his side. "Dad."

She reached out tentatively. Touched his shoulder. His head lay canted against the concrete. He was wheezing. When he breathed in, she heard a whistle.

She fought the ballistic vest off of him and yanked his shirt open, sending buttons flying. He had a gunshot wound at his waistline. And he'd been shot with nails both at his waist and high on his side, ribs obviously broken. With every heartbeat, blood pulsed from his wounds.

She put her hand against his side. Tried to put pressure on the gunshot wound. He moaned.

"We're going to get you help. Hold on."

She looked back at Sean. He was slumped over, the shotgun loose in his hands.

And the scene wasn't secure. She didn't know whether Rhone was down for good. She scanned the platform. No sign of the SIG. She crawled her three-point crawl back to Sean's side, grabbed the Remington, and staggered to her feet. Racked the action one-handed, lurched to the edge of the platform, and aimed it with a shaking arm at the tracks.

Rhone lay across them, arms out, fingers drawn into claws, head thrown back as if howling. His skin was bright red.

He looked firmly dead. Gone, ain't coming back. Had to be. And she didn't believe it. She wrenched herself down off the platform to the tracks. Thought the power was shot but found a piece of rebar and dropped it so it simultaneously touched the main track and the third rail. Nothing happened.

She approached Rhone warily. The smell was horrific. She gagged, and thought: *This is the truth of him.* A stench and heat that finally killed him. She flashed the light on his face. His lips had cracked. His pupils were wide, and when she hit them with the Maglite they continued staring without reaction.

The electricity had shot through him and created starburst cataracts in his eyes.

She held the barrel of the Remington over his chest. The SIG lay on the tracks near him. She kicked it behind her. The spool of copper wire had rolled against the base of the platform. She tossed it back up. Then she knelt at Rhone's side and dug through his pockets and found the device, the size of a bar of soap, that was stuffed in his shirt pocket. The radio frequency jammer.

She flicked a switch to turn it off. Staggered back from Rhone's empty shell. Maybe the rest of him had already gone somewhere else. Somewhere he couldn't come back from.

She collected the SIG, awkwardly holstered it, then kept the shotgun trained on him while she climbed back onto the platform.

Her shoulder-mounted radio came alive with static and chatter. She pressed the TRANSMIT button.

"Officers down. Repeat, officers down."

She gave the location, and heard confirmation.

"I scratched arrows on the wall with a rock," she said. "Follow them, you'll find us."

"We're coming," the dispatcher said. "Hold on, Detective."

She crawled back toward her dad. She needed to keep pressure on his wounds until the medics arrived.

Mack looked up and grabbed her shirt. His lips parted but no words emerged.

She pressed a hand to the bleeding wound in his abdomen. "I'm here."

He mouthed, *Love you.*

"I love you too," she choked out. "Hang on."

The wheezing stopped. His hand fell to the platform.

She dropped the shotgun and rolled him onto his back.

"Dad."

She listened for his breath, felt for his heartbeat. *"Dad."*

She knelt over him and cleared his airway and began chest compressions, one-handed.

"Dad. Mack. Wait. Look at me."

She listened and watched and knew and kept going, her own voice pressing into him, going through him, chasing after something that had fled across a divide where she couldn't follow. Calling, her voice softening, from a summons to a wish to a ragged prayer, a good-bye. But he was already gone, and couldn't hear it.

Her radio hummed. "Stay with us, Detective Hendrix. Help is on the way."

58

Caitlin emerged from the pit into a night blazing with stars and flashing lights. Detective Martinez and two Special Response Unit officers led her from the abandoned factory into a cold glare and dark, sparkling air. She held her injured right hand against her chest. Martinez ran interference, clearing her path, supporting her elbow in case she passed out. *Concussed.* She'd heard him say it into the radio.

The paramedics would get to her. First, they had to bring Sean up. On the underground train platform, she had bent over him, talking, even though he was only marginally present, floating back and forth, in and out.

No. She had rasped it. *You don't go anywhere, Rawlins.* Looking around the dark, where the black swallowed all, knowing the darkness didn't mean absence of light; it meant death. Wanting Sean to squeeze her hand and look up at her, even as an irrational thread wanted to put her lips to his ear and whisper, *Go get my father and bring him back.*

Everyone was there. ATF, sheriffs, EMTs. The bomb squad was below. The firing circuit had apparently been faulty, but they were taking no chances neutralizing the explosives. Her vision straightened, then slipped double again. She saw Lieutenant Kogara stalk through the wide rolling gate, tie and jacket flapping, looking stern and concerned.

As he approached, Martinez raised a hand, like a halfback blocking an approaching tackle.

"Getting Detective Hendrix to the ambulance, sir. She's pretty beat-up."

Kogara got a good look at her. His face was half bleached by floodlights. She squinted and tried to focus. He seemed to take in the state of her hand.

"Rhone?" he said.

"Dead."

The hum rose in her ears again, and for a moment she felt far away, weightless, looking down on the site from a depthless height. Then a hand cupped her elbow and she regained her balance.

Kogara's voice came to her as through a

tin wall. "We'll talk after you get treatment. Go."

She may have said thank you. Martinez led her away. He said, "Everybody's looking at you. Nails like claws. You're Wolverine."

He was trying to buck her up. Or keep her conscious. She walked toward the gate, toward the exit from hell, through the tunnel of kaleidoscope lights. A shout rose behind her. She tried to look back, and stumbled.

Martinez steadied her. "The EMTs are bringing Sean up, and they're moving fast. That's a good sign."

"Wait," she said.

The paramedics hustled out of the building, shepherding Sean strapped to the stretcher, already swathed in monitors and gear. Portable IV. Cervical collar. ECG monitor. A female EMT ran alongside, keeping pressure on one of the wounds in his chest.

Caitlin caught up with them and tried to run alongside. "Sean, you're out. You're safe. You're going to be okay."

The EMT looked at her like she might be mad. Caitlin hoped it was because of the way she looked, and not because of Sean's condition.

"Hear me, Sean? You're going to be okay."

He opened his eyes and looked at her. He blinked, maybe acknowledgment, maybe agreement.

"You're going to fight," she said, "like a mofo. For all of us. For you. And me." Her voice broke. "For Sadie, and Michele. Got it?"

He blinked again. She took his hand. Thought she felt him squeeze.

Overhead came the drone of a helicopter. A medevac helo swooped in off the bay, navigation lights flashing. Across the street, on a vacant lot, deputies had marked out a makeshift landing zone. The helo descended, noise echoing between the buildings, downwash blasting dust. The paramedics leaned over the stretcher, protecting Sean. The helicopter settled on its skids and the engine cycled down.

Caitlin bent and kissed Sean, and the paramedics took off with him, running for the helo.

Martinez said, "He's in good hands." He led her toward the ambulance. "Come on."

She was halfway there when a sheriff's office car came barreling down the alley, lights screaming from the light strip inside the windshield. It stopped sharply beside the ambulance. Guthrie jumped out.

Behind them, the helicopter door slid shut

and its engines spooled up. Caitlin turned and watched it lift off, pilot's face uplit in the cockpit, talking into his mic. She wished it into the air, her left hand in front of her face to block blowing grit. It rose, blades whirring against the floodlights, then dipped its nose and swooped in a broad turn, heading hard out over the bay. It beelined for the glow of the city across the water. She knew what that meant.

"San Francisco General," she said.

"That's good," Martinez said.

She didn't nod. San Francisco General Hospital was a Level 1 Trauma Center. If they were flying Sean there, it meant he needed the people who brought you back from the farthest edge.

She lost sight of the helo in the lights of the Bay Bridge. She kept looking anyway, until the engine faded into the hum in her ears. She felt she wasn't quite grounded, that the veil between this world and the other was porous, and she stood at the brink. She felt that she needed to keep her back to the hole in the concrete inside the factory, to bar anyone else from finding it. And to bar anything within the pit from getting out and pursuing Sean. To stop it from ever again reaching those seared by the Prophet's touch.

"Detective." Guthrie approached gingerly. "Caitlin. You hanging in there?"

"Yeah."

He and Martinez walked her to the waiting ambulance. More cars pulled up. Sean's boss from the ATF. A second federal vehicle, a black SUV with a whip antenna. The driver got out, a somber, hawkeyed man in a dark suit, who stood at a distance, watching her. FBI.

A paramedic jumped down from the open doors of the ambulance. He asked her to climb inside. She got as far as the rear bumper. Sat.

"In a minute," she said.

The paramedic shone a pinpoint flashlight in her eyes, asked her to follow his finger, checked her head, palpated the massive, throbbing bruise on the side of it.

"Did you lose consciousness?" he said.

"Maybe."

"Headache?"

"Like Godzilla."

"Nausea? Vomiting?"

"Not yet. But the stars and the humming and the — dizzy."

After a few seconds, it ebbed. The paramedic had a hand on her shoulder. "We need to transport you to the ER."

"In a while. San Francisco General first.

My boyfriend . . ."

"Now." He gently turned her hand. He tried to stay professional, but said, "*Damn, girl.*"

He helped her stand. She looked at Guthrie and Martinez, and a bolus of tears tried to rise in her eyes. She blinked it away. "Shanklin. Lyle."

Guthrie nodded. Martinez stared at the ground.

"They were . . . they tried . . ."

"They did," Guthrie said.

The cold seemed finally to penetrate, all the way through her.

Outside the factory building, someone whistled and called to Martinez. He leaned in and spoke quietly to Caitlin.

"You did good. Hang in, kid."

He headed off.

The paramedic said, "I'm going to leave the nails in situ. You'll need a hand surgeon to evaluate this injury. Come on."

She looked back at the factory. "My dad's still in there. I don't want to leave him alone."

Guthrie's shoulders dropped. "Detective. The crime scene team will take hours." His voice gentled. "The ME needs to attend. Dr. Azir will take care of your dad."

Her throat locked. She nodded. "Then

take me to San Francisco General."

The paramedic said, "Lake Merritt. They know you're coming. And you can't help your boyfriend in this state."

He assisted her as she climbed into the ambulance. The doors closed. They drove from the scene, and the flashing lights faded to nothing.

59

Thursday

At Calvary Cemetery, Caitlin walked beside her mother from the graveside service. The trees brimmed with pink blossoms under a cobalt sky. Behind them, white blooms covered the casket.

People in dark suits headed quietly to their cars. Sandy cinched an arm around Caitlin's waist. Caitlin was feeling stronger, but her right arm hung in a sling, swathed in a blue cast, the bones of her hand glued back together, fingers wired. Her face was a thunderstorm of bruises.

The crowd was small — loyal friends, Sandy's colleagues, a few people from the sheriff's office. Martinez wore a tie, which Caitlin found strangely touching. The plainclothes old-timer with the jowls and slouch, who had knocked on her door the night it all started, gently offered his condolences. Caitlin and Sandy both thanked him.

The last to catch up with them, as they neared Sandy's car, was Sergeant Guthrie.

He wore a suit with a crisp white shirt but looked as gaunt and wary as ever. "Mrs. Hendrix. Caitlin. I'm sorry for your loss."

"Thank you," Caitlin said.

"Mack would have appreciated your coming today," Sandy said.

She sent a last, lingering gaze toward her ex-husband's grave. Then she kissed Caitlin's cheek.

"I'll wait for you in the car." She peered at Guthrie over her sunglasses. "Five minutes, Sergeant. She was only discharged from the hospital yesterday."

"Yes, ma'am."

They stood under the trees for a moment, and Caitlin said, "Let's walk."

"You up to that?"

"I can't stand still."

They headed slowly across the lawn. Guthrie eyed her with concern. "What's the latest on Sean?"

"Touch-and-go."

That was as much as she could get out. She needed to hold every thought inside, to gather her strength and summon all the powers of earth and heaven, so that she could get back to Sean, hold his hand, talk even if he drifted half aware. Send it all to him. *Stay alive.*

Guthrie held himself to her sluggish pace. "Highway Patrol found the Dodge Ram pickup abandoned in a gully in San Francisco. Wiped clean. We haven't found the confidential informant Sean went to meet. But not all the blood on the factory floor belonged to Sean. It could be the CI's."

"You still don't know if he was for real, or somebody Rhone paid to set Sean up."

"We're working on it," Guthrie said. "Paige lawyered up, by the way."

"She's a smart little survivor."

They slowed beneath the lowering branches of an oak.

"The abandoned factory," she said.

"It was his grand finale, wasn't it?" Guthrie said.

"Yes — but not in the way he planned it to be."

Though still fighting through her shock and pain, she was trying to put the pieces together. In her mind, she heard Mack's voice.

"*Serial killers never quit.* Dad had that right. The only things that stop them are death or capture. And Rhone never planned on either."

As she had done countless times since Sunday night, she tried to rewind the

548

descent into the tunnel — to slow down the moments before the Prophet attacked, and see them with granular clarity. Her recollections were fuzzy, pointillist impressions. But as she walked with Guthrie, she tried again to put them in mental order.

"Rhone said, 'At last you come to the Ninth Circle.' Like it was part of his master plan," she said. "But when he had Dad at gunpoint . . ." The memory bloomed, vivid and hideous. "At that point, Rhone started improvising."

"Maybe he had his script worked out, but the heat of the moment, the fight, threw him off."

"Possibly." She shook her head. "But something doesn't add up."

"What doesn't?" Guthrie said.

"In the *Inferno,* the Ninth Circle of Hell punishes treachery."

"To Rhone, the fact that you're a cop was treacherous. In his mind, every move you made was intended to betray him," he said. "He was a psychopath. Ease down."

That was like telling a rocket sled to hit the brakes after it had launched into the air across the Grand Canyon.

"That isn't it. Rhone tried to force me to betray either Dad and Sean, or the people in range of the explosives. He said he'd let

549

me live if I chose which of them would die."

"There doesn't have to be an 'it,' Caitlin."

She turned to him. "This is the Prophet. Of course there does."

Her head began to pound. "In the *Inferno,* the deepest pit of hell isn't a lake of fire. It's solid ice. Betrayers are encased in it." She tried to recall how Dante categorized them. "There are those who kill their kin — Cain. Mordred. Then traitors and turncoats, who betray their people or their country. Then those who betray their guests. And finally, the center of hell . . ." She put a hand against her forehead. "I'm rambling."

"Keep talking," Guthrie said. "You're getting at something."

A breeze swept through the trees. Blossoms shook free like confetti.

Caitlin let her gaze drift with them. "The deepest pit of hell holds those who betray their lords. Brutus. Cassius. Judas. And at the very bottom is the greatest betrayer of all — Satan. Lucifer, who committed personal treachery against God. He's a giant with three faces, frozen to the waist in ice, beating his wings in vain. Trapped."

"Maybe Rhone saw himself as Satan, ruined for betraying the lord of light."

"No. He saw himself as the lord. He thought *he* was the light." She exhaled.

"The thing is — I can't believe he would ever want us to find his lair. He would never lure us there, or toy with us once we were inside."

But that was what he had done. And he had succeeded. It didn't matter whether he had died under the blast of a shotgun or the heat of a thousand volts. He had killed Lyle and Shanklin. He had taken her father.

The well of pain rose and broke over her. It felt like the scars on her arms had slit open and begun to run. The tears dropped down her cheeks. She inhaled and let out a stifled sob.

Guthrie set a hand on her shoulder.

"Sorry." She wiped her eyes. "I shouldn't . . ."

"Shut up, kid." He squeezed her shoulder. "It's catching up with you. If it didn't, I'd have you sectioned."

He shepherded her across the lawn toward her mother's car. "You take all the time you need. Think things through, and when you're ready, there are people who want to listen."

"Excuse me?"

"I'm not the only one who wants to debrief you."

He handed her a business card. She read it.

551

"Does this have to do with the black SUV parked over there?" She nodded up the road. "The one with the whip antenna and the guys in Ray-Bans. Same vehicle pulled up at the abandoned factory the other night, just before I got in the ambulance."

The card read: *C. J. Emmerich, Special Agent in Charge.* FBI Behavioral Analysis Unit.

"Early on," Guthrie said, "you asked if the Bureau would reevaluate the Prophet's profile. Now they'd like to talk to you." He held up a hand. "When you're back to fighting fit. No rush."

Disquiet was burrowing through her. Exhaustion, grief. And a gnawing certainty that she was overlooking a vital connection.

"No, now. Maybe they can help me figure out why this equation seems unsolvable."

The agent who climbed from the black SUV was the somber, hawkeyed man who had eyed her the other night. He shut the heavy car door with a click. His black mackintosh blew in the wind like a wing.

"Detective Hendrix. Pleased to meet you. I wish it were under better circumstances."

"Special Agent Emmerich," Caitlin said. "I'm trying to piece together a complete picture of Titus Rhone's last stand. I hope you can see whatever it is I'm missing."

"Tell me."

She ran over the last minutes in the subway tunnel. Emmerich listened with a kind of hungry tranquility.

"After you shot at the timer, what did he do? Moment by moment," he said.

"He screamed, 'Wolfen bitch.' Watched the timer count down to zero. When nothing happened, he looked stunned. He made a move toward it, but checked himself and turned to attack me first. Then he — got this look of shock, and stopped. He said, 'So advance the banners of the king of hell.' He grabbed the spool of copper wire. And I fired the final shot."

Once again she pictured herself on the abandoned subway platform. A fresh swell of emotion broke over her.

"Detective?" Emmerich said.

"Sean — Special Agent Rawlins — if he hadn't pushed the Remington within my reach . . ."

Guthrie's expression hardened. "Sean?"

"I never could have gotten it on my own."

"Agent Rawlins tells it exactly the other way round."

She frowned. "No."

"Yes." He glanced at Emmerich. "We spoke briefly to him. He doesn't remember much, but he remembers that. He said the shotgun was beyond his grasp, 'but not Caitlin's.' " He eyed her again, and his voice softened. "After a head injury, you can't expect perfect recall."

"No. That's not . . ."

She closed her eyes. Was back in the subway tunnel, pinned, watching her father battle Rhone. Felt a black sail descend, a shadow that seemingly tore itself from the Prophet to consume her. Heard steel scrape across the platform, and saw the barrel of the shotgun shining within her reach.

Now she opened her eyes.

She saw once more the nauseating *white-blacksnap* of the power shorting out in the tunnel, heard Sean's breathing, rat sounds, bat wings, the black sail scything down to take them all.

The shadows peeled away.

"There's a second killer," she said.

Emmerich's and Guthrie's heads turned in unison.

"What?" Guthrie said.

The ambush in the tunnel. Icy light, the recorded voice of the Prophet, Rhone attacking her father from behind, then . . .

She hadn't seen Rhone shoot her father. She had heard the nail gun, seen Mack lurch, and then. And then. The two-by-four hit her in the head. The black sail had swept over her.

She was waking up now.

A hard blow to the side of the head, stars and pain, falling. A hot, calloused hand dragging her to the cabinet before drilling the nails through her hand. While, across the platform, her dad began fighting for his life with Titus Rhone.

"Two men. There were two men who attacked us." She let out a gasp. "The CI Sean was supposed to meet. What if . . ." She touched her forehead. "There are two of them."

"A second killer. Working with Rhone?" Emmerich said.

"Not a copycat. A partner."

Her head throbbed, but she worked past it. "That's why things didn't match. The shoe prints. The voice modulation. The times when he seemed to be in two places at once."

"Because he was?"

Guthrie said, "Hendrix. You were concussed."

"Fine. But, Sergeant — that explains it. The second killer was the one who lured us to the factory and abandoned tunnel."

"A second killer."

"A young man. Obsessed with the Prophet. I saw it, and I didn't push hard

555

enough . . ."

Emmerich said, "If this is true, he was also obsessed with you."

"Someone who managed to connect with Titus Rhone. Who used Rhone to get me." She looked at him. "Someone who lured Rhone to his death."

"Why?"

"Because he wanted to take the killer's place and surpass him."

Emmerich's hawkeyed stare turned sharper. "An UNSUB."

"He was the one who nailed my hand to the cabinet in the dark."

"If so — where is he?"

"He must have escaped in the firefight."

She heard it again: scuffling, receding sounds. "I think he retreated and observed. Up the tunnel, on the stairs to the ticket hall, under the tarps, somewhere."

"He wanted to watch," Emmerich said.

"When he saw Rhone go down — when he saw me holding a twelve-gauge — and the lights went out, he fled."

"Because he thought you still had shells in the magazine?" Guthrie said.

The cool breeze couldn't compete with the cold realization taking hold inside of her. "Because he got what he came for. Rhone's defeat."

Boom — it hit her.

"The firing circuit wasn't faulty. The explosives failed to detonate because the UNSUB sabotaged it," she said.

And she understood the look of revelation and sick satisfaction that had crossed Rhone's face just before she fired the final shot.

"Rhone knew the truth. He saw the second killer, and knew he'd been set up. Knew his partner had sabotaged the bomb. Knew he was doomed." She touched her fingers to her temple. "Jesus. Rhone was *proud* that his student was taking down the king of hell."

"Because the UNSUB was completing the Prophet's fantasy?" Emmerich said.

"Because the UNSUB subverted the plan and took it to extremes even the Prophet never dreamed of. Rhone appreciated the poetic irony."

She looked at them, and shook her head. "That's why it was the Ninth Circle. The disciple was betraying the master."

Guthrie's face went dark. He was working it over in his mind. "If this is true, he wanted you alive. Why? So you could tell the tale? That doesn't strike me as enough."

The wind picked up. A crooked nail seemed to scrape down her spine.

"Because he has something else planned," she said.

Emmerich's hands hung at his sides. He looked like a gunfighter preparing to draw. "We need to find him. I want you to work with us."

She raised an eyebrow at Guthrie.

He said, "We've been talking. But it's your decision."

A gust of wind set the leaves shivering. Caitlin felt rickety on her feet, shocked, drained — yet energy pulsed through her.

"Yes. I want to get this guy. But not just him." She turned to Emmerich. "Tell me where to start."

60

The view from the hospital room was painfully bright. Morning sun through the window, lights overhead, heart monitor beeping its EKG pattern. Caitlin, sitting beside the bed.

Her red hair hung loose, soft, drying after a shower. Pale skin too pale, Sean thought, eyes too dark, the left side of her face a map of bruises, purple going green. Her right arm was in a sling, her surgically repaired hand immobilized with wire and plaster. It was a feat of engineering and skill that would let her grip her SIG and punch a bag and maybe, he hoped, give him the finger when he deserved it.

"Hey," he said.

She smiled. "Hey."

She stood up, moving like every inch of her ached, and crossed to the bed. With her left hand she brushed his hair from his forehead with her fingertips.

"Didn't think the hospital had discharged you yet," he said.

"Can't keep Wolverine locked up."

He knew it was late in the week. He wasn't sure how many days had passed since Caitlin and Mack found him. He was only now holding on to the daylight. He lifted his hand.

She took it. "Michele's here. She's been here almost the whole time."

He nodded. The thought that his ex would stalk the halls for him — and for Caitlin — briefly overwhelmed him.

"Sadie's with Michele's mom and dad. When you're ready, we'll call and you can talk to her."

"Great," he said.

It came out choked. He knew he was going to be okay. He knew Caitlin had rescued him. He knew not everybody had gotten the same second chance.

"Your dad," he said. "Above and beyond."

She pressed her lips together and blinked back tears. "Yeah. That was him."

He blew out a hard breath. "And your officers . . ."

"I know."

Silence was all either of them could give. Caitlin stood for a long moment, gripping his hand. Holding something back.

560

"What else?" he said.

"Rhone had a partner."

"Jesus."

She explained in quick strokes. He shook his head.

"A new Prophet," he said.

"No. I think this guy is something else entirely."

She held on, regarding him with an openness he rarely saw on her face. New barriers would be going up, he figured, but for the moment, she'd shed her emotional Kevlar.

He squeezed her hand. "There's more, I can tell. What?"

"The FBI offered me a job in the Behavioral Analysis Unit. I said yes."

"Holy shit. Joining the G?"

She brought him up to speed. "It means the academy at Quantico —"

"Know it well."

"— and working there, at least to begin. But none of that can happen unless I get medical clearance." She looked uneasily at her right hand.

"*Until* you get medical clearance. It'll happen."

She leaned over him and rested her left arm across his chest. Her voice grew quiet. "But I'm not going anywhere until you're back on your feet."

"Tomorrow. Weekend at the latest."

"Sean. I'm not leaving you."

"I know you're not." He took a slow breath. "Two feds? We'll work it out."

She tried to peer into him, unsure.

"Yeah, I'm drugged to the eyeballs," he said. "But it's your life's work, and important. And the chance won't come again. You'll never be able to live with yourself if you miss it."

She put her hand to his face and kissed him, carefully. "I love you."

"You know I'm Sean, right? Not Shadow."

Her expression turned mordant. "Asshole."

"Just checking. You have a concussion."

"Bark and see what I do to you."

"I love you too, Wolverine."

In her jeans pocket, Caitlin's phone rang. She flinched. Flinching at phone calls had become a habit, Sean noticed, though she didn't realize it. She stepped to the window, talked, listened, and clicked off.

"That them?" he said.

The sunlight seemed to gather around her, to infuse and energize her. Her wan skin took on a sheen, her eyes a dark focus. She nodded.

"Go," he said.

"I'll be back."

"Good. Or I'll follow you."

Then she was out the door, leaving only air and light behind.

EPILOGUE

The late-summer leaves shimmered green
in the heat. Locusts buzzed in the trees.
Even at eight A.M., Virginia was a different
world from California. Caitlin parked in the
Quantico lot, smoothed the jacket of her
new black suit, and strode into the lobby.

The FBI shield dominated the wall. Today
the sight of it made her stand straighter,
made her heart beat harder. The woman at
the desk smiled knowingly. So much for
playing it cool.

"Good morning," Caitlin said.

"Welcome to the FBI, Special Agent Hendrix."

Caitlin tried to contain her own smile as
she buzzed through the door.

SAC Emmerich's assistant met her on the
other side. The young woman extended her
hand as if ready for a firm shake, but
softened her grip at the sight of the brace
Caitlin wore.

"How's the rehab?" she said.

"A bitch, but it's done. This is precautionary."

"Glad to hear it. And glad to have you with us."

She led Caitlin deep into the cubicle maze, to a desk stacked with file folders, office supplies, and a box of books. The young woman patted the files.

"These are for your review. Team briefing is at nine." She nodded, an efficient, tidy nod. "Settle in. I'll see you afterward."

Caitlin stood there, savoring the moment. She sent Sean a text: Hey, G-man: I'm here. Fed Central, baby. Love, your G-woman. Grinning, she sat down. She pulled the stack of files toward her. The desk phone rang.

She picked up, relishing her first chance to say it. "Behavioral Analysis, Hendrix."

A coarse voice said, "So it's real. Caitlin rises anew."

The voice said *Caitlin* like the word was a snake, a slithering thing that had shed its skin and continued on in a new guise. Her gaze lengthened, across the floor, out the windows, to the rolling Virginia hills and the shimmering sky.

"Truly amazing," the voice said. "You're hard to bring down."

She put a hand against the desk to steady herself. "I'm a goddamn nightmare."

That voice . . . It was young, harsh, with a crack at the edge, like he'd once been punched or cut in the throat. She saw a man saunter past her in a biker bar, saying, *Ladies. Or should I say, lady and narc.*

He had been that close.

"But hard doesn't mean impossible," he said. "Enjoy your time. And your gift."

The call went dead. She stared at the things on the desk. Grabbing a pair of scissors, she sliced open the box of what she'd thought were books.

Inside, wrapped in a gleaming shroud of cellophane, lay a bouquet of black lilies.

ACKNOWLEDGMENTS

This novel wouldn't be what it is without the skill, support, and hard work of many people. As always, I'm grateful to Jessica Renheim and Ben Sevier; Ivan Held; and everyone at Dutton. My thanks also go to Don Winslow, and to Edward Tsai, David Koll, and the entire team at the Story Factory. For his insight, dedication, and belief in the project, my deepest thanks go to Shane Salerno.

For their steadfast encouragement, my appreciation also goes to Nancy Freund Fraser and Ann Aubrey Hanson. For educating me about Arabian horses, I thank Leslie Gardiner. For his knowledge of all things Bay Area, I'm grateful to David Lazo. And for everything, now and forever, my love and thanks go to Paul Shreve.

ABOUT THE AUTHOR

Meg Gardiner is the author of twelve critically acclaimed novels, including *China Lake,* which won the Edgar Award. Originally from Santa Barbara, California, she lives in Austin, Texas.

The employees of Thorndike Press hope you have enjoyed this Large Print book. All our Thorndike, Wheeler, and Kennebec Large Print titles are designed for easy reading, and all our books are made to last. Other Thorndike Press Large Print books are available at your library, through selected bookstores, or directly from us.

For information about titles, please call:
    (800) 223-1244

or visit our website at:
    gale.com/thorndike

To share your comments, please write:
    Publisher
    Thorndike Press
    10 Water St., Suite 310
    Waterville, ME 04901